"Bronwyn?" said Gerald. "You can't be serious?" He was halfway through his breakfast, but the name put him off his meal. "I might remind you she turned on us outside the gates of this very castle. If it hadn't been for Herdwin's quick thinking, it would've been disastrous."

"I know it's a difficult thing," said Anna, "but she's the only candidate both sides will accept."

"You mean that Hollis's nephew is willing to accept. He lost any right to an opinion when his uncle took up arms against us."

"You know as well as I that we can't let only three earls rule over Norland—there's too much bad blood."

"And so instead, we simply let them get back to the way things were?"

"No," said Anna. "We need to amend the rules of succession to allow Bronwyn to be crowned queen."

He saw the spark of mischief in her eyes. "You have something in mind."

"Yes, I do. I aim to restrict how many warriors each earl can maintain."

"And you believe they'll go for that?"

"They will if they want peace with Merceria. I'll not have the Earl of Beaconsgate sending any more raiders over our borders. Either they accept that limitation, or we'll be back on a war footing."

"We can't afford that," said Gerald.

"True, but they don't know that."

"That's a dangerous bluff."

"It's not the only surprise I have in mind for them."

Gerald looked down at his food to see sausages staring back at him. "I'm sensing I'm not going to have the stomach to finish breakfast."

"Nonsense. You're going to like this, although I daresay the earls won't."

"Now you have me intrigued."

"I will demand they recognize the Orcs' claims to Ravensguard."

"They definitely won't like that."

Also by Paul J Bennett

A PLAGUE IN ZEIDERBRUCH

TRIUMPH OF THE CROWN

Heir to the Crown: Book Ten

PAUL J BENNETT

Dedication

To those who have sacrificed for the greater benefit of all.

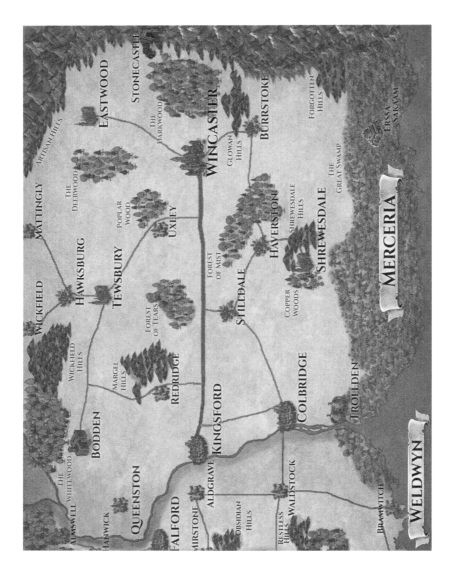

Map of Merceria

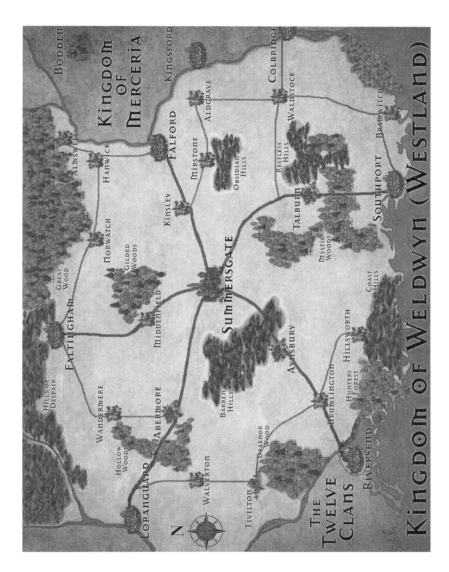

Map of Weldwyn

ONE

Norland

SUMMER 965 MC* (*MERCERIAN CALENDAR)

Anna shifted in her seat. As Queen of Merceria, she was expected to act with grace and dignity, but the infant within her had other ideas, moving around at the most inconvenient of times. A wet nose pressed against her arm, and she looked down to see Tempus, her faithful Kurathian Mastiff, staring back with concern. She reached down, stroking the dog's head before returning her attention to the rest of the room, where a heated debate raged on.

"He deserves death!" screamed out Lord Creighton, the Norland Earl of Riverhurst.

"That may well be," replied Baron Fitzwilliam, his voice calm and collected, "but this meeting's purpose is to decide on how the country will move forward, not deal out summary justice. I might remind you, there's still no agreement as to who'll be king, let alone dealing with the traitors."

"I agree," said Lord Marley, the younger. By some standards, he was barely an adult, having only eighteen years to his name, but his father, the previous Earl of Walthorne, had died in the war. "As the baron has indicated, we must select a new king. It's up to whomever we pick to decide the fate of these traitorous curs."

"Yes, but that's precisely the point, isn't it?" said Lord Waverly, the elderly Earl of Marston.

Of necessity, the queen had listened to this arguing all morning, nay, all week, for the negotiations had been tumultuous since their onset. She'd considered it an achievement to gather everyone together to discuss Norland's future, but now she wondered if she weren't better off locking everyone up and declaring martial law.

Anna closed her eyes, taking a deep breath in an attempt to calm herself. The rule of law was important to her, so much so that not long ago, she'd been forced to sit by and watch her dearest friend go on trial for murder. It had not been an easy thing to do. She'd nearly given in and called in the Royal Guard in the final moments. She thought to herself, if she could live through that, then she could put up with a few disagreeable nobles.

The baby kicked, and once more, she shifted. Sensing her discomfort, Baron Fitzwilliam turned to her, keeping his voice low. "Shall we adjourn this meeting, Your Majesty?"

"No," she replied, "although I think I might excuse myself. You are better able to deal with these men than I at the moment."

"Of course." The baron nodded to Sophie, who stepped forward, ready to pull the queen's chair out as she stood. The earls, sensing what was about to happen, all stood, bowing their heads reverentially.

"You must excuse me," said Anna, "but I tire easily these days. I shall leave you in the capable hands of Lord Fitzwilliam."

She rose, leaving the room as quickly as dignity would permit. Once through the door, she paused a moment to take in a breath of fresh air.

"Are you ill, Majesty?"

"No, Sophie, I'm fine. I need to sit and relax for a bit. All this back and forth makes my head spin."

Her lady-in-waiting took her arm, guiding her through the castle to where her rooms awaited. The Royal Guards followed in her wake, their presence a constant reminder that she was still in the Norland capital.

"Have someone find Lady Nicole," said the queen. "I should very much like to talk to her."

Sophie nodded her head at a servant, who then rushed off to deliver the summons. "Let's get you nice and comfortable, shall we?"

The guards opened the door, and Sophie led her queen into the room. "You should put your feet up, and I'll have someone fetch you something to drink."

"Yes," said Anna, "and perhaps something to eat?"

"Of course, Majesty."

"You're so good to me, Sophie. Tell me, how is Sir Preston these days?"

The woman blushed. "He is well, Majesty. Thank you for asking."

"And are we to see a wedding anytime soon?"

It was a fair question, for the Knight of the Hound had made his intentions clear with a formal proposal mere days ago.

"We have yet to set a date, Majesty, and with all this going on in Norland, I doubt it will be soon."

"Nonsense," said Anna. "You should be out and about with him instead of spending all your time fussing over an irritable pregnant woman." Sophie merely smiled.

A guard announced Lady Nicole.

"Send her in," said the queen.

Lady Nicole Arendale entered the room, curtsying in the Weldwyn style. Since the Royal Marriage, it had become the fashionable thing to do in Merceria, but Anna still found the custom strange.

"Nikki, so glad to see you. Tell me, were your twins uncomfortable to bear?"

"They were, indeed, Majesty, although there were also times of bliss. Mind you, I wasn't forced to sit through interminable meetings."

"Ah, you heard about the impasse at the Nobles Council, did you?"

"Yes. It appears you have your hands full."

"I don't suppose you can offer any advice?"

"They're not much different from the gangs of Wincaster," said Nikki.

"That's not the first time you've made that comparison."

"Nor will it likely be the last. If you want a lasting peace, you must be willing to give a little."

"Meaning?"

"For this to work, both sides need to feel like they're gaining something."

"Yes," said the queen. "But what? If we allow one of the earls to become king, there'll be a bloodbath. All they seem to care about is killing their enemies."

"You need a compromise candidate, someone who can be seen as acceptable to both sides."

"Like who?"

"I'm afraid that's not for me to say."

"Of course it is," said Anna. "You obviously already have someone in mind. Spit it out. I shan't hold it against you."

"Very well…" began Nikki.

"Bronwyn?" said Gerald. "You can't be serious?" He was halfway through his breakfast, but the name put him off his meal. "I might remind you she turned on us outside the gates of this very castle. If it hadn't been for Herdwin's quick thinking, it would've been disastrous."

"I know it's a difficult thing," said Anna, "but she's the only candidate both sides will accept."

"You mean that Hollis's nephew is willing to accept. He lost any right to an opinion when his uncle took up arms against us."

"You know as well as I that we can't let only three earls rule over Norland—there's too much bad blood."

"And so instead, we simply let them get back to the way things were?"

"No," said Anna. "We need to amend the rules of succession to allow Bronwyn to be crowned queen."

He saw the spark of mischief in her eyes. "You have something in mind."

"Yes, I do. I aim to restrict how many warriors each earl can maintain."

"And you believe they'll go for that?"

"They will if they want peace with Merceria. I'll not have the Earl of Beaconsgate sending any more raiders over our borders. Either they accept that limitation, or we'll be back on a war footing."

"We can't afford that," said Gerald.

"True, but they don't know that."

"That's a dangerous bluff."

"It's not the only surprise I have in mind for them."

Gerald looked down at his food to see sausages staring back at him. "I'm sensing I'm not going to have the stomach to finish breakfast."

"Nonsense. You're going to like this, although I daresay the earls won't."

"Now you have me intrigued."

"I will demand they recognize the Orcs' claims to Ravensguard."

"They definitely won't like that."

"It doesn't matter," said Anna. "The harsh reality is Ghodrug's Orcs already occupy the city. Should the earls attempt to retake it, Merceria would be obligated to come to the aid of our allies. After all, we are allied with ALL the Orcs, not only one or two tribes."

"A clever play," said Gerald. "I assume that would mean they'd need a seat on the Nobles Council?"

"That would be best for the Orcs and for us, as it turns out, since we'd be able to keep track of what's going on up here."

"And the rest of the earldom?"

"I have no objection to them appointing a new earl. Then again, I suppose they could choose to simply surrender Ravensguard entirely."

Gerald smiled. "Then we'd need to leave a permanent garrison there to aid the Orcs."

"Yes, and I doubt the earls would want that. Better for them to have an enemy on their council than to be left in the dark, wouldn't you say?"

"I'm not sure I follow?"

"They all know what would happen if we were to march out of Norland —they'd be back to war in a heartbeat. Like it or not, our presence is the only thing keeping the peace, and that's something we can leverage to our advantage."

. . .

That evening, Anna met informally with her closest advisors, gathered around a table loaded with food, but she was so engrossed with planning that she ate little.

"I'll be returning to Wincaster," she announced, getting to the gathering's true purpose.

"And the army?" said Fitz.

"The bulk of it will return home, but I'll leave a garrison here to keep an eye on things for the foreseeable future. Lord Richard, I hoped you would stay on as my representative. You are well versed in matters of court and are fully aware of my intentions in regard to Norland."

"I would be delighted. Might I ask the nature of the garrison?"

"I'll leave Sir Heward under your command with, shall we say, six companies of footmen?"

"Might we make that four foot and two archers?"

"I would suggest some horsemen," added Beverly, "for the simple reason that the Norlanders have great respect for them."

"Very well," said the queen. "I'll leave it up to Gerald and the baron to decide on which companies. As for the rest, I asked Albreda and Aldwyn to remain here for the time being. Their task is to create a new circle of magic. Once that's in place, it will be much easier to move back and forth as required."

"Is there any word from Weldwyn?" asked Aubrey.

"No. Since the death of King Leofric, we've heard little. We can assume Alstan is the new king, but I doubt he's had time to do much of anything. Once I return to Wincaster, we'll send a delegation to Summersgate via the Dome."

"I still can't get used to that," said Gerald. "All these magic circles make my head spin. Not that it isn't convenient, but it's hard to think of all those miles traversed in an instant."

"It was no different with the gates," said Hayley, "and you handled those quite well."

"Yes, but those were ancient. Some of these circles were actually created by us. I wonder what people on the Continent would say if they knew we could do that?"

"I imagine they do so all the time," said Aubrey. "I am assuming they know how, of course, for they have a much older understanding of magic."

"We don't know that for sure," cautioned Revi. "If you recall, pardon the expression, Albreda taught us the spell of recall."

"Yes, but the technique for creating the circle in the first place was found at the Dome."

The queen turned her attention to the chieftain of the Black Arrows. "What are your intentions, Urgon? To return to your home in the Artisan Hills?"

In answer, he clutched the hand of his bondmate, a pale Orc with hair the colour of moonlight. "Zhura and I will travel to Hawksburg and settle down there. Many of our tribemates will join us, but some still desire to return to the place of their birth."

"Will you then be considered a new tribe?" asked Gerald.

"It is a distinct possibility. I must give it some thought. Lady Aubrey was the one who graciously extended the invitation, and Zhura wishes to see it for herself."

"Now that the spirit army is destroyed, are the spirits at rest?" asked Revi.

"No," replied Zhura. "But Aubrey and Kraloch found a way to dampen their effects, a type of meditation that keeps them at bay."

"Yes," said Aubrey. "You may recall that some time ago, I discovered I could see magical auras while in spirit form. It turns out Zhura has a bright aura, indicating she may have magical potential. If I can hear the spirits by casting a spell, it's likely she can learn to silence them using something similar. In any event, we're going to give it a try in Hawksburg."

"All this is well and good," said Fitz, "but if we could just return to the issue of Norland for a moment, I have a question."

"Go on," urged the queen.

"What are we to do with the prisoners? Thurlowe and Calder are in the dungeons, but what is their ultimate fate to be? And what of Rutherford? He could resurface at any time."

"They shall remain imprisoned until the earls choose a new leader. At that point, it will be out of our hands. As for Rutherford, the man is to be considered a prisoner. If he does show up, he shall be promptly arrested and placed with the others."

"And if they decide to choose Bronwyn for their queen?"

"It's not the ideal solution, I grant you," replied Anna, "but we shall make it work. It is better to have a queen they can all agree on than a king who leads to another civil war. Just make sure we have safeguards in place."

"I've made extensive notes about this," she continued. "I'll be sure to get them to you before I leave. Is there anything else anyone would like to bring up?"

"There is the matter of Bronwyn herself," said Fitz. "The last time she was our ally, she betrayed us."

"Yes," said Beverly. "Spurred on, no doubt, by Sir Greyson and his quest for power."

"I believe," said Anna, "we can rectify that situation by assigning her a new aide, someone we trust."

"Sir Preston?" said Fitz.

"No. I wouldn't do that to poor Sophie. I was thinking of Sir Gareth. Do you believe he would approve of being made a Knight of the Hound, Baron?"

"I think he would be most honoured, Your Majesty."

"Good, and if there are any others that any of you deem worthy of the honour, I'd be glad to hear of it. It's high time we grew the order back to its original size. Let's make the arrangements for Sir Gareth to be inducted before I go. It'll give us all something to celebrate. Beverly, as Knight Commander, you'll preside over the ceremony, and I hope I can count on you, Lord Richard, to sponsor him?"

"Of course."

"Good, then I'll leave it to the Fitzwilliams to organize everything. Beverly can inform me when I'll be needed. In the meantime, I shall rest and pray that this child gives me some peace."

At this last remark, they all stood, allowing the queen to leave.

"I wonder how I should break this news to Sir Gareth?" mused Fitz.

"You think he won't like it?" said Beverly.

"No, he'll love it. I meant which do I tell him first, that he's now a Knight of the Hound or that he has to look after Bronwyn?"

"I think his induction into the order should take precedence. Better to follow with the bad news afterwards."

"Yes, I think you have the right of it." He paused a moment, staring at his daughter.

"Something wrong, Father?"

"Who would have thought it, eh? I still remember you as a little girl, wishing with all her might that she might someday become a knight. Now, here you are, Knight Commander, no less, of the most prestigious order in the kingdom."

"I don't know about that. We might have the queen's blessing, but there's only six of us."

"Nonsense. You're the premier order and the envy of the Four Kingdoms. One day your reputation shall be known throughout the land of Eiddenwerthe."

"Here we go again," said Gerald. "His pride is showing through. You better get him out of here, Albreda, before he starts waxing poetic."

"Quite right," agreed the Druid. "Come along, Richard. We all know how pleased you are to be working with your daughter again. Now, how about we search this castle to find a suitable location for the ceremony?"

She stood, taking the baron's hand and leading him from the room.

Beverly held her tongue until he left, then snorted. "Sometimes he's like a little boy."

"Come now," said Gerald. "You can't blame him. He's proud of you, that's all."

"Yes," agreed Hayley. "We should all have a father like that."

"In a sense, we do," said Aubrey. "Lord Richard is like an uncle to everyone."

"You have to say that," said Beverly. "He IS your uncle."

The late King Halfan's throne room proved the perfect location for the ceremony. Anna positioned herself in front of the throne, Tempus at her side with Dame Beverly standing before her, facing the crowd.

Word of the event had travelled quickly, and the room was packed with onlookers. Some came to offer their congratulations, while others were simply interested in seeing what strange customs these Mercerians had.

The remaining Knights of the Hound—Hayley, Arnim, Heward, and Preston, marched in and stood facing Beverly, leaving a space for the new inductee. Sir Gareth entered next with Lord Richard accompanying him. They strode across the room and came to a halt amongst the other members of the order.

"Sir Gareth," said Beverly. "Step forward."

The man did as he was bid, standing still as she struck him on the arm to prove his strength, as was the custom.

"I pronounce this man worthy," she called out, then stepped aside to give the queen an unobstructed view of the fellow.

Anna took a step closer, then waited as a hush fell over the crowd. "Since our ancestors first set foot upon this land, there have always been those who stood ready to defend our way of life. We are here today to recognize the courage and conviction of Sir Gareth and welcome him into the Royal Order of the Hound. There, he joins others, prepared to serve their country, their queen, and to protect those who cannot protect themselves."

She waited as Hayley stepped forward bearing a pillow upon which rested her Dwarven sword. Anna took it in hand, removing it from the scabbard, and holding the blade high, its edge catching the light.

"Kneel," the queen commanded.

Gareth knelt, and she placed the blade on his right shoulder. "Recite the oath."

"I do solemnly swear," said Sir Gareth, "to serve my kingdom, my queen, and the people of Merceria until the end of my days."

"Be it known to all that this brave and honourable man has been inducted into the Royal Order of the Hound. From this day, I call upon him to uphold the laws of Merceria and to serve his sovereign faithfully. Arise, Sir Gareth, Knight of the Hound."

She withdrew the sword, and her newest knight stood, and with a nod from the queen, he turned to face the crowd. The audience applauded, then the queen made her way from the room, Beverly in the lead, with the other knights following.

"Outstanding," said Fitz. "It couldn't have gone smoother if I'd planned it myself."

Albreda smiled. "But you did!"

TWO

Flight

SUMMER 965 MC

Tyrell Caracticus looked out the window of the Grand Edifice of the Arcane Wizards Council, more commonly known as the Dome. Before him, the smoking ruins of the Palace were a reminder of the day's events, although the creature who had caused such devastation had long since fled. In its wake, the dragon left death and destruction on a scale unheard of.

Even afterwards, the people continued to suffer by the hand of Brida, the High Queen of the Twelve Clans. Her father, King Dathen, was being held in the dungeons beneath the Palace when the creature unleashed by the Kurathians destroyed any chance of his survival. In retribution, the new queen ordered her troops into the streets, arresting anyone who resisted and even executing people on the spot.

Tyrell had taken Princess Edwina to the Dome, where they remained safe for the time being, as Brida had seemed reluctant to attack the place. Something had changed, however, for large groups of warriors were now assembling at the front door.

"Aegryth," he called out. "Fetch the princess. We need to get her to safety."

"About time," replied the Earth Mage. "I've been saying that since you brought her here."

Tyrell grimaced, for he knew she was right, but he'd taken an oath to protect the knowledge held within this very building and was loathe to surrender it to the enemy. "Is everything in place?"

"It is, although I don't know if the spell will allow it all to be recalled."

"Still, we must try. There are almost a thousand years of history at stake. Now, hurry. I shall meet you both in the casting circle."

He watched them run from the room, then examined his surroundings. There would be no escape for him, for he knew without a doubt he must give his life to prevent the enemy from learning the secrets held within these walls.

Tyrell stepped out into the hallway, where several students had taken it upon themselves to join him in his grand sacrifice. They stood by with torches ready, waiting only for his command to begin the destruction of the collective learnings of over nine hundred years of scholarly pursuits.

He entered the room to find Aegryth in the centre of the casting circle, Edwina at her side. Around them were stacked all manner of books and parchments—everything they deemed crucial to save. He wished they could bring more but knew it was not to be.

"Cast your recall," said Tyrell, "but do not try to return. The enemy will be upon us soon enough, and I fear one spell is all we have time to complete."

Aegryth stared back at him, shocked by his words. "Aren't you coming too?"

"No, I cannot. Someone must remain behind to deny the enemy that which they covet most. Now, begin your spell and speak no more of this." He noted her look of hesitation. "You are the future of the Dome now, you and Princess Edwina."

The Earth Mage said nothing in reply, merely nodded her head in understanding, and then her arms began moving as she cast recall. The air buzzed with energy, and then Tyrell felt a breeze as dust whirled around them. The runes glowed with magic right before a cylinder of light shot up from the floor, obstructing his view of them. A moment later, the cylinder collapsed, revealing an empty circle. He turned, leaving the place one last time.

Evard Brenton, Royal Guardsman, stood by the door. If truth be told, he was proud of his position. It meant the prestige of working for the queen with the safe job of guarding the Palace. Today, he stood before the room containing the casting circle, on the alert lest anyone unauthorized attempt entry.

He looked across at Donald Harper. The two grew up together, spending most of their later lives serving the queen, first as bodyguards back in Uxley and now here, in the capital. He was about to mention that very fact when he felt the distinctive buzz of magic in the air.

"Someone's using the circle," he said.

"Could be the queen," said Harper.

"No, she came back this morning. Did you not pay attention when the last shift briefed us?"

Harper laughed. "No, I was still half asleep."

"Well, you're awake now. Sound the alarm."

Harper reached out, ringing the bell that would alert the guard. Moments later, soldiers thundered down the hall, weapons drawn. At their head, Sergeant Fairfax looked slightly out of breath. "You raised the alarm?"

"We did," said Evard. "The circle has been activated. Are we expecting someone?"

"Not to my knowledge. Open the doors, and we'll investigate."

Brenton and Harper each grabbed a handle, swinging the double doors outward to reveal the room within. In the centre stood two women, one much younger than the other. The floor was littered with books and papers that looked like they had been flung around as if by a great wind.

"Identify yourself!" demanded the sergeant.

"I am Aegryth Malthunen, Arcanus of Summersgate, and this is Princess Edwina. We must see the queen immediately. Weldwyn has fallen!"

Alric moved closer, holding Anna in a tender embrace. Just as their lips were about to touch, the baby kicked, and both of them laughed out loud.

"That's quite the kick he's got."

"Or she," countered Anna.

"Are you sure there's no way Aubrey can determine the sex of our child?"

"No, we must wait for the birth."

A soft knock interrupted their conversation.

"Who is it?" called out Anna.

"Dame Beverly," came the response. "It's an emergency."

"Come."

The door opened, revealing the red-haired knight. "It's Princess Edwina, Your Majesty. She's just recalled to Wincaster along with Aegryth Malthunen."

"My sister?" said Alric. "Where are they?"

"Down the hall. We thought it best for Aubrey to look them over, under the circumstances."

"What circumstances? What's happened?"

"I think it best if they tell you themselves."

"Lead on," said Anna, "and let's get to the bottom of this."

As they entered the room, Aubrey was just completing a spell. The mage looked up as she finished. "Only a precaution, Your Majesty. A minor spell of healing to help with the bruising."

Edwina rushed forward, hugging her brother tightly.

"Bruising?" said Alric. "I don't understand?"

Aegryth explained the situation. "It's all my fault, Your Highness. When I cast the spell of recall, I had no idea the wind would cause the books to fly around."

"Books? What books? What in the name of Malin are you talking about?"

"Master Caracticus wanted to save as much of our knowledge as possible. I'm afraid Summersgate has fallen."

"Fallen?" said Alric. "To whom? The Clans?"

"Yes, although it would seem a large army of Kurathians aided them."

"I can't say that surprises me."

"Rumour has it they weren't mercenaries, but the personal army of a Kurathian prince."

"A prince, in Weldwyn? Why would they even consider such a thing?"

"They wouldn't," added Anna. "Not without help. I suspect there's more at play here than simple revenge."

"Are you suggesting Lady Penelope is behind this?"

Anna shrugged. "Penelope, Kythelia—it doesn't matter what you call her. She's always wanted to destroy us."

"Yes, but we defeated her army of spirits."

"And while we were tied up in Norland, she marched through Weldwyn, or so it would seem."

Alric looked down at his sister. "What about Alstan and Mother?"

"I'm afraid they're dead, Your Highness," said Aegryth. "A great dragon descended on the Palace, crushing everyone. Tyrell had the presence of mind to recall to the Dome along with the princess."

"Are you saying the rest of my family perished?"

"Your mother and brother, yes, but we believe Althea was off visiting Mirstone on the queen's behalf. However, we have no confirmation of her fate."

Alric felt the room spinning. He released his hold on his youngest sister and sought out a chair. "This is all just too much to take."

Anna moved to stand beside him, her hands instinctively going to his shoulder. "We shall get through this," she said, her voice straining to hold back tears.

"There's more," said Aegryth. "We discovered your sister Edwina has the capacity to learn magic."

"Nonsense," said Alric. "She's a member of the Royal Family. Mages can never rule Weldwyn; it has been so since our birth as a kingdom."

"Be that as it may, she's shown an aptitude for Air Magic."

"We have no Air Mages."

"Not in recent history, no, yet the fact remains she has it within her."

"What proof have you of that?" demanded Alric.

"There's an easy way to settle this," said Anna. "We shall have Aubrey enter the spirit realm. From there, she'll be able to see Edwina's magical aura."

"You can do that?" said Aegryth.

"I can," replied the Life Mage. "Although it's not something I've done lately. I suppose, now that Kythelia's hold over the spirits is broken, it will be safer."

"I'm not certain I understand."

"The Dark Queen used Blood Magic to bind spirits to her will. The last thing I wanted to do was find my spirit captured by her."

"Could she even do something like that?"

"I'm not sure, but I didn't want to find out the hard way."

Anna shifted her attention to Aegryth. "Tell us everything you know about what happened in Weldwyn."

"Are you aware of King Leofric's death?"

"Yes. Gretchen Harwell found us in the north. Is that what precipitated this invasion?"

"That was Queen Igraine's belief. Alstan was ready to lead the army, but with so many warriors lost along with the king, there was little to work with. That's why Althea went to Mirstone, to get more warriors."

Alric leaned forward. "When did all of this happen?"

"A few hours ago."

"And you didn't see fit to send Edwina here immediately? What were you thinking?"

"It was my idea," said Edwina. "We were safe within the Dome, protected by many magical defences. The priority had to be saving as much knowledge as possible."

"No," said Alric, his voice rising. "The priority was saving a princess of the realm."

"Do not be harsh," said Anna. "They did what they thought best. And in any event, she's safe now."

"My pardon," said Aegryth, "but Master Tyrell used the time wisely, gathering the most important tomes and sending them here for safety."

The door opened, revealing Gerald. "I hear we have company?" His smile soon disappeared as he saw the sombre looks. "What's happened?"

"Weldwyn has fallen," said Anna, "or at least Summersgate has. Brida led the Clans in a full-scale invasion, assisted, it would seem, by a Kurathian prince."

"I suppose we should have expected that after the loss of Leofric's army."

"What do we do now?" asked Aegryth.

"Do?" said Alric. "We reclaim Weldwyn, of course."

"I wouldn't advise that until the spring," said Gerald. "The army is battered and bruised. We'll need to raise more men if we're to be successful."

"Agreed," said Anna. "And I must take this matter to the Nobles Council. We shall need their support if we are to recruit more soldiers."

"What of your allies?" asked Aegryth.

"That's another matter entirely. The Orcs played a critical role in Norland, but they paid a heavy price. I cannot guarantee they'll be willing to risk losing even more in the west."

"The Dwarves will fight," said Gerald. "Herdwin is a big supporter of the Weldwyn Alliance, and King Thalgrun can be counted on to send a company or two."

"And the Saurians?" asked Alric.

"I'm sure they'd help, but they're better suited to scouting and guarding our supply lines."

"They have dragons," warned Aegryth.

"How many?" asked Gerald.

"We don't know for sure, but Tyrell identified at least two. The colossal creature that collapsed the Palace, and a smaller green one."

"Collapsed the Palace? It was that large?"

"Indeed," said Aegryth. "I daresay large enough to eat a horse in a single gulp."

"I know this may sound like a strange question," said Anna, "but was anyone riding these creatures?"

"Not that we could tell," replied the Earth Mage. "Then again, we only saw it from a distance. Tyrell could have told you more, but he stayed behind to destroy what was left of the library and deny it to the enemy."

"A wise choice," said Anna. "I shudder to think what Kythelia could do with such knowledge."

Lady Aubrey moved to the centre of the room. "Shall I enter the spirit realm now, Your Majesty?"

"Yes, by all means. Let us at least put one matter to rest."

The Life Mage lay down on the floor and closed her eyes.

"What is she doing?" asked Edwina.

"When she enters the spirit realm, her body becomes dormant and unable to support itself. The last thing we want is for her to fall and be injured."

Aubrey began the spell, calling on the ancient language of magic to channel the power within her. The air buzzed, and then her body went limp, her head rolling to the side.

Edwina moved closer to get a better view. "She looks like she's asleep, but she's not breathing, at least not as far as I can tell."

"That's because her spirit is now separate from her body," explained Anna.

"But where is she? I don't see her?"

"Nor would you, unless you used a spell to do so."

"So she's invisible?"

"In a manner of speaking, yes. Although my dog, Tempus, can sometimes detect her presence."

"So he's a ghost detector?"

Anna laughed. "I suppose he is, but Lady Aubrey is no ghost."

"But you said she's a spirit—aren't they the same thing?"

"A ghost no longer has a living body in which to reside. Aubrey is tethered to hers by an invisible thread—at least that's how she explained it to me."

The Life Mage opened her eyes, taking a moment to focus.

"Well?" said Alric. "What's the verdict?"

Anna held out her hand, helping the mage to her feet.

"It's true. I could see her magical aura as clearly as I can see you."

"And she has the power of Air Magic?" said Aegryth.

"As far as I can tell."

"What does that mean?" said Alric. "I thought you said you could detect her aura?"

"Yes, I can, but I've never used this technique on a potential Air Mage before. She has a blue aura, that I can say for certain, but whether that's Air Magic or something else, I don't know."

"And is this aura strong?"

"Strong enough to indicate she has some potential. Only time will tell if she's able to harness that inner power."

"It is as Tyrell suspected," said Aegryth. "He believed that somewhere along the line, the Royal Family married into a family with a hidden potential."

"Are you suggesting my mother could have used magic?" asked Alric.

"Not necessarily. Magic can often lay dormant for generations, and even then, not everyone who has the potential for such things is even aware of it."

"Yes," added Aubrey. "I've read extensively on the theory. Revi's library has several valuable essays on the matter."

"The question is," interrupted Edwina, "what happens to me now?"

"That depends on you," said the queen.

In answer, the young princess looked at her brother.

"Don't look at me," said Alric. "You're fifteen, old enough to make your own decisions."

"I should very much like to learn magic."

"That presents some difficulties," said Aegryth. "We have no Air Mage to tutor you."

"True," said Aubrey, "but you brought a lot of books with you. Surely some of those deal with the subject?"

"Yes, but how would she learn the spells with no one to teach them to her? It's not as if an Earth Mage could teach her how to control... whatever it is that Air Mages control."

"I would like to consult with Albreda."

"She's a wild mage! With all due respect, do you believe that's wise?"

"Her approach to magic has made her the most powerful mage in all the known lands. I'm not suggesting Edwina would be that powerful, but if Albreda could learn without a tutor, why not her?"

"I'm willing to try," said the young princess.

"Unless I miss my guess," said Anna, "that won't be for some time. She has to learn the magical alphabet first, doesn't she?"

"She does," said Aubrey, "but that, at least, is something any of our mages can do."

"She'll need to give up her claim to the throne," warned Alric. "The laws of Weldwyn demand it."

"Fine by me," said Edwina. "It's not as if I wanted to become queen anyway. Now I can spend my days learning magic instead of being married off to some noble."

"Come," said Aubrey. "Let's find you a nice room in the Palace and get you settled in, shall we? This must be so overwhelming."

"Actually, I find it a good distraction from all that has happened. Tell me, Lady Aubrey, how long did it take you to learn to cast spells?"

"Let's see. I was just a little older than you are now. Of course, I already knew about the magical alphabet from reading books."

"I like to read too."

"That's excellent news. It will make the initial phase of your training easier." They wandered out of the room, their voices trailing off.

"I'm glad she'll have something to distract her for a while," said Alric. "She's been through a lot."

"She's grown so much," added Anna. "She's almost a young lady now."

"That's what they do," said Gerald. "They grow up into adults. You're the living example of that."

"Come now. Queen, I may be, but deep down, I'll always be that little girl you found in the hedge maze."

THREE

Kasri

SUMMER 965 MC

K asri Ironheart made her way through the fortress of Galburn's Ridge. A summoning from her father, King Thalgrun, was no small thing, and although she knew him well, the request's wording left no doubt as to its import.

She passed through the doorway, the Hearth Guard merely nodding at her arrival. Within the makeshift throne room waited the king, flanked by Agramath, the master of rock and stone, as well as the captains of the Dwarven companies. Evidently, this was an official occasion, demanding proper decorum, so she strode right up to him, then bowed deeply.

"*You summoned me, My Vard?*" she said in her native tongue.

"*I did,*" replied Thalgrun. "*We are discussing our association with the Mercerians, and I would have your thoughts on the matter.*"

She quickly glanced around at the other captains, trying to decipher their moods by their stance, but they were all as stone-faced as her father. It suddenly struck her he might have seen fit to replace her with another heir. It was, after all, the right of a Dwarven king to choose their successor. Had he a change of heart concerning her future? A stubbornness fell over her, and she resolved to tell the truth and suffer the consequences.

"*I believe we have much to learn from the Mercerians,*" she said at last.

"*And they from us,*" replied the king. "*It has been proposed that the Life Mage, Revi Bloom, return with us to Ironcliff and commit our magic circle to memory.*"

The announcement caught her by surprise. "*We are returning home?*"

"*Not all of us, but I shall talk of that in a moment. You are the premier warrior of Ironcliff, Kasri. Do you trust these people?*"

"*I do, Father. I found them to be true to their word and generous in spirit.*"

"High praise indeed."

"What does Agramath think of the idea?" she asked.

"He believes it is an acceptable risk. In return for this act, Revi Bloom has agreed to teach the spell of recall to our master of rock and stone, thus making travel between Ironcliff and the Mercerian capital easier. My question to you is whether or not we can still secure the circle should our relationship sour."

"The Hearth Guard is more than capable of stopping any unwanted intrusion, if that's what you mean."

"That may well be, but we won't have the Hearth Guard to rely on, at least not for the foreseeable future."

She felt a slight panic. Surely he wasn't about to disband the elite company? *"It matters little. Any of our armoured warriors would be able to do so."*

"Good. That's what I hoped you'd say."

Relief washed over her, yet still, there was a nagging feeling. *"Might I ask, My Vard, why the Hearth Guard would be unable to resume that duty?"*

"As I said, we will soon be returning home to Ironcliff, but when I say 'we', I don't mean all of us."

"What are you suggesting?"

"Our alliance with the Mercerians is not over. We received word that Merceria's ally, Weldwyn, has been invaded. I intend to send a small force to assist them in their endeavours."

"How much of a force?"

"Three companies, including the Hearth Guard. You would, of course, command them."

"It is a great honour, My Vard. One that I gratefully accept."

"Good. In addition to the Hearth Guard, you shall have a company of our regular warriors and one of arbalesters. Within those restrictions, you can choose which captains you would like."

"I shall do so this very day."

"Excellent. Now, although you will command our contingent, you must operate within the established hierarchy of the Mercerian army. I will leave it to you to determine how that will work. At the very least, however, they will need to take on provisioning you, for you will be far too distant from home for us to do so."

"Understood, My Vard. I shall seek out their leaders and bring it to their attention."

"Good. The rest of us shall begin the long march home by week's end. As to your own force's disposition, I suggest you consult with their marshal. No doubt, you'll have enough marching of your own in the coming days. Let us hope it is not through the winter snow."

"Yes, My Vard." She bowed deeply before backing up and away from the makeshift throne.

"*Not so fast,*" said the king. "*I am not yet done.*"

She halted. "*Your pardon. I thought the meeting complete.*"

"*Understandable, given what I told you, but there is more.*"

She waited, noticing the indecision on his face. He was struggling with something, but she had no idea what it might be.

"*Come closer,*" he beckoned. "*I would embrace my daughter.*"

He rose as she moved forward, enfolding her in his arms for a brief moment. "*You will still succeed me as ruler of Ironcliff,*" he whispered, "*but the time has come for me to hand down Stormhammer.*"

He reached down to where the mighty weapon sat beside his chair. Forged over five centuries ago of the finest metals known to Dwarven kind, it was imbued with the magic of a mighty Air Mage.

Kasri looked on in wonderment. "*Are you sure, Father? This is your weapon!*"

"*I shall not partake of another battle, but I suspect you will face many in the years to come. Better it goes where it will be put to good use than to collect dust in a mountain fortress.*" He placed the weapon in her hands.

"*I shall not let you down, Father.*"

"*Of that, I have no doubt. Mark my words, Kasri. One day you will rule Ironcliff; on that, I will never waver, but to do so, you must survive the coming conflict. Do you understand me?*"

"*I do,*" she said, "*and I will strive to honour this weapon as you have.*"

"*Good. Now, come. We have much to discuss, you and I, and this is not the place to do so.*"

"*What more is there to talk of?*"

His eyes glinted with mischief. "*Well, for one thing, I must show you how to call on the powers of that hammer!*"

Beverly looked down at the crudely drawn map of Norland. "Are you sure you're going to have enough warriors, Father?"

"Of course," said Baron Fitzwilliam. "Gerald saw to that already. Chief Ghodrug also promised I could call on the Orcs of Ravensguard if needed. You, on the other hand, need to get the rest of this army moving south before the snow arrives."

"I'm only worried about you. I don't trust these Norland earls."

"Oh, they're not so bad once you get to know them. You concern yourself with the coming campaign in Weldwyn, and let me worry about settling things here. Remember, we'll soon have a working circle of magic, then we can travel with ease."

"I still don't trust Bronwyn."

"Nor do I," said the baron, "but we may be forced to accept her to expedite a more permanent peace. The simple matter is, we can't afford to maintain a garrison here, not if we expect to liberate Weldwyn."

"You're right, of course," said Beverly. She turned to go, then paused a moment. "I shall miss you, Father."

"And I, you, my dear, but we shall see each other again, don't you worry. If anything, I'm the one who should be worried. After all, it's you who'll be returning to battle come spring."

Beverly smiled as she left the room, her thoughts turning to other matters. Gerald had left it to her to organize the march back to Merceria, a task occupying much of her time of late. Even as she walked, she visualized the supply lists and wagons. So taken with her thoughts was she that she almost collided with Kasri.

"I beg your pardon," said Beverly. "I should've been paying more attention to where I was going."

"Quite all right," said the Dwarf. "I was just coming to speak with you. I understand you were put in charge of taking the army south?"

"Yes."

"Good, because it's that very thing I wanted to talk to you about. How do you think your queen would react if we came with you?"

"That depends," replied the knight. "What do you mean by 'we'?"

"Three companies, including the Hearth Guard."

"I assume you'd be commanding?"

"Of course."

"I think that's marvellous, and I'm sure she'd be thrilled to bits." Beverly suddenly screwed up her face.

"Something wrong?"

"No, merely that you've thrown off my calculations. I'm going to need more wagons."

"Can I help?"

"How? You don't happen to have extra horses in your quarters, do you?"

Kasri chuckled. "No, but each company has a rationeer, and they know how to make stonecakes."

"A rationeer?"

"Yes, what you might call a cook, although our rations are different from what you call food."

"I'm more than familiar with stonecakes. What is it you're proposing?"

"Given some time and access to the ovens hereabouts, we can turn out enough food to take us all the way to Wincaster."

"Then I wouldn't need extra wagons."

"Precisely," said Kasri. "And once we're in your capital, they can make more."

"Enough to feed the entire army?"

"No, but we could probably supplement a few companies, in addition to our own needs, of course."

"I'm sure Herdwin would appreciate that."

"Who's Herdwin?"

"Our Dwarven commander. He's in charge of the companies from Stonecastle."

"How many warriors does he have?"

"Four companies. Why?"

"Well," said Kasri, "if he's organized along similar lines, we can work with his own rationeers to produce even more, but we still can't feed the rest of you for long."

"Why is that?"

"Dwarves can use stonecakes indefinitely, but Humans require a more... what's the word... balanced diet, at least in the long run."

"I'll keep that in mind," replied Beverly. "When would your Dwarves be ready to march?"

"As soon as you like. When are your own troops leaving?"

"I'd like to be out of Galburn's Ridge by month's end, weather permitting. Is that enough time for you to prepare your stonecakes?"

"That's plenty."

"Good enough. Anything else?"

Kasri simply grinned back.

"What?" said Beverly.

"There's something I want to show you."

"Very well, then, what is it?"

"You must come and see."

"Right now?"

"Of course, right now! I can't keep it a secret forever!"

Beverly found the Dwarf's exuberance infectious. "Well, after that kind of endorsement, now I HAVE to see what it is."

Kasri led her through the castle, finally arriving at her quarters. There, she opened the door, then picked up Stormhammer from a nearby table.

"It's mine," she gushed. "My father gave it to me this very morning."

"Congratulations," said the knight. "This is a most wonderful gift."

"It is, isn't it? I think it's made of the same metal as Nature's Fury."

"May I hold it?"

"Of course," the Dwarf replied. She handed it over, taking delight as Beverly examined its craftsmanship.

"It's a little heavier than my own hammer, and there's much more fili-gree work on the handle, but I'd say it's definitely made of the same mate-rial—sky metal."

"It would be interesting to try them out side by side, don't you think?"

"I look forward to it," said Beverly, "but I'm afraid I've got lots of work to do. Anything else you need?"

"Yes, just a quick question."

"Go on."

"What do you know of this Herdwin?"

"He's a smith by trade and a good friend of the marshal's. Why?"

Kasri shrugged. "I wanted to know a bit about him before I go and intro-duce myself. I've got a feeling we're going to be working together closely in the coming days."

Beverly smiled. "Tell him I said hello, and if he wants to dye your hair black, tell him no."

Herdwin looked down at the broken axle. The wagon had been tipped up, the better to get at the bottom, but it quickly became apparent the metal rod was bent far too much to rotate correctly.

"How did this happen?" he grumbled.

In response, his cohorts all looked at their feet as if the answer lay between their boots.

"Oh, now I see how this is going to go. We'll need to replace this if this thing's to be of any use."

"Need help?" The voice took him by surprise. He turned to see a female Dwarf taking a great interest in his work.

"You must be Kasri Ironheart," he said.

"I am."

"Then greetings. I'm Herdwin Steelarm."

"I know who you are."

"In that case, is there something I can do for you?"

"Yes. My Dwarves are heading south, along with the Mercerians. I thought we might travel together."

Herdwin blushed.

"I meant our companies," corrected Kasri, although her face also turned crimson.

"I have two hundred warriors. You?"

"Around a hundred and fifty."

"I couldn't help but notice that many of yours wore plate armour. Are they coming too?"

"Just the Hearth Guard, although I wish it were more. The rest will be armoured much as your own warriors."

"Sounds like a grand idea. Have you spoken to Gerald about this?"

"You mean the marshal? I understood he left for Wincaster."

"He did? He didn't tell me. Who did he leave in charge?"

Kasri smiled. "Who do you think?"

"No doubt that would be Beverly. A fine commander in her own right."

"It sounds like you know her well."

"Her and her husband both. I was the one who told young Aldwin how to create a Dwarven forge to make Nature's Fury."

"I doubt the smiths guild liked the idea of that," said Kasri.

"Between you and me, the smiths guild can go and sit in a deep, dark hole for all I care."

"You have no love for the guild?"

"No. I left Stonecastle years ago because of their shenanigans."

"Shenanigans? I'm not sure I understand?"

"It's simple, really. I was more than ready to move on from my apprenticeship, but their rules said I needed to take another ten years before being eligible for promotion to full smith."

"Perhaps they felt you weren't ready?"

"They told me I was," said Herdwin, "but the guild has a limit on how many full smiths they can employ. Told me if they let me graduate, the increased production would lower prices—competition, you understand, and they couldn't have that."

"So you just left?"

"I did and never looked back. Found myself in Wincaster soon after. Mind you, it hasn't all been smooth forging, but I've done all right. Might even say I prospered."

"You couldn't have fallen completely out of favour. They gave you warriors to command."

"Yes, well, that's a completely different matter."

"I'm listening."

He looked her in the eye, expecting feigned interest, but instead saw only curiosity. "This is hardly the place to talk of such things."

"Have you people who can see to this wagon now that you've identified the problem?"

"I do."

"Then let us find somewhere more comfortable where we can find some decent mead."

"Good luck with that," said Herdwin. "The Norlanders can't brew the stuff to save their lives."

"Then ale, perhaps?"

"Now, that sounds far more promising. One of the camp followers has a fairly nice concoction."

"Camp followers? You mean all those extra people who follow behind the Mercerian army?"

"I know. It's a strange concept, isn't it? No Dwarven army worth its granite would endanger others like that, but it's their way."

It didn't take long to find the wagon he was looking for. Herdwin and Kasri soon had tankards of ale as they wandered the open courtyard.

"You're an interesting Dwarf," said Kasri. "I've never quite met anyone like you."

"Ah well, you wouldn't have, would you, you being a noble and everything. Me, on the other hand, I'm nothing but a guildless smith."

"You're being too hard on yourself. I heard what you did during the siege —that took real bravery. Not to mention how you saved the queen when the entire kingdom was looking for her."

Herdwin blushed. "That's all overblown nonsense."

"So you didn't save the queen?"

"Well, she was only a princess at the time, and I wasn't the only one helping her." He took a chug of ale. "Listen to me blathering on about myself. I hear you've had quite a distinguished career yourself."

"I've done all right."

"And if you don't mind my asking, how is it you're out here, leading a group of warriors? I thought you'd be forged by now with children of your own."

"There was certainly no shortage of possible forge-mates, but none captured my heart. I suppose I always preferred the life of a warrior over that of mere domesticity."

"Well," said Herdwin, "you'll get plenty of experience with the Mercerians. They're a kingdom that seems to be constantly at war."

"I only saw them fight once and was rather busy myself to take stock of their tactics. What's your assessment of their fighting ability?"

"Man for man, they're the best warriors this side of the mountains." He chuckled. "Of course, they're not Dwarves, but the commanders are all well-seasoned. I imagine you could learn a thing or two from any of them."

She moved slightly closer, lowering her voice. "Does that include you?"

He blushed. "I... well, er..."

"Come now," she said. "I'm only interested in your battle experience."

"Nothing more?"

"Well, let's start with that, shall we?"

FOUR

On the Move

AUTUMN 965 MC

The Mercerian companies marched in single file on the road while their cavalry trotted along on either side. The journey south had been uneventful, and eventually they passed through the border village of Wickfield. They then continued on to Hawksburg, and now, with the town coming into view, everyone looked forward to a nice rest.

Aldwin rode up beside Beverly, his horse dwarfed by the mighty Mercerian Charger.

"I wonder if Aubrey is home," he mused.

"We'll find out soon enough. We'll be there well before dark."

He looked back over his shoulder. "How many of these companies will remain here?"

"About a third. The rest will winter in Tewsbury and Wincaster."

"Does that mean we get a night off?"

"You might, but I'm far too busy."

"Meaning?"

"Albreda will take me through the circle to the capital to make my report, or Aubrey, if she's here. I'm afraid I won't be back till morning. I'd invite you to go with me, but I'll be spending all my time with the queen."

"I'm more than happy to stay here. It'll give me the chance to talk some more with Kasri's armourers."

"About what?" she asked.

"You know full well I'm learning how that plate armour works."

She gave him her most disarming smile. "And would you be making some for anyone you know?"

He laughed. "Eventually, but I'll need a proper forge for that, difficult to do when we're marching. I wonder if Albreda would take me back to Bodden for the winter?"

"I'm sure she would, although my father is still in Norland."

"Yes, but she has family up there, doesn't she?"

"She has her pack, if that's what you mean. What if I came and joined you? It would be nice to see home again, even if it's only for a few weeks."

"I would like that, but I shouldn't get my hopes up."

"What's that supposed to mean?"

"You know as well as I that you'll be spending most of the winter training warriors."

"Nobody said I couldn't train them in Bodden."

"And how would you move everyone up there? You can't expect Albreda to carry hundreds of people using her magic, surely?"

"No," said Beverly. "I suppose not."

"Cheer up. This war has to end eventually, then we'll have all the time together we want."

Anna took her seat. As the Queen of Merceria, her task was to conduct this meeting of the Nobles Council. Still, she would have given anything to have more friendly faces in attendance. As if sensing her discomfort, Tempus shifted, pressing himself against her leg. She cast a quick glance toward the loyal mastiff, then turned her attention to those at the table.

"As you doubtlessly heard," she began, "the war to subdue Norland is over. However, it has come to our attention that our ally, Weldwyn, has fallen to the Twelve Clans and their ally, a Kurathian prince."

"A sad state of affairs," said Lord Alexander Stanton, the Earl of Tewsbury. "Would that we could have stopped them, but it now appears we are too late."

"Precisely why I aim to send in our army to win it back."

"Is that wise, Your Majesty?"

"They are our allies," said the queen.

"True, but Weldwyn, as a realm, no longer exists. Thus, the alliance is rendered defunct."

"Would you to care to explain that to my husband, the Heir to the Crown of Weldwyn?"

Lord Horace Spencer, the Earl of Eastwood, shifted uncomfortably in his chair. "I'm afraid I must agree with Stanton. We took casualties in the recent campaign with Norland that leaves us with little to work with."

"Are you an expert in military matters now?" The question came from Hayley Chambers. She was the High Ranger, but more importantly, the

Baroness of Queenston, although that seemed to carry little weight with the other nobles."

Spencer grimaced. "You know as well as I another war would bankrupt us."

"You seem to think I'm here seeking your permission," said Anna. "As queen, it is my decision and mine alone as to whether or not we honour the terms of our alliance."

"Then why did you call us here?" asked Stanton. "Surely not just to gloat?"

"Not in the least. I am informing you I'm invoking the right of the monarch to call men to arms."

"That's only done in the case of invasion! And you didn't even use it when the Norlanders came across the border last year."

"There was no time to raise troops then, and well you know it."

"To do so now directly violates our law."

"Does it?" said Hayley. "If Kythelia is behind the invasion of Weldwyn, you can bet it won't be long before they come eastward."

"Oh yes," said Stanton. "The Dark Queen. You keep using her name to make us fearful, but your tactics won't work this time. If this Elf is behind the attack on Weldwyn, then where is your proof?"

"And how would I prove it?" asked the queen. "Shall I invite her here to Wincaster to talk to all of you in person?"

Lord Horace cleared his throat. "Perhaps there is a compromise we can all agree on? We have numerous allies—would they be willing to shoulder the burden of liberating Weldwyn?"

"That's not fair," said Hayley. "You're only suggesting that because they're not here to object."

"But they have representation on our council. It is not our fault they deigned to refuse the summons. Well, I say we take a vote to send them westward."

"And good riddance to them," said Stanton. "It's about time they did their fair share."

"Their fair share?" said Hayley. "If it hadn't been for them, we never would have defeated the Norland invasion. Have you so quickly forgotten the sacrifice they made at the Battle of Uxley?"

"It is clear," said the queen, "that not everyone here agrees with my decision. However, it still stands. Lady Hayley, in your capacity as High Ranger, I'm authorizing you to send word throughout the kingdom to raise arms."

"This is outrageous!" shouted Stanton.

"You are entitled to your own opinions, however wrong they may be."

. . .

Gerald stretched his legs, then took another sip of his cider. They'd gathered in the queen's quarters for an impromptu meeting of her closest advisors, taking advantage of Beverly's visit to include her in the proceedings. Also present were Hayley, Albreda, Aubrey, and Prince Alric.

"We can't do anything before winter ends," said the marshal, "and even then, we'll need to wait until the snow melts."

"I know that," said Anna, irritation straining her voice. Tempus raised his head to stare at her, concern written on his face. "Sorry," she continued. "This child is making me uncomfortable of late."

Gerald smiled. "I remember when Meredith was pregnant with Sally. She never could get comfortable."

"That's hardly reassuring. In any case, Gerald, I want you to work with Alric and come up with a plan to retake Weldwyn."

"Difficult when we don't know enemy numbers," he warned.

"That's where I come in," said Hayley. "I'm going to send in small groups of rangers. They'll each bring a shaman with them. That way, we can communicate using the spell of spirit talk."

"And the Orcs agreed to this?"

"Yes. I already broached the idea with Kraloch, and he agreed. It will also give us an up-to-date idea of garrison sizes and troop movements."

"And just how many of these groups will we have?" asked the marshal.

"That's the only problem. We're limited not by rangers but by shamans. Andurak has agreed to help, as has Urgon's sister, Kurghal, but that only gives us three, including Kraloch. Even then, that's assuming Aubrey can coordinate back here."

"Three groups it is, then," said Gerald. "I'll confer with Prince Alric once we're done here, and hopefully, together, we can determine how best to deploy these scouting groups."

"Agreed," said Alric. "I'd also suggest we send at least one group to Mirstone. Word is my sister Althea went there seeking warriors. It's possible they held out against the Clans."

"You believe they can withstand the Clans?"

"I visited the place years ago. Dwarven engineers designed its defences. I shouldn't need to tell you what that means."

"Good point," said Gerald. "I'll make sure it's a priority once we begin the campaign. Before we get that far, however, we must see to increasing the size of the army."

"Yes," agreed Anna. "To that end, I'm authorizing the raising of more troops. I'm hoping we can train and equip them by spring."

"What kind of numbers are we looking at?" asked Beverly.

"Ten companies," said the queen. "We could raise more, but there's no way the smiths could create enough weapons and armour to equip them. My intent is to raise more should the need arise, but the longer we delay that, the better. I might remind everyone we also must bear the cost of feeding and housing them."

"Speaking of which," said Hayley, "I've had reports of discontent. It seems some members of the nobility object to having Royal companies billeted in their cities over the winter."

"Any cities in particular?"

She grinned. "Care to guess?"

"Stanton," said Gerald. "I wish that fellow would hurry up and die already."

"Don't be like that," said the queen. "Everyone has a right to their opinion, however wrong it might be."

"True, but it's almost as if he's actively working against us. That's very close to treasonous, in my mind."

"I believe in the rule of law," Anna replied, "and I shall not follow in my ancestors' footsteps by arresting anyone who opposes me. That road can only lead to oppression and ruin."

"Still, we must do something!"

"You should talk to my father," said Beverly. "He's been at odds with Stanton for years."

"Why is that?" asked Hayley.

"I'm not sure, but I think it has something to do with my mother."

"Let's be thankful Stanton didn't marry her, else he'd be your father."

"No," said Beverly. "Without my father, I wouldn't be me. He was the one who made me what I am today. Well, him and Gerald here."

"Well said," added the queen. "But it still leaves us with the question of how to deal with Stanton. He still carries a lot of influence on the Nobles Council. What do you think, Albreda?"

The Druid looked up in surprise. "Me? Why would you want my opinion?"

"You are a valued member of this inner circle."

"I try to keep as far from politics as I can. I find most of the nobles of this realm to be insufferable fools, present company excluded, of course. I think it comes from all the inbreeding. Fresh blood is needed in these ancient lines if we are to make progress. If it weren't for Aubrey here, and Richard, I'd say let's get rid of them all and start afresh."

"While I am sympathetic to your opinion," said Anna, "it hardly helps us deal with the issues at hand."

"There's an old expression," said Aubrey. "You fight fire with fire."

"Who said that?" asked Gerald.

"Likely Fire Mages," she replied. "In any event, the point I'm trying to make is that we employ the earl's tactics against him."

"Meaning?"

"We spread rumours ourselves."

"Isn't that stooping to his level?"

"We don't sow dissension or false information, merely talk of how much the army is valued and what a great job it's doing."

"That could work," added Hayley. "The rangers visit all the towns and villages in the kingdom. Who better to carry the word?"

"That's all well and good," said Gerald, "but come spring, we'll need all your rangers in Weldwyn. Who would spread the word, then?"

"It's far too complicated an issue to solve today," said the queen. "Besides, we don't know for certain the earl is behind any of this, only that his city is one of the problem areas."

"Who else could it be?"

"Kythelia, for one. It would be just like her to sow discontent amongst us as we prepare to liberate Weldwyn."

"So, how do we proceed?" asked the marshal.

"For now, we do nothing. In the coming days, I shall hold discussions with the realm's nobles and see if we can't put an end to such thoughts. Until then, I suggest you put your minds towards planning our coming spring offensive."

Once she returned to Hawksburg, Beverly continued the march. Her army was now reduced after leaving several companies in Hawksburg to wait out the winter. Still, it numbered over a thousand as they made the two-day march to Tewsbury.

As they approached the city's gates, Beverly sent her Kurathian riders ahead to make arrangements for billeting the men. It didn't take them long to return with the news that the city's gates were closed. Even worse, the guards there refused to open them.

Beverly urged Lightning on, easily outdistancing her men. Tewsbury was a walled city, and she had no desire to lay siege to it, yet refusing them entry was tantamount to rejecting the queen herself.

She slowed as she approached the gate. On the battlements above, several people took an interest in her arrival.

"Who commands here?" she called out.

"What's it to you?" came the reply.

"I am Dame Beverly Fitzwilliam," she announced. "Knight of the Hound and servant of Queen Anna. In her name, I order you to open the gates."

"And if we don't?"

"Then you shall be charged with high treason. I shouldn't need to tell you the penalty for such actions."

"You still wouldn't get into Tewsbury."

"I have a battle-hardened army behind me," said Beverly, "and amongst their numbers are over three hundred Dwarven warriors, experts in siege warfare. Do you truly want to subject yourselves to something like that?"

Her words struck a chord, for there was a hurried discussion amongst the defenders. Moments later, the noise of the great winch that controlled the gates could be heard as the doors opened.

Beverly urged Lightning forward and entered the city, remaining beside the gate lest they change their minds. The first company through was the Wincaster Light Horse. She immediately ordered them to take over control of the gate. There was resistance at first, but the sight of veteran warriors marching up the steps of the gatehouse soon put such objections to rest.

A small crowd gathered once word got around about their arrival. It was not a common sight, for armies of this size were rarely on the march. Most of the townsfolk simply watched as the warriors passed, but the appearance of the Orcs led to curses and abuse hurled in the direction of her army.

She ordered the companies to camp in Tewsbury Common: a large field inside the city typically used for such things as village fairs.

That evening, she spent a sleepless night, worried the townsfolk's attitude might devolve into violence. She'd ordered the Dwarves to form a perimeter guard to counter that threat, denying entry to any but those essential to army business.

The situation was far worse than they feared, enough even to justify a permanent Royal Garrison, all at a time when every warrior was needed to retake Weldwyn.

The next morning, she summoned Captain Carlson, the leader of the Wincaster Light Horse.

"You wanted to see me, Commander?"

"Yes. Come in," said Beverly. "I'm going to appoint you as the Tewsbury garrison's provisional commander. Naturally, I'll be leaving you the Wincaster Light Horse, along with two companies of foot and two of bows, all of them Mercerian."

The man's look of relief was obvious. "Yes, Commander. I think that best, given the circumstances. Have you any particular details for me?"

"Yes. Remember, you are royal troops and not under the command of the Earl of Tewsbury. I shall inform the queen of these developments, but there is no magic circle in the city, so news travels slower than I would like.

Your men will assume the duty of garrisoning the gatehouses, but should things get out of hand, use your best judgement."

"Meaning we fight if necessary?"

"I'm hoping it won't come to that, but the preservation of the companies is your foremost responsibility."

"And the local garrison?"

"You may find their loyalties divided. Make an effort, if you can, to win them over to our side, but don't overextend yourself. I know this is a difficult situation, but you've proven yourself on the battlefield, and your loyalty to the Crown is unquestioned. See us through to the spring safely, and we shall see about making your promotion more permanent."

"Yes, Commander. Might I ask when the remainder of the army will march?"

"I was going to rest them for a couple of days, but all things considered, it might be better if we head out later today."

"Probably for the best."

"I want daily reports sent to Hawksburg. From there, they can be recalled to the capital."

"Daily reports?"

"Yes, anything from the mundane to rumours. If you hear it, write it down. I know this is a far cry from what you're used to, Carlson, but we need to keep ahead of things. Oh, and if at any time you feel you or your command is in danger of violence, I want to hear about it. Is that clear?"

"Crystal clear."

"Good." She handed him a series of papers. "These are your orders, along with authorization to draw rations and so forth." She noted his look of consternation. "Don't worry. Most of it is rather routine. With any luck, this whole situation will sort itself out."

FIVE

Winter

WINTER 965 MC

The first snow arrived early and with a vengeance, blanketing the entire kingdom in a thick layer of white. The Army of Merceria, safely spread amongst the great cities of the kingdom, dug in for the winter even as new recruits began arriving in Wincaster.

Based on the success of the closely packed Orc spearmen, Gerald decided these new Human warriors would be trained in a similar style. This meant that their weapons were much easier to produce, although it would still require the capital's smiths to work for months preparing armour in sufficient quantity.

As always, Beverly was the marshal's ears and eyes, assessing the new warriors' abilities, then developing drills to employ with these new troops. The queen also took an active part in this expansion, giving the entire army a new sense of pride.

There was a celebratory mood in the air, what with the magic circle in Galburn's Ridge and Revi back from Ironcliff. Anna's closest advisors were invited to the Royal Palace to celebrate the season at the Midwinter Feast. Even Tempus was in a good mood, chewing away at a large bone, occasionally licking his chops.

Gerald had never seen so much food in one place. He reached across, stabbing out at a nearby platter of sausages. His aim true, he speared one, but as he brought it back to his plate, it escaped, falling to the table.

Anna laughed while Tempus tilted his head, raising an ear. "I hope you're better at training than you are at capturing your dinner."

"It's these forks," he complained. "They're different from the usual ones."

"Yes," added Prince Alric. "They're from Weldwyn."

Gerald held his fork before him, displaying its end to those at the table. "It should have more tines, although I must admit the grip is nice."

"It's a fork, not a weapon, although it is made for stabbing. Perhaps we should style it after a Mercerian Broadsword to make it more to your liking?"

"Now that I can get behind." The marshal rescued the stranded sausage, this time with a firm stab. "There, that's better. In some ways, it IS like a new weapon—one only needs to become proficient in its use."

Anna turned to Hayley. "How are things in Queenston?"

"Very well, at last report. I was thinking of heading out there later this week. I hear our breeding stock is finally here."

"The mastiffs?" said Albreda. "How did they return with Weldwyn under occupation?"

"Through Trollden, actually. The river has been cleared all the way to the sea. In fact, Colbridge is being swamped with shipping."

"From the Continent?"

"No, from Weldwyn. Many of their ships fled at first sight of the enemy, taking refuge with us over the winter."

"That brings up something I'd like to discuss," said Anna. "We need some way of dealing with that Kurathian fleet."

"We could build a fleet of our own," suggested Alric.

"And we will, eventually, but there's no way we could construct enough ships to take on a Kurathian prince. Not to mention we have little experience with war at sea."

"Just a moment," said Gerald as he swallowed a mouthful of food. "There's another approach. I suggest we take the ports. Without a city to shelter in, they'll be forced to return home. Either that or sit out at sea, where the weather will play havoc with their ships. They don't call it the Sea of Storms for nothing."

"Easier said than done," said Alric. "The ports of Weldwyn are well defended."

"Yes, but there's only two of them."

"True, and while Southport is well within marching distance, Riversend is clear across the other side of the kingdom."

"A pity we don't have a Fire Mage," said Aubrey.

"Is it?" said Beverly. "We didn't need one when we torched their ships back in sixty-one."

"True, but we had control of the city back then. We're in a far different position these days."

"I suppose we'll need to give it some more thought."

Anna looked at Gerald. "What are your ideas for the campaign?"

"I've been considering that a lot. I foresee a two-pronged assault. First, we land the main army across the river from Kingsford, then march on Aldgrave. Once that's in our hands, we'll move up the road to Mirstone. Meanwhile, Alric will command the second army in the south, crossing at Colbridge. They'll march west to Waldstock, then turn south, taking Bramwitch, then Southport. All of this will be coordinated by means of Aubrey's magic."

"You mean the Orcs' magic," said the Life Mage.

"I stand corrected," said the marshal. "In any case, we'll have the advantage of being able to communicate over long distances. Of course, we can't use that for everything, or we'll wear out our mages, so we'll still use riders for the more mundane reports. To prevent the enemy from learning our plans, all official information will be written in Orcish."

"In Orc?" said Alric.

"Yes. We did that in Norland, and it worked out well."

"But they don't have a written language, do they?"

"No, but we've been writing it down as it sounds."

"You mean phonetically?" said Aubrey.

"I suppose I do," said Gerald. "To speed things up, both Alric and I will need Orcs on our respective staffs to help with translation."

"Staffs," said Alric. "It's still an idea I find strange."

"It proved very useful up north, Bronwyn aside."

"Yes," agreed Beverly. "It made it much easier to react when things went in unexpected directions."

"Unexpected directions," mused Fitz. "You have quite a way with words, my dear."

"Speaking of unexpected," said the queen. "How are things going in Galburn's Ridge?"

"You mean the negotiations? About as well as can be expected. The earls are digging their heels in, although they have, for the moment, put their differences aside when it comes to trying to kill each other."

"And are they still pushing for Bronwyn to be their queen?"

"I'm afraid so," said Lord Richard. "I think they're all of the belief that once she's crowned, they can marry her off to a son and rule Norland as they always have."

"We must put a stop to that."

"What would you propose?"

"Tell them we shall agree to Bronwyn's rule provided they adopt the succession laws of Merceria."

The baron grinned. "That would make Bronwyn queen for life, regardless of her marital status."

"Are you sure that's wise?" asked Gerald. "I still don't know if I would trust her."

"Sir Gareth has been keeping a close eye on her. I doubt she'll try anything under his watchful gaze."

"The last knight we gave her fell in love with her," said Beverly.

Her father barked out a laugh. "That won't work with Sir Gareth. He's wise to those sorts of tactics."

"When will you return north?" asked the queen.

"Albreda and I will visit Bodden, then recall there sometime next week."

"It's odd to think about how much that spell has affected us," said Gerald. "It wasn't so long ago that we'd set aside weeks for such a journey. Now it's a simple matter of casting a spell."

"Not quite simple," said Albreda. "I might remind you it took considerable power to create those circles of magic."

"And we are grateful for the sacrifice," said Anna. "One day, there'll be circles in all the cities of Merceria, and hopefully Weldwyn as well."

"That would take a lot of mages, not to mention all the gold and silver required for their construction."

"We need more mages first," said Anna. Her gaze sought out Alric's youngest sister. "Speaking of which, how is your learning going, Edwina?"

"Quite well," the young woman explained. "Aubrey is an excellent tutor."

"Indeed?" said Revi. "It seems like only yesterday she was my apprentice, and now she has become the teacher. My, how things change."

"For the better," said Anna. "That reminds me, Aubrey, what do you think of using the Saurian gates?"

The table fell quiet.

"You know those are dangerous," warned Alric. "Look what happened to Revi."

"Yes, but he is restored to us, thanks to Aubrey and Kraloch."

"What is it you're suggesting?"

A look of determination settled over the queen's face. "I'm going to Queenston, and the Saurian gate is the most efficient way to do that. I shall, of course, have Aubrey and Kraloch use their magic on my return to ensure I am in the best of health."

Alric paled. "But you are carrying the Royal Heir."

"I'm so glad you noticed, but that does not prevent me from travelling."

"You should be resting, not travelling through gates."

"And I shall be." She swivelled her gaze. "Tell me, Hayley, how is the construction going in Queenston?"

"Very well," replied the High Ranger. "The engineer, Begrin, has been making good progress. The wall is partially complete, as are several towers."

"Begrin?" piped up Kasri. "That sounds Dwarven."

"He is," said Herdwin, who sat on her right. "And a fine one, too. Why, he had the entire city planned out right from the start."

"An entire city, from nothing. I'd love to see that."

"Perhaps Her Majesty might let us accompany her?"

Anna smiled. "I would like that."

"It appears I lost the skirmish," said Alric.

"Don't think of it as a skirmish so much as a new opportunity. Come with us and see what they've been up to. Who knows, one day we may live there on a more permanent basis."

"How long have they been building there?" asked Kasri.

"They started back in the autumn of sixty-one."

"Yes," added Hayley, "and they haven't slowed down yet."

"Is there an actual reason for this visit?" said Alric. "Or are we just visiting to get out of the capital?"

"I want to find out how the mastiffs are settling in," replied Anna. "Although I must admit I am curious to see how the city is progressing."

"It's not a city," said Gerald, "merely an oversized camp."

"Not anymore," said Hayley. "It's grown by leaps and bounds."

"Yes," added Fitz. "And its proximity to Bodden has increased trade there considerably, and for that, I am truly grateful." He raised his goblet on high. "Let's toast to Queenston's success, shall we?"

The closest Saurian gate was at the village of Uxley. A train of carriages was hastily organized, and three days later, arrived at the Royal Estate where Anna had grown up.

The Royal Entourage had increased considerably since her youth, yet the enthusiasm at her arrival in the village remained as heartfelt as ever. A quick stop at the Old Oak tavern led to a longer visit than expected.

By the time the carriages rolled up to the estate, it was well past midnight, yet Hanson was there to greet them. The old fellow sported even less hair these days, but there was still fire in his eyes. Everyone at the hall fussed over the queen, and Anna clearly loved the attention.

That night she sat in the trophy room, warming herself by the fire, Alric at her side and Tempus by her feet, the great mastiff stretching out towards the fireplace. Gerald took a separate seat closer to the flames, casting his gaze around.

"It's been a long time since we sat here," he said. "I still remember when we pranked Fitz."

Anna giggled. "Yes, that was fun, although I believe this room looks better without all the trophies on the walls." She'd ordered them replaced with paintings, giving the place a much calmer feeling.

"It will be odd going to the gate without Lily," said Gerald.

"True, but the winter is hard on the Saurians. Better they weather it out back in Erssa Saka'am. Don't worry. They'll return in plenty of time to help with the campaign."

"I'm sure they will." He looked over at Alric, who'd dozed off. "Have you two come up with a name yet?"

"Several, in fact, but it's hard to narrow it down to one. I'm hoping that will become easier once we know if it's a boy or girl."

He smiled. "You'll make a wonderful mother."

"What makes you say that?"

"Because I know you. You plan for everything, and despite your present discomfort, I sense you're excited about the birth."

Now it was her turn to smile. She stretched her legs, revelling in the feeling. Alric let out a snore, then shifted slightly, causing her to giggle.

"I'm hesitant to bring this up," said Anna, "but I think you need someone."

"I'm not sure I follow?" said Gerald.

"You've been alone for so long. You should have someone to share your life with." She held up her hand. "Yes, I know. You're part of my family, and I shall always consider you my father, but you deserve so much more. I'd like to see you happy."

"I AM happy."

"Are you, truly? You throw yourself into your work, but beneath that tough exterior, I sense a sadness."

He stared at the flames, his soul in turmoil. "I suppose that's true. I see what you and Alric have, and it reminds me of Meredith." He turned to look at her, tears welling up. "I know it's been years, but a part of me still longs to be with her, not to mention Sally."

"And you will, one day," said Anna, then added, "A long time from now, though, Saxnor willing. I still need you."

He smiled, although his heart wasn't in it. "You have a long life ahead of you, Anna, one filled with love and happiness, but my time is coming to an end."

"Don't say that!"

He caught the panic in her voice. "Don't worry. I'm not going anywhere, just ruminating in my old age. Anyway, with the coming invasion, I have no time for falling in love—not to suggest anyone is lining up to become the new Duchess of Wincaster."

"I'm not proposing you marry for convenience's sake; merely keep your heart open to the possibility. If you remember, Alric and I didn't get along so well when we first met."

He smiled, this time meaning it. "I remember it well, and I hear what you're saying. I shall indeed keep my heart open to the possibility, although I doubt a military campaign is an ideal location for such a thing."

"Good. Now summon Sophie, will you? I'm going to need help getting this stomach of mine out of this chair."

Queenston differed greatly from what Gerald remembered. Of course, the basic elements were still there, including the three hills that defined the area, but they were now within the confines of a nearly complete stone wall. The town had grown significantly, with a Palace now atop the cave containing the Saurian Temple. Before it lay a grand avenue leading south, bordered by lush green grass and well-ordered buildings.

Around the town wandered Humans and Orcs, along with possibly the largest population of Dwarves outside of their mountain enclaves.

Hayley had been the first to travel through the gate, allowing her to organize a welcoming committee for the queen. Anna, upon her arrival, made straight for the kennels, where the Kurathian handler Montag oversaw the breeding of the mastiffs.

Tempus, despite his age, rushed towards them, barking as he went. It only took a moment for the great war dogs to respond, sending deafening howls rolling across the fields.

"Look at his energy," said Gerald. "You'd think he was just a pup."

Anna smiled. "It's nice to see him enjoying himself."

He chuckled. "Yes, although it might be a tad more enjoyable if they weren't so loud."

Across from them, the Dwarven militia practiced their tactics on the training grounds, moving in precision through various formations. Gerald leaned against the wooden fence that marked off the area.

"What do you think?" asked Anna, coming to stand beside him.

"They're impressive, I'll grant you, and a wonderful addition to the local garrison. I have no doubt they'd defend the place with great gusto."

"Gusto?" she laughed. "Where ever did you get that from?"

"Lanaka, if you must know. He says it's a Kurathian word."

"I doubt that. They probably picked it up somewhere back in the old country."

"Where's Tempus?"

"Saying hello to his new friends. They managed to procure quite a few for breeding."

"And when you say 'quite a few'?"

"Two dozen, with the promise of more to come. You shall have a full two companies to march into Weldwyn, although you'll still need to use them sparingly. It takes years to properly train them."

"Of that, I'm well aware. I can assure you I shall only deploy them if cavalry threaten." Anna's gaze drifted to the neatly organized buildings. "It's odd, seeing everything so..."

"Uniform?"

"Yes, but there's something else I can't quite put my finger on."

"I know what you mean," said Gerald. "It's the drainage. The Dwarves constructed a completely subterranean sewer system."

"Wincaster has one of those."

"True, but Wincaster added them years after the city was built. Queenston, on the other hand, was built from the beginning with all those tunnels. Apparently, it's much easier to deal with when the houses don't keep getting in the way. The streets are also straight, not to mention spread out."

"I hear they also marked out a spot for the new magical academy."

"I thought that was going in the old Royal Estate in Hawksburg?"

"And it will, for now, but eventually, they'll need something bigger."

"Just how big were you thinking?"

"I want dozens of mages in Merceria, maybe even a hundred or more."

"So many?"

"I used to believe a dozen was a good number, but look at what happened in Weldwyn? We need to secure the future of magic, and we can't do that with so few. In any case, the new academy will be purpose-built for the training of mages. It's still some years away, of course, but you know how much I like to plan."

"Yes," said Gerald. "It is your defining characteristic."

"I'll take that as a compliment."

"As it was meant to be."

Alric's voice drifted towards them. "If you two are done watching the Dwarves, I've got a little surprise for you."

Anna whirled around a little too quickly, for she temporarily lost her balance. Gerald reached out, grabbing her arm before she fell.

She regained her composure quickly. "What kind of surprise?"

"I'm told they built a rather nice tavern, and there's Dwarven ale."

"Then lead on," said Anna. "Although, I might limit myself to a nice cider for now."

SIX

Summersgate

WINTER 965 MC

James Goodwin sat in his carriage, watching from afar as warriors broke into a nearby manor house. Moments later, they emerged, gripping the occupant's arms and tossing him into the back of a wagon.

"That marks the end of Lord Stafford," he mused. "How many more on the list?"

"Only three," replied Lord Godfrey. "The opposition is simply melting away."

"It's a pity we couldn't account for the rest of the Royal Family."

"We knew Prince Alric was always beyond our reach. It matters little in the long run if one of his sisters survived."

"And you're sure the others are dead?"

"You saw what's left of the Palace," said Lord Godfrey. "We know Queen Igraine was present, along with Prince Alstan and Princess Edwina. There's no way any of them could have escaped that catastrophe."

"What about Althea?"

His mentor shrugged. "Who cares? Althea can't inherit, and she's hardly a military threat to our new rulers. No, I think we can safely assume she's fled, in which case she is of little concern to us."

James nodded at the letter. "And the rest of the names on that list?"

"They will be dealt with in time. I doubt any of them are left in Summersgate but don't worry, I have agents combing through the other cities of Weldwyn. If they haven't crossed the border into Merceria, we shall find them."

The wagon rolled off, the screams of its prisoners echoing down the street. James Goodwin chuckled. "This is all so easy."

"See? What did I tell you? One by one, we pick off our opponents, and there's nothing they can do about it. Even as their star sets, ours arises anew, with the promise of a bright, prosperous future." He chuckled. "You know what would be interesting? Think of what we could do if we had Princess Althea within our grasp?"

"She would be worth a handsome reward, I'd wager," said James.

"No, no. Think bigger."

"Bigger?"

"Yes," said Lord Godfrey. "We could have her marry you. That would make you the legitimate claimant to the throne."

"I doubt Brida would like that. She's seized the throne for herself."

"Yes, but she can't rule Weldwyn forever. She still has her homeland to contend with."

"I wonder how long she'll remain here?"

"Likely some months yet. By all accounts, she has some matters to attend to before she leaves."

"And by 'accounts', you mean?"

"Personal vendettas. She's determined to punish anyone who had anything to do with her father's imprisonment."

"Even the guards?"

"Especially the guards. She's not satisfied with just the bodies of the Royal Family—anybody who held any rank in the army of Weldwyn is fair game. That, of course, is precisely what we want. After all, neither of us is a warrior, so we have nothing to worry about."

"And," added James, "we also provided our new masters with a list of enemies."

"That too. I tell you, my friend, our future has never looked brighter."

"Shall we go and celebrate our victory?"

"I can't," said Lord Godfrey. "I'm afraid I have some urgent business to attend to. I would suggest you get some rest. It's likely to be a busy day tomorrow. Shall I drop you at your home?"

"If you would be so kind."

"Very well." He rapped his cane on the top of the carriage. "Onward, driver, to the Goodwin estate."

The carriage sprang forward, jostling them as it sped through the streets of Summersgate.

James Goodwin stepped from the carriage, chuckling as his feet hit the ground.

"You find something amusing?" said Lord Godfrey.

"Only my mother's absolute trust in me. The woman will believe anything I tell her."

"Indeed. Shall I drop by tomorrow morning? We can go over our plans one more time before heading off to the Palace."

"That is most agreeable," said James.

He stood back, waiting as the driver cracked the whip and the carriage rolled on. Turning to face the door to his home, he took a moment to look over the place. It was not the most ostentatious of houses, and he briefly considered laying claim to the manor house of Lord Stafford. It would be a significant improvement over his present lodgings, but then again, he might do even better still. The thought of Princess Althea came to mind, and he was struck by how right it felt. Doubtless, King Leofric's daughter might object to the union, but once she whelped a child, she would no longer be needed. A smile crept over his face as he thought of her, grovelling on her knees for her life.

James Goodwin had always been a man easily swayed by his emotions. Unfortunately, such thoughts generally led to a dark place for those around him, as many had discovered.

He stepped up to the door and entered his home, where servants immediately greeted him. After divesting himself of his cloak, he made his way to the library, his mother's favourite place of solitude. She sat silently by the window, book in hand.

"Good day, Mother."

"Good evening, James. I trust all is well?"

He adopted a somewhat concerned expression. "Unfortunately, it is not. There has been some trouble of late, and I fear my name may have been mentioned."

"What kind of trouble?"

"Our new overlord has ordered the arrest of several noble families. It's only a matter of time before we find our own name on the list." He noted the quick intake of breath, her look of worry.

"I'm afraid," he continued, "that I've been approached by unscrupulous individuals. I fear they may force me into something I do not want to do, all in the name of survival."

"We must get you help, James."

"Help? From who? In case you haven't noticed, Mother, the entire realm is now under the rule of the Twelve Clans. We can expect little from them in the way of mercy." He saw the tears forming and knew his lie had struck home.

"Then you must do what is necessary to survive," she said as she closed her book and rose. "I shall go to the chapel and pray to Malin for your deliverance from this curse."

"Curse? It is no curse. Rather, the action of a superior foe. One who will brook no interference with their... schemes."

There, he saw it. The utter resignation that they were trapped in an impossible situation. It was almost too hard to maintain his worried façade. Instead, he averted his gaze, lest his manner give away his deceit.

"One day," he said, "I may be called upon to do something I might regret."

His mother moved closer, touching his arm. "You must do what is necessary to survive. We all must."

At that point, he knew he had her. She was trapped as surely as a fly in a spider's web.

James nodded his head. "You're right, of course." He steeled himself before meeting her gaze. Her tears were building. He saw her struggling to keep them at bay and marvelled at how easily he'd strung her along.

"I shall retire to my office to contemplate my future, however bleak it might appear. Call me when dinner is served."

"I will," his mother promised.

Morning found James once again in the company of his co-conspirator. They rode to the Palace in silence, speaking only when the ruins of the place came into view.

"I still find the view shocking," said Lord Godfrey. "Don't you?"

"I must confess I do, although it grieves me not to be rid of all of Leofric's family."

"I imagine they suffered greatly as the Palace collapsed."

"It pleases me to think they did," said James. "Although I believe it more likely they died quickly."

"How can you be so sure?"

"I've heard reports from first-hand witnesses. They say it collapsed as soon as the dragon landed upon it. By all accounts, it was all over in but a moment."

"Be that as it may, we are not here to visit the old Palace itself, rather that of Brida's new Palace, a large mansion seized in her name. I hear the Mercerian queen stayed there when she visited Weldwyn back in sixty."

"And how did the High Queen of the Clans take that news?"

"Quite well. In fact, she insisted on staying there."

The carriage rolled to a stop.

"Before we enter," said Lord Godfrey, "I feel I should warn you."

"About what?"

"Brida can be temperamental at times. It is often better to spare the details and stick to the facts."

"Surely she's not upset with us?"

"No," said Lord Godfrey, "but she is frustrated with the slow pace of conquest. You need to understand, occupying a kingdom such as Weldwyn is one thing; running it, quite another. Back in the Clanholdings, she wasn't a queen so much as a local chieftain."

"Yet she is called the High Queen?"

"Just as Dathen was called High King, but it didn't help him when he was crushed beneath that dragon."

James Goodwin shuddered. "I hate to think of that monstrosity flying over us."

"You should be thanking Prince Tarak. If it weren't for those dragons of his, the men of Weldwyn would have put up more of a fight, and then where would we be?" Lord Godfrey climbed down from the carriage, making for the door, leaving his companion to play catch-up.

A pair of guards halted them, but they were let in after identifying themselves. A servant waited, a man of Weldwyn, by the look of him, leading James to wonder if he was a leftover from the Royal Family or simply someone hired off the streets.

"This way," the man said. "I'll take you to see Her Majesty."

They were led down a hall and into what looked to be a dining room converted into a makeshift throne room, where Brida sat on an ornate wooden chair. A massive bare-chested warrior stood behind her, his axe resting head-first on the floor.

"Your Majesty," said Lord Godfrey. "You honour us."

The High Queen's gaze flitted to his companion. "And who do we have here?"

"This is Lord James Goodwin," he replied. "His name is, I believe, known to you?"

"Ah yes, I remember now. Welcome, Lord James. Lord Godfrey speaks highly of you."

"I'm flattered, Your Majesty," responded James.

"I am led to understand the two of you have been most helpful of late."

"You are referring to the capture of Lord Stafford?"

"Indeed. His arrest has almost completed my collection."

"Collection?" said James.

"Yes, of all the top nobles of Weldwyn. Some eluded my grasp by dying before we could arrest them, but I'm confident the rest will soon be in the dungeons where they belong."

"I am glad we could be of service, Your Majesty."

"You've proven to be of great service," continued the queen, "but the job is far from over. As you know, there are still three names on that list I want tracked down."

"Yes," said Lord Godfrey. "Lady Lindsey Martindale, Lord Tulfar Axehand, and Lord Parvan Luminor, if I'm not mistaken."

"I already have people travelling to Tivilton to arrest Lord Parvan. What I require from you two is to track down Lady Lindsey and the Dwarf, Lord Tulfar."

James stiffened. "Tulfar is Lord of Mirstone. The last I heard, we have yet to capture that town."

"You are correct, but once it falls, I want him in my hands. As for Lady Lindsey, she has somehow eluded my men. We believe she may be fleeing east, towards Merceria."

"Rest assured," said Lord Godfrey, "we shall do all we can to locate her."

"See that you do. A man is only of use to me when he continues to serve. Fail me in this, and there will be no second chance."

"Understood, Your Majesty."

"Good, now be off about your business. I have many things awaiting my attention." They both bowed deeply and backed from the room.

By the time they returned to the carriage, James was sweating profusely. "By Malin, that was a most distressing audience. I can see what you mean when you say she can be temperamental."

"Yes," said Lord Godfrey, "and I'm afraid it puts us in a rather distressing situation. I don't know about you, but I'm loathe to leave the safety of Summersgate on the mad hopes of locating this Viscountess Lindsey, not to mention the thought of sifting through a Dwarven stronghold."

"What do you think she meant about Lord Parvan?"

"You mean about sending people to arrest him? I daresay that won't be easy if his reputation is anything to go on."

"I thought we considered him a potential ally?"

"And so we did, but when the wind shifts, so, too, must we."

"And am I to one day be as carelessly discarded?"

"Of course not," said Lord Godfrey. "Lord Parvan is an Elf, hardly a trustworthy ally to begin with. We, on the other hand, see eye to eye on many issues. Fear not, my friend, we are in this together to the end."

"Yes, but to what end?"

"I understand your reservations, but there's an old saying I like that says, 'the man who doesn't gamble will never win.'"

"Is this nothing more than a gamble?"

"I prefer to think of it more as a calculated strategy. It has done well for us so far. I see no reason to doubt it will continue to do so."

Lord James took a deep breath. "Very well, I suppose we're too far in now to back out, anyway. We shall stay the course, whatever that may bring."

"That's the spirit."

"What is our next step?"

"We make a pretence of engaging in an active search for these nobles. My hope is we can delay it long enough for her to lose interest."

"And if she doesn't?"

"Then we'll decide on a different course of action, but I'm hoping we can at least delay till spring. Say, you don't think you could talk your mother into working for us, do you?"

James smiled. "I can make her do anything. Why? What have you got in mind?"

"Sooner or later, Prince Alric will bring an army to liberate his precious Weldwyn, and even convince the Mercerians to join him. When that happens, we shall need as much information about their numbers as possible."

"Are you suggesting I send her into their camp as a spy?"

"Why not?"

"Well, how would she get word back to us?"

Lord Godfrey waved his hand. "We can work out the details later. Do you think you could convince her or not?"

"By spring? Easily. I'm just not sure how effective she would be."

"One thing at a time. We'll start by having her carry out some head counting here in the city. That will tell us if she's trustworthy enough."

James smiled. "Ah, I see what you're getting at. An excellent idea."

"Yes, it is, isn't it? I must say I'm rather proud of myself for that."

"And rightly so."

"What do you say we celebrate with a tankard of ale down at the Amber Shard?"

"Only one?"

"Well," replied Lord Godfrey, "let's start with one. After all, we wouldn't want to appear too eager for all the ladies in attendance."

"You truly think there'll be women there after all this city has been through?"

"My dear fellow, it is precisely because of all that has transpired they WILL be present. They still need to make a living, and what better way than by entertaining the victorious?"

"You make a compelling case."

"Trust me, it is no idle boast." He held his hand over his heart. "I swear to you in the name of Malin there shall be plenty of women there to entertain the likes of you."

"Plenty being how many?"

Lord Godfrey let out a laugh. "More than enough to satisfy you, you rogue. And here I thought I was the randy one. Has this something to do with the idea of coupling with a princess? If you like, I can arrange for a woman to be suitably adorned in a fashionable dress."

A smile creased the lips of James Goodwin. "I just might take you up on that offer. Mind you, she would have to bear more than a passing resemblance to the princess. How tall would you say Althea was?"

"I can't really say. I never actually met her in person."

"Then I shall settle for someone of average height."

Lord Godfrey grinned. "Consider it done."

SEVEN

Resistance

WINTER 965 MC

Toby Whitaker looked down at his waterlogged boots, noticing the seams were beginning to wear thin. And to make matters worse, the constant trudging through the snow had turned his feet numb.

"I hate this," he said, his breath frosting in the air before him. "Why couldn't we wait until spring?"

His older companion smiled, showing off his missing teeth. "Now, now," said Angus. "Our job is to fight when we're told, not complain about every minor inconvenience."

"Inconvenience? I could lose my toes!"

"We'll rest soon, then you can warm yourself up."

Toby glanced at the troops in front of them. "Don't they ever tire?"

Angus followed his gaze. The mail-clad warriors of Prince Tarak kept a steady pace despite the cold weather, surprising considering where they came from. He wondered if the Kurathian Isles ever saw snow, then shook his head.

"Never mind them. They're all show."

"They can afford to be," said Toby. "They have decent boots."

"I tell you what; next time we fight the enemy, find yourself a new pair."

"You mean take them off a dead man? That's ghoulish."

Angus shrugged. "Given the choice between plundering a dead man's boots or freezing your toes off, I think the answer is obvious, don't you?"

"I suppose. It wasn't like this back in sixty-one."

"I might remind you we lost the war in sixty-one. This time, we conquered the entire kingdom." He paused a moment, considering his words. "Well, all right, maybe not the whole country, but we'll rectify that once we reach Mirstone."

Toby cast his eyes around nervously.

"What are you doing?" asked his older companion.

"Just checking to make sure there are no blackbirds around."

"That's a load of superstitious nonsense."

"Is it? We saw one when we last invaded this wretched place, and look what happened to us. I told you then, and I'll repeat it here—a blackbird is a sign of doom."

"And here you are looking for them," said Angus. "It's the middle of winter, my friend. You won't see their like in weather like this."

Toby opened his mouth to say more, but a horn sounded in the distance, grabbing his attention. "What was that?"

"I don't know, but it's got the Kurathians all riled up."

The armoured warriors in front of them picked up the pace, deploying into a three-deep line. In answer, the leader of the Clansmen berated their troops, shoving them into a rough mimicry of their ally.

"I don't like this," said Toby.

"Hush now, and keep your eyes to your front." Angus drew his sword, a rusty, old thing that had been in his family for three generations. He unslung his shield and held it ready, his eyes peering through the early morning fog.

"See anything?" the younger man asked.

Everything went quiet, and for a moment, it was easy to believe they were the only living souls for miles around. The first sign of trouble was a clattering as bolts struck the Kurathians, rattling off shields and digging into chainmail hauberks, with the screams of the wounded and dying quickly following.

Toby felt his skin crawl. His eyes darted around, seeking out the enemy, but all he saw were the backs of the prince's warriors.

"What's happening?" he shouted.

"It's an ambush," replied Angus. "But whoever it is has met their match. A few stray bolts won't stop those Kurathians."

More bolts dug in, thinning the ranks before another horn sounded. Everyone held their breath, expecting the enemy to reveal themselves, but instead, all they heard was a woman's voice.

"Surrender," she called out, "and we shall spare your lives."

Toby heard the Kurathian captain cursing in his own language—at least that was what it sounded like to him—followed immediately by orders, for the elite warriors raised shields and readied their weapons.

"Here they come," said Angus. "Prepare yourself."

Boots crunched on snow, the sound coming closer with every passing moment. The men in front of them suddenly advanced, disappearing into the mist, leaving the Clansmen in their ragged line.

The clang of steel on steel rang out. Clearly, they'd engaged the enemy, yet nothing could be seen. The sounds, however, told a story of their own. Yells and screams came back, all of them in Kurathian—who were they fighting, and why was the enemy not suffering?

The struggle continued for some time, and all the while, the Clansmen grew more uncertain of what to do. Even their captain, an experienced warrior, stood there just to Toby's right, apparently unable to make a decision.

The sound of fighting finally died down and then came hurried footsteps. Out of the mist burst the Kurathians, fleeing for their lives. They were experienced enough to keep a grip on their weapons, but the looks on their faces told the world they knew they were outmatched. They streamed past, pushing their way through the Clan lines, and continuing up the road, heading back towards the capital.

Everything got eerily quiet. Toby watched the mist as it thinned out and a grey shape came towards them. At first, he took it for a wall, for it was long and not quite the height of a warrior. He wondered if it might be some form of magic, but then it drew closer, revealing a solid line of mailed Dwarves, shoulder to shoulder, with large square shields held so close together they looked like they were joined. Above their heads, he saw axes and hammers, ready to bring death and destruction.

Toby Whitaker considered himself a brave man, but something in the faces of these dour warriors drove all thought of standing his ground from his mind. He looked around at his comrades, but his captain had already turned to run. It only took a moment for the rest to follow his example.

The company of Clansmen soon became a mass of panicking individuals. Toby went down, slipping in the snow and ice. Angus grabbed his arm, hauling his friend to his feet, only to be struck down as a fellow warrior pushed him out of the way.

When they'd started out, they had been a confident army, marching to an almost certain victory. Now, they were nothing more than a chaotic mob, intent only on survival.

Toby looked up as the Dwarves neared. Axes rose and fell, slicing through the few who dared resist their advance. He threw down his sword and put his arms up, praying to the Gods to spare his life.

Althea watched with satisfaction as the enemy broke. The Kurathians had shown some backbone, but their collapse precipitated the disintegration of their lines. A large enemy group now streamed westward, lost to her sight in the early morning mist. She nodded to the Dwarf beside her, who then put a horn to his lips. Three single notes echoed through the air, the signal for Lord Tulfar to begin his part.

Brogar Hammerhand came up beside her. "What shall we do with the prisoners, Highness?"

"Please," she said. "Call me commander."

"Certainly, Commander, but the question still remains."

"Gather their weapons and keep a close watch on them. Once Lord Tulfar has done his part, we shall consult with him on the fate of these invaders."

"I must say I'm surprised. I expected the Clansmen to put up more of a fight."

"These are not their best warriors," said Althea. "I suspect their elite troops are waiting out the winter back in Summersgate. In the meantime, we at least bloodied their nose."

"I have to admit," said the Dwarf, "your idea to cut off their retreat was inspired. Tell me, have you read much of military tactics?"

"Not particularly, but it seemed like the logical thing to do."

He nodded sagely. "You are truly a great warrior, as this battle proved."

"This was not a battle, merely a skirmish, but I thank you for the kind words. In truth, the victory here is entirely due to the stalwart warriors of Mirstone. Without their discipline and training, none of this would've been possible. It's a pity my father didn't have any of you when he marched into Norland. It could well have saved him."

"We cannot change the past," said Brogar, "but you have shown us the way forward. The Army of the Clans will think twice about coming down this road again, at least this winter."

"Yes, but come spring, they'll throw everything they have at us." She looked skyward. The sun was out in full force now, the mist burning away quickly. Off in the distance, she heard more fighting.

Brogar chuckled. "It appears Lord Tulfar has engaged the enemy."

"Detail twenty warriors to guard the prisoners," she ordered, "then have the line advance. It's time to place the enemy between the hammer and anvil."

"Yes, Commander."

The Dwarves advanced, maintaining their tight formation. They had gone no more than fifty paces when they heard Lord Tulfar's signal.

"It is done," said Brogar. "Victory is ours!"

The snow was splattered red, while swords and shields lay discarded everywhere. Off to the north side of the road huddled a group of Clansmen, their faces full of despair. Clearly, they expected death. The thought struck a chord in Althea's heart. She had no love for Clansmen, had even sworn to make them pay, but now, seeing them like this, her resolve wavered. These were no longer faceless warriors but living men, each with parents, possibly even children of their own. At that instant, she understood the burden of command. Their fate was now in her hands—they would live or die based on what she did next.

Althea halted her warriors. "Set up a perimeter guard," she ordered. "The rest can take a break while we deal with the survivors."

She walked over to the Clansmen, Brogar close at hand. There was no opposition amongst them, merely a look of utter defeat.

"You," she said, standing before a young man. "What's your name?"

"Toby," he replied. "Toby Whitaker."

"Where are you from?"

"Halsworth."

"Why did you come here?"

He looked up in confusion. "We were ordered here?"

"No, I mean, why did you invade Weldwyn?"

"We were told King Leofric was dead, along with a good portion of his army. My Clan Chief ordered us to follow the High Queen, Brida."

"Brida? Would this be the same woman who wanted to marry Prince Alric?"

"I wouldn't know. I am but a humble soldier."

"Not anymore, you're not."

He cast his eyes downward. "No, I suppose not. What's to become of us?"

"That largely depends on you."

"Me?"

Althea smiled. "Well, not you, specifically, but the actions of your people. I'm willing to spare your lives if you agree to my terms."

"I'm no officer. I can't speak for my people."

"Then who can?"

Toby looked around, but his old captain wasn't amongst the prisoners. His gaze came to rest on Angus.

"You're the oldest," he said to his friend. "It looks like you're in charge now."

Angus stood. "Aye, I suppose it falls on me to speak for the Clansmen. What are your terms?"

"Each and every one of you must swear never again to take up arms against Weldwyn. In addition, you will serve out the remainder of this war working the mines of Mirstone."

"That's it, then? We are to be slaves for the rest of our lives?"

"You are not slaves, but prisoners. Once this war is over and the throne restored, you shall be released. You have my word on it."

Angus looked around at his fellow Clansmen—they all seemed to be in agreement. He returned his gaze to their captor. "It appears we have little choice. Very well, we agree, although I would be curious to know who it is that has dealt us such a harsh defeat."

"I am Princess Althea, of the Royal House of Weldwyn."

It was late in the evening by the time they marched into Mirstone. With the prisoners sent to the mines, and the warriors dismissed, Althea and Brogar made their way to where Lord Tulfar waited for them, handing them both drinks as they arrived.

"Come, sit," the lord said. "There is much to discuss." They all took their seats, Althea closest to the raging fire. "You did well today," he continued. "You have a gift for this."

"I only did as I thought best," replied Althea.

"And that was outstanding, but our war has only just begun."

"How long can Mirstone remain free?"

"That largely depends on how many soldiers Brida sends to attack us. Cracking into a Dwarven stronghold is not an easy task, and the mines here are purpose-built to be defensible."

"Yes, but you had to evacuate everyone from above ground. That puts a tremendous strain on your resources, especially food."

"It's true, I'll not deny it, but surely the Mercerians will come to our aid?"

"I cannot say," said Althea. "The last I heard, they were still fighting in Norland. Even if they are successful there, they may lack the resources to assist us."

"Then we must decide on a course of action for ourselves. I'm curious to hear your assessment of our current situation."

"There are only two options: either we evacuate Mirstone and push eastward to Merceria, or we dig in and wait things out."

Lord Tulfar nodded. "I am of a similar mind. We have plenty of freshwater, thanks to underground springs. However, food becomes a more pressing matter, especially now that we have all these prisoners to look after."

"I won't apologize for that. They are still living people, with families back home."

The Dwarf held up his hand. "I'm not condemning you for your actions. This war will be over one day, and we'll need to live once more beside our traditional enemy. The only way to do that is to make peace with our neighbour, and that starts here."

"You surprise me," said Althea. "I expected you to be more ruthless."

"Why? Because I'm a Dwarf? I can't say I blame you. After all, we're known as a stubborn, prideful people."

"Yet, in truth, you are as cultured and refined as any people I have ever met. My father's folly was not including your people in his decisions about running the kingdom. I shall strive to ensure my brother Alstan does not repeat his mistakes."

"I'm afraid it won't be Alstan who'll be king."

She felt her heart stop. "Whatever do you mean?"

"We've been talking to the prisoners. Alstan is dead, as is the queen."

Panic rose within her. "Edwina?" she squeaked out.

Tulfar shook his head. "She was in the Palace when the dragon descended. It appears no one survived."

Althea felt the tears building, yet they would not come. "That makes Alric king," she said, her voice husky with emotion. "He will not stand by and let these invaders have free rein."

"No," agreed Lord Tulfar. "Nor will his warrior queen accept anything but complete victory. My guess is it won't be long before we see a response."

"They won't have the army, especially after all they must have gone through in Norland."

"I hate to say it," said Brogar, "but for all we know, they may have lost the war in the north. Leofric certainly didn't fare well."

"I loved my father," said Althea, "and he was known as a great leader, but his military skills pale in comparison to the Mercerians. You forget—I spent time amongst them."

"You did?" said Lord Tulfar. "I didn't know that."

She nodded. "I was at my brother's wedding."

"That must've been quite the trip."

"It was. It took us weeks to get there. Mind you, that was before they started using their magic to travel back and forth."

"Magic? What magic?"

"The Mercerians have access to a spell called recall. I believe the wild mage created it or discovered it; I'm not sure of the details."

"And how does this recall spell work?"

"Alric tried to explain it to me once, but it was a tad confusing. He said their mages could only travel to places they'd been before, and they could only arrive within a magic circle."

"And what type of magic was this? Earth Magic, perhaps?"

"No, it couldn't be. Albreda is an Earth Mage, of course, but Lady Aubrey could use it as well, and she's a healer."

"Fascinating," said Lord Tulfar. "Not that it helps us at all as we don't possess any mages here at Mirstone. Although I suppose it does mean they could return directly to Summersgate."

"Likely not their best option when the city is overrun."

"Agreed. We must get word to them."

"I hope that has been done already. I can't imagine Arcanus Tyrell not sending word about the city falling."

"Good. That means even as we speak, the Mercerians will likely be planning their return to our soil."

"In that case," said Althea, "let's see how we can assist in their coming campaign."

"What did you have in mind?"

"The most appropriate invasion route from Merceria has always been the road from Falford to Summersgate."

"Aye, it's the best road in terms of quality."

"Yes, but if they crossed from Kingsford, they could bypass Falford altogether and march through Mirstone."

"True," said Tulfar. "Then up to Kinsley and on to the capital. But I still don't see how that helps us."

"The first thing we do is get word to Kingsford with everything we know and convince them to take the Mirstone road. While they're doing that, we'll move west towards Kinsley and secure the area. With any luck, the advancing Mercerians will be able to outmanoeuvre the Clansmen stationed in Falford."

Lord Tulfar rubbed his hands together. "I like your thinking. Now, let's talk details, shall we?"

EIGHT

Preparations

Beverly stood atop the walls of Kingsford, looking down at the docks. After so many years of being cut off from the sea, it was strange to see masts jutting up from below. The river itself was frozen solid, locking these ships in until the spring thaw.

The first thing she'd done upon arriving had been to send scouts to the river's western banks to give advanced warning should the enemy make an appearance. However, it appeared the Clans were content to sit out the winter in the warmth of their cities.

She made her way to the stairs, then descended into the practice yard. Hayley was there, along with close to a hundred rangers, loosing arrows at targets to keep their skills sharp. The High Ranger, spotting the red-headed knight, wandered over to meet her.

"See anything interesting?" Hayley asked.

"Nothing but ice and snow."

"Hardly surprising, considering the season."

"I thought we'd at least see a scout or two. It's what I would've done had I been them."

"Then let's thank Saxnor you're with us."

"How are the rangers doing?"

"We needed to make some allowances for the cold weather, but aside from that, everything's proceeding on schedule."

"And when will you take them out?"

"Gorath will lead the first group early next week. We're just waiting on Kiren-Jool."

"That's a good idea," said Beverly, "taking along a mage. It'll let you recall to safety, should the situation warrant it."

"It only works because we're keeping the numbers small."

"Why small? You have close to a hundred rangers."

"So we can rotate them in and out. The plan is for each group to only be out for about two weeks at a time. That allows them to come back and rest. It also reduces how much food we need to carry, both important issues when you're in enemy territory. I don't suppose your pickets have anything to report?"

"Not yet," said Beverly, "but the enemy will make an appearance sooner or later if only to confirm we're here."

"And if they come in force?"

"The garrison is more than capable of holding them off until reinforcements arrive."

"And how about your own training?"

Beverly smiled. "Our new companies trickled in over the last couple of weeks, and now they're eager to march into Weldwyn. I'll have them out on the common this afternoon. You should drop by and see for yourself."

"I think I shall," said Hayley. "It'll give me something to pass the time."

"Missing Revi?"

"I haven't seen him for weeks. Ever since he got back from Ironcliff, he's been deep in study."

"Let me guess: he's on the verge of a great breakthrough?"

The ranger laughed. "Not quite. He and Aubrey are working on a syllabus for their school of magic."

"Whatever that means."

"He said it's important for mages to know how all magic works, not just their own specialty. We're no different. I'm a ranger, but I still learned about all those melee weapons I'll never use. You must have done the same?"

"Not really," said Beverly. "I mastered every weapon I ever learned about."

"Of course you did. I forgot who I was talking to. I imagine Kraloch could explain it better if you're interested. He worked with Aubrey quite a bit."

"That's all right. I know my cousin well enough to know she's a hard worker. If she says they've got work to do, that's good enough for me."

"I haven't seen that husband of yours?" said Hayley.

"And likely won't till spring. He's holed up in Wincaster studying that Dwarven plate armour. The queen gave him access to the Royal Smithy, so no doubt he's already hard at work on a brand new set of armour for me."

"Must be nice, being married to a master armourer."

"To be honest, I'd prefer he were here with me, but I suppose it's good he's not, less distraction for me."

"Perhaps I should look at things the same way."

"Well," said Beverly, "as long as we're both here without our men, we might as well make the best of it."

"What are you suggesting?"

"Merely that we dine together. It'll help fight off the loneliness of command, not to mention allowing us to keep up to date on what the other is doing."

"Sounds good to me," said Hayley. "You're staying at the duke's estate, aren't you?"

"Yes. He's away in Wincaster."

"When do you want me there?"

"Anytime you like. I usually eat around dusk."

"Dusk it is. Should I bring wine?"

The answer never came, for there was a call from a sentry on the wall.

"Someone's approaching, Commander."

"One of our pickets?" called out Beverly.

"No. They're on foot."

Beverly looked at her comrade. "How did they get past the pickets?"

"I have no idea," said Hayley, "but I bet the wall would afford us a better view." They ran up the steps, halting at the battlements.

Beverly scanned the horizon. "There's your answer." She pointed.

An individual sprinted across the snow while a group of horsemen engaged in a skirmish farther west. At this range, it was difficult to make out details, but one thing was for sure, the pickets were outnumbered. Beverly looked down the wall to where the sentry stood.

"Raise the alarm," she said. "Hayley, bring your rangers to the wall, if you please."

"Why? What are you going to do?"

"Ride out with a company of cavalry."

"You think you'll get there in time?"

"We'll soon see."

Beverly descended the steps and was across the training ground in no time, all the while yelling for the heavy horse to mount up. In emergencies like this, they didn't wait to don their heavy armour, choosing instead only their gambesons and helmets to save time.

Beverly soon had Lightning saddled and mounted quickly enough to lead them out the western gate towards the docks. Of necessity, they travelled two abreast, but the frozen river soon allowed them to spread out as they cleared the ships.

She slowed, allowing those following to catch up. They were soon in a line, weapons drawn, and ready to engage the enemy. Riding on, they closed in on the solitary figure and quickly realized he was one of the mountain folk, looking exhausted as he made his way through the knee-deep snow.

Off in the distance, Beverly's pickets withdrew from the skirmish and headed towards her, the enemy following. She called to her men to halt, then waited as their opponents closed the range. Her pickets, noticing her waiting, slowed their mounts and took up positions on either flank, ready to fight once more.

She watched the enemy horsemen slow as they beheld her preparations for a moment, before they all turned in a well-practiced manoeuvre and rode off westward. There was no denying their nationality, for their precision and the manner of their turn told her all she needed to know. Kurathians had come to Kingsford, and not light horse like the ones employed by Merceria. Her own warriors stayed in line until the enemy riders were well out of sight.

Beverly rode back through the gates, the Dwarf sitting just behind her. It wasn't the most comfortable of seats, but in his state of exhaustion, he was happy not to need to walk. Lightning slowed as they approached the practice field, and then she helped the fellow down.

Hayley, upon seeing their return, came down off the wall. "What have we here?" she called out.

The Dwarf bowed. "My name is Caldrim. Lord Tulfar of Mirstone sent me to inform you the city of Dwarves still stands."

"Are they besieged?" asked Beverly, dismounting.

"Not at the moment. Commander Althea led a successful ambush against the forces of our enemies. It has kept them at bay for the moment, but come spring, they will undoubtedly return."

"Anything else?"

"Yes. We hold a large number of prisoners, Clan warriors all, but they are fast depleting our food stores."

"How far is Mirstone from here?"

"Nigh on a hundred miles."

"Too far to send wagons," mused Hayley. "Although, maybe horses could get through?"

"The biggest issue is those horsemen," said Beverly. "If they show up again, we'll have our hands full." She returned her attention to the Dwarf. "If we were to take the prisoners off your hands, would that leave you enough food till spring?"

"Most assuredly," said Caldrim.

"But how would we do that with those horsemen out there?" asked Hayley.

"Simple," said Beverly. "We deploy Kurathians of our own. If nothing else, it should confuse them."

"You are in league with the Kurathians?" said a wide-eyed Caldrim.

"We took several companies of them into service, yes, but I assure you they are loyal to us."

"How can you be so certain?"

"Commander Lanaka has served us for years. I trust him with my life."

"Yes, but do you trust him with OUR lives?"

"I do," said Beverly, meeting his stare.

"Very well, then I accept he is trustworthy."

"Come, let us feed you, and then you can fill us in on details."

Commander Lanaka rode out with two companies of his cavalry early the next morning. They headed due west, then separated, each company spreading out to watch an ever-expanding area.

By noon, he spotted what he was looking for—a group of heavily armoured Kurathians riding eastward. He recalled his company and formed up into one of their old formations. As a former mercenary, he'd often led his men in four-wide columns, but the Mercerian custom was to ride two abreast. However, for this ruse to work, he must rely on the old traditions.

He kept them at a sedate pace, altering course to intercept his country-men. He soon recognized their livery as they closed, for they carried the pennant of none other than Prince Tarak of Kouras. Not only that, but as they came within hailing distance, he recognized the voice that called out.

"Identify yourself!"

"I am Captain Lanaka," he replied, using his old Kurathian rank. "Do my ears deceive me, or is that Captain Haralan I hear?"

The prince's man halted his column before trotting over. "Lanaka? I didn't know the prince brought mercenaries?"

"He didn't. We are employed by the Clans."

The man nodded. "That makes sense. They are weak in cavalry. Not that their footmen are much better." He laughed at his own jest, Lanaka quickly joining in.

"What brings you here, to the east?" Lanaka asked.

Haralan sobered. "We are on the lookout for Mercerian scouts, but I doubt they would be foolish enough to ride out in this weather."

"And where are you off to at present?"

"To the walls of Kingsford to spy out their garrison."

"Let me spare you the effort," said Lanaka. "We just returned from there with little to report."

"Have they amassed an army?"

"If they have, there's no evidence of it. I believe it is more likely they are tucked away in their capital in fear for their lives."

The captain stared back, judging Lanaka's character before responding. "I shall be pleased to take your word." He was about to turn around and return to his men when he noticed Lanaka's saddle. "You are not using a Kurathian rig?"

"It's too difficult for these Clansmen to replace. It took some adjustment, but we became used to it."

Haralan shook his head. "You mercenaries, you compromise your principles far too easily."

"It is the price we pay for gainful employment. Not everyone has a wealthy prince to sponsor them."

"Nor will you with an attitude like that. I suggest you be on your way, Lanaka, before I take insult."

The commander bowed. "My apologies, Captain. I did not mean to offend."

Lanaka led his men south, keeping the pace slow to watch for Haralan's response. When the prince's man turned north, away from Kingsford, he breathed a sigh of relief.

Beverly watched as the prisoners were brought out. They had a look of defeat in their eyes, not too surprising considering they'd been stuck in the mines for the last few weeks.

Princess Althea rode over towards her. "Dame Beverly, it's been some time since last we met."

"So it has, Your Highness. I see you've been busy in the interim."

"That I have. It appears the Dwarves of Mirstone have adopted me as their own."

"And rightly so. You've proven yourself a highly competent military commander from what I heard. It seems you take after your brother Prince Alric."

"High praise coming from you. I only wish I knew the rest of my family's fate."

"Edwina is safe in Wincaster," said Beverly. "Aegryth Malthunen took her there when Summersgate fell, but we know of no others who survived."

A shadow fell across the young princess's face. "I feared as much. Any idea how the city fell?"

"Treachery, I would warrant. That and an immense dragon."

"A dragon?"

"Aye, massive enough to collapse the Palace beneath its weight. Unfortunately, that's where the queen and Prince Alstan were last reported to be."

"You mentioned treachery?"

"Yes. Based on Aegryth's account, the city fell quickly without resorting to a siege. I'm sorry. Treachery is the only explanation that makes sense."

"Any idea who's responsible?"

"No, but I'll make sure you're informed if we discover anything new. Not that it's likely, under the current circumstances, but sooner or later, we'll retake Summersgate, and then we can get to the bottom of it."

"Thank you," said Althea. "Your words give me hope. I only wish your men could remain here at Mirstone to help us."

"We'll be back. I promise you, but right now, the best way we can be of assistance is to take these prisoners off your hands."

"That alone will help immensely. I assume you will march come spring?"

"Indeed, as soon as the roads permit. In the meantime, we'll have ranger groups patrolling. If any should find themselves in the area, I'll have them stop by."

"To what end?"

Beverly smiled. "Each group has an Orc shaman with them, capable of communicating over great distances. If you have any messages, they can reach us within mere moments."

"Impressive. Would that we had some of our own."

"Are there any mages here?"

"Unfortunately not, but they certainly don't lack for warriors."

"How many are there?"

"Two hundred who are battle-hardened, but if need be, the entire population can fight. Taking Mirstone would be costly for the Clans."

"Let's hope it doesn't come to that," said Beverly. "We'll need your help to take the war to the enemy."

"They shall be at your disposal come spring."

"Thank you, Highness. I'm sure Her Majesty will appreciate it."

"Any idea how they might be employed?"

"The marshal has great respect for the mountain folk," said Beverly, "and we already number over three hundred of them. The addition of your own forces will probably lead to the creation of a Dwarven brigade, although who is to command it, I can't say."

"Understood. In the meantime, I shall continue to carry out patrols of my own."

Beverly looked at the doors of Mirstone. "It would take a massive army to capture this place. I doubt they'll attempt it any time soon."

"That will not deter me from taking the fight to the enemy."

"Nor would I want it to, but the more I look at what you have here, the more I believe it would be of use to us. I should very much like our ranger groups to operate out of here. It would allow them to coordinate their actions with you and also serve as a reserve should the enemy try to make a move."

"That's a splendid idea. I'm sure Lord Tulfar would be amenable. And who knows, by spring, there may be more warriors ready to march."

"I wouldn't want you to strip the defences."

"Nonsense. The real restriction here is time and armour, both of which will be eased by a few more months of training and smithing."

"And the expense?"

"It'll be difficult," said Althea. "Of that, there can be no doubt, but the Dwarves of Mirstone took an oath to restore the Crown. I, in return, promised them a seat at the table."

Beverly nodded. "That's exactly what we did back in Wincaster, and I must say it's been a welcome change. The only challenge now is finally reaching a state of peace so we can all enjoy it."

"And you believe you can defeat the Clans?"

"I know we can. Gerald defeated them in the past, and that was without the battle-hardened veterans of Merceria."

"You're very confident."

"That's because we wouldn't undertake a campaign if we didn't believe it could be won."

"Good to hear," said Althea. "Now, you best be on your way before some of Prince Tarak's horsemen make an appearance."

"Unlikely. We have Kurathians of our own out screening us. That does, however, mean they'll require a Royal Pardon once the war is over."

"I'm not sure I understand?"

"We took the Kurathian mercenaries with us back to Merceria, under the condition that they never set foot in Weldwyn again."

"I'm sure my father would see the wisdom in employing them, were he still alive. In any case, it matters little now. Alric is now Heir to the Crown of Weldwyn, assuming he's approved."

"Approved?"

"Yes," said Althea. "Don't you know? The Earls Council must approve all Weldwyn kings."

"What a strange custom. Although, perhaps Merceria would be better off had we adopted a similar practice."

"Wasn't it your current system that led to the crowning of Queen Anna?"

Beverly laughed. "Clearly, I am outmatched. I concede the point."

NINE

Spring

SPRING 966 MC

Anna was sweating profusely.

"We should have remained in Wincaster," said Alric.

"Nonsense," she panted. "This way, I can stay close to..." Her voice trailed off as a contraction began anew. She gripped his hand tightly.

"Breathe through it," said the midwife.

"Easy for you to say. You're not the one about to push out a baby the size of a melon! Aubrey, where are you?"

"I am here, Majesty," replied the Life Mage, coming closer.

"Should I leave?" said Alric.

Aubrey looked at him in surprise. "Why would you do that?"

"It's the custom in Weldwyn for the father to wait in another room."

"That is not the custom here. You forget, Highness, warriors founded our kingdom, and we don't leave our women to undergo the trials of birth alone, at least not if we can help it."

"Then I shall stay. Not that I could leave even if I wanted. My wife's firm grip has seen to that."

Anna let out a grunt as another contraction lanced through her.

"It is almost time," said Aubrey.

Gerald looked up from his notes. He'd been going over a map of Weldwyn, once more fussing over the details of the coming campaign. It had all been planned for months, but the enforced delay only caused him to second-guess his decisions.

"It is a good plan," said Urgon, "as I said many times before. Why do you still fret?"

"Lives are at stake. It weighs heavily on my mind."

"And so it should, but you must trust in your decisions."

"I'll be fine once the army starts moving. It's all this waiting that's getting to me."

"It is more than that, I would hazard," said the Orc. "You are worried about the queen."

Gerald took a deep breath, letting it out slowly. "Yes, I am. Childbirth can be a difficult process. There is much that can go wrong."

"Lady Aubrey is with her. She is the most gifted healer in all of Merceria."

"I'm surprised to hear you say that. I would have thought Kraloch more powerful."

"It is not a matter of raw power," said Urgon, "but her ability to heal. Kraloch is an expert in things of a spiritual nature, but Aubrey has a gift with the restoration of flesh. The queen will be fine. You will see."

"I suppose it wouldn't be so bad if it wasn't for all this waiting."

The Orc grinned. "Ah, now we get to the root of the problem. You Humans are always in a hurry to get things done. There is an old Orc proverb that says the longer the wait, the greater the prize."

"Wisdom from the Ancestors?"

"You know our culture well, old friend."

"How is Zhura?"

"She is well. Aubrey's teachings enabled her to shut out the spirits' voices. It appears she has an affinity for the spirit realm."

"But you knew that already?" said Gerald. "She's a ghostwalker."

"She has always heard the spirits; that much is true, but it now appears she has a great potential to use magic as well."

"And Aubrey will teach her?"

"She and Kraloch taught her some techniques, but Zhura is not young, nor am I, for that matter."

"None of us are," said Gerald, "but that doesn't prevent us from learning something new."

"Nor will it, but for now, I think she will be able to live a normal life."

"And will she be joining us on campaign?"

"Yes, although she will not participate directly. She is content to become… what is the word?"

"A camp follower?"

"Yes," said Urgon. "She will accompany those who follow in the army's wake."

"At least you'll be able to see her."

"That I shall, and it pleases me greatly."

The door opened, revealing Beverly. "I have news," she said.

"Go on, then," replied Gerald.

"Queen Anna has given birth to a son."

"And the queen?"

"She is tired but otherwise in good health."

Gerald smiled. "This calls for a celebration. Grab some wine from that cabinet, Beverly, and join us, won't you?"

"I'd be honoured." She pulled out three goblets, filling them with wine.

Gerald took one, then held it up. "To Her Majesty, Queen Anna." They each took a sip.

"And to Prince..." His voice trailed off, and his gaze went to Beverly. "What name did they pick?"

The knight stared back for a moment. "I have no idea. Sorry, I should have asked."

"Don't worry about it. We'll find out, eventually. The important thing is everyone is hale and hearty."

"Should we go and congratulate her?" asked Urgon.

"No," Gerald replied. "Let her rest. She'll likely be sleeping."

"To the prince, then. Whatever his name shall be."

They all toasted the newborn's health.

Jack Marlowe made his way through the keep. The duke's residence in Kingsford wasn't as opulent as the Royal Palace in Wincaster, but it was far nicer than the inn he'd been billeted in. He halted by a door, the guards posted there offering no protest.

"Highness?" he called out.

"Come in, Jack."

"My heartfelt congratulations on the birth of your son," said Jack as he entered the room.

Prince Alric smiled. "Thank you, Jack. That means a lot to me."

"Did you settle on a name?"

"Several, in fact, but Anna is sleeping. I shouldn't want to spoil her announcement."

"So you agreed on one?"

"More or less. Let's just say there are still several we're considering."

"You know, Jack would be quite the name for a prince."

Alric laughed. "I hate to disappoint you, but that is not one of the contenders."

"Ah well, I tried. Still, it's a momentous day."

"It's a child, Jack, not the coming of a new god."

"This is not only a child, Highness. He is the heir to two kingdoms. That doesn't happen every day."

Alric sobered. "I suppose that's true. I never really thought of it that way, but with Alstan all but confirmed dead, that puts me in line for the Crown of Weldwyn."

"So it does. One day, you shall be prince no longer, but a king. Then, you must get used to everyone calling you, Your Majesty."

"Yes, and that would make Anna queen of both Merceria and Weldwyn."

"Now, that," said Jack, "is something I didn't consider. This child of yours will inherit both crowns. Does that mean Merceria and Weldwyn will become one kingdom?"

"I suppose that's possible, but there would be a lot of things to consider."

"Such as?"

"Well, for one, our laws of succession are different, not to mention our Nobles Council has to approve the next heir."

"It's not as if they have an alternative."

"Ah, but they do," said Alric. "In theory, any of the earls could be chosen as the king."

"Assuming there are any left. I don't imagine Brida would allow them to continue with their previous titles. The real question is whether or not she allows them to survive."

"You believe she might purge them?"

"It's likely," said Jack. "After all, she wants to rule Weldwyn. She can hardly do that if there are other potential rulers out there."

"In other words, she wants me dead."

"Undoubtedly. You did choose Princess Anna over her, remember? Things like that tend to leave a lasting impression."

"Yes, that was the reason behind the first invasion, back in sixty-one. But surely we put an end to all of that?"

"It would appear not. This time, we'll be required to arrive at a more permanent solution."

"You mean kill her?"

"Do you know any better way to secure your throne?"

"No," said Alric. "I suppose not."

"Let's not ruin the day, Highness. You should be celebrating the birth of your son, Jack."

The prince laughed. "As I said, that name was not amongst those we considered."

"Still, in the absence of anything else, I shall use it to refer to the Royal Family's newest member."

"Perhaps you'd be willing to marry Brida?"

The cavalier paled. "Me? Why ever would you suggest something like that?"

"Well, you are noble-born, after all, and marriage to Brida would cement peace between our peoples. Of course, you couldn't do anything till after this war is over."

"Are you suggesting this because I insisted on calling your son Jack?"

Alric grinned. "Come now, we both know there can be only one Jack."

"You make a compelling case, Highness. Very well, I shall accept your logic, providing you never mention the idea of marriage again."

"You hate marriage that much?"

"As I've mentioned on multiple occasions, I consider it a wonderful state of existence… for others. But to tie myself down to but a single woman would be doing a great disservice to the realm."

Alric laughed. "Ah, but she wouldn't be a single woman."

"She wouldn't?"

"No, she'd be married to you." The prince's laughter echoed down the hall.

Kasri watched as a barge poled its way across the river to where the army had assembled on the western bank, guarded by cavalry to ensure their safety. Other barges lined the quay in Kingsford, filled with warriors ready to fight.

"Quite the sight, isn't it?" said Herdwin.

"It is indeed, although I can't say I'm eager to make the crossing."

"Let me guess; you don't like the idea of floating on water?"

"How'd you guess?"

"I was the same way when I first came to Merceria. Not that I spent much time doing so. Still, the very thought of drowning was enough to keep me away from rivers."

"And now?"

"I accept it's just part of life."

"You've lived amongst Humans for so long," said Kasri, "yet within you still beats the heart of a Dwarf."

He blushed. "Well, we can hardly give up all our traditions."

"There are some I would gladly dispose of."

"Such as?"

"The pressure to forge."

"Marriage isn't so bad," said Herdwin.

"I have nothing against it," she continued, "but the expectation that I must choose someone can be so overwhelming."

"That's to be expected. After all, you're the heir to Ironcliff. You could have anyone you choose."

"What of you? Ever been forged?"

"No. I left Stonecastle long before that became an option, and you don't see too many female Dwarves in the Human lands."

"You've done well for yourself," said Kasri. "I hear you're reckoned a master smith—that's rare amongst Humans. Has the guild ever extended you an offer of membership since you left?"

"They contacted me some years ago, but I wasn't interested."

"I'm sure that didn't sit well with them."

Herdwin coughed up a laugh. "No, it didn't, but the King of Stonecastle still insisted I take command of their army when the time came to help Merceria."

"I don't imagine the guild liked that."

"No, they didn't, but what the king wants, the king gets."

"Had you much military experience at that time?"

"None whatsoever," said Herdwin, "but I was good friends with Gerald."

"So they picked you for political expediency," said Kasri. "Some things never change. Not that I object to your presence; far from it, in fact. I've come to see you as a close friend."

"And I you," he replied. "It will be nice to fight side by side with other Dwarven companies for a change."

"You don't enjoy working with the Mercerians?"

"I like them well enough, but our tactics are not theirs, and that hampers us on the battlefield."

"I should very much like to discuss this further," said Kasri, "but I fear our turn has come to cross the river."

"So it has."

She paused a moment, wracked by indecision. Finally, she turned to Herdwin, looking him in the eyes. "I would deem it a great favour if you would accompany me across the river. I must admit to some trepidation at the thought, and your presence would be of great comfort to me."

"I would be delighted."

～

Beverly watched the men forming up on the western bank. The cavalry had crossed late last night, spreading out to keep an eye on things while the foot assembled. The Mercerians were the first across, followed by the Orcs. All that remained were the Dwarves, which would bring their army to full strength.

No, that was not quite right, for the last to cross would be the mastiffs. The great hounds were organized into two companies, although perhaps the term company was not correct. These creatures would be used sparingly but could prove devastating against cavalry.

She wondered if Prince Tarak had any mastiffs within his own army? The thought made her shiver. Not much made Beverly fearful, but she'd witnessed the aftermath of a mastiff attack at Colbridge. There, they'd been released on the Knights of the Sword to enormous effect. Indeed, it had decimated almost half the order in one charge. They had not been employed since, mainly due to the inability to replace losses. With breeding stock now available, the situation had changed dramatically.

A smiling Revi Bloom rode over and joined her at the river's edge.

"You're in a good mood, Master Bloom," she said.

"And why shouldn't I be?" the mage replied. "It's a nice, warm spring day, and the might of Merceria is on full display."

"It's not like you to praise the army. You're usually complaining that the war is interfering with your studies."

"And it still is, but at least now we're doing something to end this conflict."

"This has to do with Aubrey, doesn't it? You're happy she's the one helping to look after the new prince."

He smiled. "Does it show that much? Don't get me wrong; I like children, but infants can be an awful drain on one's energy, don't you think?"

"Not at all," said Beverly. "It's work. I'll grant you that, but the rewards far outpace the challenges."

"Spoken like someone who has no children."

"I might remind you that you're in the same boat. Unless there's something you're not telling me?"

Revi blushed. "I can assure you that is not the case."

"Does that preclude the idea of you and Hayley having children in the future?"

"Not at all. I would hope we should enjoy the fruits of childbirth at some point, but let's not get ahead of ourselves."

"Meaning?"

"We are not yet married."

"That doesn't mean you can't have children."

She tried to hold back her laughter as he turned an even deeper shade of crimson, but it was of little use. She imagined a cluster of small children clutching at the mage's robes, and the thought was just too much to bear. She laughed aloud.

"I'm glad this is amusing you," said Revi, his manner indicating precisely the opposite.

"I'm sorry. I meant no disrespect."

"And what of you? Are children in your future?"

"They must be," said Beverly. "Eventually, I'll be Baroness of Bodden, and someone needs to carry on the name."

A group of Orcs rode by, interrupting their conversation.

"I must say," said Revi, "the sight of Orcs upon horses seems wrong somehow."

"Actually, they've proven remarkably useful."

"In what way?"

"They pack a punch like the heavys but aren't held back by the weight of armour. I wouldn't put them up against knights, but given the right circumstances, they're very effective."

"How many of them do we have?"

"Only two companies."

"I thought there'd be more."

"There is, but we left them behind to help garrison Merceria. It frees up our knights to fight in Weldwyn."

"What of Prince Alric?"

"I expect he's on his way to Colbridge by now. His army will cross once he's arrived."

"And is it as large as ours?"

"Not quite, but then again, we're marching more or less straight for the capital. Our thought is the enemy will send everything they have against us, making his job in the south that much easier."

"Easier? He has to siege a city, doesn't he?"

"He does," said Beverly. "Southport, to be exact. None of the other towns are fortified."

"Has he enough soldiers for that?"

"He and Gerald seem to believe so, and it's thought he may be able to recruit from the towns he liberates along the way."

"I wish him well, although I doubt it will be that easy. Who's going with him?"

"Lord Jack, of course, not to mention Tog and his Trolls. Aubrey will be with them as well, so I suppose that means you'll be required to take over the responsibility of looking after our new princeling."

"You mean Braedon," corrected Revi. "That's the name they finally decided on, although, for some strange reason, they gave him a second name."

"Which is?"

"Gerald," said the mage. "Hardly surprising considering her love for the marshal."

"Braedon Gerald," said Beverly. "I like it."

"Well, I'm glad someone approves. If you ask me, the entire concept is foreign."

"That he has two names?"

"Yes, it's very… Weldwynian."

"Weldwynian? Is that what you do now? Make up new words?"

"Somebody has to advance the language."

"And did it occur to you that Prince Braedon would inherit both the throne of Merceria and of Weldwyn?"

"No," said Revi, looking genuinely shocked. "It did not." He shrugged. "Well, in that case, I shall excuse the odd custom."

TEN

The South

SPRING 966 MC

With Alric's army finally across the river, they marched to the west, effortlessly capturing the town of Waldstock. Warned of their approach, the Kurathians withdrew southward, taking as much with them as possible. The garrison had consisted of Prince Tarak's forces—that much was gleaned from the townsfolk, but more surprising still was that they withdrew in good order.

With estimates putting the opposition at close to six hundred souls, the pressure was on to bring them to battle before they could seek the refuge of Southport.

Thankfully, the marshal had seen fit to send Lanaka's brigade south with the prince, giving him access to a fast scouting force familiar with Kurathian tactics. It turned out to be a good choice, for Tarak's men kept up a rearguard action that hampered the advance and kept the Mercerian cavalry on its toes.

The trip from Waldstock to Bramwitch was a long one, made all the more so by the poor state of the roads. Added to this, the constant threat of raids by Tarak's men slowed the advance down to a crawl.

Two weeks after entering Weldwyn, they finally encountered the enemy formed up for battle. The tail end of the Great Swamp was on their eastern flank, while to the west archers stood atop a slight rise. The bulk of the Kurathian army was in a line between them, the town standing behind them with their heavier cavalry held in reserve. Although the army's standard was on display, the Royal Standard of Prince Tarak was nowhere to be seen. It appeared his commanders would decide this battle rather than the prince himself.

Alric set his footmen in a line opposite, with his own archers placed on either side to counter this. Lanaka massed his men to the west, ready to exploit any flanking opportunity that might present itself. The prince placed their secret weapon, the Trolls, on his eastern flank, for they were unaffected by the swamp as it was their natural habitat.

The entire Mercerian army advanced at once. With no arbalests or rangers present amongst the enemy ranks, there was no fear of Kurathian arrows, so the early advance offered little in the way of danger. However, the real test would come once the range closed and the combatants committed to the attack.

Alric kept the line steady, their ranks tightly packed, the better to concentrate their attack once contact was made. The archers moved in from the flanks, taking positions on either side of the main force rather than being spread out.

The collective roar as the two armies came within melee distance was quickly replaced by the clash of arms. All the while, the Mercerian cavalry waited just behind their line, ready to push through a gap should one appear. Alric was eager to get into the fray, yet years of tutelage under Marshal Matheson had taught him well. Instead of succumbing to the glory of battle, he held back, allowing his captains to do the work. His time would come, of that he was sure, but for now, his job was to lead the army, not seek individual honour.

The men fought with ferocity, but the Kurathians held their positions. The footmen of Merceria took many casualties, causing Alric much consternation. However, things looked much better in the west as Lanaka's riders charged into the enemy archers.

He turned to his aide. "Jack, prepare the heavy cavalry. You know what to do."

"Aye, Highness, and not a moment too soon. These Kurathians are a stubborn bunch."

The battle wore on, with both sides suffering greatly, yet the prince knew he would soon gain the upper hand despite the apparent setback. As he watched, Tog and his Trolls made their way through the swamp, emerging on the eastern end of the Kurathian line, taking the defenders by surprise on the flank. The footmen's weapons were of little use against the Trolls' thick skins, and the line soon disintegrated into chaos.

Jack Marlowe launched his attack to the west, hitting a weak spot between the foe's archers and their light cavalry. Soon he fought side by side with the forces of Lanaka, the resistance crumbling before them.

Outflanked, the Kurathians morale broke, and within moments, they fled back to the safety of the streets of Bramwitch.

The Trolls, coming from the swamp, tore into the Kurathian reserve, engaging the last of them. The Mercerians kept up the advance, taking advantage of the enemy's chaotic lines, pushing ever closer to Bramwitch.

Alric ordered his personal cavalry through a gap in the line, and the town was soon theirs. Small pockets of resistance fought on, but they surrendered in large numbers.

Jack appeared at his side. "Victory is ours, Highness. The enemy is broken!"

"So it is," said the prince. "Secure Bramwitch and round up any prisoners."

"And those who don't wish to surrender?"

"Surround them, and we'll finish them off with archers. And collect as many horses as you can. We'll need them in the days to come."

Lady Aubrey approached, looking dour.

"It is a great victory," said Alric. "Why the long face?"

"So many died," the mage replied, "and many more need healing. Your part this day might be done, but mine is only just beginning."

"Yes, you're right. I'm sorry."

"Shall I report your success to the marshal?"

"No, look after the wounded first. News of our success can wait until tomorrow when we have a better idea of our losses."

The Life Mage rode off to see to her healing duties.

That evening saw Prince Alric comfortably ensconced at an inn, the window of his room facing the water. A group of Kurathian ships sat farther out to sea—not sufficient to threaten his occupation of Bramwitch but enough to carry away a significant number of Kurathians who'd fled the battle.

"Frustrating, isn't it?" said Jack. "I suppose they'll sail for Southport, and then we'll be obliged to fight them all over again."

"It can't be helped," replied the prince. "We have no ships at hand with which to engage them."

"Pity."

"Yes, and something I'll not see happen again. Once this war's over, I shall take measures to build a fleet of our own."

"That will be costly, Highness."

"It is the price we must pay if we are to keep those Kurathian pirates at bay."

"Pirates?"

Alric waved away the remark. "You know what I mean."

"I do, although I wonder why a Prince of Kurathia brought his army here in the first place. Wouldn't the Continent be closer?"

"That would be my assumption as well, but we cannot overlook the possibility Kythelia is behind all of this."

"You honestly believe the Clans would follow an Elf?"

"Merceria did without even realizing it. Remember, she can assume the guise of a Human when it suits her purposes."

"That may be true," said Jack, "but why convince a Kurathian prince to sail all the way here?"

"Why indeed? No doubt she promised him something in return. My guess would be Merceria."

"What makes you say that?"

"It's the only thing that makes sense. I can't see Brida agreeing to give away half of Weldwyn, can you?"

"No, I suppose not, but if that's the case, why hasn't he invaded?"

"That's an excellent question. It might be as simple as securing Weldwyn before invading Merceria."

"Or," suggested Jack, "they wanted to lure us back here to deal us a blow from which we won't be able to recover?"

"If that's their plan, they'll be sorely disappointed. The Marshal of Merceria won't fall for a trap like that."

"Then what's their strategy?"

"I wish I knew."

"We have reports of dragons. You don't think they'll send those against us, do you?"

"It's impossible to say for certain. They'll use them somewhere, but I think the greater threat to them, at the moment, is the army up north. They're the ones threatening the capital with their advance. It would help if we knew how many of the creatures they possessed."

"According to Arcanus Tyrell, they possess at least two."

"Yes, but there could be more. The mere threat of their presence is enough to affect all our plans."

"What do we do if they show up here?" asked Jack.

"We would rely on our archers."

"We don't have many of those."

"Yes, I know, and it's something that's been troubling me for some time. How many did we recruit from Waldstock?"

"Only fifty, although we might get twice that here in Bramwitch."

"We still need to equip them with bows."

"Easy enough," said Jack. "If I had to guess, I'd say the Kurathians provided us with more than a hundred."

"How long does it take to become a trained archer?"

"Months, even longer if you want them to be competent. It's too bad we don't have crossbows; those are much easier to learn."

"That's an excellent idea. I'll send word to the marshal, and hopefully, the fletchers back in Merceria can construct them for us."

"That would still take time. Southport would have some in its armoury. For Malin's sake, there might even be some here. If I recall, the Baron of Bramwitch had a thing for archery, didn't he? I seem to recall him hunting with your father."

"That's right, he did—in the Gilded Woods, and they used crossbows. The men should search his estate. He may have some there."

"I doubt there would be enough to equip a company of archers."

"No, but by sharing them, we could at least commence training. Each bow we put into use is one more bolt we can loose off at a dragon. Malin knows we're going to need all the help we can get."

"Consider it done."

"How many prisoners did we take?" asked Alric.

"By last count, over two hundred."

"Is that all? I would've assumed more."

"And so it would have been, but Lady Aubrey can only heal so many, and the priority must be given to our own warriors first."

"Yes, of course. It's a pity we don't have more healers."

"Not only healers," added Jack, "ANY mages would be helpful, especially considering we'll likely be sieging Southport. You'd think the Mercerians could have at least spared an Earth Mage or two."

"Don't worry, they'd send them if I asked, but right now, we don't even know what's happening in the north. The marshal came up with the idea to keep them in reserve until needed."

"We need them now if we want them here in time to attack Southport."

"I shall be sure to have Lady Aubrey pass that along."

"That reminds me," said Jack. "I created a tally of our losses, as well as the enemy casualties." He passed over a folded note.

"Thank you. That's most helpful."

"I live to serve, Highness."

"No, you don't," said Alric. "You live for the glory."

"Well, I suppose that's true, but only for YOUR glory, Highness. To do otherwise would ruin my reputation."

"I swear by Malin's tears, you could charm the venom from a snake, Jack."

The cavalier grinned. "That's what I'm here for, Highness."

Aubrey knelt, closing her eyes as she called on her inner magic to heal the wound. She put her glowing hands on the injured man, and the colour drained into him, lingering where the flesh knitted.

Her head spun as she stood, and she recognized the exhaustion. She must take care, lest she overuse her magic, and take physical damage herself. The injured lay spread out on the floor all around here, with little to comfort them save for a blanket on which to lie. These were not Mercerians, or men of Weldwyn, for that matter, for they had all been healed. No, these men were Kurathians, the very same enemy who had so recently stood against them.

A hand reached up, clutching at her skirts. "*Thank you,*" the man said, using the language of his people.

"*You are welcome,*" she replied. "*May Saint Mathew watch over you.*"

His eyes lit up. "*You speak our language?*"

"*Some. Amongst our people are many Kurathians, and I've needed to treat them over the years. It has proven helpful to learn their language.*"

"*And you worship the Saints?*"

"*My people worship Saxnor,*" she replied, "*but I understand your beliefs and seek to give you comfort.*"

"*What will happen to us?*"

"*That is difficult to answer. In the short term, you shall be marched back to Merceria where we can keep an eye on you.*"

"*And then?*"

"*That largely depends on how this war goes. Many of your people have decided to live in Merceria as free men. Perhaps you will someday do the same?*"

"*My prince will not allow it.*"

"*It is not his decision to make.*"

"*Ah,*" the man said, "*but it is. He owns us.*"

"*I understand you're in service to him, but each may choose their own path, surely?*"

"*No, you do not understand. We all took an oath of lifelong service. Our lives are his to control.*"

"*And if he should die?*"

The thought appeared to surprise the fellow. "*Prince Tarak cannot die.*"

"*Everyone dies, eventually.*"

"*Of old age, yes, but he is a man in his prime. He will not depart this world for the land of spirits any time soon.*"

"*People die in battle all the time.*"

"*Not Prince Tarak. He is untouchable in battle.*"

"*I might remind you our army just defeated you.*"

"*True, but had our prince been present, it would have been a far different outcome.*"

"*Are you suggesting he's immune to wounds?*"

"*He has had his share over the years, but he is far too cunning to be killed in battle.*"

Aubrey chuckled. "*He wouldn't be the first general to succumb to Mercerian might.*"

"*This is no jest,*" the man said. "*He is a ruthless man and will stop at nothing to achieve his aims. Do you really believe a group of misfits bred from mercenaries could defeat him?*"

Aubrey's voice turned icy. "*You have no idea who you're dealing with. Our marshal has taken on enemies far superior to a rogue Kurathian prince. Now, rest, and while you're at it, you might consider your future. Your prince can't help you now.*"

She left him, but the conversation haunted her so much, she sought out Prince Alric. His Highness sat at a table, going over lists of some sort.

"I hope I'm not interrupting," she said.

He put down the paper he'd been holding. "Lady Aubrey, this is a pleasant surprise. What can I do for you?"

"I just came from attending to the wounded."

"I was unaware we had any left which required your services."

"I was referring to the Kurathians," she replied.

"And?"

"Apparently, their prince is an accomplished leader."

"So claims every military commander ever."

"This is different. It's almost as if their soldiers worship him, while at the same time, fear him."

"Not the best way to inspire the men, I'd warrant."

"This is no jest, Highness. They believe him to be unbeatable."

"An easy claim to make when he hasn't seen battle."

"Perhaps."

Alric rose, moving around the table. "Come, let us discuss the matter further in more comfortable surroundings." He walked over to a small table that rested against the wall. "Would you like some wine?"

"That would be nice, thank you."

He poured two goblets, then passed one to her. "Take a seat."

She sat on a nearby chair, the prince taking one opposite her.

"I can see this has had quite an impact on you," said Alric. "Tell me, how well do you know Kurathians?"

"I dealt with Lanaka's men on many occasions and always found them to be honourable. I even learned their language, although most of them speak the same tongue as us."

"Well," said Alric, "they would have to, wouldn't they, being mercenaries and all. They couldn't very well seek employment if they couldn't communicate with those who hire them. As for myself, I've read much about them. They are, by all accounts, a ruthless people, some might even say fanatical."

"Your knowledge of them is biased by the fact that they are your enemy."

"I will freely admit to that. I've not spent much time amongst Lanaka's men, but I do admire their military prowess, even if their beliefs are a little strange."

"Because they worship the Saints?"

Alric grinned. "You must admit, it's a strange religion."

"Why? Because the Saints were mortals?"

"Precisely. Gods are the creators of all. Who are we to claim otherwise?"

"How much do you know about their Saints?"

"Not much, and I've little desire to learn more."

"You denigrate their religion, yet your own beliefs clash with those of the queen. You worship Malin, while she worships Saxnor."

"Yes, but they're both Gods."

She took a sip of her wine, thinking things through. "May I speak freely?"

"Of course," he said, leaning forward in interest.

"You should be more accepting of others."

"Who says I'm not?"

"Your actions," said Aubrey. "Aside from the Trolls, there are no other races in your army, and those were only chosen for their military prowess. You've got a blindness when it comes to Orcs and Dwarves, one your father shared."

He sat back, stunned by her statement. He took a drink, thinking things over. "I must admit it's true," he said at last. "This is not something I was conscious of, but now you mention it, I recognize it for what it is. I've seen, first-hand, the value the Orcs and Dwarves add to the army of Merceria, yet I refused the offer of their services."

"The question," said Aubrey, "is why?"

"This is my first independent command, and coming to grips with that has been hard enough without dealing with all the different tactics these people offer."

"I can understand your reticence about Orcs. After all, in Weldwyn, they are a mostly unknown people. But Dwarves make up an entire barony, and they proved crucial to King Leofric's defence against the first Clan invasion."

"You're right," said Alric. "I should have considered that, but I'm still wary of non-Humans. I think it has to do with the actions of Lord Parvan."

"He's an Elf, not a Dwarf. The two are not at all similar."

"And I thank you for reminding me of that, Aubrey. I shall endeavour to put aside my prejudices in future."

ELEVEN

Treachery

SPRING 966 MC

Lord Alexander Stanton, Earl of Tewsbury, looked across the table at the few who had assembled. He'd summoned the Nobles Council in Wincaster to discuss a matter of great import. It was hardly his fault the queen's faction was woefully underrepresented due to their efforts of liberating Weldwyn.

Lord Markham Anglesley, Duke of Colbridge, shifted in his seat. "Can we get on with this? I haven't got all day."

"Have big plans, do you?" This question came from Lord Horace Spencer, Earl of Eastwood. "What's her name?"

"Very funny. I'll have you know I'm expected at the Grand."

"Oh? I didn't realize you were a devotee of the theatre."

"It is a work I commissioned, if you must know."

"Indeed?" said Spencer. "How intriguing. Please, tell us more."

"Yes," added the newly appointed Earl of Shrewesdale, Lord Heath Morris, the previous earl's distant cousin. It had taken forever to learn of his existence and even longer to find him. He was, by trade, a carpenter. However, the elevation to earl had well suited his nature, and the fellow adapted to the life of luxury quickly, spending most of his time in Wincaster.

"It's an accounting of my father's legacy," said Anglesley, "and I'm quite proud of it."

"Does it include his treachery?" asked Lord Avery Somerset, Duke of Kingsford.

Colbridge reddened.

"Now, now," said Stanton. "Let us not get distracted by personal matters."

"Quite right," added Spencer. "There is the business of the realm to discuss. I believe you had an issue to raise, Lord Stanton?"

"I do," replied Stanton. "Word has reached me of unrest within the kingdom. If we do not suppress this as quickly as possible, it could spread, jeopardizing the entire campaign to retake Weldwyn."

"Unrest?" said Somerset. "Why have I heard nothing of this?"

"It is contained, for the moment, but I fear it will spread."

"We should put an end to it immediately," said Spencer.

Stanton smiled. "And how would you suggest we do that?"

"Why, send in warriors, naturally. How else would we react?"

"I'm with Spencer," said Anglesley. "The last thing we want is for the queen to return to a land in turmoil."

"On the contrary," said Somerset. "We should send word to Her Majesty and seek her thoughts."

"What's wrong with you? Are you not capable of making a decision?" Anglesley stood. "I move that we immediately send troops to put down this insurrection."

"I second the motion," added Morris, eager to be heard.

"Very well," said Stanton. "The motion has been raised to send troops to the insurrection. Let us vote, shall we?"

"We hardly discussed it!" said Somerset.

"Still, the motion has been raised. We must take the vote."

Hands were raised around the table, all but the Duke of Kingsford.

"The motion is passed," said Stanton, obviously pleased with the result. "Now, the matter before us is how many soldiers we send?"

"And what type," added Spencer.

"That, too. I would recommend cavalry be employed. We can send it from the garrison at Tewsbury."

"Where are we sending them to?" asked Somerset.

"Hawksburg."

"You can't be serious?"

"I am quite serious, my friend. The Orcs there have proven difficult of late, even going so far as to claim land as their own."

"Preposterous," said Spencer. "If we're not careful, they'll take over the entire realm."

"Come now," said Somerset. "You're overreacting. The Orcs of Hawksburg have long been considered friendly. I might remind you the baroness insisted on their remaining there after the rebuilding."

"Did she?" said Stanton. "Or was she fearful of reprisals should she refuse their offer?"

"He makes a good point," said Spencer. "My predecessor had all manner of problems with the Orcs."

"Really?" said Somerset. "If I recall, he hired them to try to usurp the throne."

"Precisely the reason they can't be trusted," replied Stanton. "You see? History is on our side."

"How many men can we send?" asked Spencer.

"Enough to see them off our land. I would recommend a company of horse and two of foot."

"And who would command this expedition?"

"Whomever we choose."

"Obviously, but you must have someone particular in mind?"

"I do," said Stanton. "I propose we give command to Lord Arnim Caster, Viscount Haverston."

"He's the queen's man," said Morris. "Are you sure that's a good idea?"

"He is a man known for following orders, and as an ally of the queen, his presence will hold much weight. In addition, he is a seasoned commander, having participated in many battles."

Lord Horace Spencer smiled. "And should he fail, it will deflect blame on to the queen."

"I don't like this," said Somerset. "This is a matter to be laid before Her Majesty, not decided by the whim of the Nobles Council."

"I disagree," said Stanton. "It is the duty of this council to run the country in the queen's absence."

"Half the nobles are out of the kingdom. You know, were they here, there would be no way this motion would pass."

"And still, we are presented with this matter. I move we appoint Lord Arnim Caster as head of this expedition and send it to Hawksburg. Will anyone second the motion?"

Lord Markham Anglesley raised his hand. "I shall."

"Then let us tally the vote."

Once more, hands were raised. "The motion is carried," Stanton proclaimed.

"It cannot," said Somerset. "Only the marshal can appoint a military commander, or the queen, if need be."

"And yet it is done. Let us adjourn now, gentlemen, content that we did our duty this day."

"I must object!"

"You may object all you like, Somerset, but the fact of the matter is you were outmanoeuvred, my friend. I suggest you console yourself with the knowledge we shall finally rid this kingdom of the green scourge."

"And now you show your true colours," said Somerset. "Do you hate the Orcs so much?"

"Not at all. My desire to remove them has nothing to do with their race. Rather, the weakening of their power will only strengthen ours."

Nikki collapsed in the chair. "They're finally asleep. I thought they'd never go down."

"They were fussing a lot today," said Arnim. "I think they miss the queen."

"Well, the queen and all her friends. They seem to be particularly attached to Beverly."

"It must be her red hair."

"Why would you say that?"

"Come, come," said Arnim. "It's her most striking feature, and you know what children are like."

"Clearly, you don't."

"What's that supposed to mean?"

"Nothing. I'm sorry, I'm just so exhausted. The twins are far more work than I ever thought possible."

"We can afford servants to help."

"And surrender my duties as a mother? I think not!"

"Have it your way, then." He was about to say more when a knock on the door interrupted him. A guard opened it a moment later. "I beg your pardon, Lord Arnim, but the Duke of Kingsford is here to see you."

"Somerset? Here to see me? Are you sure?"

"Of course, he's sure," said Nikki. "He's hardly likely to say so if he wasn't."

"Yes, good point. Send him in, please." He turned to his wife. "This is what we get for staying in the Palace."

"Well," said Nikki, "we are looking after things for the queen."

"So we are. I wonder what the duke wants?"

"We'll soon see."

The Duke of Kingsford entered the room. "I hope I'm not disturbing you?"

"Not at all," said Arnim.

Nikki began to rise, but the duke interjected. "Don't rise on my account."

"What can I do for you, Your Grace?" asked Arnim.

"I'm here in an unofficial capacity. I just came from the Nobles Council."

"And?"

"You will soon be receiving orders to assume command of a small expedition."

"To join the war?"

"No, to suppress an uprising."

"Where?" said Arnim. "In Merceria?"

"So the reports say, but I am of the opinion they are greatly exaggerated."

"Yet I am to take warriors there to suppress it?"

"Those will be your orders," replied Somerset.

"And where is this uprising?"

"In Hawksburg."

Arnim laughed. "You can't be serious?"

"These orders cannot be refused. They bear the authority of the Nobles Council. In the queen's absence, they are considered the equivalent of a Royal Proclamation."

"You know the queen would never condone such an act."

"That is something in which you and I agree. The Earl of Tewsbury is without a doubt orchestrating this problem; he as much as admitted it to me himself."

"To what end?"

"He feels that by ejecting the Orcs from Mercerian soil, they will possess less influence at court."

"Thus giving him more."

"Precisely. I understand this puts you in a difficult position. The situation at Hawksburg must be handled with considerable tact and diplomacy, not at the end of a sword."

"Understood," said Arnim. "And you may rest assured I shall play my part in this affair in the interest of the queen. Speaking of which, is she returning to Wincaster any time soon?"

"I'm afraid not. After the birth of the heir, she elected to remain in Kingsford so she can be closer to the army."

"A pity. She could have sorted out this mess in short order. You said you were against this. Who voted in favour?"

"The Duke of Colbridge, along with the Earls of Shrewesdale, Tewsbury, and Eastwood. It appears Lord Alexander Stanton used his time wisely while you were all traipsing around in Norland."

"For Saxnor's sake," said Arnim. "It's bad enough we need to fight off the Clans. Now we must deal with this lot as well!"

"We will win through," said Nikki.

"Of course we will," said the duke. "Thanks mainly to men like you, Lord Arnim."

"I will do what I can, but you must get word to the queen. We cannot take this act sitting down."

"Nor shall we, I assure you. I'll send word to Her Majesty immediately. In the meantime, I suggest you proceed with caution, and if anyone asks, I was never here."

"Understood, Your Grace."

"I shall leave you now, having disrupted your day. My apologies, Lady Caster."

"That's quite all right, Your Grace. I'm used to it. Shall I see you out?"

"No, I can do that myself. I've been enough of a burden today."

He turned, exiting the room.

"I should talk to the guard," said Arnim, "and make sure he mentions this to no one."

"The guards are not gossips," said Nikki, "and have the queen's complete trust. Best not to impugn their loyalty by bringing it up."

"And when the orders arrive?"

"Then act as if they are a complete surprise. Come now, you were a member of the town watch for years. If you can deal with the gangs of Wincaster, you can deal with the whims of nobles."

"High-ranking nobles," he added.

"That may well be, but beneath that fancy exterior, they're still just men. It wasn't so long ago you would tell someone like that to go jump off a cliff."

"That's different. I'm a father now; I have more to risk."

"It is precisely because of that very fact you MUST take a stand. Do you want our children growing up under the thumb of oppression?"

"You know I don't."

"Then do what you feel you must to protect us all."

He nodded. "I will. Thank you, Nikki, for giving me the clarity I needed."

She rose from her seat, her exhaustion all but forgotten. "Come," she said. "It's time we were abed."

"And the so-called uprising?"

"It is distant," she replied, "and I would have my husband's company before he marches to save the kingdom."

He grinned. "Then lead on, and I shall follow."

Arnim received his official orders early the next morning. As chance would have it, Albreda arrived in Wincaster shortly thereafter, bringing reports from Lord Richard. It appeared the nobles of Norland were no further along in their negotiations than last winter, but at least they hadn't given up altogether.

The Druid waited until Arnim finished reading through the letters before speaking. "If there's nothing else you need, I'll be returning to Galburn's Ridge."

"There's nothing for the baron, but I wonder if you might be free to take me to Hawksburg?"

"To what end?"

"I'm to report to Tewsbury to assemble a small force."

"Do I detect a note of annoyance?"

"You do. The Nobles Council of Merceria has ordered me to suppress an uprising in Hawksburg."

"Don't be absurd. The people of Hawksburg love Lady Aubrey."

"And well I know it, but the writ carries the official seal. I am duty-bound to investigate."

"And so you will go to Hawksburg and then ride to Tewsbury only to return? That seems like a waste of time if ever I've heard of one. As for your request, I shall be happy to accompany you, even as far as Tewsbury. I suspect the earl's motives are an attempt to cover up something else."

"You mean he doesn't want the Orcs evicted?"

"Did Beverly tell you what she encountered when she marched the army through Tewsbury last fall?"

"No," said Arnim. "Why? What happened?"

"The city garrison refused to open the gates for the Royal Army."

"Were you there?"

"No. I was back in Galburn's Ridge, but I heard it from Richard. He, in turn, heard it directly from Beverly when he last visited Wincaster. I suspect our precious Lord Alexander wants the Royal Garrison out of his city and feels this is the best way to accomplish it."

"That would fit with what I know of the man."

"Very well," said Albreda. "You've made a mundane visit more enticing. When would you like to leave?"

"There are few arrangements for me to make, but that shouldn't take long."

"What arrangements?"

"Well," said Arnim, "I was left as the queen's representative in her absence. I must be careful about who I turn over the reins of power to."

"That's easy; give them to Aldwin."

"Aldwin? But he's a smith?"

Albreda bristled. "And you were once a farmer. Am I to hold that against you, or are you now so full of yourself at being a noble that you have forsaken your past?"

"I apologize," said Arnim. "I did not mean to offend."

"Aldwin is a master smith and also the husband of the queen's champion. You give him too little credit."

"But he lacks experience in politics."

"True, but he has others he can lean on: the Duke of Kingsford for one, not to mention your wife, Lady Nicole. He also has the advantage of being true to his word. He would never do anything to jeopardize the queen's rule, and I'll check in on him regularly to see how he's getting on. Does that make you feel any better?"

"It does."

"Good, then the matter is settled. Now, write that letter of yours naming him as the person in charge, and let us be off to Hawksburg. With any luck, we could ride to Tewsbury before the sun sets."

"That's close to thirty miles?"

"Your point?" said Albreda.

"That's a long ride for a horse, especially this time of year when the roads are still muddy."

"Do you think I would suggest such a thing if I didn't believe it was possible? Naturally, I will talk to the horses and find only those steeds willing to undertake the trip."

"Is this something you do on a regular basis?"

"I'm the Witch of the Whitewood," she replied. "To do otherwise would be contrary to my nature."

It didn't take long for Arnim to arrange things with Aldwin. The smith was surprised with the appointment but took it in stride, especially after Albreda's reassurances that she would check in on him from time to time.

Albreda cast her spell, not even deigning to use the Palace's magic circle. The wind picked up, swirling around them, obliterating all sight of the area, and then they were standing in Hawksburg, a pair of Orc guards looking on in interest.

"Greetings, Lahzak," said the Druid. "I trust all is well here?"

The Orc bowed. "It is, wise one. What brings you to Hawksburg?"

"Let me start by saying your mastery of the common tongue is remarkable."

"Thank you, mistress."

"Now, as to our reason for being here, we are on our way to Tewsbury. Can you make a couple of horses available for us? I shall chat with them before we leave, so make sure you choose two sturdy animals."

"As you wish," said Lahzak.

"Now," said Albreda, turning her attention to Arnim, "let's see what the weather is like, shall we?" She led him out of the building to gaze up at a clear blue sky. "This bodes well."

"I don't wish to seem ungrateful," said Arnim, "but perhaps it would be better if I travelled to Tewsbury by myself?"

"Nonsense. This is the queen's business, and I shan't permit anyone to interfere."

"Even you?"

"Don't be impertinent. You know I adore the queen—she's one of the few sensible people in positions of power. I have only her best interests at heart. Now, let's see to those horses, shall we?"

"But you just sent the Orc off to get some?"

"That Orc has a name. I suggest you learn it unless you prefer being known simply as 'that Human'?"

"You seem particularly ill-tempered this morning," said Arnim. "I hope I haven't upset you?"

"No more than usual. The truth is I can't stand people who plot behind their leaders' backs. That's not you, of course, but you have the luck to be the only person around while I rant about it."

"Understood. I shan't take offence."

"Good. Then we understand each other perfectly."

TWELVE

Dragon Fire

SPRING 966 MC

"We're behind schedule," grumbled Gerald. "We should've been in Falford a week ago."

"Couldn't be helped, sir," said Sergeant Blackwood. "The weather's not been cooperating of late."

"How long have we known each other?"

"Longer than I care to admit. Why?"

"Then stop calling me sir."

"It's only proper," replied the sergeant. "After all, you're the marshal."

"Yes, and you're the Sergeant-at-Arms of Bodden Keep."

"Not anymore, sir. I was lent to you for this staff of yours."

"You make it sound like a punishment."

"Not at all, but a good sergeant must know his place."

"How is the rest of the staff?"

"Oh, grumbling as always. You remember what the baron used to say, if they stop grumbling, there's a real problem."

Gerald laughed. "He always did have a way with words."

Since their time in Norland, the marshal's staff had grown and now numbered twenty individuals. That didn't include the many runners meant to carry messages to the individual commanders, only those needed to interpret Gerald's orders.

"You know," said the marshal, "it wasn't so long ago that I could command the army without all these extra people around."

"True, but then again, you weren't required to deal with all the messages coming in from rangers and mages."

"Yes, but do I genuinely need so many people?"

"Why not?" said Blackwood. "It frees you up to do the more important tasks."

"Like complaining about how slow we are?"

"Precisely."

"Is this how you ingratiated yourself to Fitz—by simply agreeing with everything he said?"

"Of course. How else was I to do it?"

Gerald looked skyward. The clouds were rolling in again. Tomorrow promised another day of slogging through mud. "Give the order to make camp. We'll get no farther today."

"Yes, sir." Blackwood rode off, yelling orders as he went.

The action caught the attention of Revi Bloom. Taking advantage of the marshal's solitude, the Life Mage rode over, a smile creasing his lips.

"You're in a good mood," said Gerald. "Saw Hayley, did you?"

"Not for some days. The last I heard, she was in the area, though, so there's a good chance we'll run across her before we reach Falford."

"I assume you were scouting with Shellbreaker?"

"Yes, I was. The good news is there's no sign of the enemy close by."

"And the bad news?"

"We're going to get more rain, a lot of it, if I don't miss my guess."

"That's hardly news."

"There's more, I'm afraid. There are some problems with the supply wagons."

"What problems?"

"They're overdue. We were expecting a group last night, but we've heard nothing so far. Were it not for the weather, I'd send Shellbreaker out looking for them, but that would only put his life at risk."

"I'll send some light cavalry back towards Aldgrave. Let's hope they can discover what happened to them."

"A wise choice," said the mage. "Even with all these rangers about, we can't dismiss the possibility of raiders getting through. They are Kurathians, after all. Of course, we might be worrying over nothing. Could they have followed the Dwarves by mistake?"

Gerald weighed the situation. He'd dispatched the Dwarves to Mirstone, along with the Orcs of the Black Arrow. That army, under Urgon's command, needed little in the way of supplies, each individual carrying two weeks of food in the form of stonecakes.

"No," he said at last. "Something's wrong. Those wagoneers followed us all the way into Norland. They're not the sort to take the wrong path."

"You might consider sending more horsemen. If the Kurathians are hopping around, it could spell trouble."

"Good point. I'll send Beverly. Have you seen her?"

"As a matter of fact, I have—she's just over there." Revi pointed. "Shall I fetch her for you?"

"No, I'll ride over to her. There are still some things I can do myself."

"Meaning?"

"Nothing," replied Gerald. "Just something my sergeant said." He spurred on his horse, sending clumps of mud flying as he galloped across the field. Beverly brought Lightning to a halt as soon as she noticed him approaching.

"Something wrong?" she asked.

"Unfortunately, yes. Some of our wagons have gone astray."

"They're probably bogged down in the mud."

"Quite possibly, but we can't ignore it. Kurathians are known to use raiding tactics and may have found a way past us. I want you to take some men and investigate."

"How many?"

"As many as you need, but leave me with at least one company of horse-men, will you?"

She laughed. "I'll do my best. How about I take two companies of light horse for scouting purposes and one heavy, in case we run into a fight?"

"Sounds good, although I must warn you more rain is on the way."

"For Saxnor's sake, more? We should have prayed to Akosia, then we'd have decent weather."

"She's the goddess of the sea, not rain," said Gerald, "but at this point, I'm willing to try anything."

"I'll take care of it," she said, "and then meet you in Falford."

"Thank you, Beverly. I knew I could count on you."

She winked. "My pleasure, Marshal."

"Keep that up, and I may need to make you general."

"You can't. That would be too confusing."

"Confusing, how?"

"Can you imagine having two General Fitzwilliams?"

He laughed. "There is that. I suppose that means you'll have to wait until he retires."

"Fine by me. I'm in no hurry to command an army."

"You handled the spirit army well enough."

"Only after you showed us the way."

"You're only complimenting me to get on my good side."

"Am I?" said the knight. "Is it working?"

"You know it is. Now, get out of here, and go find out what happened to my wagons."

. . .

Two days later found Beverly examining the ground. "There's never a ranger around when you need one," she grumbled. She stood, realizing just how much she sounded like Gerald.

Captain Nevin moved closer. "Find something useful?"

"Maybe. It looks like a group of wagons turned west for some reason, and abruptly, if these tracks are any indication."

"You're suggesting they were attacked?"

"Undoubtedly. The real question is, by whom? I can see no tracks other than our own, and that of the wagons, of course."

"So, what do we do now?"

"That's the easy part; we follow the tracks, but stay on alert. Whoever is responsible for this may still be in the area. I want your company watching to our north, Captain Linton's to the south. I'll keep the heavy cavalry with me."

"Aye, Commander."

Beverly looked skyward. The rain had ceased for the moment, but more dark clouds threatened. She wandered back to Lightning and hauled herself into the saddle. Tracking was not her area of expertise, but even she could tell the tracks were reasonably fresh. With any luck, they would find the wayward wagons before dark. She urged Lightning forward, heading west, the heavy cavalry falling in behind.

It wasn't long before they rode into some hills. Not enough to make navigation difficult, but still sufficient to limit their view of the distance. The first sign of concern was when a rider from Captain Nevin's group came galloping towards her.

"Trouble?" she called out.

"The captain reports we're being watched."

"By whom?"

"That has yet to be determined. They're over that hill." He pointed north.

"Well then, let's ride over and find out who has taken such an interest in us, shall we?"

"Just like that?"

In answer, she turned to her men. "Sergeant, take ten men and circle to the north."

"Aye, Commander." A group of riders split from her company, carrying out their orders.

"We'll give them a moment to get into position," she continued, "then we'll make our move. Ride to your captain and tell him to maintain his current heading."

"Yes, Commander." The man headed back to his own company.

Beverly waited long enough for her sergeant to reach his position before turning north, advancing at a canter. Once their watchers were in full view, she would consider a charge, but for now, she wanted to conserve the horses' strength.

Lightning began climbing the hill, and then someone stood up, waving their hands in the air to get her attention. She slowed her pace as she drew closer.

"Thank Saxnor, you're here," the woman called out.

"I know you," said Beverly. "Vivian, isn't it?"

"It is," the woman replied. "I'm one of the wagon drivers."

"Where are the rest of you?"

"Scattered in amongst these hills. We needed to spread out to survive."

"Raiders?"

"No, worse—a dragon."

"A dragon? Here?"

Vivian nodded. "I saw it myself. If you come with me, I'll show you the damage it's done." She led Beverly down the reverse side of the hill. At the bottom lay a long scorch mark, along with what looked like the burned remains of a wagon.

"Is this the fate of all the wagons?"

"I'm afraid so, as well as at least a dozen people."

"This is grim news. We certainly didn't expect the enemy to employ dragons this far from Summersgate. What can you tell us about it? Was it large?"

"Aye, at least twice the size of your horse, and green, as near as I could tell, not that I spent much time looking at it. We first spotted it coming in from the west, heading straight for us."

"Are you sure it wasn't just flying around and discovered you?"

"It flew in a straight line."

"How long ago was this?"

"Three days."

"Let's get back to safety. I'll send riders out to locate any other survivors. You'll ride double with one of my warriors, but I'll need you to answer any questions the marshal may have. Don't worry, no one's blaming you."

"Still," said Vivian, "the wagons' loss will be a heavy blow."

"Wagons we can replace," said Beverly. "I'm more concerned with the loss of life, as I know the marshal will be."

She ordered her men to spread out to look for survivors. More wagons were located, and those that weren't burned had suffered from broken axles, a result of their attempt to flee over rocky terrain. In total, they rounded up six additional survivors, a far cry from the two dozen who'd accompanied the wagons. What remained of the supplies themselves were abandoned, for there were no spare horses on which barrels and crates could be packed.

Sergeant Blackwood entered the building. "They're back," he announced.

The marshal looked up from his desk. He'd been going over lists of supplies, overwhelmed by all the calculations needed to feed an army. Blackwood admitted Beverly, who made straight for the marshal.

"You found them?" Gerald asked.

"I did," she said, "although I'm afraid it's not good news. A dragon attacked our wagons."

"Are you sure?"

"Absolutely. We saw the scorch marks, not to mention what was left of the wagons."

"And our people?"

"Seven survived, and even then, four are wounded. Revi's seeing to them even as we speak."

Gerald looked around a room that was so packed with his staff, it was challenging to speak above the noise. "Come," he said at last. "Let's go for a walk."

He led her outside, then started up the street. Falford was a reasonably large town, and the army's presence only added to the congestion.

"What's bothering you?" said Beverly. "It's not like you to step outside for a stroll, not when there's army business to attend to."

He halted, looking her in the eyes. "I think we have a spy amongst us."

"A spy? Who?"

"I wish I knew."

"Are you sure you're not imagining things?"

"We have yet to encounter the enemy in any meaningful numbers," he said, "but it's almost as if they know what we're doing."

"But Prince Alric defeated them in the south. We have Aubrey's report."

"True, but then again, his campaign isn't handled through my staff."

"You believe the spy is actually on your staff? How could that be? You hand-picked them yourself."

"I did, and that's what worries me."

"It could be a coincidence. Aubrey told us Prince Tarak is some sort of military genius. Couldn't he just be outmanoeuvring us?"

Gerald continued his walk. "While that's definitely possible, the attack on the wagons would seem to indicate otherwise."

"Not at all. The dragon could have spotted them from miles away."

"True, but to do that, it would've needed to fly over either our pickets or those of Urgon. Tell me, where did it happen?"

"Just north of Waldstock. Why?"

"We have rangers watching to the west of Waldstock, and they reported no dragon sightings. For a beast to attack us there without being sighted, it must have flown a very specific route. Surely that can't be mere coincidence."

"You make a compelling case, but very few knew the timing of those supplies."

"Except for everyone who works on my staff, and that's what has me worried."

"Does the loss of the wagons affect our campaign?"

"No, but a few more incidents like this, and we'll be required to call a halt. An army marches on its stomach, and we can't besiege Summersgate with men who are starving."

Beverly gritted her teeth. "This is so frustrating."

"It is, admittedly, but at least we're aware of it."

"And if you're wrong?"

Gerald shrugged. "It wouldn't hurt me to be a little more careful with who I pick for my staff."

"What do we do now?"

"I want you to investigate."

"Me? I'm a knight, not a scholar. You need someone like Aubrey."

"Unfortunately, she's down south, and I need someone I can trust here."

"And I am to do this without raising suspicion?"

"I never said it was easy."

"No," said Beverly. "You most assuredly did not, but what you're asking is difficult, especially considering we're in the middle of a campaign."

"I'll have Blackwood help you. We've both known him for years."

"How long do I have?"

"I can't tell you. What I do know is we won't be moving on the capital any time soon, not with a dragon threatening our supply lines."

"And how do you intend to solve that problem?"

"In the short term, I'll assign warriors to guard each group of wagons."

"And in the long term?"

"That's where you come in. We can't realistically stop a dragon, but we can stop information about our wagons from reaching enemy hands. Plug that hole in our shield wall, and the problem will fix itself."

"I'll do what I can."

"Good, because I received word Anna is coming to Falford. The last thing we need is her carriage being attacked on the road."

"The queen is coming here?"

"She is. Why? Does that surprise you?"

"I would've thought she'd want to stay in Kingsford, considering she's only just given birth."

"That was weeks ago, and you know what she's like when she gets an idea in her head."

"Shouldn't I be going to Kingsford to escort her?"

"No," said Gerald. "That's already been taken care of. Sir Preston now commands the new Guard Cavalry, so he'll accompany her."

"I assume she's crossing near Aldgrave?"

"I'm not sure. I thought it best she make her own arrangements and keep them to herself."

"Do we at least know when she intends to arrive?"

"Of course not. That would make things far too easy."

"So, all I need to do is root out a traitor who may or may not exist before the queen arrives at an unspecified time?"

"That about sums it up, yes."

"You're not exactly making this easy for me," said Beverly.

"True, but if it was easy, I could do it myself. Besides, who else can I trust with something like this? Consider it the price you must pay for all those years of flattering me. Of course, if you'd prefer not to help the man who taught you everything you know about weapons…"

"All right, you win. I'll do it, although, for the life of me, I have no idea where I'll start."

"Good. I hoped you'd say that."

"Come, come," said Beverly. "You knew I would never refuse an order."

"I never really considered this an order, rather more of a request, if I'm being honest."

"And the difference is?"

"Nothing regarding your investigation is written down. You'll report to me directly and only when nobody's around."

"Not even the queen?"

"Well, the queen can be trusted, obviously, but no one else unless she says so."

"Very well. I'll have a chat with Sergeant Blackwood, and together, we'll come up with a way forward."

"Good, and in the meantime, I'll concentrate on getting this army ready to advance on Summersgate."

"Any word on Mirstone?"

"Gorath's rangers report Urgon arrived there two days ago. There's been no sign of the enemy, and they joined forces with Princess Althea. They're waiting on us to advance to Kinsley so we can concentrate our forces."

"Finally, some good news for a change."

"I'm not sure I'd call it good," said Gerald. "Prince Tarak is out there somewhere, waiting to spring on us like a pack of wolves."

"You worry too much. He might have a reputation as a brilliant tactician, but we have the Wolf of Merceria."

He looked at her in confusion.

"That's you, Gerald."

"Me? Wherever did you come up with that one?"

"I just thought of it, but somehow it suits you. It's meant purely as a compliment, of course. You must admit it makes sense, considering your past."

Gerald mulled it over. "The Wolf of Merceria. I suppose it could be worse. What are they calling you these days?"

Beverly smiled. "Redblade. What else?"

The marshal laughed. "They need a new name. You use a hammer now."

"True, but Redhammer doesn't have the same ring to it."

THIRTEEN

Encounters

SPRING 966 MC

C aptain Carlson looked back in disbelief. Since last fall, he'd been in command of Tewsbury's garrison, but the news that he would be ordered to march on a Mercerian town seemed incredulous. "You can't be serious?"

"Do I not look serious?" asked Arnim. "The Nobles Council ordered us to Hawksburg."

"What has the queen to say on the matter?"

"I wish I knew, but she remains with the army. In her absence, the council carries the weight of the law."

"I shall follow orders, naturally, but I feel it my duty to inform you there's been some concerning developments here of late."

"Can you be more specific?"

Captain Carlson looked at Albreda.

"Spit it out, man," ordered the Druid. "I'm a trusted agent of the queen, for Saxnor's sake."

"There's been growing resentment against non-Humans. It started as mere whispers in the taverns, but now it's talked about openly in the streets." He chuckled.

"I'm glad you find that amusing," said Albreda.

"It's only that most of the people here have never even seen an Orc, let alone know anything about their contributions to the war in Norland."

"Still," said Arnim, "we have our orders, no matter how ridiculous they seem."

"Your orders," said Albreda. "They call on you to march to Hawksburg, correct?"

"Yes, and suppress the uprising."

"But with no details as to how it is to be accomplished?"

"Correct. I am to use my own discretion."

"Then I suggest you do just that."

"You can't be serious?"

"Go to Hawksburg with your footmen. That should take you two days. Obviously, there is no uprising, so then you can return having fulfilled your obligation."

"The council won't like that."

"I don't care. You and I both know the queen would never condone this ridiculous waste of time."

"And what will you do in my absence?"

"Oh, you know, the usual."

"The usual?"

"Yes," said Albreda. "I shall convince everyone here of the error of their ways."

"That won't make you very popular."

"I gave up trying to be popular years ago. No, I tell a lie; I never tried to be popular. In any case, I'm not constrained by duty. Unlike you, I didn't take an oath to serve the Crown or obey and defend the laws of the land."

A look of panic crossed Arnim's face.

"Don't worry," she soothed. "I have only the queen's best interests in mind."

"And if Tewsbury refuses us entry on our return?"

"I'll destroy the gates. I did so at Bodden, and I can easily do the same here."

"Bodden was only an iron grating from what I heard. The doors of Tewsbury are much larger."

"It's merely a matter of scale," explained the Druid, "and my power has grown considerably since then."

"I believe you."

"Good. Then I shall leave you to your duties, gentlemen. It's time for me to go for a walk."

She left without further discussion.

"I wouldn't want to be on her bad side," noted Captain Carlson.

"Nor I," replied Arnim.

The docks in Falford were packed as the ship bearing the Royal Flag of Merceria butted up against the quay. It wasn't the first time Anna had visited this Weldwyn town, but it would mark the first time a foreign queen had officially set foot on Weldwyn soil.

The guards came first, forming up at the bottom of the ramp. Then Sir Preston led the queen down, followed by her faithful dog, Tempus, and her chief lady-in-waiting, Sophie. The rest of her entourage followed along behind at a suitable distance.

Gerald met her as she stepped ashore. "Your Majesty," he said. "You honour us with your presence."

Anna smiled. "So formal."

"There is a crowd," he reminded her.

"Yes, of course. Shall we go inside? I haven't eaten all morning."

"Where's Prince Braedon?"

"Napping, if you can believe it. Matron Crawley will bring him along shortly." She looked at the crowd gathered in the distance. "Is this all for me?"

"Naturally. It's not every day a Queen of Merceria comes to Weldwyn."

"It feels like we've done this all before."

Gerald chuckled. "We have, in a sense, although I daresay it won't be as easy to evict the Clansmen this time."

"From what I hear, it's not the Clansmen who are the problem. Rather, it is the army of Prince Tarak."

"You've been keeping up to date with matters."

"I read every report you send me. That's one of the reasons I'm here now."

"Did I give you the impression we were in trouble?"

"No, of course not, but I can't have you wasting all your time writing letters to me, can I? It's far more efficient to tell me in person."

Tempus ears pricked up as a wail issued from the ship. "Ah," said Anna. "It appears the princeling has awoken."

An older woman emerged from the aft cabin, bearing a bundled infant. They both watched as she descended the ramp to stand beside the queen and curtsy. Tempus took an immediate interest in the proceedings, sniffing the air, causing Matron Crawly to hold Braedon even higher as if he was in danger. Anna took the child, then knelt, letting the great hound gaze down upon her son.

"That's Tempus," she said in a soothing voice. "He's here to keep you safe like he does me." The child's eyes were full of wonderment while Tempus stared back, wagging his tail. "These two have been getting along famously." She stood, then held him up for Gerald to see. "Say hello to your grandfather."

Gerald felt tears welling up.

"Would you like to hold him?" Anna asked.

The matron gave him a withering glare. "Surely not, Your Majesty?"

Anna suppressed a grin and handed over the Heir to the Crown of Merceria. "See?" she said. "Gerald knows how to hold a baby."

"My goodness, he's big," said the marshal.

"And so he should be. He eats like there's no tomorrow."

"The boy has a healthy appetite," added the matron.

"Did you find somewhere for us to stay?"

"Yes," said Gerald. "The same place we stayed at last time, the Earl of Falford's home."

"Good. Then lead on. I'm eager to get to work."

"Shall I take the child?" asked the matron.

"No," said Gerald, a little too quickly. "I've got him. Provided that's all right with Her Majesty?"

Anna smiled. "Nothing would make me happier."

Sir Preston watched as a well-dressed woman rode through Falford, her carriage liberally splattered with mud.

He felt a tug on his arm. "Someone you know?" asked Sophie.

"No, but the presence of a noble here in Falford is unusual, to say the least."

"Excepting Mercerian ones," she added.

"That's true, of course, yet I wonder who that might be. I don't recognize the coat of arms, do you?"

"No, but I suspect that's because it's from Weldwyn. What about the Earl of Falford's wife?"

"I thought he was a widower?"

Sophie shrugged. "I don't know. Prince Alric never mentioned the topic, at least not that I can recall."

He halted, turning to face her. "There's something I want to discuss with you."

"Go on," she said, her eyes staring up in wonder.

"It's just that—" A yell came from his left, and he turned abruptly, quickly noticing the carriage had come to a sudden halt. The woman within, whoever she was, was haranguing a Mercerian soldier who happened to be walking by. "Wait here," he pleaded. "I should see to this."

Sophie's face fell. "I will not. If you're going to see who this woman is, then I'm coming with you. Don't think for a moment you're going to get off that easily."

They approached the carriage cautiously. Sir Preston appeared tense and ready to spring into action at a moment's notice, but Sophie was more accepting of the circumstances. As the queen's lady-in-waiting, she was used to how some nobles treated their social inferiors.

"Is there a problem here?" called out the knight.

"I should say there is," came back the woman's voice. An elderly face appeared at the carriage window. "This buffoon cannot tell me the way to the earl's estate."

"Of course not," said Sir Preston. "He's a Mercerian."

The woman looked as if someone had slapped her. "A Mercerian? Here in Falford?"

"Yes. Like many of my countrymen, he's come here to help liberate Weldwyn."

He watched the relief flooding the woman's face. "Thank Malin for that. And who are you?"

"I might ask you the same question, madame. My name is Sir Preston, Knight of the Hound and a commander in the Army of Merceria."

"I am Lady Lindsey Martindale, Viscountess of Talburn."

"Honoured to meet you, Lady Lindsay. Might I ask the purpose of your visit?"

"Not that it's any business of yours, but I fled the capital some weeks past and have been seeking a place of refuge for some time."

"Summersgate fell last fall."

"I know that, of course. I spent several months in Norwatch, but then the enemy came there. I struck out across the countryside, eager to make Kinsley, only to find that it, too, was in the hands of the usurper."

"Usurper?"

"Yes," said Lady Lindsey. "The self-styled Queen of Weldwyn, Brida."

"Are you suggesting Brida was in Kinsley?"

"No, of course not, you silly man. I meant her army."

Sophie found her temper rising. "He's not a silly man."

The noble raised her eyebrows. "And you are?"

"Sophie."

"She means Lady Sophie," added Sir Preston, "confidante to the queen."

"Indeed? Perhaps I am mistaken in my assessment of you two. Does that mean the Queen of Merceria is here in the city?"

"It does," said Sir Preston, "and I have the honour of commanding her guard."

"Well, I suppose someone has to bear that responsibility."

Sir Preston began turning red, and Sophie clutched his arm, speaking before he could, "Would you like to pay your respects?"

"Yes, of course," the woman replied. "I shall need somewhere to make myself presentable first, though."

"There's an inn down the street, my lady, a place called the White Stag."

"Finally," said Lady Lindsey. "The answer I needed. Thank you, my dear. You may inform Her Majesty I will pay my respects at court as soon as I am able."

"Yes, my lady."

Lady Lindsey rapped the roof of the carriage with her walking stick. "You heard the woman. Carry on to the White Stag." They rolled off down the street.

"I can't help but feel this is a bad omen," said Sir Preston.

"Never mind that," said Sophie. "You were about to say something to me before that horrid woman interrupted?"

"Yes. It has been some time since we announced our engagement. I should very much like—"

At that precise moment, a nearby door opened, and two men tumbled out into the street, gripped in a deathlike hold.

"Oh, for Saxnor's sake," shouted the knight as he strode across the street and pulled them apart. When they tried to strike out again, he drew his sword. "Desist now, or I shall be forced to place you both under arrest!"

Duly chastised, the two men simply stared at him.

"Shake hands and stop this nonsense!"

They did what they were told, for it was not wise to refuse a Knight of the Hound.

"Good. Now go your separate ways, and if I hear of this happening again, I'll see you both hung from the nearest tree. Do you hear me?"

They backed away, then turned, heading in different directions.

"Saxnor's balls," said Sir Preston. "Can a man get no peace these days?" He turned his attention back to Sophie. "Let's get married."

"We're already engaged," she replied.

"No, I mean actually married. I don't want to wait any longer."

"What of your parents?"

"They will understand. Of course, if you'd prefer to wait—"

"No," she quickly replied. "But we should at least wait until tomorrow, if only to gather friends."

"Then tomorrow it shall be." He moved closer, holding her in an embrace. "Oh, Sophie, you've made me so very happy."

She blushed. "Preston, we're in public!"

"So we are, but I don't care. I want the entire city to know how much I love you."

A giggle escaped her lips. "I'm sure they all know, my love; they talk of little else. Now you must let me go, or we shall not have sufficient time to make all the arrangements."

"I shall find someone to marry us."

"And I'll ask the queen's permission."

A look of dismay crossed his face. "What if she refuses?"

"Don't be ridiculous. Why would you say such a thing?"

"A queen's lady-in-waiting has to be unmarried."

"And you think that will hold much water with the queen?"

He grinned. "No, I suppose not."

"Good. Now, be on your way and prepare yourself for tomorrow's wedding. I have things of my own to attend to."

"This is marvellous news," said Anna. "You must let me host it in your honour."

"Thank you, Your Majesty," said Sophie.

"You seem a little nervous, although that's only natural, considering you're getting married."

"To tell the truth, there is something on my mind, Majesty."

"Then tell me, Sophie, and let's forget this majesty nonsense for a moment, shall we?"

"Sir Preston believes a lady-in-waiting must be unmarried."

"Nonsense. That may have been the custom in the past, but who am I to follow the rules? You will be my lady-in-waiting until you decide otherwise. Is that clear?"

"Thank you, Majes…"

"There," said the queen. "That wasn't so hard, was it? Just think, after tomorrow, we'll be addressing you as Lady Sophie… I hate to admit it, but I don't know Sir Preston's family name."

"It's Wright."

"Is it? I suppose that makes sense. After all, his family is descended from wainwrights. So there you have it—you shall soon be known as Lady Sophie Wright."

They gathered the next day at the baron's residence. Word of the celebration had travelled quickly, and the place was soon deluged with requests for invitations. The queen kept the invitees to people who Sophie knew, although she did allow one or two others of import to attend. Thus, Lady Lindsay Martindale found herself at the festivities as the only Weldwyn noble in attendance.

She made her way through the guests, consisting mainly of military officers. Most were men in their prime, far too young to her aged eyes, but at least one turned out to be a striking individual of a suitable age. He moved to the front of the room, capturing everyone's attention, including Lady Lindsey. The fellow cleared his throat before speaking.

"Since the days of our ancestors, military commanders have enjoyed the privilege of performing the marriage ceremony for those under their command. In that tradition, we are gathered here today to witness the union of Sir Preston Wright and Lady Sophie Fairborn."

The ceremony continued, but Lady Lindsey's attention strayed elsewhere. She tapped a red-headed woman on the shoulders.

"Who is that man conducting the ceremony?" the lady asked. "He doesn't look like a Holy Father."

"He's not," the woman replied. "That's Gerald Matheson, the Marshal of Merceria."

"And he is conducting the ceremony? This Sir Preston must be someone very important, indeed."

"He is a Knight of the Hound—one of only six."

"Ah, a knight? That's something like a cavalier, isn't it?"

"I suppose you might see it that way, but the truth is we knights are far more than mere warriors."

"We knights? Are you proposing that you yourself are a knight?"

"I am. The Knight Commander, to be exact. Dame Beverly Fitzwilliam, and you are?"

"Lady Lindsey Martindale, Viscountess of Talburn."

"Talburn? That's a Mercerian name. We had a prince named Talburn who tried to usurp the Crown. He went on to found Norland."

"Yes, and in celebration of his attempt, we named a village after him. Of course, it's grown significantly since then, and fortunately, our kingdoms are no longer bitter enemies. However, it now lies in the hands of our enemies."

"Did you speak to the queen?"

"Not yet. I didn't want to interrupt the ceremony."

"I can arrange a meeting if you like?"

"I would greatly appreciate that, thank you. If you don't mind my saying, you sound very cultured."

"My father is Lord Richard Fitzwilliam, Baron of Bodden."

"Ah, then you'll make someone a proud husband someday."

"I already have," Beverly replied, not bothering to hide her smile.

"And what is his title, if I might ask?"

"The Master Smith of Bodden." She watched the woman's face fall—clearly not the answer she'd expected.

"Are you suggesting he is a commoner?"

"Not anymore. His name is Lord Aldwin."

"And is that a commonplace thing in Merceria?"

Beverly thought for a moment. "Now you mention it, it has been of late. Why, the marshal IS the Duke of Wincaster."

"A duke? Indeed? How fascinating. Is there a Duchess?"

"No," said Beverly. She was about to say more, but something told her it was none of her business. "Rest assured, I shall speak to Her Majesty once the ceremony is complete and have an answer for you before you leave."

"Excellent." Lady Lindsey turned her attention once more to the newly married couple as people surged forward to offer their best wishes for a happy union.

She shook her head. Marriage was not about love—it was about duty, power, and influence. A good marriage could cement an alliance: a bad one doom a family to the history books. Sometimes, it was hard to tell which was which, but she had no doubt a union such as this could only lead to trouble. A cavalier, or a knight for that matter, was not sufficiently well off to take a wife, and neither was a lady-in-waiting any prize considered worthy. It was amazing that these Mercerians had managed to thrive with ideas like this.

The marshal made his way through the room, obviously in a good mood. Perhaps now was the time to introduce herself? After all, a duke needed a duchess, and who better to provide that service than a noble of Weldwyn?

FOURTEEN

Traitor

SPRING 966 MC

"I know you." Albreda had looked up from her table at the tavern to notice a young man staring back at her. "Manson, isn't it?"

His mouth fell open. "Yes, I'm surprised you remember."

"I met you back in sixty-two. You worked at the stables at that time."

"I did, and you helped me with the horses."

"I remember it well."

"May I join you?"

"By all means," said Albreda. She waited until he sat down before ordering him a tankard of ale. "Are you still looking after Mercerian Chargers?"

"Not since the knights left, no."

"But you're still at the stable?"

"Yes, and still only a stable hand. I'm afraid we're not as busy as we once were."

"You should go to Hawksburg. I hear they need people to help look after all those horses. You know, they breed them there."

"So I hear," said Manson, "but they also say the place is swarming with greenskins."

"You mean Orcs? They're not monsters."

"That's not what I heard."

Albreda caught the eye of their server. "Another couple of rounds here, if you please." She leaned forward. "I find this whole thing most fascinating. Tell me more."

"About the Orcs?"

"Yes. What, precisely, have you heard?"

"They are said to be a very warlike race, intent on conquering the civilized lands. Their plan is to infiltrate the cities of Merceria and then rise up and take over."

"That is the most absurd thing I've ever heard," said Albreda. "I'm surprised you would believe such a ridiculous accusation."

Her statement caught the attention of a man at the next table. "It's true," he insisted.

"Of course it's not," said Albreda. "And a simple examination of the numbers proves it. How many Orcs do you believe there are?"

"Hundreds," the man replied.

"And have you any idea how many Humans live within Merceria?"

He shook his head.

"Then let's look at Tewsbury, shall we? This city has a population of, oh, I don't know, maybe twenty thousand or so? Even if all the Orcs were here, it's doubtful they could seize power, let alone across all the cities of the realm, and that's even assuming they wanted to."

"But they took over Hawksburg."

"I can assure you they most certainly did not. They helped rebuild Hawksburg after the war, and the people there welcomed them with open arms. The Orc hunters kept the people fed after the place was burned to the ground."

"Then their work is done," the man persisted. "It's time for them to go home."

"Home? And where would that be?"

"Who cares!"

"The Orcs of the Black Arrow live in the Artisan Hills, a most desolate place. Why should they return there to a life of starvation and solitude when Hawksburg invites them to stay?"

"Easy for you to say. You're not the one who has to deal with them creeping around the streets at night."

"Where in Saxnor's name did you hear that?"

The fellow grew defensive. "It's true. I heard it from a merchant who travelled through Hawksburg."

"I see. And was he, perchance, talking of the town watch? Because the Orcs and Humans share the responsibility of keeping the streets safe. I might also add that their presence has reduced crime considerably."

"Oh yes? And how would you know that?"

"You clearly do not know who I am."

"Nor do I care."

"Ignore him," pleaded Manson. "He's a notorious know-it-all."

"Watch your tongue," the man warned.

Albreda stood, commanding the entire room. "I expect few here would recognize me by sight, but my name is Albreda, also known as the Witch of the Whitewood." Such was the reputation of her name that all within fell silent.

"You were deceived, all of you. The Orcs are our allies. Had it not been for their assistance, a tyrannical king would still rule over you."

"He kept us safe," a voice called out.

"Did he? His rule led to the Earl of Eastwood plotting his overthrow, not to mention the fact that he failed to bring Norland to its heels."

"And what has your so-called queen done for us?"

"Why, you ungrateful fool. She established laws to protect you all and allow you to live in relative peace."

"That didn't stop the Norland invasion."

"True, but her army defeated it, then marched north to put an end to such threats once and for all. Not that anyone here suffered much—you were all safely behind the walls of your city when the enemy marched past. I might also remind you that Queen Anna welcomed you back into the kingdom once the war was over. Had the situation been reversed, I doubt your precious king would have spared a city that took up arms against him. It would be your city that lies in ruins, not Hawksburg."

"They got what they deserved."

Albreda stepped closer to the fellow. She was not a tall woman, by any means, yet somehow she seemed to tower over him. So much so that he turned quite pale.

"Look at you," she mocked. "You believe yourselves men of honour and loyalty, yet you feed on gossip like a dog with a bone. Did it cross no one's mind to question these outrageous lies?" She stared down at the fellow. "What is your name?"

"Conrad."

"Well, Conrad, it seems there is only one way I can convince you. Come with me!"

"To where?"

"I will take you to Hawksburg to see the place for yourself."

He snickered. "Don't be ridiculous. It's a two-day trip."

"I can have you there before you need to empty your bladder. Now come, or else I'll be forced to do something more drastic."

She heard the gasps, and a smile creased her lips. She looked around the room. "I shall take Conrad to meet the Orcs. Don't worry, I'll bring him back safely, then he can tell you first-hand what they are really like. Would that satisfy you?"

No one spoke out, but there were nods everywhere. Obviously, nobody wanted to upset the Witch of the Whitewood.

"Good. Now come, Conrad. We need to step outside."

He gulped. "We do?"

"Yes, we do. Casting my spell here would only upset the other patrons of this fine establishment."

Conrad stood, looking like he was under a sentence of death. Albreda gripped his arm and steered him out into the street. Many swarmed out behind them, eager to see what was about to happen.

"Manson," she said. "I wonder if you would do me a kindness and keep an eye on my horse for a couple of days?"

"Of course," replied the stable hand. "Where it is?"

"In the Wincaster Light's stables. Do you know it?"

"I do."

"Good. Now, the rest of you back up. There's likely to be some dirt flying around when I cast my spell."

The crowd did as instructed. People along the street now joined the audience, attracted by the strange development.

"Stand still, Conrad, and don't be alarmed. Nothing's going to hurt you." She looked skyward and let the power flow through her. Arcane words tumbled from her lips, and then the air buzzed with magic. Albreda closed her eyes and held her hands on high as wind swirled around them, lifting dirt into a vortex that surrounded them and blocked out all signs of Tewsbury.

She completed the spell and felt the familiar tug, then the air stilled, and they were standing in the Hawksburg circle.

"Mistress Albreda," came a familiar voice. "You honour us with your presence."

"Lahzak," she replied. "You have such a way with words. This is Conrad. He hails from Tewsbury. I wonder if I might rely on you to show him around?"

"Certainly," said the Orc.

The man stared back in shock. "He speaks our language."

"Of course he does," said Albreda. "You'd hardly understand him otherwise." She switched to Orc. "*Show him the city, particularly those areas where Orcs and Humans work together.*"

"*Yes, Mistress Albreda.*"

"*Come now, we've known each other far too long for such formality. I am Albreda, nothing more.*"

The Orc grinned. "*Yes, Albreda. It would be my privilege.*"

"What did he say?" asked Conrad.

"Nothing that need concern you. Lahzak will give you a tour of the town and then bring you back here by dinnertime."

"And how am I to pay for my food?"

"Don't worry about that. There's plenty for everyone."

He still looked confused.

"Did I not mention we'll be staying at the baroness's estate?" Albreda didn't believe it was possible, but Conrad grew even paler.

"Not to worry, you won't be required to watch your manners; Lady Aubrey isn't here. We'll put you up at her house, then ride back to Tewsbury tomorrow. I assume you can ride a horse?"

"I've never tried."

"Ah, well then. I'll have a chat with the horses and pick you a gentle ride."

"You can talk to horses?"

"Of course," said Albreda, winking at Lahzak. "I'm the Witch of the Whitewood."

Back in Falford, Lady Lindsay sat, eating her breakfast. It had been a late night, and her introduction to the marshal had been limited to a simple hello and curtsy, but she suspected it would soon lead to more.

She smiled at the thought. In her youth, she'd been the talk of the town, her beauty and grace the envy of all. It was true she'd lived a long life, but she still prided herself on her appearance. Her servant placed a goblet of wine to her right.

"No," she snapped. "You stupid girl, I said the red, not the white."

The young woman removed the offending cup and quickly replaced its contents.

Lady Lindsey took a sip, then rolled her eyes. "Honestly, I don't know why I've kept you on for so long. You can't even choose a decent vintage." She rose, her breakfast all but forgotten. "Have the carriage pull up around front. I shall be visiting what passes for the Royal Court this morning."

"Yes, my lady."

Her servant ran off, eager to escape the room. Lady Lindsey moved across to a small side table, opened a jewellery box, selected a necklace to highlight her plunging neckline, and then looked in the mirror. "There. Now, what man could resist that?"

Next, was the selection of a suitable cloak. She chose the one in royal blue to accentuate her matching eyes, then tied the golden clasp around her neck.

"I wonder," she mused aloud. "What will the marshal say?" She laughed at her own words. "He won't be able to resist me. True, it's been some time since I was actively on the hunt, but a duke is no laughing matter."

The door opened. "Did you call, my lady?"

Lady Lindsey turned in irritation. "I did not. But while you're here, where is the carriage?"

"I have called for it, my lady, but it takes time to prepare the horses."

The noble's eyes looked up at the ceiling. "Malin's tears, I am surrounded by incompetents."

Sometime later, Lady Lindsey finally arrived at the Duke of Falford's estate. She waited as a servant ran forth to open the carriage door, then descended to the street. The house looked much as it did the previous day, save for a distinct lack of decorations. The other difference was that warriors guarded the gates instead of servants, giving the place a very martial feel.

"I am here to visit with the marshal, His Grace, Lord Gerald Matheson."

The servant raised his eyebrows. "His Grace?"

"Yes. Is that not the correct form of address?"

"It is, my lady."

"Then don't just stand there gaping. Take me to him."

"Of course, my lady."

He led her past the guards and into the house. On the occasion of the wedding, they'd been hosted in the great hall, but today she was led past that magnificent room into a much more work-like environment. Many were present, some guarding doors, others walking briskly about their business, whatever that was.

Finally, they halted by a door, and the servant announced her presence to one of the guards. He stepped inside, leaving her to wait in the hallway while he discussed matters with his master. After only a short delay, the door opened wide.

"Lady Lindsey," said the duke. "What brings you here today?"

She moved closer. "I came to see you, Your Grace."

"Please, no one calls me, 'Your Grace'. Call me Gerald."

"Very well, Gerald," she said in reply, putting on her best smile. She'd hoped to have a private moment with the marshal, but the room was packed with people. "What is this place?"

"Ah, this is my staff."

"They don't look like servants?"

He laughed. "That's because they're not. These men and women are all warriors."

"Men AND women?"

"Yes. I understand you already met Dame Beverly?"

The red-headed knight waved from across the room.

"That's one woman."

"Yes, the other is Sam—she's over there." He pointed.

"Sam? What an unusual name for a girl."

"It's short for Samantha."

"Then that is how she should be addressed."

"Our customs differ from yours," said Gerald. "You said you wanted to see me?"

"Yes." She moved closer, lowering her voice and pouring on the charm. "I thought, considering the circumstances, that we might get to know each other a little better."

"Circumstances?"

"Yes. We're both nobles of a certain age and, by all accounts, unattached?"

He blushed. "I'm sorry to disappoint you, but my duties as head of the army keep me far too busy for such things."

"But you must eat on occasion, surely?"

"I take my meals with the queen."

"Excellent, then I shall join you. It's only proper that I offer her my counsel as a noble of Weldwyn."

"I…"

"He would be happy to accept," piped in Beverly. She looked at the marshal, who wore a look of surprise. "Come now, Gerald, it's time you learned how to socialize. This war won't last forever." She turned her attention to Lady Lindsey. "You must excuse the marshal; he's been rather consumed with the war of late."

"A quality I admire," said Lady Lindsey. "Might I enquire when we shall dine, Marshal?" This last remark was directed at the duke, who plainly preferred this form of address.

"Dusk?" he suggested.

"Dusk it is." She pretended to trip, allowing herself to brush up against him. "I look forward to it," she whispered, then turned and left, leaving him utterly stunned as the door closed behind her.

"What was that all about?" asked Gerald.

"It's obvious, isn't it?" replied a smirking Beverly. "She wants you."

"Wants me?"

"Come now, must I spell it out for you?"

He blushed. "I don't have time for all this nonsense. In any case, what do I have to offer?"

"Plenty," said Beverly. "You're the Duke of Wincaster and a close friend of the queen."

"Those are only titles."

"True, but you're also a caring individual, and that shows in the way you look after your warriors. Everyone likes you, Gerald. Why is it so hard to believe a woman might take an interest in you?"

"I suppose you're right, but I only just met her."

"No one's saying you're obliged to marry her, but you should at least give her a chance."

He stared back. "I haven't done that sort of thing in years."

She chuckled. "Don't worry. You have plenty of friends who can give you advice."

"And become a laughingstock? That's the last thing I want."

"Fine, then just me and the queen. Will that suffice?"

"Yes, that's much better."

"Good, now let's have a look at you." She walked around him while he stood there, dumbfounded.

"What are you doing?" he asked.

"When was the last time you trimmed that beard of yours?"

"I beg your pardon?"

"And you could use a good wash."

"I've been up for two days straight. The army doesn't run itself."

"Well," said Beverly, "that explains the attitude. Go and get some sleep. I'll have Blackwood come get you in plenty of time to get ready for dinner."

"It's still early."

"It is, and you need sleep."

"Who's going to look after all this?" He spread his arms out wide to encompass the entire room.

"Me," she replied. "It's not as if I haven't done it before." Her voice lowered. "It'll also give me the opportunity to deal one-on-one with some of these people and find out what's going on."

"Very well, you convinced me, but send word if anything important happens."

"I promise," said Beverly. "Now, get out of here before you find something else to consume you."

He left, although, admittedly, not before reminding everyone of their duties. Beverly felt a presence to one side and turned to see Sergeant Blackwood.

"Did you know his wife?" she asked.

"Meredith? Aye, she was full of life. You would have liked her. When she died, he lost a part of himself. Of course, that was years ago, long before you were born."

"I should have liked to know him back then. It's hard to imagine what he must have been like."

"You see glimpses of it occasionally. He seems to have a soft spot for young Prince Braedon."

"That I can believe. He was always kind to me, especially when I was younger. I was lucky he took me under his wing."

"Took you under his wing? Your father ordered him to train you."

"True," said Beverly, "but he could have just played the part of the dutiful soldier and only taught me the basics. Instead, he helped me become a knight, and I couldn't have done that without him."

FIFTEEN

Lord James

SPRING 966 MC

Lady Jane Goodwin sat alone in the dining hall, eating her meal. Since the occupation, the days seemed to drag on, and she seldom saw her son. Spearing another piece of meat, she popped it in her mouth, barely tasting it at all. Footsteps echoed in the hallway, and she held her breath. Could he have finally returned? The door opened, revealing Lord James Goodwin.

"Good evening, Mother."

"James, it's so nice to see you. I trust everything is well?"

"Well? I'd hardly say that."

"Why? Whatever is the matter?"

He sat opposite her, taking a moment to gather his thoughts. "I'm in a somewhat difficult position," he said at last. "As you are aware, the Clans have overrun all of Weldwyn. We hoped they might content themselves with putting their own ruler on the throne, but it now appears they are intent on being far more ruthless."

Jane felt a fist close over her heart. "What are you saying?"

"They're rounding up nobles, Mother, and taking them away."

"Away to where?"

"That's just it. No one knows. There are rumours, of course, but nothing that can be proven."

"What kind of rumours?"

"I'd hate to say."

"Come now, I'm your mother. I've lived through two invasions. There's little you can say that would shock me."

"Well," began James, "they took away Lord Stafford, and he was never seen again. They say his barony has been given to another, and that can only mean one thing."

"Are you suggesting they murdered him?"

"I can see little other explanation, can you?"

"If this is true, we must flee."

"To where?" he asked. "The entire kingdom is under their control."

"Then we should go east, to Merceria. Prince Alric married their queen. Surely they would give us shelter?"

"And risk war with the Clans? You give them too much credit."

"But they are our allies!"

"They WERE," corrected James, the lie coming easily to his lips, "but with the fall of Leofric, so, too, died the alliance. I'm afraid we're on our own, Mother."

Jane felt her panic rising. "And so we simply wait for them to take us away?"

"Not quite. It seems I was given another option, although I daresay I am reluctant to consider it."

"You must do what is necessary to survive. What is this option you speak of?"

"They want me to spy on the Mercerians."

"Why? You just said they weren't coming to help us?"

"That was my belief, but Prince Alric has apparently scraped together a group of rebels. Unfortunately, their presence endangers us all."

"How?"

"Our new queen, Brida, claims that for every Clansmen the rebels kill, she'll execute three of us."

"That's nothing more than a bluff."

"I'm afraid it isn't. Today, I witnessed an execution first-hand. Quite frankly, it's only by luck I wasn't one of the victims myself."

"And so you intend to agree to their demands?"

"What else can I do? I WAS going to continue my work here, in Summersgate."

"What work?"

He looked around the room quickly before lowering his voice. "We are attempting to rally opposition against Brida."

"A rebellion of your own?"

"Not quite. We are trying to identify Clansmen who might be more sympathetic to our cause. Of course, all that work will be for naught if I'm sent to spy on Prince Alric."

"Is there no other choice for this mission?"

"I could refuse," said James, "but I fear that act of defiance would be my last."

"There must be another way."

"If there is, I'm open to it."

Lady Jane pushed the plate away from her. "I'll go in your place."

"You?"

"Why not me? And, if I were to make it to Prince Alric's army, he would never suspect I was there to spy."

"You make a good point, but it would likely be perilous."

"I am not afraid to die," she replied. "And even if I did, it would at least be with the knowledge that I did so to save your life."

"I can't let you do this, Mother."

"You must. There is no other way."

Lady Jane stared into his eyes, but he cast them down in shame.

"You are my son," she continued, "and I would do anything to keep you from harm."

He reached across the table, taking her hand in his. "Thank you, Mother. There are no words to express my gratitude."

"I shall need details."

"Such as?"

"How am I to get word back to Summersgate?"

"Someone was to contact me once I was in the rebel camp. At least, that's what they told me when they offered me the opportunity."

"And when would I leave?"

"The sooner, the better. They wanted me out of the city by first light tomorrow."

"Then I shall go and gather my things. It will likely be a difficult trip. Am I to walk or take a horse?"

"I'm afraid our invaders have decreed no horses are permitted to leave the city."

"Then I must choose a good pair of walking shoes. As for you, I will need you to return to our conquerors and inform them I'll be going in your stead. I wouldn't like to be arrested for trying to leave the city."

"Understood. I'll do as you ask." He stood, finally looking deep into her eyes. "I shall never forget your sacrifice, Mother."

Lady Jane was too upset to speak. Instead, she just nodded, the tears running down her cheeks.

. . .

Lord James left the house by way of the back door to where a carriage drawn by four horses waited. He hopped inside, taking the seat opposite Lord Godfrey.

"Well?" the older man said. "Did it go according to plan?"

"It couldn't have gone better if I planned it myself. Oh, wait a moment, I did!" James laughed at his own jest.

"So your mother believed you?"

"I had her eating out of the palm of my hand. I have only to play the part of the remorseful son for a little longer, and then I shall be rid of her."

"And she'll spy on the Mercerians?"

"She will. I told her they were rebels, and the Clansmen were threatening reprisals."

"And when she learns they're not rebels?"

"It'll be too late to change her mind. She fully believes my life is at stake, and she's desperate to save me from the noose."

Dark clouds gathered overhead as Lady Jane Goodwin stepped into the carriage. It would be a quick trip to the gate, and then she would need to abandon her ride, making the rest of the journey eastward on foot.

She'd chosen to travel light, but as she sat within the confines of her carriage, she began to think that trying to lug anything across the wilderness was a bad idea. The carriage jolted forward, and then the horses settled into a regular rhythm as they trotted down the cobblestone streets. The effect was hypnotic, and soon she closed her eyes, contemplating her current situation.

Her life had been one of privilege, but it had taken its toll. As a young woman of means, her marriage had been arranged long before she was old enough to understand the ramifications. Even after her nuptials, she knew little of such things, for her education was limited. Still, she understood her obligations as a wife and mother.

She'd given Lord Goodwin a son, yet that hadn't impressed the man. Theirs had been a loveless marriage, leading her to turn her affections towards her son, the only person who showed her any kindness. However, as he grew older, he began to exhibit the same behaviours she found so abhorrent in her husband.

James was a spendthrift and a notorious womanizer. She'd tried to broach the subject with him on numerous occasions, only to be rebuked. Unfortunately, his attitude towards women was much the same as his father—they were little more than objects to be used and discarded.

The thought brought her to tears, and to distract herself, she looked out the window, watching those on the street as her carriage took her through the city.

Summersgate was not what it used to be. As a girl, she could walk these streets freely, but now, with the Clansmen roaming the place, nowhere was safe, not even out in the open. They'd born a grudge against Weldwyn for centuries, and with their revenge complete, they took what they wanted, whether it be riches or people.

No, that wasn't quite true. Her own maid had been spared such a fate, even rescued from it by a concerned Clansman—maybe they weren't all barbarians.

The carriage rolled past the Dome, a magnificent building topped by a copper roof that would forever retain its original lustre, thanks to magic. Unfortunately, the mages had all fled, leaving the building to be occupied by the enemy. She expected to see Clansmen there but instead, spied green-clad warriors in full helms armed with long spears. So unexpected was the sight, she ordered a temporary halt to her trip.

The guards stood motionless, forming a line facing the street. People passing by crossed over the road to stay well clear of these warriors, whoever they were, and even the Clansmen kept their distance.

Jane watched them for only a short time before tapping the top of the carriage to continue her journey. The gates soon drew closer, bringing about the time for her to be on her way.

It took only a moment for the coachman to open the door after reaching their destination. "We are here, my lady."

She stepped out. "Thank you. You can take my things back to the house. I shan't be needing them."

This surprised the fellow, but Lady Jane shook her head. "No, there is far too much for me to carry. Better I travel light."

She took a moment to pull her pass from her belt. It was nothing more than a letter authorizing her to leave the city, yet she brandished it at the gate with some trepidation. Would they accept this, or would they place her under arrest for attempting to flee?

A guard spotted her approach and waved her over. He was an older man with a kindly face, though from the Clanholdings, if his manner of dress was any indication.

"You're leaving us?" he said.

"I am," she replied. "I must see to a rather pressing business on behalf of the High Queen."

"Impressive, but the road eastward can be dangerous. Are you not taking an escort?"

"I'm afraid my mission precludes that possibility."

He looked at her a moment, trying to gauge the honesty of her response. She worried he would order her arrest, and all would be for naught. The Clans would hang her son, and then the only important thing she'd ever done in her life would be erased from existence.

The guard merely smiled. "I wish you well in your travels. You may proceed."

Lady Jane almost fainted with relief. "Thank you," she said.

She passed through the gate and into the fields beyond. After a hundred paces or so, she hesitated, looking back at Summersgate. Was she on a fool's errand? A trap of some sort to lead her into danger? She quickly dismissed the thought. James was in trouble, and her duty as his mother was to do all she could to keep him safe. A calmness came over her, and then she hiked up her dress and proceeded down the road heading east.

It was drizzling by noon, and by mid-afternoon, the clouds unleashed the thunderous fury of a storm. Lady Jane was soaked in mere moments, her dress becoming heavy, her boots thoroughly waterlogged.

In her youth, she would have exalted in the rain, but now, in her declining years, she yearned for nothing more than a comfortable seat by a raging fire.

To make matters worse, the wind was determined to ravage the countryside, plastering her face with rain and causing no end of discomfort. She sought refuge beneath the arms of a great oak tree, still chilled but at least partially protected from the elements. There she sat, pondering the grim circumstances that had brought her to this place.

She blamed herself, something she often did. In her mind, her husband's lack of attention was due entirely to her own absence of desire. Everyone told her this was natural, that a wife would learn, in time, to appreciate her husband, but it had never happened to her.

Even their son's birth had little effect on the man. If anything, he became even more consumed with life at court, cozying up to those in positions of power and influence. Not that it had done any good. Oh, they'd had a reasonably comfortable life, and she never felt in want of food or clothing, but she would gladly have traded all that for any sign of affection, even so much as a simple peck on the cheek.

The rain continued as she sat there in the middle of the field. She briefly considered returning to Summersgate, returning to her mission once the weather changed, but to do so might threaten her son's deal with their new masters.

Her stomach growled, and she realized she'd brought no food. Of course, she had coins, yet there was nowhere nearby to spend them. Resolving to take matters into her own hands, she returned to the road. The downpour finally ceased by late afternoon, although dark clouds still lingered.

Darkness had already fallen when she noticed lights ahead. Along the kingdom's roadways were inns where travellers could find refuge. One such building now lit up the countryside, a beacon of hope after what had been a torrential downpour.

Jane made her way towards it, trudging through mud that clung to her feet like ponderous weights. By the time she arrived, she was exhausted. She reached for the handle just as someone opened the door.

"We saw you approaching," said a friendly face. "Come in and warm yourself by the fire."

"Thank you," she squeaked out. "And perhaps something to eat?"

The man let her in, then peered outside, looking left and right. "Have you no carriage?"

"I have not," she said. "It was damaged some miles back."

"I'll send out a rider to help."

"Don't bother. They're already on their way back to Summersgate."

"And you chose not to accompany them?"

"My presence is required elsewhere."

He led her to a chair. "Here, this is nice and close to the fire. Some ale, perhaps?"

"If you would be so kind."

The next morning found her dry and refreshed. She set out at first light, determined to get as far east as possible, this time carrying extra food purchased at the inn. The weather held, and by noon, she felt she'd made enough progress to stop for a rest.

She chose a hill upon which to sit. The view was breathtaking, consisting of rolling grassland with patches of trees scattered around the countryside. It reminded her of her childhood, and she yearned for the freedom of her youth. Those had been happier times, days when she lacked for nothing and lived life to its fullest. All that had come crashing to a halt on her wedding night.

She rose, shaking off the memory. Dwelling on the past would do no good. She must look to the future. Making her way back to the road, she continued eastward.

Not long afterwards, she heard horses, and then a group of six horsemen came into view—Kurathians, by the look of them. They slowed as they neared, and then one of their number dismounted.

"Well, well," he said, using the common tongue of Weldwyn. "What have we here?"

She stood her ground, although her heart grew faint. "I am on important business for the High Queen," she said.

The man crossed his arms. "Oh yes? And what type of business might that be?"

"It's a s-s-secret," she stammered. "I cannot speak of it."

He moved closer. "And you have some proof of this?"

She reached into her skirts and pulled forth the letter. The heavy rain and damp clothes of yesterday's journey had done their work, for now it was nothing more than smudges of ink on a damp and torn piece of paper. All she could do was stare down at it in disbelief.

The Kurathian laughed, then moved forward, grabbing her by the arms before she could react. "Then I shall take what I want!"

He threw her to the ground, and she feared the worst. The man grabbed at her dress, and she screamed. But it had little effect, for the rider was only interested in one thing—her purse, and once he had it, he stood, not even deigning to say anything further to her. Instead, out of his mouth came something in his native tongue, and his comrades laughed, then he climbed back aboard his horse, and they rode off.

Jane lay there for some time, shaken to the core. She'd been nothing to them save a source of coins, easily discarded like the bones of a fish. She'd lost everything—her husband, her son, even her dignity. All she could do was weep.

SIXTEEN

Rumours

SPRING 966 MC

Lady Lindsey Martindale threw herself into a chair, taking a break from getting ready to meet the Queen of Merceria, though the actual target was Marshal Matheson.

She'd done her research to prepare for this, familiarizing herself with everyone in the Mercerian queen's inner circle of confidence. Not that she could identify them by sight, but at least she knew their names. It appeared the young woman had gathered a long list of sycophants over the years. That gave Lady Lindsey hope, for if that were the case, it should be easy enough for her to do likewise.

She waited while the servant brought in her best dress, then stood, holding out her arms, allowing herself to be garbed in the fine clothing. Next, followed some focused attention on her hair and then a careful selection of jewellery to match. With her ensemble finally complete, she left her rooms to make her way to the earl's estate.

Expected as she was, servants quickly ushered her into the large dining room, where the queen sat, along with the marshal and a third person Lady Lindsey struggled to identify. The woman looked familiar, but she couldn't recall her name for the life of her.

"Greetings," said Anna. "You are familiar with Arcanus Aegryth Malthunen, of course?"

"I am," she replied, "if only by reputation."

"I hope you don't mind," said Gerald. "Aegryth has just returned, and we thought it might be nice for you to be in the company of a fellow country-man, or perhaps I should say, countrywoman."

Lady Lindsey played along, laughing at the jest. "Indeed, it is a most welcome surprise." Her gaze took in the table. "You have had quite the meal prepared. I hope this isn't all on my behalf?"

"Come, sit," said the queen. "We thought it important to make a favourable impression. And in any case, I must ensure Gerald eats his fill. He's prone to skipping meals when he gets busy."

"Gerald? You mean, His Grace, the duke?"

"Nobody calls me that," insisted Gerald.

"But it is the proper form of address, is it not? How many dukes do you have in Merceria, if I may be so bold?"

"Three," said Anna. "Wincaster, of course, and then there's Kingsford and Colbridge."

"There is no such noble rank in Weldwyn. Have you earls as well?"

"We do, and they rank just below duke in terms of precedence, although when you speak of influence and prestige, they are essentially the same."

"And you have lesser nobles," said Lady Lindsey. "I remember someone being introduced as the Baron of Bodden's daughter."

"That would be Beverly," said Gerald. "She's an indispensable part of the army."

"She is a woman! In Weldwyn, she would never be permitted to participate in such a vulgar thing as war."

"Our traditions are different," said the queen. "Women play a critical role in the day-to-day management of the kingdom."

"How curious," said Lady Lindsey. "It's no wonder you've been so successful. After all, you combine the might of men with the intelligence of women."

Anna laughed. "I suppose that's one way of looking at it."

"I'm not so sure," said Gerald. "I can't make up my mind if I've been insulted or not."

Lady Lindsay put her hand on his forearm. "I meant it purely in jest."

He turned crimson, pulling his arm away to scratch at his beard.

"Come now, Gerald," said Anna. "I had them cook those sausages just for you."

He speared one, then transferred it to his plate. From somewhere below the table came a loud rumble.

"What was that?" asked Lady Lindsey, looking around the room.

"Only Tempus," said the queen. "He can smell the sausages."

At the mention of his name, the huge mastiff sat up, his head reaching up to tower over the table top.

Lady Lindsey paled, but quickly regained her composure. "Perhaps the servants should take him away and feed him?"

Gerald laughed. "You won't get him to leave Anna's side."

"You mean Her Majesty," corrected Lady Lindsey.

The marshal sobered. "Yes, of course."

"I hear congratulations are in order, Your Majesty, on the birth of your son?"

"Yes, Prince Braedon."

"He's the spitting image of his father," said Aegryth.

"I wasn't aware you knew him as a child?" said Lady Lindsey, an edge of frost to her voice.

"Oh yes, I was there at his birth, along with Arcanus Roxanne. It seems so long ago now."

"And now he has a son," said the queen with a smile.

Lady Lindsey wasn't finished. "Now tell me, and be honest, Your Majesty... will there be other children in your future? After all, you know what they say: first the heir, then the spare."

"That is something I've yet to discuss with Prince Alric."

"And how is His Highness? He's in the south, isn't he?"

"You're remarkably well informed," said Gerald.

"I try to remain abreast of things."

"He is well," said Anna. "We hear from him regularly. In fact, his reports are due any day now."

"It must be lonely without him around to keep you company."

"Not at all. I have many friends."

"Still," continued Lady Lindsey, "the warmth of a husband is something to be cherished."

"I miss him, of course, but I know we shall be together soon enough. What of yourself? Is there a Viscount of Talburn?"

"Not for many years, now. He died in a border skirmish with the Clans over thirty years ago."

"I can sympathize," said Gerald. "I lost my family to raiders from Norland."

She saw her chance. "It's terrible, isn't it? I mourned the loss of my husband for years."

"And have you any other family?" he asked.

"None whatsoever. To be honest, it's a matter that greatly concerns the court, or it did before this invasion happened. I am without any heir to inherit my lands, you see; not that I've been without suitors." She let her gaze drift over the marshal. "What of you, Your Grace? Have you any suitors?"

He blushed. "It's not something I've ever considered. For one thing, I'm far too old for children. I don't need them, if I'm being honest. I have the queen here."

Lady Lindsey tried to grasp his meaning, but it made little sense to her. In the end, she had to admit failure. "I'm afraid I don't understand."

"What he's saying," said Anna, "is I'm like a daughter to him."

"That's a little odd, isn't it?"

"Not at all. Of course, Gerald is not my real father, but he might as well be. He's always been there for me through thick and thin, and if that's not family, what is?"

"But your father was King Andred, wasn't he?"

"This isn't the place for such a discussion," he said. "Perhaps we should change the subject?"

"No," said Anna. "I have nothing to hide. If you must know, Lady Lindsey, my mother was King Andred's wife, but as to my father, someone else was involved."

"Not the marshal?"

"No, of course not. Gerald would never be so uncouth as to lie with another man's wife."

"I AM right here," said the marshal, his face growing red with embarrassment.

"I took the throne by force, if you must know," the queen said. "Upon the death of Andred, my brother Henry became king, but he tried to have me murdered. And not only me, Gerald was there in the dungeons, along with Dame Beverly."

"And somehow, you survived all that to become queen. How remarkable."

"She's a remarkable woman," said the marshal. "Anyone else would have given up."

"I get that from you," said Anna.

Obviously, there was a close bond between the young woman and her marshal, something Lady Lindsey thought she could exploit to her own advantage. "Might I ask how you two met?"

"The queen was a little girl, living at the Royal Estate in Uxley."

"Yes," said Anna, "and Gerald was wounded in service to the king... well, the baron, actually. In any event, after some trouble in Wincaster, he was sent to the Uxley estate to look after the grounds."

"Trouble in Wincaster, you say?"

"Nothing that bears repeating. One day, I was playing in the hedge maze, and he found me."

"She'd been stealing my tools," he added.

"Yes, that's right, and we've been firm friends ever since."

"Remarkable," said Lady Lindsey. "I had no idea the tale was so... convoluted." Her gaze turned once more to the marshal. "You said Norlanders killed your family?"

"Yes, many years ago now. I had a wife and daughter."

She saw the look of loss and wisely chose not to pursue the matter. "And now you are the equivalent of a grandfather. That must make you exceedingly proud!"

"It does," he replied. He suddenly looked down at her empty plate. "Are you not hungry?"

"My pardon, I was simply too engrossed in the conversation." In truth, she'd been waiting for someone to serve her, but apparently, that was not the custom amongst these people. She speared a sausage much as she had witnessed the marshal had done. "This looks most appetizing."

"It's one of Gerald's favourite foods," said the queen.

"Mine also," she replied. "What an amazing coincidence. We appear to have many things in common." She poked it with a knife, only to be splattered with hot grease, the result almost breaking her calm demeanour. At the Royal Court in Weldwyn, such a mistake in etiquette would be unthinkable, yet here, it garnered no attention at all. She continued, cutting off a small piece and popping it in her mouth. It was not at all to her taste, but after her earlier remark, she could do little but smother her dislike and continue on with the meal.

"Tell me, Your Grace," asked Lady Lindsey, "have you been a soldier for long?"

"Almost my entire life," he replied. "For many years, I was a Sergeant-at-Arms."

"A sergeant? And here I thought you were born noble?"

"Noble? Me? Far from it. My parents were farmers."

"But I don't understand. If you were a farmer, how did you become a duke?"

"I awarded him that title after the war," said the queen. "It's usually reserved for the Heir to the Crown of Merceria."

"Wouldn't that mean your son?"

"Ordinarily, but he's already a prince and, therefore, has no need for additional titles. In any case, Gerald more than deserved it."

"And does this title come with estates?"

"It does," said the marshal, "but I gave the manor house over to Prince Alric to act as a permanent residence for the Weldwyn ambassador."

"Then where do you live?"

"In the Palace," said Anna, "with Alric and I."

"I must admit, the court of Merceria is far different from what I imagined."

"In what way?"

"King Leofric always insisted on a rigid code of conduct when hosting meals. Not that there's anything wrong with your own approach, of course. It is merely... different."

"I'll take that as a compliment," said Anna.

Aegryth looked at the queen. "With your permission, Majesty, I will turn in for the night. It has been a hectic day. I shall make a full report of the ranger's activities tomorrow morning, if that is all right with you?"

"Of course," said Anna. "Good night, Aegryth, and sleep well."

The Weldwyn mage left them to continue their meal.

It was late in the evening when they finally finished eating—eating being a strange word to describe how they picked away at their food. The queen had proved to be quite a conversationalist, the duke less so, but Lady Lindsey was convinced more than ever that she was a perfect match for the Marshal of Merceria. To that end, she extracted from him the promise of another meal, this time only the two of them. She left close to midnight, content she'd advanced her plans this evening.

As for the queen, the extensive network of close friends surrounding the throne would prove a hindrance to her intentions. She must come up with some way of thinning their ranks without implicating herself.

Queen Anna was young, her marriage still fresh. Lady Lindsey remembered well the passion of youth, and with that memory came her answer. There was nothing like a scandal to divide a court, and the biggest scandal of all would be an illicit affair.

She'd learned Prince Alric had taken an army south, and along with them went Lady Aubrey Brandon. Lady Lindsey knew little of the woman's character, save that she was said to be fair of face and young. A few discreet enquiries at dinner confirmed she was unmarried and, better yet, not promised to any suitor, the very best attributes to have when plotting a fictitious affair. The woman also had no real family, having lost everyone in the civil war to retake the throne.

Early morning found Lady Lindsey still awake, her mind having churned over every conceivable scenario she could imagine. She looked down at the paper before her and smiled. It had taken her all night long to draft it, but the result pleased her. Written from the point of view of an interested observer, it hinted at an unhealthy relationship between Prince Alric and Lady Aubrey.

She considered it some of her finest work, for Lady Aubrey, by reputation, at least, was just the kind of young woman who men would find appealing. And Prince Alric, separated from his devoted wife, would doubtless be missing the intimacy of their marriage.

Lady Lindsey folded the letter carefully, then applied a simple seal of wax, foregoing the use of her ring to mark it as her own. Now, the only question was how to bring it to the queen's attention. To have it show up on her doorstep would raise too much suspicion, but what if it came in with dispatches from the south?

The thought sent a thrill down her spine. It had been years since she played such games at the court of Weldwyn, yet the prospect of spreading a little mayhem still excited her. Of course, it was the Weldwyn way to play a constant game of cat and mouse with the other nobles. True, not many were left these days, and taking on a royal was a new experience, but there was little joy in the reward without significant risk.

Now, all that remained was to put it in the hands of a military courier. To that end, she began the habit of frequenting a tavern near the earl's estate that was usually packed with warriors, many of them leaders in their own right. A few coins ensured her popularity with the patrons, allowing her to learn all manner of things, including the fact that couriers typically stopped off there before delivering their messages.

It made sense, of course, for a man who rode all day would often require a drink to slake their thirst before making their report.

Thus, she was present when the next rider came in from the south. A few crowns spent, and she was able to surreptitiously drop the letter into the man's satchel while he was busy wetting his whistle. Pleased with her success, she waited long after the man left for the earl's estate, lest the regular patrons take note of her quick exit.

That night, she lay awake, her mind in turmoil. Although she hated to admit it, the thought she might get away with it both exhilarated and terrified her. She had not felt this alive in decades, let alone this powerful. It was as if everyone had strings attached to them, and she the one who controlled them.

Gerald made his way down to the breakfast table. As usual, Tempus lay on the floor, eating bacon dropped before him. Anna pored over letters of all kinds while Beverly picked away at some eggs.

"Good morning," he said. "And how are you two this morning?"

"Well enough," said the queen, dropping another slice of bacon for her hound. "A message from Wincaster came in last night. It appears that in our absence, the Earl of Tewsbury has been making a nuisance of himself. Would you care to read it? It's from the Duke of Kingsford."

"Not unless you want me to. I'm far too busy dealing with army matters."

"That's his way of saying he's overworked," added Beverly.

"You're the one to talk," said Gerald. "How's your investigation going?"

"I've made some discreet enquiries, but nothing to report yet. Honestly, I'm just about ready to believe the whole thing merely a coincidence."

"You're talking about the attack on our wagons?" asked Anna.

"Yes," replied the knight. "Gerald believes someone on his staff might be feeding information to our enemies. There's no actual proof, but you must admit, the chance of a dragon accidentally locating them is a little hard to stomach, especially when they had to fly over our scouts."

"It's a fair enough concern. Let me know if you discover anything of interest."

"I will." Beverly stuffed a piece of bacon into her mouth.

The queen fell silent, and Gerald immediately noticed.

"Something wrong?"

"There is most definitely something wrong." She handed a letter to Gerald. "Tell me what you think of that?"

He looked over the missive before passing it to Beverly, who did likewise.

"This is ridiculous," said the knight. "Aubrey would never do something like that."

"Agreed," said Anna. "Nor would Alric, but someone wants us to believe it to be so. The question is, who?"

Beverly turned the paper over, examining both sides carefully. "There's no indication of who wrote it, although I must admit their hand is well-practiced. I would guess whoever is behind this has an education. Shall we investigate?"

"No," said the queen. "We've far too much on our plates at this moment. Say nothing of this to anyone, but keep your eyes out for anybody spreading malicious gossip."

SEVENTEEN

Investigation

SPRING 966 MC

"This is just too much!" Gerald slammed his fist down. "First our wagons are attacked, then the blasted Earl of Tewsbury starts making trouble, and now someone is trying to play with the queen's emotions." His gaze strayed to the other side of the table where Beverly sat. "Please tell me you, at least, made some progress?"

"Not much, I'm afraid. Every single member of your staff has an exemplary record. It's hard to imagine any of them acting contrary to our plans. Have we suffered any more attacks?"

"No, thank Saxnor. I arranged for our supplies to come up the river by ships, but I had to assign our archers to protect them, lest a dragon appears. We just can't seem to win. In Norland, we were short of cavalry. Now, we find ourselves drastically lacking in bowmen. What's next, footmen?"

"We never have enough men, but that hasn't stopped us from winning battle after battle."

"True, but I wish I'd kept some of those Dwarven arbalesters instead of sending them all to Mirstone."

"You can't start questioning every decision."

"No," said Gerald, "I suppose not. Still, it would be nice to make some actual progress. Without bowmen, I can't risk advancing the army. If we eliminated the spy amongst us, at least it would free up those archers."

"If there even is one," said Beverly. "I'm still not convinced. In any event, questioning people isn't going to get us any further."

"Could be we're looking at this all wrong."

The knight was intrigued. "What do you have in mind?"

"We're assuming someone willingly supplied intelligence to the enemy. What if they were coerced?"

"You mean forced?"

"Yes, maybe through blackmail?"

"I hadn't considered that possibility, but now you mention it, it's a far more reasonable explanation. Coerced or not, they must get the information to their contact somehow, which means an outside entity, someone who can freely pass both our lines and those of the enemy."

"There are hundreds of camp followers who easily fit that description. We can't possibly investigate all of them."

"Then let's look at your staff as potential blackmail victims. What if someone was carrying on an affair while married? They might pay quite a bit to keep things quiet."

"Or what if they were wanted for some kind of crime?"

"Both are possibilities," said Beverly. "They might also have some form of connection to a gang. Saxnor knows Wincaster is crawling with enough of them."

"Yes, but why would a gang want to endanger the army? That seems a bit of a stretch to me."

"How many of your staff are married?"

Gerald laughed. "Only you, as far as I know. I think we can safely put that theory to bed unless there's something you'd care to admit?"

"Very funny," said Beverly. "You know I would never do anything of the kind."

"Of course, I know that."

"What kinds of things would a man wish to hide from his friends?"

"Let's see, now," said Gerald. "I remember when I first went to Uxley, I had an addiction to numbleaf."

"You never told me that. Was that from the wound you received up in Bodden?"

"It was. It started as a way to numb the pain, but the more I took, the more resistant I became to its effects. Eventually, I just couldn't get enough to ease the pain."

"That's terrible. What happened?"

"After I was set upon by bandits, Andronicus healed me. With my flesh restored, all pain was gone."

"And you didn't still crave the numbleaf?"

"Not really, but then again, I was at a good place in my life. Had I been back in Wincaster, I can see how I might have turned back to it."

"Do you believe one of your staff could be addicted to numbleaf?"

"No," he said. "I'm sure I'd notice the effects, but that doesn't preclude some other combination of herbs."

"What about alcohol?"

"Drinking is commonplace, but no one has let it affect their worth. Let's face it; everyone I picked is highly competent when it comes to their jobs."

"So it has to be something that didn't affect the performance of their duties."

"Wait a moment," said Gerald. "You made me think of something."

"Care to elaborate?"

"Yes. Years ago, when I was at Uxley, I was dismissed from service."

"I remember. You took the princess into Wincaster and nearly caused a riot."

"Nearly? There was no nearly about it. In any case, I returned to the village of Uxley and took up the life of a farmer."

"You're not suggesting someone is addicted to cabbages?"

"Cabbages? No, but I seem to recall Anna visiting me one time. She convinced a man in a carriage to purchase a Royal Cabbage."

"Surely there's no such thing?" said Beverly.

"That's just it. There isn't, but she convinced the fellow it had the same effects as blueseed, and you know what that's for?"

"No, I'm afraid I'm not."

Gerald blushed. "Well, let's just say it enhances a man's... you know."

"No, I don't."

"His... virility?"

Now it was Beverly's turn to blush. "Oh, now I see what you mean. Yes, I suppose that would be something to be ashamed of."

"Not that it's illegal or anything, but if word got around that a man needed help in that area, there would be no end to his shame."

"Really? Wouldn't he just seek help from a healer?"

"I don't think you grasp how men feel about these things. I'm sure Aldwin would understand."

Beverly turned an even darker shade of crimson. "Aldwin most certainly does not need any help in the performance of his husbandly duties!"

"I'm not trying to infer he does," said Gerald, equally as embarrassed. "I merely wished to demonstrate how it could be used against a man."

"Well, you made your point. Can we move on to another subject?"

"Such as?"

"Where would a person find such a thing?"

Gerald chuckled. "I thought you wanted to change the subject?"

"I am. We are no longer talking about Aldwin."

"Ah, now I understand. As to blueseed, I imagine it could be found easily enough amongst the camp followers."

"Yes, but we're too well-known. If we go asking for something like that, everyone will be suspicious, especially if they're blackmailing someone."

"We'll get Blackwood to ask after it," said Gerald. "That should arouse little suspicion."

"Blackwood?"

"Aye, he's had his fair share of misadventures in the past. I doubt looking for blueseed will trouble his conscience."

"And if he finds it?"

"Then we'll set a watch on whoever is selling it."

"Ah," said Beverly. "Now I see where you're going with this. Whoever is selling it must have some way of getting word to the enemy."

"Precisely, and once we have that, we can round them all up and find out who purchased the stuff."

"You believe they'll cooperate?"

"They can either help or face a charge of treason, and I don't have to tell you the punishment for that."

"The plan makes sense."

"Good," said Gerald. "Then you'll talk to Blackwood?"

"About blueseed?" said Beverly. "I think it would be easier coming from you."

He looked at her a moment, noticing her embarrassment. "Very well. Go and find him, and let him know I want to speak with him."

Relief flooded the knight's face. "Anything else?"

"Yes, we need trusted men to keep an eye on whoever is selling the stuff."

"That, I can take care of."

Orlan Turnbull shifted his gaze. He was standing near the farrier, ostensibly to watch as his mount's horseshoe was replaced, but the reality was far from it. Across from him, a woman sold herbal remedies from a wagon.

As a member of the Guard Cavalry, he was used to carrying out all sorts of strange orders, but this one had them all beat. According to Dame Beverly, there were spies within their camp. Although he personally thought that unlikely, he was too good a soldier not to follow a superior's orders, particularly one as well-respected as the knight commander.

The task was simple enough: observe whoever the herbalist came in contact with, the object being to identify any co-conspirators. The problem lay in standing around all afternoon without raising suspicions. The farrier was one such tactic, but the man's work would soon be done, leaving Turnbull in the embarrassing situation of no longer having an excuse to be in amongst the camp followers.

He and his companions had found reasons to visit the marshal's staff for the express purpose of memorizing faces. Easily done, considering the number of messages travelling between their location and the rest of the army. It only remained to wait until one of them showed up here to purchase blueseed.

Turnbull couldn't help but laugh at the thought. Some poor old sod must be desperate indeed to require such a thing. He'd never partaken of it himself, of course, but there was a curious side to his nature that wondered what kind of effect it might have on someone who was fully capable to begin with. The thoughts of a night of debauchery came to mind, then he shook his head, clearing such things from memory.

"Won't be much longer," said the farrier. "You sure you don't want to come back later?"

"No, it's fine," Orlan replied. "I'm in no hurry. I'll wait."

"Suit yourself." The man grabbed his pick and began removing dirt and stones from the horse's hoof.

Turnbull returned his attention to the herbalist, where someone now stood there talking to her, his back to the warrior, making it impossible to identify the fellow.

He cursed, for one moment was all it took to distract him from his assignment. His gaze stayed glued to his target as they talked in low voices. He couldn't hear what they discussed, but it looked like they were haggling over the price.

Turnbull shifted his position, acting as though he were simply walking by. He stopped after a few paces, stooping to pretend a stone was lodged in his boot. The voices, no more distinct, were in the final stages of the conversation. The woman selling the herbs handed over a tiny pouch containing the Gods knew what. In return, the man of interest handed over some coins.

The cavalryman knew he needed to act if only to determine what the fellow had bought. He rose, moving quickly to bump into the other man. The pouch fell to the ground, just before both Turnbull and his victim did likewise.

"Pardon me," said Orlan. "I was in a hurry and wasn't watching where I was going."

The other fellow sat up, revealing the countenance of Captain Kendall, one of the marshal's staff.

"Quite all right. Accidents happen."

"You dropped something," said Turnbull. "Here, let me get it for you." He reached out, grabbing the pouch and making sure he held it upside down. Small seeds fell to the ground.

"Oh, how clumsy of me." Turnbull began scooping them up.

Captain Kendall looked mortified. "I have it well in hand, sir. Leave it to me."

"Very well, and once again, my apologies." Turnbull rose, making a show of wiping his hands. He got to his feet and was soon on his way. Once free of the area, he halted, opening the palm of his hand to examine the seeds he'd stolen.

"Good work," said Beverly.

"Thank you, Commander," replied Turnbull, "but I'm afraid this has only become more complicated."

"What makes you say that?"

"Well, I'm no expert in such things, but that doesn't look much like blue-seed. For one thing, look at its colour; it's more red than blue."

"Then what is it?" asked the knight commander.

"I was hoping you'd tell me."

She held the concoction to her nose. "It has a rather unique smell to it, but I don't think it's a seed at all."

"Have we anyone who could help identify it?"

Beverly smiled. "Revi Bloom. His parents are both herbalists. I'm sure he'll know something. Is this all there is?"

"It's all I could take without arousing suspicion."

"And you're sure it was Captain Kendall?"

"Absolutely. I'm just thankful he didn't recognize me. Do you want me to continue watching him?"

"No, you may return to your company. I'll take it from here."

Revi Bloom concentrated on the tankard. He called forth the power of magic, yet still, it refused his attempts to move the stupid thing. This was all so frustrating!

"Am I interrupting something?" He looked up to see Dame Beverly.

"If you must know, I'm attempting to perfect a spell."

"Oh? What does it do?"

"It moves things."

"I can do that," said Beverly.

"You can?"

"Yes. Watch." She took a step forward and pushed the tankard over.

"Very funny," said the mage. "Did you come here for the sole purpose of mocking my studies, or is there something more important?"

"I'm wondering if you could identify something for me."

"I can certainly try. What is it?"

Beverly passed over a carefully folded paper. "It's in here. Careful not to spill it. We don't have much for you to analyze."

Ever intrigued, Revi took the note, moving to the table to carefully unfold it. Within were what looked like three tiny beans. His first thought was they might be seeds, but then he cast an orb of light, illuminating the area.

"Interesting. Where did you get this?"

"I can't tell you, other than to say it was purchased from an herbalist. Do you recognize it?"

In answer, the mage lifted one, crushing it between finger and thumb. It left a red smear on his fingers, which he then lifted to smell.

"How curious."

"Meaning?"

"I'd need to do a few tests to confirm it, but I believe you found a rare concoction of herbs and mushrooms, called heartseed."

"Is it difficult to make?"

"Very. I'm surprised you would even find it anywhere hereabouts."

"I see," said Beverly. "Any idea as to its use?"

"Yes. I know exactly what it's used for."

The knight waited, but the mage offered no further explanation.

"Well?" she asked.

"Well, what?"

"Aren't you going to explain its properties?"

"Oh yes, of course. It's a highly addictive substance used for the treatment of anxiety."

"Anxiety? Not for a… well, that is to say…"

"Spit it out, Beverly. I'm not a mind reader."

She gathered her composure. "Could it be used for enhancing a man's desire?"

"No, in fact, it's more likely to have the opposite effect. Look, this is a rare compound. Very few would even know how to make it. However, I can't remark on its efficacy since I'm unaware of how potent the ingredients were. Further testing would be required to know that, but I'm afraid the sample is too small, not to mention I'm lacking the tools for such tests here in Falford. Is the dosage important?"

Beverly's face fell. "No, not really. I hoped it would be evidence of something more compelling going on."

"More compelling? Whatever do you mean?"

"Gerald and I believe someone was being blackmailed for using blueseed."

"It may not be blueseed," said Revi, "but this is likely far worse. As I mentioned, this is highly addictive. Do we know how much was purchased?"

"I was told a small pouch's worth. Why?"

"Heartseed is so-called because it soothes the heart, planting the seed of calm, if you will. Yes, I know it looks like a seed as well, but that is mere coincidence. A person would have to suffer terribly to even consider such a medication. Why, its side effects alone are most alarming."

"Side effects?"

"Yes, the unwanted effects of taking it. Think of mead: everyone likes the taste, but drink too much of the stuff, and the hangover in the morning will feel like it's killing you."

"And this is what it's like to take heartseed?"

"Taking the wrong amount could lead to a quickened pulse, so much so, the heart might rupture."

"And how is this concoction taken?"

"It is ground to a fine powder, then placed on the gums." He used his finger to separate one of the small balls. "This would be the right dose for an individual. Anything more might drive him mad with agony."

"Agony? I thought you said it would be the heart that would suffer?"

"And it would," said Revi, "accompanied by massive chest pains. Whoever is taking this stuff must be stopped immediately. His very life depends on it."

"And could this same man survive without it?"

Revi thought it over. It had been some years since he'd learned about mixing such compounds, but his parents' warnings had been quite pronounced. "He would, although his anxiety might return tenfold, at least in the short term. It would be best to sedate the victim, or at least tie him up, lest he hurt himself."

"Could your Life Magic help him?"

"I could detoxify him. That would definitely be of some assistance, but I'm afraid his dependency on the heartseed is more a matter of the mind over body."

"Meaning?"

"He would crave more of the compound. It would wear off in time, of course, but that could be anywhere from days to weeks." He watched Beverly's face for any sign of further questions. "Does that help?"

"It does," she replied, "although not in the way I expected. I hoped we'd have time to track down who's leaking information to the enemy, but if the man's life is in danger, we must act sooner rather than later."

"Are you trying to tell me there's a spy amongst us?"

"That's what we believe."

"And I assume whoever was taking this heartseed was being forced to reveal information?"

"That's my theory."

"Well, at least by arresting the fellow, you'll be stopping all of that. Perhaps he can tell you what you need to know about the others?"

"We can only hope."

EIGHTEEN

Suspicion

SPRING 966 MC

Gerald sighed. "I'm afraid we're no closer to finding the courier who took the information to the enemy."

"What about the herbalist?" asked Anna. "Wasn't she the one who passed it on?"

"We have her in custody, but she refuses to cooperate. Claims she was only providing the medication the captain needed. That would've been the end of it if Kendall hadn't confessed to passing our plans on to her."

"And this Captain Kendall has been placed under arrest?"

"He has," replied Gerald. "Unfortunately, with the herbalist not talking, there's no way to find out who she passed it on to. Which means somebody is still out there who can interfere with our plans."

"That's disappointing. I hoped we'd put an end to all of this."

"Well," said Gerald, "at least we cut off that particular leak. With that out of the way, I'm confident we can resume our offensive."

"About time too," said Anna. "I was beginning to feel like we'd never march on Summersgate."

"I thought you'd be happier?"

"Ordinarily, I would be, but I received another one of those disturbing letters."

"You mean accusing Alric of being unfaithful?"

"Yes, and they've grown bolder. The first letter merely hinted at something untoward. This new one comes out and claims they've been intimate."

"Is it in the same handwriting?"

"It is," said Anna. "I don't want to believe it, but it's difficult when he's so far away."

"It's time we put an end to this immediately," said Gerald.

"How?"

"Hayley's rangers came back this morning, which means Kraloch is back amongst us. It's easy enough to have him contact Aubrey."

"Yes, but that would prove nothing. If she were guilty, she wouldn't admit anything."

"Do you believe Aubrey the kind of person who would tempt your husband?"

"I'd like to think not, but—"

"But nothing," he said. "Aubrey is a woman of high morals. If you don't believe me, talk to Beverly. This also smacks of a Clan plot."

"How?"

"If they could discredit Alric, he'd lose his position of commander of the southern army. That alone is enough to doubt the veracity of this report. There's also the matter of his army. Most of the men under his command are Mercerians, all loyal to you. Do you believe they would simply accept their prince carrying on with another woman?"

"I suppose not, but then where are these letters coming from?"

"That's a good question. Either they were placed in the satchel before leaving the south or after delivery here."

"Or sometime during the trip," added Anna.

"When did you receive this last letter?"

"Only this morning."

"Good. Then the messenger is likely still here. I'll have Beverly interview him. That might give us some idea of where the letter came from."

"Is there anything else we can do?"

"Yes. I'll have Kraloch contact Aubrey. He knows her well enough to determine if she's lying. She can also relate whether or not there are any rumours down there concerning the two of them."

"I'm not sure I'd like this to come out in the open."

"And it won't," said Gerald. "Kraloch can be trusted not to speak of it to anyone."

"Very well, but in the meantime, you must make plans to get this army moving. I won't permit my personal troubles to hold up the liberation of Weldwyn."

"Understood."

"Are you sure this will work?" Anna asked.

"I assure you it will," said Kraloch. "I can cast the spell of spirit talk on another, thus allowing them to participate in the conversation. It will be as though we were all in the same room, but the remote individuals will look ghostlike as if they were spirit walking."

"Very well, you may begin."

Kraloch took up a position in the centre of the room, planting his bare feet firmly on the floor. With his hands raised into the air, he looked towards the ceiling even though his eyes were closed. Arcane words flowed from his mouth, echoing off the walls as his power built. The familiar buzzing in the air was apparent to all as the hairs on the back of their necks rose up.

"The first part of the spell is complete," said the Orc. "I joined you to me through your spirits. The next step will be to contact Aubrey." More words of power issued forth, and the room once again hummed with energy. A ghostly image appeared before them.

"Lady Aubrey," said Kraloch. "I am glad to see you well."

"As am I," the Life Mage replied. "Although I must admit to some confusion as to the reason for this contact. Has something gone wrong?" She paused only a moment, but it was clear from her actions that she noticed the others present in their spirit forms. "Wait, is that the queen?"

"It is," said the Orc, "along with the marshal and your cousin, Beverly."

"What's wrong?"

"We've heard disturbing rumours of late," said Beverly, taking her cue from the queen.

"Rumours?"

"Yes, of trouble in the south."

"I can assure you everything is going well here. We expect to surround Southport by the week's end. The siege will commence almost immediately. Tog assures me—"

"It's not about Southport," said Beverly. "I'm afraid we received a report suggesting you and Alric have become close."

"Well, of course, we're close. I'm one of his advisors." Even in her ghostly form, the full meaning of her words became evident, for she suddenly turned crimson. "Surely you're not suggesting something untoward?"

"Sorry, Cousin, but that's the rumour."

"I can assure you, there is nothing of the sort going on here. The fact is I'm far too busy to consider something like that. And besides, I haven't ever been intimate with anyone!"

"Too much information, Aubrey. We're not accusing you of taking part in anything... untoward, as you put it, but the rumour started somewhere."

"Well, there's no hint of it here. I can tell you that."

"I believe you, but can you think of anyone who would start such a rumour? Could it be someone you wronged?"

"Like who? I'm a healer. I don't exactly go around upsetting people."

"What about the prince?"

"After our victory at Bramwitch, there's been nothing but good wishes for our continued success. Naturally, the prisoners might think otherwise, but it's not as if any of them have access to our reports. How about someone at your end?"

"Possibly."

Aubrey looked at the queen. "I'm sorry for all of this, Your Majesty, but I can assure you I am on my best behaviour when it comes to His Highness."

"I believe you," said Anna, the hint of a smile coming through. "The truth is I never should have doubted you."

"Shall I fetch Prince Alric?" asked Aubrey. "You could speak to him yourself, if you wish?"

"Maybe later. I don't want to keep him from his duties. I know how much work leading an army can be. I would have you pass on my congratulations, however, and best wishes for his continued success."

"I will do that. I promise."

Anna turned to Gerald. "Did the messenger have any insights?"

"He did, as a matter of fact. The man's been with us for years and has never shown any reason for us to doubt his loyalty. The only stop he made around others was after he arrived in Falford."

"Why would he not come straight to your office?"

"It's common for couriers to get a quick drink before reporting, mainly to wash the dirt of the road from their throats before answering any questions we might have."

"And do we know where he stopped?"

Gerald smiled. "We do. A place called the Sword and Shield. It's around the corner from us. It's a common place for our warriors to drink."

"We should send someone there to find out more."

"Already done," said Gerald. "Even as we speak, Sergeant Blackwood is making enquiries. Don't worry. If somebody slipped a note into a messenger's satchel, someone's bound to have noticed something."

"It seems we have wasted your time, Aubrey," said Anna. "For that, I am truly sorry."

"Not at all, Your Majesty. Your reaction is completely understandable, given the circumstances. I'll pass on your message to His Highness and pay more attention to rumours down here. If I hear anything questionable, I'll be sure to contact Kraloch."

"Thank you, Aubrey. You are a true friend."

"With your permission, Majesty," said Kraloch, "I shall end the spell. Each moment it lasts consumes more of my power."

"Of course," said Anna.

The Orc broke the connection, Aubrey's image fading from view.

"That was most illuminating," said Beverly. "But right now, I'd like permission to head down to the Sword and Shield."

"By all means," said the queen. "Please keep me informed of any developments."

The tavern was a busy place, particularly amongst the men of the Mercerian army. Spotting Sergeant Blackwood, Beverly headed over to his table and sat beside him. His companion took her by surprise.

"Sam? I didn't expect to see you here?"

The woman shrugged. "Blackwood asked if I'd be willing to help."

"Have you been here long?"

"Since early this morning. I've been keeping my ears open and my mouth shut."

"I sent her," said Blackwood. "I thought it likely she'd have better success at getting the men to open up about anything they saw."

"Because she's a fellow soldier?"

"No, because she's a woman. You might find this hard to believe, but most men like to impress members of the opposite sex. That means a lot of sweet-talking."

"I'm not sure I approve of your methods," said Beverly.

"It worked though," said Sam.

"Why? What have you discovered?"

"Soldiers mostly frequent this place, but they're not the only patrons."

"Meaning?"

"There was one, in particular," said Sam, "who was free with her coins."

Beverly looked around. "Is she here now?"

"No, but she was here both days the letters arrived."

"Have you a name?"

"No, but I do have a description. Apparently, she was well-dressed, most likely a noble, if her manners are any clue. She was also old."

"How old?" asked Beverly.

"Ancient, maybe even as old as the marshal."

"Marshal Matheson isn't that old!"

The archer shrugged. "If you say so. In any case, it sounds like she and the marshal are of a similar age. Any idea who that might be?"

Beverly sat back in her chair. "Oh yes. I know exactly who that sounds like, although for the life of me, I have no idea why she would do such a thing."

"Do tell," said Blackwood.

Beverly lowered her voice. "Lady Lindsey Martindale, the Viscount of Talburn, although I guess I should say the viscountess."

"What is a viscount?" asked Sam. "Is that above a baron?"

"I think so," said the knight. "At least it is in Merceria. I assume it's no different here in Weldwyn."

"That makes things difficult, then," said the sergeant. "We can't up and arrest a Weldwyn noble. Saxnor knows they have few enough of them."

"I'll report this to the queen, but I can't say she'll be happy."

"Far from it, considering what she's been insinuating."

"Do you think she's working with the Clans?" asked Sam.

"I have a hard time believing that," said Beverly, "but I suppose anything is possible. In any case, it'll be up to the queen to decide what to do about her."

Blackwood shifted uncomfortably. "What do we do now?"

"Nothing until I've relayed this to Her Majesty. Do we know where she's staying?"

"I don't imagine it would be too hard to find out. Shall I make a few enquiries?"

"Yes, and take Sam with you. When you locate the viscountess, send word to me at the earl's estate, but once you find her, make sure one of you keeps her in sight at all times."

"Yes, Commander."

Lady Lindsey Martindale approached the door to the queen's temporary residence with a spring in her step. Things had gone well over the last few days, and now a personal invitation from Her Majesty to attend a luncheon! She hoped the marshal would be present, for she'd seen nothing of him recently, likely due to his commitment to the army.

Servants opened the door, admitting her into the earl's estate. The new Earl of Falford had been given that title after his predecessor plotted against the throne of Merceria—an act that had very nearly resulted in war between the two kingdoms. Lord Erick Lanford was more loyal to King Leofric, but his presence in Summersgate when the enemy attacked meant his current status was unknown. Lady Lindsey suspected he was imprisoned somewhere, but there was a chance Brida, the High Queen of the Clans, executed him rather than take him hostage.

She was led down a hallway, and then the servant paused, announcing, "Her Majesty is in here."

Something about the woman looked familiar, and then she placed her face. "You're the one who married that knight."

"Yes, Lady Sophie Wright."

"And yet you act as a servant to the queen? I should have thought that beneath a woman of means?"

"We all serve in different ways," said Sophie. Her expression left no doubt she would not entertain further questions on the matter. Instead, she turned her back on the viscountess as she opened the door. Inside was an office of some sort where the queen sat behind an enormous desk, making her look exceedingly small. To make matters worse, that wretched hound sat at her side, his eyes staring at her like it wanted to kill something. The marshal sat on one side of the room, while on the other stood Dame Beverly. Judging from their faces, this was to be a less informal gathering than she had hoped for.

"Lady Lindsey," said Anna. "Do come in and take a seat."

"I hope I've not come at an inopportune time, Your Majesty. I should hate to be a bother."

"Not at all. In fact, we've been meaning to have you around for some time, but you know how it is."

"I completely understand. It's not an easy thing to oversee an army, let alone a kingdom as well."

She noted the queen's eyes flick to Lady Sophie along with an ever-so-slight nod. Something was going on here, something Lady Lindsey couldn't quite grasp.

"How has your stay been?" asked the queen. "In Falford, I mean."

"I found suitable lodgings, although they pale in comparison to my house in Summersgate."

"And the food?"

"Adequate, at best."

"I hear the Sword and Shield offers up a nice Mercerian pudding," added the marshal.

Lady Lindsey's eyes swivelled to the Duke of Wincaster. "Does it? I wouldn't know. It's not the sort of place I frequent."

"And yet you've been there several times in the last week," said Dame Beverly.

"What are you trying to insinuate?"

"Merely that with you, all is not as it seems."

"And so you invited me here to insult me?"

"Insult you, no," said Anna, "but we will get to the bottom of this matter, I assure you."

"And what matter is that?" Lady Lindsey began to sweat.

"Come now. To continue to play innocent serves no one."

"I don't know what you're talking about."

"Maybe this will refresh your memory." The queen tossed two letters onto the desk.

The Weldwyn noble recognized them immediately but said nothing. Inside she felt like a little girl, trapped after lying to her parents. She fought down the urge to panic.

"What are those?" she finally asked.

"You know full well what they are."

"Do I?"

"You can deny it all you want," added the marshal, "but as you sit here, my men are searching your lodgings. It won't take long for us to find a sample of your handwriting. Then there'll be no denying the truth."

"I'm not about to admit to any knowledge of what those letters contain, but let's say for a moment I did? What would you have me do?"

"Well, for a start, stop making any more baseless accusations."

"And if I didn't?"

"In that event," said the queen, "I would be forced to place you under arrest."

"On what charge?"

"That's easy," replied the marshal. "Treason."

"I might remind you I am not of Merceria nor are you of Weldwyn. Your laws have no hold over me. Now, had I committed such a crime in your own kingdom, that would be an entirely different matter, I grant you, but as it is..." She let her voice trail off.

"This is outrageous," said Beverly.

The Queen of Merceria merely smiled. "Tell me, Lady Lindsey, what would you do were the situation reversed?"

"Well," the woman replied, "for one thing, I would tread carefully. If Prince Alric ever hopes to sit upon the throne of Weldwyn, he'll need a Council of Nobles to support his claim."

"A Council of Earls," corrected Dame Beverly. "You, on the other hand, are only a viscountess."

"True, on both accounts, yet the kingdom is lacking any earls at the moment. I imagine once the dust settles, there'll be all kinds of titles being handed out. You would do well to cultivate support for your husband's claim now, before others get involved."

Queen Anna tapped the letters. "These I can overlook, if only for political reasons, but what I don't understand is why? What possible motive could you have for discrediting Prince Alric? Don't you support his claim to the throne?"

"Oh, I do," said Lady Lindsey, "but there are far too many Mercerians within his circle of advisors."

"I see, now," said Beverly. "It wasn't His Highness you were trying to embarrass, but Lady Aubrey."

"Perhaps you should demand satisfaction," suggested the queen. "I understand it's allowed in Weldwyn."

"I don't understand," said Lady Lindsey. "Why would Dame Beverly demand satisfaction? It is not her I maligned!" No sooner were the words out of her mouth than she realized her mistake. It had not been her intention to admit to anything, but now it was out in the open.

"She is my cousin," said Beverly. "By impugning her reputation, you slighted my family."

"You are merely a knight, and she but a baroness."

"My father is the Baron of Bodden," said Beverly, "and I, his heir. As such, I am well within my rights to demand trial by combat."

Lady Lindsey paled. Had the circumstances been different, she would have accepted the demand without flinching, for it would have been easy enough to find someone to stand as her champion. Here, though, hampered by a lack of Weldwyn warriors, she could do little more; thus, she must adjust her strategy.

"Then let me offer you my heartfelt apologies, Dame Beverly. I admit it was wrong of me to pursue the matter and give weight to such scandalous rumours. I promise you shall hear no more of this."

"And that's it?" said the marshal. "You believe that by simply apologizing, everything will be forgiven?"

The queen rose, coming around the desk. The movement caught everyone's attention, especially when she paused beside Gerald, placing her hand upon his shoulder.

"Everyone is upset," Anna said. "And while it is unforgivable to make such accusations, we must allow that the war has been hard on everyone. You are free to leave us, Lady Lindsey, but know that your presence will no longer be tolerated at my court or in my presence."

"Of course, Your Majesty, and once again, let me say how truly sorry I am." She turned to face the marshal, but he refused to meet her gaze. She rose, making her way to where Lady Sophie waited at the door.

"I shall trouble you no more," she said as she left their presence.

NINETEEN

Kythelia

SPRING 966 MC

Queen Kythelia looked out the window as the carriage passed through the gate.

"Finally," she said. "After all these years, I have returned."

"You've been here before?"

The queen looked at Princess Margaret. The Human had proven to be of great benefit over the last few years, learning the art of Necromancy with ease.

"Yes, but not for some time," the Elf admitted. "I have not set foot in Summersgate for over two thousand years."

"I wasn't aware the capital of Weldwyn was that old?"

"It isn't, but long before Summersgate was built, an Elven kingdom stretched all the way to what you call the Thunder Mountains."

"But that would include all of Merceria!"

"And so it did, and right here, at this very location, was the Elven city of Mith-Drunuin."

"An Elven city? Here in the heart of Weldwyn?"

"Oh no, that wasn't for another thousand years. In any case, it was destroyed in the Great War, centuries before the coming of your kind."

"Yet you still consider it home?"

"I do," said the Dark Queen. "I've plotted my return for centuries, and finally, I am here."

Margaret looked out the window. "And now that you're here, what will you do?"

"The first step will be to visit our erstwhile allies, starting with the so-called High Queen."

"So-called? Did she not do exactly as you asked?"

"She did, but my need of her is almost at an end, and I must take steps to re-evaluate her usefulness."

"Is that what you're going to do with me once I'm no longer of use to you?"

Kythelia looked into her eyes. "You are one of us now, Margaret. Never forget that. Your place amongst us is assured."

"And when Brida's usefulness is at an end?"

"Then we shall simply eliminate her. There is little reason to keep her alive once my rule has been firmly established. As for your own part in all of this, I have a mind to make you ruler of Merceria once we subjugate it."

"Me? Queen?"

Kythelia smiled. "Would you prefer the title of Empress of Merceria?"

"Empress? I like that."

"Then empress it shall be, but remember, queen or empress, you still owe your fealty to me."

"Of course," said Margaret. "I would have it no other way."

The carriage rolled up before an ornate mansion.

"We are here," said the Elven queen.

"And where is here?"

"Why, this is where the High Queen holds court. Come, Margaret. Let us go and visit our supposed ally."

"Supposed?"

"She has been plotting behind our backs."

"And you know this, how?"

Kythelia smiled. "I kept her on a short leash."

"And is that a leash I shall share?"

"Remain loyal to me, and there is nothing to fear. Cross me, however, and I will not soon forget. Now, come. We have work to do."

An Elven guard opened the door, then stood back, his face masked by a helmet. More such Elves lined up along the left and right, forming a corridor down which the two Necromancers walked, their soft footfalls in stark contrast to the heavy boots of their guards.

Several Human warriors guarded doors, but as the Elves drew closer, they backed away, allowing the new arrivals full access to the High Queen.

Kythelia beckoned Margaret to take the lead. "You do the talking," she urged. "It will allow me to see how she handles things."

The former Princess of Merceria stepped through the doorway, only to be met with scorn.

"Who dares disturb the High Queen?" Brida demanded.

"I do. Margaret of Wincaster, rightful Queen of Merceria."

"Queen you might be, but I am the High Queen. Bow before me, and show me the proper respect."

"I bow to no one save for Queen Kythelia." Margaret stood aside, allowing her mistress to be seen.

Brida leaned forward on her makeshift throne. "I rule here!"

"For now, but the time will soon come to pay your debt."

"Debt? What are you talking about?"

"Come now," said Margaret. "Did you think someone would go to the trouble of helping you conquer Weldwyn without asking for something in return?"

She saw Brida gulp. The Clanswoman must have suspected there would eventually be a price to pay, although doubtless, she thought she'd have more time.

Kythelia stepped forward. "I made you, Brida of the Twelve Clans, and I can just as easily unmake you. You rule here only at my pleasure. Is that understood?"

"Do not talk to me like that. I am the High Queen!"

"So you keep saying, yet the words mean little to me." The Dark Queen moved closer, then paused, looking over the Clanswoman. "You are young, so I will forgive the harsh words, but cross me again, and there shall be no more chances."

"Do not threaten me!"

"It is not a threat. It is a promise. Allow me to demonstrate." She cast a spell, then threw her arms out wide, sending black tendrils shooting across the room to wrap themselves around one of Brida's guards and begin crushing the man. Kythelia, meanwhile, basked in the darkness as the black mist contracted around her victim, sucking the very life out of him before turning him into a withered husk. Even as his presence diminished, hers only seemed to increase.

Eventually, she released her magic, and what was left of the poor fool crumbled to the floor, nothing more than dust.

Brida was shaking. "W-w-what do you want?" she stammered.

The room darkened. "What is rightfully mine!"

Lochlan looked up from his food. "Then what happened?"

"What do you think?" replied Brida. "She dismissed me from my own throne room."

"And you just let her?"

"What choice did I have? I didn't want to end up like that guard."

"I told you we never should have trusted that Elf Lysandil."

"He gave us Weldwyn."

"A poor reward indeed if we are not alive to enjoy it."

"I did not conquer this land only for someone to take it from me."

"What are you suggesting?"

"That we eliminate the threat. Elves may not die from natural causes, but a blade can still silence them."

"You can't be serious? Kythelia has lived for thousands of years. You couldn't even begin to understand what she's capable of."

"I cannot let go of this. Conquering Weldwyn was our father's dream. It is unconscionable that I should let it slip from my grasp now that Summersgate is ours."

"Be careful, Sister. I've read all I can about this Elven queen, and nothing hints at any mercy on her part. If she discovers you plot against her, it will be your undoing."

"It would not be the first time others conspired against me."

"Perhaps not," said Lochlan, "but it may well prove to be the last. And what about that army of Elves she brought with her?"

"Are you suggesting they would be a match for our warriors?"

"You know as well as I our Clansmen are ill-trained and undisciplined. If it hadn't been for the treachery of certain members of the Weldwyn nobility, we wouldn't be sitting here talking."

"You dare to speak so of your own kinsmen?"

"I speak the truth. Something you seem to be ignoring these days. How many times did the Clanholdings try to conquer Weldwyn only to be driven back across the border?"

"It matters little, for this time, we were victorious."

"And would victory have come without the aid of Prince Tarak? I think not."

"Prince Tarak is a fool if he thinks I'll help him invade Merceria."

Lochlan shook his head. "So it has come down to this. You would betray your ally—the very ally, I might add, who allowed you to complete our father's dream."

"Do not lecture me on politics. Tarak is no longer of use to me; thus, he is discarded."

"And so now you chose not only to abandon him but to insult him as well?"

"Don't tell me what I can and can't do!"

"You risk everything we've accomplished."

"You mean everything I'VE accomplished. I didn't see you leading the army."

"And you did?" said Lochlan. "I don't see any blood on your sword."

"I am a warrior queen."

"Then start acting like one."

"And what would you have me do? Roll over and lick the boots of this Elf?"

"Better to rule under her than not rule at all."

"Is it? I would beg to differ. We are Humans, Lochlan, the strongest people who have ever graced these lands. It is our destiny to rule over all the other races."

"Now you would rule them? And here I thought you harboured nothing but disdain for the other races. Are you then to welcome Dwarves and Elves to our lands?"

"You've spent your life immersed in books, Brother, so I will forgive your lack of knowledge about the ways of kings."

"The ways of kings, is it? It wasn't so long ago our father was nothing more than a Clan Chief and proud to be so, but I suppose now that you sit upon the throne of Weldwyn, you are content to adopt their ways."

"This throne should have always been mine!" screamed Brida. "And it would have been had that stupid Mercerian girl not intervened."

Lochlan shook his head. "Even had you married Alric, he had two older brothers. His fate was never to be king, or you, his queen."

"And yet it could've been arranged."

"How? By killing off his brothers? And how would you do that without raising suspicions? Not that it matters now, of course, but I am curious."

"Power is there for the taking," said Brida. "Has studying history taught you nothing?"

"If history tells us anything, it's that such plots rarely succeed, a lesson you'd do well to remember. You've been given a golden opportunity here, a chance to rule over Weldwyn as its queen. What does it matter if you must pay tribute to someone above you?"

"It matters to me. I shall be beholden to no one, especially not an Elf."

"Can I not convince you otherwise?"

"No. In this, I am determined."

"A pity," said Lochlan, "for I think, in the end, it will be your undoing."

"You need to have more faith."

"Faith? You talk to me of faith? I don't remember ever seeing you pray to the Gods."

"It is not the Gods who will determine if we are successful. It is the actions of people like us."

"No, I cannot believe that. Everything that has come to pass was due to individuals—that I'll freely admit, but it wasn't you and I who made them happen. Prince Tarak convinced the Clans to follow him into Weldwyn, and he was only here because of Queen Kythelia's actions."

"What does it matter? We are here now, right where we want to be. Don't you understand?"

"It is not I who must understand," pleaded Lochlan. "It is you. If the Elf queen doesn't support you as High Queen, your reign is doomed."

"You give her far too much credit."

"Do I? We know so little of her, but what we do know shows her to be both ruthless and unforgiving—a dangerous combination if ever there was one."

"I can be equally as dangerous."

"This spell you witnessed. Can you describe it?"

"She pointed at one of the guards," said Brida, "and then black tendrils flew forth, wrapping around him."

"Then what happened?"

"He had the very life drained out of him, even as she appeared to grow stronger."

Lochlan looked at the floor. "It is as I feared."

"Which is?"

"Kythelia is not only an Elf who has lived for thousands of years, but likely a Necromancer as well."

"A Death Mage? Surely not!"

"How else would you explain the effects of that spell?"

"An enchantment?"

Her brother laughed. "An enchantment that sucks the life out of someone? I understand we lack mages in the Clanholdings, but even I know that's not the kind of thing that enchantments do. No, this is something far more dangerous—the magic of death, which greatly complicates matters."

"Necromancer or not, she is not beyond my reach."

Lochlan sighed. "We do not see eye to eye on this. I seek to warn you against rash actions, yet you are determined to see this through, regardless of the dangers. I wish you well, Sister, but I cannot be a part of whatever it is you're planning."

"But will you stand in my way?"

"No, of course not. I wish you all success and pray you will get what you truly desire. As for me, I shall attempt to stay out of your way lest I inadvertently interfere with your designs. Farewell, Sister. You shall not see me again."

He turned with a heavy heart, leaving the room with one last glance as he paused at the door. This is how he would remember her: as the High Queen, sitting upon the throne of Weldwyn in solitude.

· · ·

Lochlan wandered the streets of Summersgate. With the locals under curfew, little could threaten him, and so he made his way through the city, taking in his surroundings. Summersgate was immense, far more so than any place in the Clanholdings. Buildings towered over him, making him feel small and insignificant, and he wondered how many people had laboured to build this city.

Of course, he knew its history, for studying ancient tales was one of his passions, yet books did not always reveal the heart behind those who built such things.

His meandering brought him to the east end of town, where he caught sight of the Dome. Even after centuries of being exposed to the elements, its copper roof retained its lustre thanks to an ancient enchantment.

Its real name was the Grand Edifice of the Arcane Wizards Council, but that being a mouthful, people simply referred to it as the Dome. According to his research, it was built over the span of a hundred years to a plan devised by the grand wizard Weldwyn, after whom the kingdom itself was named.

It was, in a word, magnificent, although he had thus far resisted the urge to enter it. When they'd first taken Summersgate, the Clans had attacked the place under Brida's orders. The defenders held out for hours, using magic to inflict terrible casualties on his countrymen.

In the end, the mages had been defeated, for they'd been vastly outnumbered. The victors had slaughtered all within, yet the place's mystique, coupled with the death and destruction wrought by magic, could not be forgotten. Their task complete, the Clansmen withdrew, fearful of lingering in a site of such power.

The assault had taken its toll, not just on the army but on their leader as well. Unwilling to suffer further losses, Brida ordered the place sealed, and it had remained thus until the arrival of Kythelia.

Lochlan stood there, staring for some time, simply taking in the building's majesty. The thought gave Lochlan pause. The Clans had no mages of their own. His father had wanted to employ a Fire Mage, but when he couldn't find any in the Clanholdings, he'd resorted to sending overseas for one. At the time, it had been hoped the great mage Carmus might take on an apprentice, but alas, he had died before doing so. Instead, his death left the Clans once again without any magic.

The Dome was said to house everything the mages of Weldwyn knew about magic. Could its contents be used to teach others the arcane arts? The thought excited him so much that he resolved to go there this very instant despite his sister's orders to the contrary.

With a new determination, Lochlan sped up but soon came to his senses. Before the building was a large, open area with long marble stairs and several statues. At first, he took the green-garbed warriors standing guard for statues themselves, but then he noticed the horsehair that topped their helmets blew freely in the wind. He had never seen Elven troops in person, yet there could be no doubt as to who these warriors were, for they were tall, much more so than Humans. However, that could be accounted for by the conical helmets that only seemed to accentuate their height. The illusion was enhanced even more by their unnaturally thin frames, which, even adorned with armour, made them look like strange creatures of the night.

Lochlan was well-read, yet even he knew little of the forest folk. From what he could glean, they were immortal or at least extremely long-lived, depending mainly on whose account you could trust. Did they possess souls like Humans, or were they godsforsaken creatures of the night, like the savage Orcs? He could easily believe the latter, standing here, looking at their unmoving forms, but he realized life was seldom so simple.

Like all good Clansmen, he had been taught Humans were the only race with souls, that only they would travel to the Afterlife, where the Gods would reward them. Did Elves even have gods? Obviously, they were intelligent creatures, but they had no qualms about killing those not of their own race.

It suddenly dawned on him his own people were just as bad. His father had spoken ill of the other races, the same as his sister was prone to. Then again, if he put his mind to it, he was hard-pressed to think of anyone he knew who had even met a non-Human up until the arrival of an emissary from Queen Kythelia.

He felt a sudden panic grip him as if he had just discovered he was on the wrong side of history. Perhaps the Elves would soon rule this land, the race of Humans to be enslaved forever more?

Lochlan tried to fight it, but the more he tried, the worse the feeling. Unable to bear it any longer, he turned and fled back into the streets of Summersgate, trying to get as far away from the Dome as possible.

TWENTY

Unmasking

Albreda took a slice of meat and placed it on her plate.

"I'm surprised to see you eat that," said Arnim. "I thought animals were your friends?"

"They are," replied the Druid, "but does not the wolf eat the deer? It's the natural way of things. Of course, I prefer my meat cooked as opposed to raw, so I'm not quite as wild as some people seem to think." Her eyes looked left to where the commoner, Conrad, sat. "How is your food?"

"A mite rich for my taste," the fellow responded, "although I appreciate the gesture."

"And how has your visit been so far?"

"Eye-opening, to say the least. I must admit to some intimidation at the sight of all the greenskins—"

"Orcs," said Albreda. "To call them anything else is an insult."

"My pardon. The Orcs were, at first, quite frightening, but once you get used to all their ways, they're not so bad."

"Are you suggesting you actually liked them?"

"I'll admit it surprised me, too, but yes, despite appearances, they are not so different from Humans. They have families, form friendships, even help out when needed. It's clear they've built a lot of goodwill here."

"And will you take this knowledge back to Tewsbury?"

"I will. I promise."

"Could you answer me a question?" said Arnim.

"If I can," said Conrad.

"Where did you first hear talk of rebellion?"

"You mean here, in Hawksburg? It's been floating around the city for sometime now. I first heard word of it over the winter. I was at the Lucky Dog, and that fellow, the man with the copperhead, was going on about all the troubles up here."

"Copperhead?"

"I believe he means redhead," said Albreda, "which will make it much easier to identify him." She turned her attention back to Conrad. "Please, don't let me interrupt. You were saying?"

"Yes, he was telling everyone how he saw the townsfolk being herded into buildings like so much cattle."

"I expect," said Arnim, "that the Orcs were doing the herding?"

"Yes, although I can see now that was likely made up."

"And had you seen this man previously?"

"Yes. He's a regular, but no one seems to know much about him."

"Why do you suppose that is?"

"I have no idea," said Conrad.

"Any idea what he does for a living? Could he be a farmer?"

"I doubt it if his appearance is any indication."

"Why would you say that?"

"A farmer has calloused hands and typically smells like livestock. Copperhead, on the other hand, is always clean."

Arnim looked at Albreda. "This bears further investigation."

"So it does," said the Druid, "but not by us. We would be too easily recognized. We shall talk of this in private, but for now, I'd like to see Conrad returned to Tewsbury. Have you any men you could spare to escort him?"

"Plenty, if I'm being honest. I had thought to return the companies to Tewsbury myself."

"Leave that to Captain Carlson. He's more than capable of marching them back without your help."

"Should I not do that in person?"

"No, you're needed in Wincaster."

"Not according to the Nobles Council," replied Arnim.

"I couldn't care less what that so-called council wants. We are dealing with matters of import here, not selecting a decent wine. Why, if Richard wasn't still dealing with Norland, I'd take him back to Wincaster myself and have him sort them all out, but it seems I must rely on your presence. After all, you are the Viscount of Haverston."

Her gaze turned back to Conrad. "What of you? Are you willing to serve the Crown?"

"Of course, but what can I do? I'm nothing but a commoner."

"So was the Marshal of Merceria. We all have to start somewhere."

"What do you want me to do?"

"Return to Tewsbury with Captain Carlson's men. A few days after your arrival, I'll send someone to find you. All I want you to do is take her to the Lucky Dog and identify this man you call 'Copperhead'."

"I can do that."

"You must speak of this to no one."

"Understood."

"Good. Now let us finish our meal, and then you can be on your way."

Captain Carlson did not lead the companies out of Hawksburg until well past noon.

"Finally," said Arnim. "We can put this matter to rest."

"Not quite yet," said Albreda. "There's still work to be done."

"But we know who's spreading these rumours."

"Yes, but not who is ultimately behind them. That's the real prize."

"And so you're going to call on Nikki to find out?"

Albreda turned to look at him. "You surprise me. For a soldier, you have a well-developed mind."

Arnim wasn't sure if he'd been insulted or not, but he kept quiet. Albreda was known to be particularly prickly when it came to certain things, so engaging in an exchange such as this could often lead to an argument few could win.

"We shall have Nikki enter Tewsbury in disguise," said Albreda. "Once she meets this Copperhead, she can follow him."

"Thus exposing his master."

"Precisely."

"I have a feeling I already know who's responsible," said Arnim.

"And that would be?"

"The Earl of Tewsbury himself, Lord Alexander Stanton."

"That was my suspicion as well, but we must have proof if we are to act against him."

"That won't be easy," said Arnim. "He's been a thorn in the queen's side since her coronation."

"And even before that, according to Richard. He and Tewsbury were rivals for the same hand in marriage. Well, I say rivals, but the truth is he only wanted Evelyn for her influence. After all, she was sister to the future Baron of Hawksburg."

"I never knew that. It explains so much."

"Doesn't it? That's what I thought when Richard first told me the story."

"I'm surprised he would have talked of it. Evelyn Brandon was his wife."

"And why wouldn't he talk of her?"

"Well..." he said, struggling to find the words, "aren't you two... involved?"

"Not that it's any business of yours, but yes, we are. Still, that doesn't mean he didn't love his wife—far from it. In fact, they were soulmates. To my mind, that's not something to be ashamed of. Rather, it should be celebrated."

"And so this animosity goes back how far?"

"Years," said Albreda. "Let's see, now. Richard first met Evelyn back in... I think he said twenty-four, or thereabouts."

"Saxnor's sake, that's over forty years ago!"

"Yes, and they've borne a grudge ever since. Not that I can blame Richard for any of this. Tewsbury could have surrendered to the fact she was in love with Richard, but no, he had to bear this lifelong animosity."

"Do you reckon that relates to all the trouble we have now?"

"Undoubtedly. The Earl of Stanton would like nothing better than to ruin Hawksburg."

"Because of Lord Richard? That seems a little off the mark, don't you think?"

"Not at all. You must remember, Aubrey is Richard's niece. Alexander Stanton is a petty man. To his mind, he can't risk hurting Richard directly, but his family is another matter entirely."

"But why now?"

"I'm afraid Beverly likely precipitated all this when she returned from Norland."

"I'm not sure I follow?"

"The garrison at Tewsbury hesitated to admit royal troops into the city. Beverly took it upon herself to order Captain Carlson to take over the duties as garrison commander."

"And Lord Alexander took it as a slap in the face."

"Precisely. In his mind, she was doing her father's bidding, adding insult to injury."

"But that wasn't her intent, surely?"

"Of course not, but we must strive to see things from Lord Alexander's point of view."

"So, what do we do now?"

"I shall take you back to Wincaster, so you can take over the stewardship of Merceria while your good wife looks into things in Tewsbury."

"Very well. When do you want to leave?"

Albreda smiled. "There's no time like the present."

. . .

Zale Halfen smiled. The crowd was getting involved in his tales, always a good sign. He took another sip of his ale before standing once more.

"We are all in danger," he said. "Those filthy greenskins threaten our very way of life." He paused, waiting for the murmurs of agreement. It hadn't taken much, merely a few words to influential people and an endless parade of drinks, courtesy of his employer. Ale seemed to work the best while having the added benefit of being relatively inexpensive, which meant more coins remaining in his own pocket.

"I say the filthy savages should be sent back where they belong."

Hands thumped tables, and Zale sat back down. He'd riled up the patrons of the Lucky Dog; now all he had to do was let them take care of the rest. It wouldn't be long before the entire city was ready to take on the greenskins.

His hand instinctively went to his belt pouch, and he reached inside to feel the coins. He'd been given them for the express purpose of spreading rumours, yet to his mind, the excess of drink was a poor investment. Far better to hire thugs to create an incident and blame it on the Orcs. The thought gave him some pleasure, for Zale Halfen had always been a thug at heart. At one time, he'd even been tempted to suggest this very plan to his employer, but the wealthy were easily insulted, and he had no wish to close off the flow of coins he so eagerly devoured.

He let the patrons of the Lucky Dog drift off into their own discussions, then drained his tankard and rose, making his way outside.

Grey clouds loomed off to the west, but he doubted the rain would hit Tewsbury until well after sundown. His thoughts drifted once more to the coins he carried. His funds were running low, the signal he must make his way once more to his employer. He set off down the street.

Nikki watched as the man made his way towards the earl's estate. To her mind, there could be little doubt as to who was behind this plot, yet she knew the queen would demand proof. She briefly considered lying and simply telling Her Majesty she'd witnessed an exchange between the earl and this Zale Halfen, but the queen had a way of seeing through such things.

In some ways, life had been simpler in the slums of Wincaster. The gangs had been brutal, but they were easily understood—cross the wrong person, and it would cost you your life. However, amongst the nobles of Merceria, it was an entirely different matter.

They were still largely motivated by greed, but not always. Influence drove these people—the ability to control events to their liking. Queen

Anna, bless her soul, was determined to have the rule of law. A noble thought, in the purest sense of the word, and there was no denying it helped those who would otherwise have no voice, but the truth was, it made things like this so much more complicated.

Nikki kept well back from her target. Following someone through city streets had been second nature to her, yet she was surprised by how easily she had fallen back into old habits. No, that wasn't quite true. She could still follow someone easy enough, but now that she had children, her survival instinct was even more heightened.

Halfen finally reached the gate that kept the commoners from entering the earl's estate. A guard challenged him, and after a brief exchange of words, the fellow was admitted.

Nikki swore. Following this fool had proven nothing. Unless she could put him together with the earl, his presence here could be explained away.

She looked up and down the street. The earl's residence was surrounded by a brick wall topped with metal spikes, easy enough to climb since the spikes were more for decoration than anything else. Back up the street she went, seeking a position beyond sight of the guard.

It took only a moment for her to climb over, and then she was moving across a well-manicured garden, using the trees and bushes to hide her progress.

There was only a brief glimpse of her target entering the building before he disappeared, then once more, she cursed. The thought of following him came to mind, but she would stand out too much in her current attire. A quick glance around confirmed no one else was in the vicinity, so she approached the house, seeking a window.

After a peek inside revealed an empty room, she continued along the side of the estate. Finally, at the third window, she spotted Lord Alexander Stanton, standing before a fireplace, drink in hand. As luck would have it, a servant opened the door at that precise moment, admitting Zale Halfen. Nikki stayed low, straining to hear their conversation.

"Ah, there you are," said Stanton. "I trust everything is going well?"

"It is, my lord. We have the people in the palm of our hands."

"You mean MY hands. Let us not forget who's in charge here."

"Of course, my lord."

"Is that all you have to report?"

"Not quite, my lord. Word is spreading quickly, but I fear, so, too, is the expense."

"You rogue. You want more coins!"

"I do, my lord, although only to serve your interests."

"Between you and the rest, I've little left to spare."

"The rest?"

"Of course," said the earl. "You don't think Tewsbury is the only place I'm doing this, do you?"

"No, of course not, my lord."

"And the other matter we spoke of?"

"That is still in the works. It's one thing to direct people's ire towards the greenskins, but quite another to speak badly of the queen."

"Still, you must persist if this is to work."

"But she controls the army, my lord."

"Yes, but they're largely away in Weldwyn. We shall not have another opportunity like this."

"Understood, my lord. I'll accelerate my efforts."

"Good. That's exactly what I wanted to hear. Now, how much more do you need? Would fifty crowns suffice?"

"More than sufficient, my lord."

"Very well. I'll have Nathaniel fetch it, then you'd best be off before someone sees you."

"Yes, my lord."

Nikki waited until she heard the door close before making her way back across the garden and over the wall. There could no longer be any doubt about the earl's part in all of this, yet his conversation hinted at so much more. Was the earl plotting to raise a rebellion himself or merely furthering his own influence by speaking ill of the queen? Had she been working for the gangs of old, murder would have set everything to rights, but killing an earl was not something the queen would agree to, at least not without a fair trial first.

Nikki felt out of her depth, a strange feeling, considering her background. She was alone, and that was the problem. In her early days in Wincaster, she had the backing of a gang, then much later, the queen herself, all within easy reach. Here in Tewsbury, however, the nearest help was days away. Even worse, if something were to happen to her before she got word back to Hawksburg, all would be lost.

She was well away from the earl's estate when she spotted a Mercerian warrior, a horseman, by the look of him, standing out front of a tavern, chatting away with a woman. It dawned on her that the garrison here consisted of royal troops. She wracked her brain, trying to remember the commander's name. Carlson—that was it. The former captain of the

Wincaster Light Horse, Dame Beverly's old company. If they couldn't be trusted, then who could? Nikki took a moment to calm herself before heading north towards their barracks.

She entered to notice a man standing by the fire. He turned as the door closed behind her.

"Can I help you with something?" he asked.

"Yes," said Nikki. "I'm here to see Captain Carlson."

"Oh yes?" The man grinned. "Here to warm him up, are you?"

"Do you know who I am?"

"No, although judging from what you're wearing, I know what you do."

Nikki looked down at her commoner's dress. In her rush to get here, she'd forgotten her attire, a ruse to enable her to spy out these traitors.

"I am Lady Nicole Arendale," she said, "and I'm working on behalf of Her Majesty, Queen Anna."

The man's smirk quickly vanished. "My apologies, my lady."

"Is Captain Carlson here?"

"He is. I shall fetch him immediately."

Nikki waited as he disappeared into the next room. Voices echoed back through the door, although she couldn't discern much of the conversation, then the captain emerged.

"Lady Nicole," he said, "this is an unexpected surprise. Is there something I can do for you?"

"There is," she replied. "I require a quill, ink, and paper to make a report."

"I'll have the sergeant fetch them immediately. Might I ask what this is concerning?"

"An act of treason," said Nicole, "by none other than the Earl of Tewsbury himself."

TWENTY-ONE

Brida

SPRING 966 MC

The lone candle in the room sputtered, shadows dancing across the wall. Brida stepped closer to the flame, where six Clansfolk huddled around the meagre light.

"This is all your fault," said Warnoch, Chief of Clan Drakewell. "Had you not been so eager to avenge your father's death, we wouldn't be here now."

Calindre, Chief of Windbourne, loomed close, the light flickering on her face. "We all supported her as High Queen. I suggest you let her have her say."

"Easy for you to say. Your child wasn't murdered on the orders of that foul Kurathian."

"It is clear now that we were deceived," said Brida. "Yes, we conquered Weldwyn, but the Dark Queen has arrived to enforce her dominance."

"Can we not simply defeat her army?" asked Erlach, Chief of Glanfrayden.

Rurik shook his head. As the Chief of Halsworth, he was known as the most stubborn of Clansmen, yet he was here, evidence of the import of this meeting. "Have you seen her warriors? They'll not be easy to defeat."

"Still," said Erlach, "we must try, mustn't we?"

Conner of Clan Hillsfar cleared his throat. "If you ask me, it's not the army we need fight, it's this Dark Queen herself."

"Not a simple task," said Brida. "She is a powerful Necromancer."

"How do you know this?"

"I saw it myself when she used her magic to suck the life out of one of my guards." Brida looked around, grim faces reflecting back at her. "Whatever we decide must be done soon. With every passing day, her grip on this city becomes even tighter."

"Killing her is not the answer." Everyone looked at Rurik.

"Go on," urged Brida.

"Weldwyn is a rich kingdom. Why not use its riches to send her on her way?"

"Are you suggesting we bribe her?"

"Why not?" said Rurik. "Everyone craves gold, even Elves."

Brida wasn't having it. "No. She's waited thousands of years to return here—she told me so herself. She won't throw that away just to fill her coffers."

"Then blackmail?"

Conner laughed. "You would have us try to blackmail a Death Mage? Have you truly lost your wits?"

"At least I'm suggesting something," defended Rurik. "You, on the other hand, are doing no such thing!"

"I suggested we kill her."

"Hardly a well-thought-out idea."

"Calm yourselves," said Brida. "Such animosity will only serve our enemies."

Calindre spoke next. "What of your brother, Lochlan? Has he any ideas?"

"Other than disagreeing with the invasion in general? No. He tried to warn me about the Elves, but I wouldn't listen. The thought of conquering Weldwyn was too great a lure."

"And now?"

"I admit I might have been hasty, but what is done is done."

"At least," said Rurik, "we can console ourselves knowing Weldwyn will never rise again. It's a pity we didn't manage to capture any of their Royal Family."

"We retrieved Alstan's body," said Brida, "along with his mother, but his sisters are unaccounted for. We shall, of course, continue the search, but I don't hold out much hope for finding them."

"Probably fled to Merceria," said Conner. "Which brings up another matter altogether. What do we do about them?"

"Merceria?" said Warnoch. "I believe you give them too much credit. They won't invade Weldwyn now that it's in our hands. They don't have the men for it."

"But they already have."

Everyone's attention turned to Conner.

"And how would you know?" asked Brida.

"I kept my eyes open and my mouth shut. It seems our Kurathian allies have had a brush or two with the Mercerians, most recently in the south."

"And?"

"The Mercerians won a battle at a place called Bramwitch, or so I'm led to believe."

"Meaning?" pressed Brida.

"Prince Tarak is not one to admit to a defeat, not that he was there himself, of course, but still, having his army suffer a loss would be a tremendous blow to his ego."

"Who led these Mercerians?" asked Brida.

"Prince Alric, if the accounts are to be believed."

"We must send a force to crush him," said Warnoch. "Every day he remains in Weldwyn, he weakens our claim."

"We cannot spare the men," said the High Queen. "The fact is it's taking far too many warriors to subjugate this wretched kingdom."

"There's more," said Conner.

Once more, all eyes turned towards the Clan Chief of Hillsfar.

"Mirstone has yet to fall to our allies."

"Mirstone?" said Brida.

"Yes, a Dwarven town on the road to Kingsford. It's important for the Mercerians if they want to secure an advance on Summersgate."

"They don't have the numbers for such an attack."

"So Warnoch claimed, but their history suggests they're used to being outnumbered, and it most assuredly didn't stop them from defeating your father's invasion."

"Leofric was lucky," said Brida. "That's all."

"Luck? Luck didn't lead to your father's capture—it was those despicable Mercerians."

"They were, in truth, Weldwyn troops," said Conner, "but the Mercerian general was the one who led them."

"And where is he now?" demanded Erlach. "Down south with Prince Alric?"

"No. He appears to be holed up in Falford."

"Falford?" said Rurik. "That's in Weldwyn, isn't it? Why weren't we informed of this?"

"I've taken steps to slow their progress," offered Brida. "They won't be advancing any time soon."

"How did you manage that?"

"By carefully manipulating Prince Tarak into a judicial use of one of his dragons."

The mention of dragons made them all shiver.

"How long before he turns those beasts on us?" said Rurik.

"That, I cannot answer, but for now, at least, we are working towards the same goal—that of total victory."

"Except they're still out there," said Calindre. "It will take an army to push them out of Weldwyn, not just a dragon."

"Just a dragon?" said Brida. "Did you hear yourself say that? A dragon is a terrifying sight—not the sort of thing one can simply shrug off."

"And yet a dragon cannot occupy a city. You need warriors for that."

"We are getting off topic," said Calindre. "We are here to discuss action against the Dark Queen, not battle the Mercerians."

"I wonder," said Erlach. "Could we somehow convince the Mercerians to take on Kythelia?"

"I'm sure they'd love to, but we can't exactly let them march into Summersgate to storm the Dome and leave the rest of the city to us, now, can we?"

"She makes a good point," said Conner. "Kythelia's elite guards are there. I doubt they'd be easy to overcome."

"What if we could lure her out?" asked Calindre.

"I'm listening," replied Brida. "What did you have in mind?"

"It seems to me she doesn't receive visitors, yet she did bring herself to visit you, Brida, when she first arrived."

"That's no guarantee she would do so again."

"Hence the lure."

"It's a good idea," said Erlach. "The best one so far, but what might draw her out?"

"You have all those captured Weldwyn nobles," suggested Warnoch. "Might one of them provide the excuse we need?"

"And then what?" said Brida. "Am I to send word to Kythelia that someone wishes to speak with her? I doubt she would find that enticing."

"What if they had knowledge of the missing royals?"

"That might work," said Erlach.

Brida wasn't impressed. "News of that nature would interest us, but the Elf queen is a Necromancer. I would hazard a guess she cares little for such things."

"This so-called plan has its problems," said Conner, "but we have the time to mull it over, don't we?"

"Look," said Erlach. "I still maintain the best way to deal with her is to eliminate her army. We control Summersgate. That gives us far more warriors in the area than she can muster."

"I hate to agree with him," said Calindre, "but he has a point. The Elven guards are, at least, warriors, not Death Mages, which means they can be killed. Throw enough soldiers at them, and they will eventually fall."

"And who is to lead this assault?" asked Brida. "It's one thing to suggest such an approach, quite another to carry it out."

"We are all in this together; thus, it's the responsibility of all of us to see this through."

The room grew quiet, for plotting such an act was a big step, one that did not come easily.

Warnoch broke the silence. "I'm in."

"As am I," offered Calindre.

"Count me in," said Erlach.

"And me," said Conner.

All eyes turned to Rurik. The older man hemmed and hawed for a moment before he shrugged his shoulders. "Very well, you can count on my support."

Warnoch looked at their High Queen. "What of yourself?"

"I can see no other option," said Brida. "I shall support the endeavour."

"Good. Now, we must consider how to proceed. What do we know of Kythelia's defences?"

"She has those guards of hers outside the Dome," offered Conner.

"How many?" asked Brida.

"I'd say at least fifty, but it would be easy enough to confirm that number. It might be judicious to assume there's an equal force inside the building."

"Then counting warriors will be our first step. Does anybody have any details on their armour?"

"It is no more than chainmail," offered Warnoch. "Although, I'll admit, it's handsomely decorated."

"Yes," said Rurik, "and they all have those full helms."

"That could work to our advantage," said Brida. "Their vision will be more restricted than that of our own warriors."

"Their weapons consist primarily of spears and shields. I suspect their defence will involve a shield wall."

"That's good," said Calindre. "It means their flanks will be vulnerable. With enough men, we can get in behind, destroying their formation."

"You make this sound all too easy," said Conner, "but let us not forget, these are Elves. They've had centuries to perfect their tactics. I doubt they will succumb so easily to our attacks."

"The men of Weldwyn did," said Brida.

"True, but that was more through happy circumstance than any inspiring tactics on our part. Had Leofric not lost the bulk of his army in Norland, the result could have been far different."

"You need to have more faith in the prowess of our own warriors."

"And you need to learn to not so easily dismiss the capabilities of our enemies. Can we destroy Kythelia's army? Most definitely, but at what cost to our own? It would be a small victory indeed to destroy her only for the Mercerians to recapture Summersgate."

"Precisely why we must throw everything we have against her. Sheer numbers will win out in the end!" Brida turned to Warnoch. "What is the strength of our garrison here?"

"Close to a thousand warriors."

"There," said Erlach. "You see? A thousand warriors to crush a hundred Elves. It almost seems unfair, doesn't it?"

"Surely you're not suggesting we use less?" said Warnoch.

"No, of course not, but with such a numerical advantage, how can we fail to be victorious?"

"A numerical advantage is always a good thing," said Brida, "but there's still the matter of getting them into position without being seen."

"Why should that even matter?" questioned Warnoch.

"If the Elf queen realizes such a large army is coming for her, she'll order the troops into the Dome, and then we'll have a siege on our hands. I shouldn't need to tell you what that would entail." She turned to Calindre. "What do we know of the Dome?"

"It's old," the woman replied. "One of the oldest buildings in the city, in fact. In our initial assault, it was protected with all sorts of magical traps, not to mention walls strengthened by spells."

"I could hardly forget," said Brida, "but could Kythelia have reset those traps, or even laid her own?"

"There's no way to know."

"That's unfortunate. It means we'd be going in blind."

"Perhaps it's better that way," suggested Warnoch. "Knowledge of what awaits them would only weigh on the minds of our warriors."

Conner snorted. "Is that how you treat your men? Personally, I'd like mine to know enough to keep them safe."

"Keep them safe! A warrior's life is given willingly to his Clan Chief."

"True, but use them indiscriminately, and you will soon have none left to command!"

"Enough, you two," said Brida. "Such bickering will get us nowhere. Entering the Dome will prove difficult, but if we can take those outside by surprise, we'll force Kythelia to negotiate."

"Negotiate?" said Calindre. "And with what would we negotiate? What do we have that she even wants?"

"Her life. Even an Elf can't live without food, and with us controlling all access to the Dome, it wouldn't take long for starvation to set in."

"Are you forgetting her magic?"

"She is a Death Mage," said Brida. "Are you now suggesting she could use magic to create food?"

"No, of course not, but that doesn't preclude the possibility she might be able to use her magic to travel great distances."

"Why in the name of the Gods would you even suggest something like that?"

"Simple," said Calindre. "Look at what we know of her. She came from… Oh, that's right. We don't know where she's from, do we?"

"Yes, we do," said Brida. "She's from the Kingdom of Estlaneth."

"And where might that lie, exactly?"

The High Queen fell silent.

"See?" said Calindre. "Not so easy to ignore, is it? Let's face it, we know very little of Queen Kythelia. Who knows if she's even a queen?"

"No," said Brida, finding her voice. "Lochlan read about her."

"But who knows if the person he read about is the same as this foul Elf? Supposing she's merely using that name to spread more fear and doubt?"

"She's still proven herself to be capable of using Death Magic. That should be cause enough for alarm."

"The point I was trying to make was we don't know from where she came. Is it possible she used magic to travel here?"

"No," said Warnoch. "She rode in through the west gate."

"And where in the west did she come from? Definitely not the Clanholdings."

"I'll admit," said Brida. "I had not considered that option. It would help if we knew more about the capabilities of a Death Mage, but such knowledge is locked up in the Dome, and I refuse to send more men into that place only to have them killed by magic. Who knows, perhaps that's the very reason she chose it as her stronghold? We must now also consider the possibility she could use magic to escape, in which case there would be little we could do to prevent it. Then again, she would still be gone from Summersgate, so perhaps it's not as far-fetched as I thought."

"I'd prefer she were dead," said Warnoch. "Then, at least, we wouldn't be looking over our shoulders in years to come, dreading her return."

"Cavalry," said Conner.

"I beg your pardon?"

"While you lot were arguing over the Elf queen, I figured out how to cut off those guards and prevent them from escaping into the Dome. If a force of horsemen were to appear out of nowhere, they could cut off the guard's possible retreat."

"Oh?" said Warnoch. "You have invisible horsemen, now, do you?"

"Clearly not," defended Conner, "but if we threaten them with a smaller force to engage their attention, we might be able to get some horsemen in behind them."

"And you expect that to work?"

"It has its merits," noted Brida. "There are many streets leading to the Dome. It's not inconceivable that we could manoeuvre a suitable group of horsemen in unobserved. The trick to it would be getting them close enough, so the Elves don't have time to react."

"How about archers?" said Erlach. "That might help pin them in place."

"Arrows wouldn't do much against a shield wall," said Warnoch.

"True, but it would force them to maintain their formation, which means they wouldn't be able to move."

"Shield walls can move," said Brida. "It just takes tremendous discipline to maintain the formation, but I believe we're close to having a solution. We must take a full account of the warriors at our disposal. Only then can we finalize our plan of attack. I suggest we meet again in two days. In the meantime, gather what information you can. We need to confirm the number of Elves guarding the Dome, at least those we can see, but we must also take a look at the roads leading to it if we are to make this work."

"And what are we looking for?" said Erlach. "Surely a road is just a road?"

"Roads come in many shapes and sizes," replied Brida. "How many men can ride abreast, and what impediments stand in their way? The last thing we want is for a cavalry charge to be held up by a trader's stall."

"I'll take care of the roads," said Conner.

"And I'll count the guards," offered Calindre.

Brida smiled. "Good, and while you're all at it, give a prayer to the Gods. With any luck, we'll be free of this so-called Elf queen by the end of the week."

TWENTY-TWO

The Mystic Woods

SPRING 966 MC

Lady Hayley Chambers, Baroness of Queenston, lay on the hill, looking at the road below, where half a dozen wagons made their way southward.

"What do you make of it?" asked Kraloch.

"I took them for supply wagons, but now that we have a better view, I'm beginning to wonder. Unless I miss my guess, those wagons are full of digging equipment, not food."

"Could they be on their way to Southport to help withstand the siege?"

"No. It's already too late for that. Most of the area south of us is under Prince Alric's control. They must know that."

"Still, they persist in heading south."

"Not quite," said Hayley. "This road heads south eventually, that's true, but for now, it only curves around the forest."

"The question still remains, where are they going?"

"Let's find out, shall we? Bring up the rest of the rangers."

The Orc disappeared back down the hill, keeping well out of sight of their target while Hayley remained watching the wagons. Of particular interest was the last one, for it carried a dozen individuals who wore no armour, merely faded and worn surcoats. Even without any visible weapons, they had the look of warriors to them.

Kraloch soon returned. "They are here," he announced, "but will remain behind the hill to avoid discovery."

"Good. Princess Althea should come into sight shortly. We'll wait till the enemy sees her before making our move."

She'd expected their allies to have made their appearance by now, but her timing must be off. Instead, she fretted while the wagons below continued advancing down the road.

A horn sounded, announcing the arrival of the Dwarves of Mirstone. The lead wagon rolled to a stop, the wagoneers behind it already starting to panic. Upon Hayley's command, the rangers advanced, taking up positions atop the hill, arrows nocked.

She called out to those below, "Surrender yourselves, in the name of Queen Anna of Merceria!"

The enemy had to have heard her, yet their actions indicated otherwise. Instead of taking their hands off the reins, they whipped the horses into a frenzy. Within moments, they were all over the place, each attempting to turn around in their own way.

It dawned on Hayley that these might be Kurathians, and she cursed herself for not realizing it sooner. She quickly ordered them to halt, in their own tongue, and three wagons stopped. More concerned with escaping, the others tried heading back up the road, away from Althea's approaching Dwarves. They didn't get far before the Dwarves of Ironcliff made an appearance of their own, cutting off any possible escape.

"It appears our work here is done," said the High Ranger. She lowered her bow and began walking down the incline, Kraloch following.

Althea's Dwarves broke their formation, taking control of the horses while those of Kasri's group took charge of the errant wagons, bringing them back to where the others waited.

"Good work," said Hayley. "And all with no losses on either side. Keep this up, and the war will be over by summer." She made her way to the warriors in the wagon, only to see ropes around their wrists. "What's going on here?"

"We are prisoners," said the oldest of the group. "My name is Captain Woodward, from the Summersgate militia."

"Greetings, Captain. I am Dame Hayley Chambers, High Ranger of Merceria. Might I ask how you came to be here?"

"When the Clans invaded the capital, many threw down their arms, but others, like us, resisted; hence, our current predicament."

"Any idea where they're taking you?"

"A little. I don't speak Kurathian, but I'm almost positive they mentioned a place called Lyndenthorpe. Are you familiar with it?"

"I can't say I am, nor is it on any maps in our possession."

"That's hardly surprising as it's only a small village that used to sit astride a quarry."

"Used to?"

"Yes. It was abandoned decades ago in favour of the one at Mirstone."

"And the villagers?"

The captain shrugged. "I can only assume they all moved on to other things."

Her gaze wandered to the other wagons. "I see a lot of shovels and picks. That must mean they're digging for something. Any idea what?"

"I'm afraid not. Do you have someone who speaks their language?"

"Unfortunately, I only know a few words. Were I back with the rest of the army, I'd have no trouble."

"I'm not sure I understand what you're inferring?"

"We number Kurathians amongst our allies. Not those of Prince Tarak, naturally, but loyal servants of the queen. Now, let's get you out of those bindings and get some food into you. Looks like it's been some time since you had a decent meal."

"Thank you," said Captain Woodward. "It's far more than we could have hoped for."

Kraloch informed the rest of the army of their discovery while the rangers took over command of the wagons. The trip back to Mirstone across the open countryside would be long, yet Hayley knew the wagons would be a welcome addition to the supply lines. Hayley rode up to where Princess Althea led the Dwarves.

"You did well today," said the High Ranger.

"As did you. I must admit, I never imagined I'd see the day where Orcs and Humans worked together in a single company." She suddenly laughed out loud. "Then again, I never imagined I'd see myself leading Dwarves."

Althea looked over her shoulder at the Dwarves marching at a steady pace, but the wagons behind them captured her attention. She brought her gaze back to Hayley. "I'd love to know what Prince Tarak was up to."

"So would we all."

"No. I mean with these wagons. It's a little odd, don't you think?"

Hayley chuckled. "More than a little, I'd say. Captain Woodward believes they were heading to a place called Lyndenthorpe. Ever hear of it?"

"I believe the walls of Summersgate are made of stone from there. It lies at the northernmost point of the Mystic Woods."

"Is that near here?"

"It depends on your definition of near. I've never been there myself, but my understanding is it would only be a day or two from our present position. Why? You're not thinking of going there now, are you?"

"No," said Hayley. "Not until we get a better idea of what's there. I'd hate to alert them to the fact we learned of it."

Althea nodded. "Likely the best course of action."

They rode on in silence, but the princess was obviously mulling things over. She finally returned her attention to the High Ranger. "Tell me, what do you think is going on there?"

"At a quarry? I can only assume they decided to dig out more rock."

"I suppose that makes sense, especially considering all those tools. Still, it's a long way to go just to get stone?"

"It didn't stop your people from digging there when they built the walls of Summersgate."

"True, but the Obsidian Hills are easier to mine."

"Yes, but we control those."

"I understand that," said Althea, "but their invasion is far from over. Why send a small group like this?"

"Could they need to make repairs?"

"It's possible, but why only a dozen miners? Wouldn't you need more than that? Plus, they'd need more wagons to haul away the stone?"

"You don't think this would be enough?"

"Have you looked at them?" asked Althea.

"I'm not sure I understand what you're suggesting?"

"Stone is heavy, and those wagons wouldn't be able to carry much of it. And to be honest, look at the state they're in; I bet they wouldn't last more than a few miles with a heavy load."

"Then why all the picks and shovels?"

"That," said Althea, "is an excellent question."

Determined to get to the bottom of things, Hayley dropped back to the rear of the column to speak with Kasri Ironheart.

The Dwarf saw her coming. "Decided to become a northerner, did you? Maybe one day I'll take you to Ironcliff."

"I'd willingly take you up on that offer. For now, however, I'd like to pick your brain."

"That sounds painful, but go ahead."

"I was talking with Princess Althea, and we were discussing what these Kurathians are up to."

"It's obvious, isn't it?"

"If it is, I'm not seeing it."

Kasri smiled. "That's because you're not looking at this the right way. What do we know about these people? And I mean this specific group."

"They have picks and shovels."

"Which tells us?"

"They're intending to dig?"

"And?"

"Let me think," said Hayley. "Hmm, a dozen men to do the labour."

"Now you're getting warmer."

"But Lyndenthorpe was a stone quarry. Why send only twelve men? If they were repairing walls, wouldn't they need more?"

"They probably would."

"Which means they're not there to quarry stone."

"Well," said Kasri, "they're definitely going to be digging out stone, or they wouldn't need those tools."

"So they're not interested in carting stone away to repair walls?"

"Now you understand."

Hayley shook her head. "No, I'm afraid I don't. There's something I'm not seeing."

"Picks and shovels are used to dig stone, that's true, but there are only a dozen men to do the manual labour. Seems to me like they're more interested in finding something."

"Like what?"

"Treasure!" said Kasri, a gleam coming to her eyes. "Let's suppose someone discovered something about that quarry."

"Such as?"

"I have no idea. Maybe there's a collapsed mine shaft hiding a hidden treasure?"

"It's a quarry, not a mine," said Hayley. "That means it's open-topped."

"Oh yes," said the Dwarf. "I suppose it does. Still, my theory holds—they're looking for something. Something that's most likely buried."

"Who buries things in an abandoned quarry?"

"That's a good question. The other matter that comes to mind is why now? The Kurathians are interested in this place. Maybe we should be too?"

"I'll definitely bring it to the marshal's attention."

They continued onward, silent for a moment before both tried to speak simultaneously, causing no end of laughter.

"You first," said Kasri.

"It occurs to me that if there were something valuable at that quarry, the Crown of Weldwyn would already have looked into it. What were you going to say?"

"I was thinking along similar lines, actually. A recent discovery must have led them here, like a long-lost journal entry or something."

"That makes sense. Once we reach the rest of the army, maybe one of our new prisoners will be forthcoming?"

"We can only hope," said Kasri.

. . .

The trip back to Mirstone was uneventful. Two days later, some of Lanaka's men arrived to interrogate the prisoners. Hayley, Kasri, and Princess Althea were left to pace the hall while their own Kurathians carried out their duties. Herdwin rounded the corner, obviously in some hurry, and almost collided with the High Ranger.

"What's this, now?" he called out. "Clogging up the corridors?" His gaze came to rest on Kasri, and he blushed. "My pardon, Your Majesty." Then he spotted Princess Althea. "I mean Your Majesties. Say, I didn't miss an invitation, did I?"

"No," said Kasri. "We're waiting on Captain Caluman. He's having a chat with the prisoners."

"Is he, now? Have they revealed anything of interest?"

"We don't know yet. We're still waiting."

Herdwin rubbed his hands together. "That sounds exciting."

He began pacing himself, making for a crowded hallway. As he walked, he stared at the floor, his favourite way of concentrating, absently bumping into Kasri, who apparently possessed a similar predilection.

"Perhaps we would be better served to walk side by side," she suggested.

"Yes," he said, smiling. "An excellent idea."

The door opened, revealing a stern-looking Kurathian.

"Captain Caluman," said Hayley. "Have you any news for us?"

"I do, not that it makes much sense. These men were sent to an abandoned quarry to dig caves."

"What are they looking for?" asked Herdwin.

"As far as I can tell, nothing."

"That makes no sense."

"I am not claiming it does, yet that is what they revealed."

"Wait a moment," said Kasri. "How big were these caves to be?"

"Why?" said Herdwin. "You have an idea what they're up to?"

"Maybe, but I need more details."

"I shall go back in and ask them," said Caluman. He turned around and entered the room, closing the door behind him.

"Well, that was disappointing," said Althea. "I hoped he'd be able to tell us something we didn't already know."

"But he did," said Kasri. "He told us they were going to dig caves."

"Yes," said Herdwin, "but does that mean digging out existing caves or making new ones?"

"Does it matter?" asked Althea.

"To be honest, I don't really know."

Kasri stared at the door, her face pale. Herdwin moved up beside her.

"Something wrong? You're not ill, are you? I told you not to eat those stonecakes. They were far too old."

"No, no. It's not that."

"Then what is it?"

"These men are part of Prince Tarak's army, yes?"

"Of course," said Herdwin, "but we already knew that."

She turned to him, a look of determination crossing her features. "What raided our supply wagons?"

Now it was her companion's turn to pale. "Are you suggesting this has something to do with dragons?"

"I am."

"Surely they haven't discovered another one?"

"No," said Kasri. "Of course not. Wild dragons only live in the mountains. Everyone knows that."

"Wild dragons? Aren't all dragons wild?"

"Not those the Kurathian princes kept in servitude."

Herdwin snapped his fingers. "Of course. It all makes sense now." He paused a moment. "No, on second thought, I'm still not seeing it."

"Dragons are here, in Weldwyn," said Kasri. "That, we know already."

"Go on."

"The trip from the Kurathian Isles is far too great a distance for them to fly, so they were likely carried aboard ships."

"And?" prompted Herdwin.

"Well, once they arrived, the prince would need someplace to keep them, wouldn't he?"

"And you believe an abandoned quarry suitable?"

"It would be if they dug caves to house them."

"You may be onto something there, although I don't much like the idea of them being so close to us."

"No," said Kasri. "Don't you see, this is good news."

"It is?"

"Yes. It would put them in a place where we could find them."

"Are you proposing we take on a dragon in battle?"

"Not a good idea," said Hayley. "I was there when we fought drakes in Tivilton, and that was bad enough. Personally, I'm fine with viewing dragons from a safe, respectful distance."

"Ah," said Kasri. "Where's your sense of adventure?"

"You're enjoying this far too much," said Herdwin.

"Ever since I was little, I've loved dragons."

"I didn't know you ever met any."

"I haven't, but that didn't stop me from reading all I could about them."

"Oh yes?" said Herdwin. "And what did you learn?"

"Well, for one thing, they're highly intelligent."

"So is a dog."

"No," said Kasri. "I mean smart enough to speak. Legend says a dragon taught us the first use of magic."

"I thought that was the Elves," said Althea.

"Really?" said Hayley. "And here I thought it was the Orcs."

"Well," continued Kasri, "it doesn't matter what you heard. The fact is, dragons speak the ancient tongue, common to all elder races, way back when."

"Wait a moment," said the princess. "Are you saying you had a common language before we Humans came along?"

"That's what I just said, didn't I? Although these days, we've all developed our own dialects, but the core of our languages remain the same."

"Aye," said Herdwin. "It's the main reason why the Dwarves of Stonecastle trade with the Elves of the Darkwood and the Orcs of the Artisan Hills. Did your research indicate anything about them employing magic?"

"No," replied Kasri. "But then again, all the accounts were second-hand."

"Have you dragons up at Ironcliff?" asked Althea.

"If we do, I never saw one. Some legends say they lived in the Thunder Mountains thousands of years ago, but no one's ever found any remains. Not that we spend much time looking for them, mind you."

"And now they've come to Weldwyn," said Herdwin. "No wonder you're so worked up."

"Worked up? Is that an insult?"

"Not at all. Merely an indication that you're very passionate."

Kasri blushed. "Why, thank you, Herdwin. I think that's the nicest thing anyone's ever said to me."

TWENTY-THREE

Jane

SPRING 966 MC

Gerald brought his horse to a halt. The rain started late in the afternoon as a drizzle, but now, as dusk approached, it cascaded down, threatening to completely wash away the road. Not that there was much of a road to begin with, for the feet of hundreds of marching men had all but obliterated any sign of it, aside from the mud, of course.

Sir Preston reined in beside him. "It's getting worse, Your Grace."

"I know," the marshal replied, "and stop calling me 'Your Grace'. You make me sound like some ancient relic. If you must use a title, then just say 'sir' and be done with it."

"Yes, sir."

"I must apologize, Sir Preston. I'm not in the best of moods."

"I can well understand. This weather could dampen the most ardent of souls."

"It's not the weather so much as the delay. We should've been in Kinsley days ago. How much farther?"

"Not much more. Maybe as little as a mile or two? Our advance scouts should bring back word any moment now, assuming they can find us in this downpour."

Gerald chuckled. "It hasn't completely washed away the road, at least not yet." He edged his horse to the side, allowing a group of archers to march past. "I'm getting too old for this."

"Sir?"

"Oh, don't worry, I'm not going anywhere. I just find of late, it's getting harder and harder to get out of bed each morning."

"It's the weather. I have the same problem."

"Liar," said Gerald, his face betraying some mirth. "You don't want to get out of bed because you've got a nice new wife keeping you warm there. Trust me, I'm not that old. I can still remember the lure of it."

Sir Preston blushed. "If you don't mind me asking, sir, how long ago did your wife pass?"

"She died back in thirty-two."

"And there's been no one since?"

"The guilt was a heavy burden for many years."

"Guilt? I thought Norland raiders killed her?"

"They did, but I wasn't there to protect her."

"There was nothing you could have done—they would've killed you too."

"I know that up here"—Gerald pointed at his head—"but here?" He pointed at his heart. "That's a wound that has taken much longer to heal. I had a daughter, too, bright as sunshine, she was, the very apple of my eye. She died alongside her mother." His face grew grim.

"I'm sorry. I didn't mean to upset you."

"No, it's all right. It took me a long time, but I have a new family now."

"You mean the queen?"

"Yes, she's like a daughter to me."

Sir Preston forced a smile. "And now you have a grandson!"

"I do, although hopefully he's bundled up nice and warm and not freezing in this dreadful rain." He spotted Beverly riding towards them, her mighty horse, Lightning, trotting along as if on parade.

"Good news?" the marshal called out.

She slowed Lightning, coming to rest to his left. "Yes. Kinsley is up the road. The entire army should be within the town before nightfall."

"That's the first good news I've heard all day." He turned to the third member of their little group. "Sir Preston, perhaps you'd care to ride ahead and see to billeting?"

"Of course, Your Gra… I mean, of course, sir." He rode off.

"What was that all about?"

"I'm trying to break him of some of his more annoying habits," replied Gerald.

"Such as?"

"An overabundance of manners."

Beverly laughed. "You can't fault him for trying."

"He's a good man. He'll make a fine general one day."

"General? Aren't you rushing things a little? You're not thinking of hanging up your shield, I hope?"

"No, of course not, but I won't live forever, and neither will your father. You must give some consideration to the army."

"You're the marshal."

"For now, but eventually, that job will be yours, and you'll need to foster competent generals. Preston and Heward are the most likely candidates."

"Not Hayley?"

"Hayley is a good leader, but her position of High Ranger would keep her far too busy for such a responsibility. Make her commander of archers, if feel you need to, but leave the army to those with little else to do."

"Like me?"

"You are the greatest warrior Merceria has ever produced, Beverly, and I don't say that lightly. You're ready to be promoted to general. You showed that back in Norland when you defeated the spirit army. Had I an army for you to command, you would be one already."

"You humble me."

"Good. A leader who begins to believe their own reputation becomes a threat to the very warriors they command. Now, let's get to Kinsley and out of this rain, shall we? I don't know about you, but I'm thoroughly soaked."

Kinsley, roughly halfway between Falford and Summersgate, was unwalled, as was common amongst the smaller towns of Weldwyn. At the same time, the narrow streets and closed-in nature of the place would still make an attack a difficult undertaking. Thankfully, the Kurathian invaders there had fled at the first sign of the Mercerian scouts, leaving the army of Merceria to be welcomed as liberators.

Gerald dismounted, passing his reins off to one of his staff. In years past, he would have insisted on seeing to the beast himself, but after a long ride and drenched as he was, he knew he lacked the strength for it.

Beverly's duties took her elsewhere, leaving the marshal alone with his thoughts. He stepped inside, moving closer to the roaring fire. Sir Preston, who'd made all the arrangements, chose this tavern as the army's new headquarters. He now strode across the room to place a warm tankard in Gerald's hand.

"Here you are," said the knight. "A nice hot cider to warm your bones."

"Thank you," the old warrior replied. "It's just what I needed." He downed half the tankard in one go and then leaned against the fireplace, staring into the flames.

"Is there anything else I can get for you, sir? Some food, perhaps?"

Gerald turned to look at the knight. "I'm more than capable of seeing to that myself. You get yourself to that wife of yours, and make sure she's all right."

Sir Preston grinned back. "Yes, sir!"

The warmth slowly seeped back into the marshal's limbs, so much so he removed his cloak, throwing it across the back of a chair. He absently watched the water run off it to pool on the floor. Around him, warriors came and went, reporting to his staff, who kept track of numbers and tallies. The job was never-ending, yet it proved to be most effective. He was reminded of Baron Fitzwilliam's advice years ago, "Look after your men, and they'll look after you."

A nearby soldier overheard him. "Did you say something, Your Grace?"

"No. Just mumbling to myself." Gerald edged farther away from the fellow, only to find himself near a window consisting of small glass panes bound together by a criss-cross of metal poles—a most unusual arrangement.

A movement outside caught his attention, but the glass distorted his view. He rubbed at it, trying to see better, but all it did was make things worse. Something had moved in the alleyway opposite; Gerald was sure of it, yet try as he might, he could not determine what it was.

With his suspicions aroused, he moved to the door, opening it to peer across the street. Something definitely crouched in the alley, a person by the look of it. He stepped outside, forgetting his cloak in his desire to unravel this mystery.

A column of spearmen marching by delayed him, leading him to curse at the enforced idleness. As soon as they had passed, he crossed the street, his hand instinctively resting on the hilt of his sword.

The figure crouched, shivering in the alley, their back to one wall, knees brought up to their chest. Gerald reached to remove his cloak, only to remember he'd left it back at the tavern. He moved closer, looking down at the poor soul, startled when the pale face of a woman stared back.

"Don't hurt me, sir, I beg of you."

He knelt before her, although his knees complained. "No one's going to harm you. Are you hurt?"

"No, my lord, only frozen and starving."

"Come. Let's get you inside where it's nice and warm, shall we?" He held out his hand.

She hesitantly reached up, her hand cold and clammy as she placed it in his. He straightened, feeling the strain on his knees once more.

"There's a tavern across the street," he said. "I'll take you there, and you can warm up by the fire."

"Thank you, my lord." Her voice was soft, almost non-existent, making it difficult to hear her over the constant downpour. He led her into the street only to see another company of spearmen marching towards them. This time, instead of waiting, he ordered them to halt, then helped the woman across to the tavern.

The men continued on their way even as Gerald pushed open the door. The room fell quiet as he ushered her in, closing the door behind them.

"Your Grace?" said Sergeant Blackwood.

"Get this woman a hot drink," said Gerald, "and something to eat." His gaze flicked to the barmaid. "Have you any spare clothing?"

"Of course, my lord." The barmaid disappeared into a back room.

"Come. Sit by the fire," said Gerald, his attention once more on his discovery.

She took a seat before lifting the hood from her head, revealing a woman of a similar age to the marshal.

"I must thank you, sir, although I'm unsure how I can repay your kindness."

"Nonsense. I couldn't just let you freeze out there. Who are you?"

"I'm Lady Jane Goodwin. Might I ask the name of my benefactor?"

"Gerald Matheson, Marshal of Merceria."

"And Duke of Wincaster," called out Blackwood.

Gerald waved away the remark.

"A duke?" she said, trying to stand. "I'm sorry, Your Grace. I didn't mean to—"

"Please, sit. You need to rest, and we are yet to get some food into you." He turned to the rest of the room. "Where is that drink?"

"I've got it," came the reply. Moments later, Sergeant Blackwood appeared, two tankards in hand. Gerald looked at the man to spot a wink and a smile.

"That's enough of that," said the marshal. "I'm only helping a woman in distress."

"Of course, sir." The smile persisted.

"Haven't you got better things to do?"

The smile disappeared. "Yes, sir. I'll leave you two alone, shall I? Not that you're alone. There's a whole tavern full of people here. Say, you don't want me to clear the room, do you?"

"Enough!" said Gerald.

Blackwood, ever the dutiful sergeant, edged away.

"Your man is devoted," said Jane.

"He's only teasing."

"Still, it's evident everyone here holds you in great esteem."

"Never mind that. How did you come to be here?"

"It's a long story."

"We appear to have plenty of time?"

"I fled Summersgate."

"On foot?"

"Yes," she admitted. "I slipped away while the Clansmen at the gates were distracted. Unfortunately, I was the victim of a robbery sometime later and now find myself devoid of funds. I'm afraid I shall be unable to pay for this drink, let alone any food."

"Don't worry about that. The important thing is you're safe. You said your name was Lady Jane. Is your husband an earl?"

"No, although my uncle is, or rather was Earl of Faltingham, Lord Edwin Weldridge. Had you met him?"

"I seem to recall Lord Edwin was a close friend of King Leofric."

"That was him. Upon his death, my elder brother should have inherited the title, but the Clans executed him."

"Did your husband suffer a similar fate?"

"No, he died years ago. Now, it's only me and my son, James."

"I assume he's all grown up?"

"Yes. How did you know?" She paused a moment. "Of course, I should have realized. It's my age, isn't it? I sometimes forget my advanced years. It's only natural for you to assume my son is an adult. He is, of course, just to be clear."

"I'm surprised he didn't flee with you."

"He couldn't," she said rather hastily. "Agents of the High Queen were watching him."

"High Queen?"

"Yes, Brida. Surely you've heard of her?"

"Oh, I know all about Brida."

"So you've met her before?"

"You might say that."

A smile appeared, lighting up the face of Lady Jane. "Evidently, you don't like her. Unless it's a Mercerian custom to frown when mentioning friends?"

"It's that obvious, is it? We met her several years ago. She travelled to Loranguard with a plan to marry Prince Alric."

"How is His Highness?"

"He is well. In fact, he's a new father."

"He is? How splendid."

Sergeant Blackwood arrived at the table, bearing two bowls. "The food you requested, sir."

"Thank you, William."

"William, is it? You haven't called me that in years."

"You two have known each other for some time?" said Jane.

"Indeed we have, ma'am."

"We served together in Bodden," explained Gerald. "Now he helps me run the army."

The door opened, revealing a familiar face.

"Ah, Beverly. Come here. There's someone over here I want you to meet."

The knight stepped closer, surprised by the presence of a woman at the marshal's table.

"This is Dame Beverly Fitzwilliam, one of my commanders," said Gerald. "Her father is the Baron of Bodden."

"Pleased to meet you," said Jane. "Although I wish it were under better circumstances. I'm afraid you're not seeing me at my best. I'm Lady Jane Goodwin."

"How do you do?" said Beverly, struggling to decide how to react.

"Lady Jane has come from Summersgate," he said, "and has been on the road for some time."

"Has she, now?" The knight's gaze turned towards their new visitor. "Might I ask if you saw any signs of Prince Tarak's army during your trip?"

"I encountered some horsemen several days ago, but nothing since."

"They robbed her," explained Gerald. "At least I assume that was who you mentioned earlier?"

"It was," said Jane. "Though they spared me any further terror."

The barmaid pushed past, depositing a bundle of clothes on the table. "That's all I could find, Lord."

"That will do nicely," said Gerald. "Thank you."

Jane stood. "With your permission, Your Grace, I shall go and change." Her gaze went to the barmaid. "Is there somewhere I could have a little privacy?"

"Certainly," the woman replied. "Come with me, and I'll show you."

They made their way from the room, then Beverly sat down. "I see you've been busy."

"It was happenstance, that's all."

"Was it? I might remind you, not so long ago, we had to deal with Lady Lindsey."

"What are you inferring?"

"Merely this woman may not be what she seems."

"Are you suggesting she's a spy?"

"She wouldn't be the first," said Beverly. "Isn't it a little strange she should show up here right as we arrive? You can call it providence if you like, but I can't help but have the feeling there's more to her story than she's letting on."

"That's to be expected, isn't it? She's only just met us."

"Yet here she is, chatting with the marshal of the army."

"Come now. Don't you think you're being a tad overly dramatic?"

Beverly softened her features. "Look, I'm not saying she IS a spy, merely that we must entertain the possibility she's not all she seems. I don't want to see you get hurt."

"Me? Why would you think I would be hurt?"

"Truly? Is that what you're going to go with? It's obvious you feel sympathy for this woman."

"Let me put your fears to rest," said Gerald. "I only just met her, and I most assuredly don't harbour any intention of pursuing her or anyone else, for that matter, if that's what you're getting at?"

"Good. Then the matter is settled. Now, what are you going to do with her?"

"I'm not sure what you're asking?"

"You took on the responsibility for her well-being when you brought her in here. You can't just put her back on the street."

"I hadn't thought of that," said Gerald. "I guess we'll need to send her back to Falford."

"That means dispatching warriors to escort her. I'm not convinced we can afford the men."

"You've got a better idea?"

"You could put her up here in Kinsley. What about the queen?"

"What about her?"

"Should we introduce her to your new friend? She is a Weldwyn noble after all."

"I suppose that would be acceptable."

Beverly laughed. "Are you sure you're not enamoured of her? I would imagine she'd be an attractive woman once she's cleaned up... for her age, I mean."

"What has her age got to do with anything?"

"Oh, so you DO think she's attractive?"

"I refuse to participate any further in this discussion."

"I'll tell you what," said Beverly. "I'm on my way to see the queen. Why don't I let her know there's a new Weldwyn noble amongst us?"

"I can do that," said Gerald, somewhat defensively. "You have far too many other duties to attend to."

TWENTY-FOUR

The Quarry

SPRING 966 MC

K asri Ironheart stepped into the tavern, along with Herdwin Steelarm. The place was packed, as one might expect when the marshal was addressing his senior commanders, yet even so, drinks flowed freely.

Kasri grabbed a tankard, passing it to her companion before filching another. She took a sip, then made a face. "Not the freshest of mead."

"It'll do in a pinch," said Herdwin. "And after the long march from Mirstone, I'll take anything I can get."

They'd arrived in Kinsley only last night, putting them two days behind the rest of the army. Now, with the northern forces of Merceria finally combined, they could begin discussions on making a move towards the Weldwyn capital. The general hubbub died down as the marshal took up a position near the fire.

"Thank you all for coming," he said.

"As if we had a choice!" someone called out to much laughter.

"I can see the drinks are popular," said Gerald, continuing his speech. "We've now amassed nearly fifteen hundred men in our bid to strike back against the Clan invasion of Weldwyn. The path before us is clear, for the road west leads to only one destination—Summersgate. Once there, we shall assault the city and defeat our enemies once and for all."

A hand went up, and the marshal singled out the man responsible. "Yes, Sir Preston?"

"Might I ask how we intend to take the city?"

"We're still discussing details, but suffice it to say the situation is well in hand."

"With only fifteen hundred?" The voice came from the crowd, although Kasri couldn't see who it belonged to.

The marshal smiled. "I've been keeping a secret from you." His gaze turned to Beverly. "All of you, and for that, I apologize, but I felt it best I kept this quiet until now." He stood on his toes and nodded at Sergeant Blackwood, who waited silently at the back of the room. All eyes followed the marshal's gaze as the old warrior opened the door, revealing none other than Lord Arandil Greycloak. The Elf made his way through the crowd, halting by Gerald's side.

"Lord Arandil," said the marshal, "is here with six hundred warriors of his own, swelling our numbers."

"The time has come," said the Elven lord, "to put aside our differences. A great darkness is upon us, one which will take the combined might of all the free races to defeat."

Confusion swept the room. "I thought we were fighting Clansmen?" called out a voice.

"And so we are," continued Lord Arandil. "They are guided by an evil Necromancer who goes by the title of Queen Kythelia." He noted the looks. "I see you recognize the name. Yes, she is the same one who conjured the spirit army that plagued you in the north. Now, she has reached the culmination of her centuries-long plan and installed herself as ruler of Weldwyn. Soon, she will turn her attention away from the subjugation of this land and turn her anger against us, the Army of Merceria. We must be sure that we are ready to meet her head-on."

"And to that end," said Gerald, "I broke the army into three brigades. Lord Greycloak will command the Elven host, Kasri Ironheart, the Dwarves. The Orcs and Humans will fall under my command for the time being, although that may change. Simply marching our army up the road to Summersgate would invite attack from our enemies, so I aim to send three separate columns westward, each taking a slightly different route. It means many of you will march cross-country. Still, should we encounter any resistance, all companies would be able to gather to overwhelm any opposition."

He paused a moment, taking in the room. Everyone stared back at him, a sight he would've found terrifying years ago, but now, after such a long and distinguished career, he took it all in stride.

"Specific orders have been drafted for each of you. My staff will ensure you have those in your hands shortly. In the meantime, I must press upon you the need for strict discipline and professionalism. We are undoubtedly outnumbered by our Kurathian adversaries, to say nothing of the Clansmen. Yet, we Mercerians and our allies have a history of defeating those who dare stand against us, a classic case of quality over quantity. Now, with all that said and done, I shall allow you to read over your specific orders."

His men passed them out, and the noise in the room escalated as each table talked amongst themselves.

"It is a good plan," said Lord Arandil, after a quick read, "but everything hangs on Kythelia's response."

"She's a force to be reckoned with, I grant you," replied Gerald, "but we must deal with each enemy one at a time. First, we need to pin down Prince Tarak before we can consider moving against the Clansmen."

"And if the Dark Queen commits her own warriors?"

"Then we shall take care of them, but I doubt that will be necessary, not until we assault Summersgate itself."

"What makes you so sure?"

"She risked everything she had in the north, but still, we defeated her army of shadows. We've taken the measure of her Elves and learned how to defeat them. I mean no offence to your own warriors, of course."

"And I take none," said Lord Arandil.

"To be honest, I'm surprised you decided to aid us. I remember you saying Elf did not kill Elf?"

"For thousands of years, we retreated into the deep woods of the land, hidden from sight and mourning the loss of life. As a race, we are now childless. That, more than anything else, has prevented us from taking part in the affairs of Humans, for while you replenish life, we only suffer its loss."

"What convinced you otherwise?"

"A letter Lady Aubrey Brandon wrote, delivered by a queen's courier, a Human by the name of Edgar Greenfield."

"Edgar? Why, he must be ancient by now?"

"He risked his very life by daring to bring hope to the Darkwood."

"Hope?"

"Yes. Lady Aubrey and the Orc shaman Kraloch found a way to bring life once more to my people."

"And your help was the price you had to pay in return?"

"No. She made no such demand, but the time to act is nigh. No longer can we sit back and simply watch events unfold before our eyes. We must take our rightful place amongst the living, not hide away in shadows. The day has come to settle our affairs, once and for all. If that must be at the side of Humans, Orcs, and Dwarves, then that is the way of it."

"I can't thank you enough," said Gerald. "Your presence will give us a much better chance of ensuring victory."

. . .

Kasri pushed her way through everyone, dragging Herdwin along with her. "Come," she said. "I need to speak to the marshal."

They found him, still standing by the fire, a cup of mead in hand. "Marshal Matheson," she said. "I wonder if I might have a moment of your time?"

"Of course. What can I do for you?"

"You've read the reports of the Mystic Woods?"

"You mean the speculation about why they sent an expedition to dig out an abandoned quarry? Yes. Why do you ask?"

The Dwarf steeled herself. "I would like to lead an expedition of our own there."

"To what end?"

"I believe they're setting up a breeding ground for dragons."

Gerald stared back, although what he was thinking was anyone's guess. He finally turned to Herdwin. "What say you, my friend?"

"You should hear her out, Gerald. She makes a very compelling case."

Once more, the marshal's attention focused on Kasri. "Very well. I'm all ears."

"Those men we intercepted were heading to the quarry at Lyndenthorpe."

"Yes, I know. That much has been confirmed from the prisoner's interrogation."

"And, they sent a dozen men to do all the digging. That would seem to me to be a rather small group? I mean, there were Kurathians to oversee everything, but only twelve labourers? What kind of digging can you do with that?"

"My understanding is they were to dig caves."

"Yes," said Kasri, "but why?"

"I presume they intended to look for something."

"In a quarry that hasn't been used in decades? Don't you think if there was anything valuable there, it would've been plundered long ago?"

"You make a good point, but how do you get from there to dragons?"

"I've spent a lifetime fascinated by dragons, reading every book Ironcliff has on the subject. They say there are even dragon bones up in the Thunder Mountains, although I've never seen them myself."

"Your knowledge will likely prove important in the coming weeks, but I still don't see the relevance here. Why would this Kurathian prince want to put his dragons in some old quarry? Wouldn't he want them closer at hand?"

"Ah, but to his mind, the war is nearly over. Don't you see?"

Gerald shook his head. "No, I'm afraid I don't. What is it I'm missing?"

"I believe he wants to breed them. When you think about it, it makes sense."

"Yes," chimed in Herdwin, "and he does have two dragons. That much, at least, has been confirmed."

"Actually," said Kasri, "I doubt that matters much."

Her companion was taken aback. "What does that mean?"

"Dragons can reproduce all by themselves."

"You mean without mating? How does that work?"

"Does a hen need a rooster to lay eggs?"

"She does if she wants them to hatch."

Kasri frowned. "You make a good point. However, my research over the years has led me to believe that's not required, at least not for dragons. Of course, I can only speculate based on what I've read."

"Hold on a moment," said Gerald. He looked through the crowd, finally locating who he was searching for. "Sir Preston?" he called out. "Would you do me a favour and go and find Dame Hayley?"

"You mean the baroness? Certainly." He disappeared back into the crowd.

"I would value her opinion on this," said Gerald, his attention once more firmly focused on the two Dwarves. "She has a knack for this sort of thing. I am curious, though. Suppose you were to find a dragon? What then?"

"I suppose we'd need to kill it," said Herdwin. "Not that I much fancy the prospect of going toe to toe with a humongous serpent, but someone has to take on the responsibility."

"Couldn't we reason with it?" said Kasri. "They are said to be intelligent creatures, capable of speech."

"And you expect them to see reason?" said Gerald. "That might be wishful thinking on your part. After all, they serve Prince Tarak. Do you honestly believe they would turn on him?"

"I can't say for sure, but I doubt they like living a life of servitude."

"How do you know they're servile?"

"I beg your pardon?"

"Let me put this another way. How do you know they're not willing participants in this war?"

"If I'm being completely honest, I don't, but even if there's a slight chance of success, shouldn't we seize it?" She saw the look of indecision on the marshal's face. "And if they don't see reason, we can always kill them!"

"And how does one kill a dragon, exactly? We took on a pair of drakes in Tivilton years ago, and that was hard work."

"I won't lie to you; it wouldn't be easy, but I have Stormhammer here, not to mention the Hearth Guard."

Hayley pushed her way towards them. "You wanted to see me, Gerald?"

"Yes. Kasri here thinks they may be breeding dragons down by Lyndenthorpe."

"I read the reports."

"And?"

"I'd say she has a pretty convincing argument."

"What makes you say that?"

"Well," said Hayley, "for one thing, the Kurathians are known to use dragons, and if our reports are accurate, there's at least two of them."

"And?"

"Prince Tarak came all the way from the Kurathian Isles. I don't know exactly how far away that is, but the dragons must have been brought here by ship. I can't imagine they would keep them cooped up below decks forever."

"Yes," said Gerald, "but at least one of them attacked our supply wagons. It couldn't possibly have flown here from the coast. Wouldn't that seem to indicate they already found a home?"

"A base of operations, yes, but a home is where such a creature would breed, and dragons live in caves, or so I'm led to believe."

"It would seem she agrees with you, Kasri."

"So you'll allow me to investigate?" asked the Dwarf.

"Very well," said Gerald, "but you'll take Hayley with you, along with some rangers. They may come in handy."

"And?" said Hayley.

"And what?"

"You must send Revi."

"Why in Saxnor's name would I do that?"

"Two reasons," said the High Ranger. "Number one, he's got that spell of tongues. We might need it if we're trying to talk to a dragon."

"And number two?"

"If we do find dragons, it would put him front and centre of a great discovery!"

The marshal laughed.

Kasri looked at Herdwin. "I don't understand. What's so funny?"

"You'd need to know the Life Mage. I'll explain it later."

"I'm not sure about losing our healer," said Gerald. "The last time we were in this part of the country, someone tried to kill the queen."

"I'll leave Kraloch to replace him," said Hayley. She noted his hesitation. "Please?"

"All right. You can have him, but you just go there and back, no traipsing around the countryside. Understood?"

"No traipsing. Agreed."

"You should set out first thing in the morning." He turned to Kasri. "Is that acceptable?"

"It is. Thank you."

"Good. Now, if you'll excuse me, I must make sure everyone understands their orders."

He wandered off, leaving Kasri with Herdwin and Hayley.

"This is so exciting," said the ranger. "I've never seen a dragon before."

"We don't know there's even one there," said Herdwin. "Only that they're preparing the place for them. It could be months before any show up."

"Who died and made you the commander of the gloom patrol?"

"Pardon?"

"She means," said Kasri, "that you should have more of an open mind."

"Don't look at me. I wasn't even invited."

"Much as I would like you to be there, your presence is needed here to take care of the rest of my warriors."

He perked up. "You want me to look after royal troops?"

"Of course. You're an experienced commander with a solid knowledge of our tactics."

"Anything else?"

"Yes," she replied, "but we can discuss that later when we're not in a crowded room."

Herdwin blushed.

Kasri, her victory complete, looked at the ranger. "Do you think Revi Bloom will agree to accompany us?"

"I'm sure he would. This is just the type of thing that gets his mind racing."

"Were you present when they fought the drake?"

"Oh? You heard about that, did you?"

"Yes, although the story lacked much in the way of details. I assume the battle was difficult?"

"It was. Likely the toughest thing we've ever faced aside from the blights."

"Blights?"

"Never mind. It's another long story and one better told by Beverly, if I'm being honest."

"Never mind that," said Kasri. "Tell me about the drakes."

"We found them in Tivilton, a town in the western reaches of Weldwyn, ruled by an Elven lord named Parvan Luminor."

"The name means nothing to me."

"Nor would I expect it to. In any case, something was attacking cattle, and we stepped in to help track it down. Strangely enough, we considered the possibility that a dragon was responsible, but we quickly dismissed the idea."

"Why is that?"

"Whatever attacked dragged the victims away, rather than flying."

"So you followed the trail, I presume?"

"We did," said Hayley. "There were two drakes, laired in some old ruins. We sent in a trio of warriors to lure them out."

"Were you one of them?"

"No, but Gerald was, along with Beverly and Jack Marlowe. I don't believe you've met him yet. He's down south with Prince Alric."

"We drew them out easily enough," continued Hayley, "but let me tell you, that hide of theirs was tough to penetrate. In the end, Beverly killed the larger of the two using a lance. Jack finished the smaller one by getting in under its soft underbelly. Its hide is somewhere back in Wincaster. Perhaps, once this war is over, you'd like to go and see it?"

"You kept the hide?"

"Not me, no, but Lord Arnim did. He thought it might make a nice suit of armour one day, but I don't believe he ever found someone willing to do the smithing."

"Remarkable," said Kasri. "I've seen Beverly in battle, but I had no idea she'd taken on a drake! And you say Gerald helped? The same Gerald who is the marshal?"

Hayley nodded. "Of course, he wasn't the marshal back then, but yes. He actually put himself in harm's way to give Beverly time to ready her charge."

"You Mercerians are a remarkable people. We have our own heroes, but I've never heard of so many brave souls serving one queen all at the same time."

"And I knew Gerald long before then," said Herdwin. "Did I ever tell you the story of how I helped rescue them from the vile clutches of the evil Dark Queen?"

"No," said Kasri with a smile, "but it's a story I'd very much like to hear. Why don't we leave this dreadfully noisy place and find somewhere a little more secluded, then you can tell me all about it?"

TWENTY-FIVE

Betrayal

Gerald stepped out into the sunshine, only to sink up to his ankles in mud. He cursed as he pulled free, then made his way to the side of the road. Today was the first decent weather they'd had in almost a week, but it would likely be some time before the army could continue the advance. The march to Summersgate had been discussed for days on end, every possibility accounted for, yet still he felt nervous.

It wasn't that he was afraid of a siege. He had, after all, successfully taken Wincaster at the end of the civil war, but the threat of dragons loomed over everything. His saving grace was the presence of Dwarven arbalesters and Elven archers, both of which, he hoped, would be able to penetrate the thick scales of such a beast. He was reminded of the fight against the drakes back in Tivilton. Those creatures, lesser cousins to dragons, had proven a tough fight. Would dragons be any less so?

Even as the thought entered his head, he knew such an encounter would be far worse. Dragons could breathe fire. What could he possibly do to counter that?

He walked as he thought things through, determined to see how the men of his command were holding up. It had been a tough week for most of them, forced as they were to camp out in the fields north of Kinsley.

He noticed a wagon serving hot cider to a long line of warriors standing by, ready to spend their meagre coins on the treat. A woman ladled it out of a pot, one of many such camp followers eking out a living.

Gerald nodded his head in greeting as he passed by a trio of army wives hanging laundry out to dry, repeating the action a moment later as he watched a young woman playing with a small child.

He spotted the Guard Cavalry's pennant and altered his course, deter-mined to find out how Sir Preston's new command was doing. Less than halfway there, he halted, taken aback by the presence of Lady Jane Goodwin moving amongst the camp followers, much as he was, offering words of encouragement and prayer. He didn't object to the behaviour. Far from it, but he suddenly felt as if he were intruding on a private matter. Determined not to interfere, he steered away from her, but it was too late.

"Marshal?" she called out. "Is that you?"

He turned, his cheeks burning. "It is, madame. Sorry, I didn't mean to interrupt you."

She moved closer, a smile gracing her features. "Not at all. I was just chatting with some of the womenfolk. What brings you here today?"

"This is my army. I often come here to see to the well-being of my warriors. And their families," he hastily added.

"You are a rare breed," said Lady Jane.

"Rare? Do the generals of Weldwyn not care for their armies?"

"We have no generals, or rather, we had none. Only the royals possess the right to lead armies in Weldwyn."

"It used to be so in Merceria, but the times changed, and with it, our customs."

She looked around, taking in their surroundings. "And tell me," she said absently, "what do you think of this merry band of adventurers you assembled?"

"Adventurers?" said Gerald. "This is not a play, put on for the amusement of others. This is war!" He suddenly realized he'd overreacted and blushed profusely.

She, in turn, swivelled her gaze to look him directly in the eyes. "You are a passionate man. I am sorry if I gave offence."

"No, it's me. I'm the one who's sorry. You didn't deserve any of that."

"Sounds like things are not going well?"

"This weather's hampering our advance. I had high hopes of being within sight of the walls of Summersgate by now, but it seems it is not to be."

"But you'll get there eventually, won't you?"

"Of course, but not until the roads dry. The last thing I want is for everyone to spend their days digging wagons out of the mud." She was staring back at him, and he suddenly felt awkward. "You don't need to be burdened with any of this."

"A burden shared is less weight to carry."

He couldn't help but smile. "Wise words, but there are some things a marshal must bear alone."

"Then let me help you with those that CAN be shared."

"I'm not sure what those would be?"

"I can talk to the camp followers," she suggested, "and even some of the warriors, if need be, freeing you up for more pressing issues."

"Then how would I know how they fare?"

"I must admit I hadn't considered that. I suppose I could visit you at your headquarters to fill you in?"

"That would be… acceptable."

"When would you like me?"

Gerald blushed for the third time today. "Pardon me?"

"When would you like me to come to the tavern you use as your basis of command?"

"Oh… er… I suppose dinnertime would be the best. I shall have someone make you some food, of course."

"So we are to dine together on a regular basis?"

"I…" Words failed him.

Lady Jane merely smiled. "Good. Then I look forward to seeing you tonight."

"Tonight?"

"Why, yes. How else am I to fill you in on all I learn?"

She turned and walked back towards more camp followers, leaving him watching her departure. Was he seeing something more in her words? She seemed pleased with the prospect of dining with him, but was that because she felt she was contributing to their success, or she looked forward to enjoying his company? He shook his head, trying to dispel the emotions welling up inside him.

Later that week found him back at the tavern, hard at work, going over endless lists. The armies of old had lived off the land, stripping food from locals as they advanced, but Gerald hated the notion that an army must deprive others of food to survive. As a result, the Mercerians developed a supply system that brought food from home or purchased it locally. It meant constantly checking on supplies, for spoilage and theft were an ever-present threat, but it garnered goodwill wherever they went. In Norland, it convinced the locals that Merceria was liberating them, not conquering as they'd been told by their nobles.

Here in Weldwyn, Gerald led the forces that were attempting to take back the throne for Prince Alric. Unfortunately, Prince Tarak's army was not inclined to pay for their supplies, doing things the old way, despite the rumour he was exceptionally wealthy. As a result, the Mercerians fed the locals along with the army, adding to an already stretched supply system.

It galled him that the Kurathian prince could show so little regard for people, but he had to admit to little surprise at the thought. Had it not been for the influence of Baron Richard Fitzwilliam, he himself might've had similar ideas.

"Trouble?"

He glanced up to see Beverly. "Why would you think that?"

"I noticed you some time ago staring at that note."

"Oh, this?" he replied, lifting the note. "It's merely a tally of the last supply run. It's fine, by the way."

"Then what's on your mind?"

"Nothing. Why?"

"Come now," said the knight. "I've known you all my life. I can tell when something perplexes you." She lowered her voice. "Has this something to do with Lady Jane? I've noticed you two sharing meals over the last few nights."

He tried to bluff his way out of it. "No, of course not."

"Would you like to try that again, without the crimson cheeks?"

"All right, you've got me. I can't stop thinking about the woman."

"That's good, isn't it?"

"Is it?" he said. "The last thing I need right now is a distraction."

"On the contrary. It helps remind us of what we're fighting for. You're no different from the rest of us."

"I'm too old for that sort of thing."

"Are you? I would have said the same thing about my father, but then Albreda came back into his life." She took a seat. "That's not it, is it?"

He stared back, unable to share what was in his heart.

"You feel guilty," said Beverly. "That's only natural, but Meredith has been gone for decades. She'd want you to move on with your life. You deserve happiness."

"Perhaps, but how do I know when it's right?"

"You'll feel it in your heart."

"What? Like Lady Lindsey did when she tried to get her claws into me?"

"Admittedly, that was a mistake on our part. It wasn't fair for us to force you into that, but we only had your best interests at heart."

"I understand that, but it doesn't make any of this easier." He paused, gathering his thoughts. "I've spent a lifetime in battle, faced certain death dozens of times, yet the thought of opening my heart to someone again truly terrifies me."

"You opened it for Anna when you first met her; you can do so again. If this woman occupies your mind, then it's time you talked about it, with her, not with others."

"I've forgotten how to talk to a woman that way."

"Nonsense," said Beverly. "You're talking to me right now."

"Yes, but you're practically family."

"And proud I am to be considered so, but each of us must find our own path to happiness. Tell me this—do you enjoy her company?"

"I do," said Gerald.

"Then that's all you need concentrate on at present. Enjoy each other's company, and if something else develops, then so be it."

"You're the last person I ever expected to be giving me advice on such things."

"I know what it is to love and be loved," said Beverly. "Gerald, I can only imagine the hurt you must have felt when you lost your beloved Meredith, but the heart is like a muscle. It needs to be exercised, or it will wither away to nothing."

He nodded, too overcome with emotion to speak. Beverly sat with him in silence, waving away Sergeant Blackwood when he came to retrieve some notes.

Gerald sat back, his eyes locking with Beverly's. "Thank you," he said. "You've given me much to think about."

"I'm here whenever you need me, as is the queen, I'm sure."

"You know, I don't believe I could talk about this with Anna."

"Because she's the queen?"

"No, because she's still so young. I don't know that she would understand."

"Are you suggesting I'm old?" said Beverly with a wry smile.

"No, merely seasoned."

"I'll take that as a compliment."

He reached for his cup and took a sip, mulling things over.

"What will you do now?" asked Beverly.

"Heed your advice. I shall go and visit Lady Jane and talk to her. If nothing else, it will allow us to clear the air." He smiled, although it was obviously forced. "There's always the possibility I'm misreading her intentions, in which case I'm worrying over nothing."

"It's never nothing where the heart is concerned."

"More words of wisdom? You're starting to sound like what's his name."

"Califax?"

"Yes," said Gerald. "That's the fellow. Your father would be proud. Then again, he's never been anything but where you're concerned."

"And both of us have always been proud of you, Gerald." She reached out and placed her hand on his. "Saxnor be with you, my friend."

The house of Nigel Wharton was a modest affair. He'd made a name for himself as a barrel maker, although he'd given up the profession in his declining years in favour of his son. Nowadays, he arranged shipments to the villages and towns of Weldwyn, or at least he'd done so before the invasion. Since then, he and his wife made do with what they'd saved, the coins trickling through their fingers like so much rain.

With the Mercerians' arrival, things started to improve. First, was the sudden demand for barrels, a demand so high, he once more carved wood to keep up with their requests. He also rented a room out to a Weldwyn noble, the coins coming from one of the Queen of Merceria's retinue. Even still, he was surprised to answer his door only to come face to face with the Duke of Wincaster himself.

"Your Grace," Nigel said, bowing deeply. "You honour us with your presence."

"Please," said Gerald. "There's no need for such formalities. I'm here to speak with Lady Jane Goodwin. Is she in?"

"I'm afraid not, my lord, but we are expecting her return shortly. Would you like us to notify you when she arrives?"

"I hoped to talk to her straight away. Might I wait here for her?"

Nigel Wharton turned to take note of his messy abode. "We weren't expecting visitors, Your Grace. The place is a complete disaster at the moment."

"Very well. I'll return later." The duke turned, ready to leave.

"Perhaps," said Nigel, "you might consider waiting in Her Ladyship's room? That might be more fitting for one of your station?"

"I shouldn't like to intrude."

"Nonsense. I'm sure she'd be delighted at the prospect of entertaining guests."

"Very well. Lead on, and I shall follow."

The landlord led him up the stairs to the end of the hall. "Her room is right here," he said, extracting a key from his belt and opening the door.

The apartment was barely more than a single chamber, with a bed occupying a good portion of the floor space. In terms of furniture, there was little, save for a table, two chairs, and a wardrobe that looked like it had seen better days. Clothes had been hastily discarded onto the table, and he recognized the rags the barmaid had supplied some days ago.

"This will do fine. Thank you."

"You're most welcome, Your Grace, and if there's any other way we can be of assistance, call out, and we'll be happy to oblige."

"I doubt that will be necessary," said Gerald, "but I appreciate the offer." Nigel left the room.

Gerald took a seat and soon found his mind wandering. There was little in here to spark any interest, not too surprising considering how Lady Jane had been found in Kinsley. Still, he could sense her presence here as if her soul had made an indelible mark on these premises.

He turned back to the discarded clothes, cast aside much as she'd been when he found her in the alley. Then he spotted a piece of paper poking out from beneath. At first, he thought it a figment of his imagination, for where would she possibly have gotten ink and paper from? It took some moments for him to reason things out, for the landlord would obviously have access to such items.

His eyes once more perused the room's contents, but they kept returning to that bit of paper. Why in the name of Saxnor would she need such a thing? Was she writing to someone, and if so, how did she hope for it to be delivered? He kept telling himself this was none of his business, but there it sat, staring at him.

He tried to distract himself, to think about military matters, but soon found it impossible to think of anything but her. Finally, he stood, moving closer to the offending paper. If it was a letter, he would find someone to deliver it, no matter the cost.

Gerald reached for it but paused, not wishing to invade her privacy. He pulled his hand away quickly, only to dislodge the garments, causing them to fall to the floor.

He stooped, picking them up, intending to return them to the table, but as he turned to place them, he saw the writing:

300 Footmen, 100 archers, 200 assorted horsemen...

There was more, but he stopped, a tightness gripping his chest. Gerald wanted desperately to pretend he hadn't seen it, but the damage was done. He felt sadness descend, but he knew he must do his duty. Lifting the page, he perused the rest. It detailed out the army's numbers—his army—and he knew, without a doubt, that they had been betrayed once more.

He'd allowed himself to be tricked into giving this woman free rein, even going so far as to convince himself she had feelings for him. Now, she had a detailed account of the warriors under his command. This was a betrayal of the worst kind. He slumped down into the chair, his eyes glued to the letter he held in a deathlike grip.

He wasn't sure how long he sat there, his mind in turmoil, but then he heard sounds coming from downstairs. By the muffled voices and the tread of feet on the steps drawing ever closer, he knew Lady Jane had arrived.

TWENTY-SIX

Melethandil

SPRING 966 MC

K asri advanced past the warriors scattered around the top of the cliff. "Your rangers are most efficient," she said, pausing at the quarry's edge, gazing into its depths. "They're definitely up to something down there."

Hayley was soon beside her, crouching to conceal her presence while her wolf pup, Gryph, sniffed at the air. "How many people would you say are down there?"

"Dozens, and note the strange spears? I've never seen their like."

Revi came up beside them. "Let's have a closer look, shall we?" He closed his eyes, calling upon his magic to link with his familiar.

Hayley, alarmed by his closeness to the edge, pulled him back, avoiding his arms as he leaned left and right, deep in the throes of his spell. His movements ceased, replaced by the gentle swaying that was common as he looked through the eyes of Shellbreaker.

"I'm swooping down to take a better look," said Revi.

The Black Coaster flew overhead, its wings silent in the early morning light. Down below, men advanced towards one of the caves, long spears with what looked like blades rather than tips held before them.

"They remind me of our poleaxes," said Kasri, "but much, much longer. Why in the name of the Gods would they need such length? They must be challenging to wield."

"There's something in the cave," said Revi. "Shellbreaker can smell it. I'm going to get closer." He ducked his head as if swooping, a movement that almost caused Hayley to break out in a fit of giggles. It wasn't that she hadn't seen it all before. Still, when the Life Mage was looking through his familiar's eyes, he darted his head around like a chicken, a sight she still found quite entertaining.

"Sulphur," he said unexpectedly. "Shellbreaker won't go any closer."

"I thought you controlled him?" said Kasri.

"We share consciousness, but I would not put him in danger. I'm afraid if we want to know more, we are the ones who must get closer."

"I'll take my Dwarves along the edge to the north. There's a ramp over there they can use. In the meantime, I would suggest you line the edge here with the rangers. Gundar knows we could certainly use the extra help."

"That's it?" said Revi. "All you intend to do is march down there and attack?"

"Of course. Why else would we be here?"

"We still don't know what's in the cave."

"Don't we?" said Kasri. "You said that bird of yours smelled sulphur. If that doesn't signify a dragon, I don't know what does?"

"That must be why they have those long poles," said Hayley. "It's likely the only thing that would penetrate a dragon's scales."

"Agreed, and it would likely make quick work of our armour as well."

"Should we reconsider our plan?" said the mage.

"Not at all. Once my Dwarves get within the reach of those things, they'll be useless. In any event, they are used to controlling a dragon; that's a far cry from using them in combat against seasoned warriors."

"So you're suggesting they're—what? Handlers?"

"If that's what you want to call them, then yes. Not so different from those who control your mastiffs, when you think of it, only on a larger scale."

"There's what looks like a gigantic cage over there," said Hayley, "but it's been disassembled. I shudder to imagine how large its occupant was."

"It would have taken a large team of horses to transport that thing here. Wouldn't it have been far easier for the creature to simply fly to the quarry?"

"An interesting observation," said Revi, "but I'm afraid we'll learn little more unless we take more direct action. I propose Kasri takes her Dwarves down the ramp. As they near the bottom, your rangers can let off a volley or two of arrows. That ought to disrupt any organized defence rather effectively."

"And if the dragon comes out?" asked Hayley.

Kasri shrugged. "Then we're just not meant to survive."

"That's a bit fatalistic, isn't it?"

"If we die, we die. At least we would do so having seen a real, live dragon."

"Personally," said Hayley, "I'd like to live a little longer."

Kasri donned her helmet, the fake beard making her look like any other Dwarven warrior. "Well," she said, her voice echoing slightly, "one thing's for certain, we can't stand around here all day doing nothing." She barked out orders in the Dwarven tongue, and her Hearth Guard began marching north towards the top of the ramp.

"She'll be fine," said Revi, his gaze flitting to Hayley.

"How can you be so sure?"

He smiled. "Simple. You're our lucky charm."

"I thought I was YOUR lucky charm?"

"You are, but as I see it, my luck is also our luck. Now, come. Get your rangers in position before the enemy can react."

Hayley gave the command, and the archers took a position along the quarry's edge. The sudden presence of fifty-odd bowmen formed in line was cause for alarm, and down in the quarry, men yelled, pointing up towards the warriors of Merceria.

"Draw," said Hayley. The rangers drew back their bowstrings and took aim.

"Pick your targets. Loose in your own time."

Arrows flew at the enemy, felling three and wounding four. More volleys followed, causing panic amongst their targets. Men ran in all directions, many discarding their long spears to aid in their escape.

Hayley noticed a smaller cave off to their left, iron bars holding back a group of individuals. "It appears they have prisoners."

"Likely more captured warriors," said Revi. "That group Kasri intercepted can't be the only ones they're utilizing."

The Dwarves of Ironcliff began descending the ramp, their tightly packed ranks marching in step, their footfalls echoing off the quarry walls. An impressive sight, made all the more so by their plate armour.

At least one Kurathian fell to his death after trying to scale the opposite wall in a bid to escape. A small group, no more than a dozen, attempted to form a defensive line. However, as the Hearth Guard drew within a few paces, they broke, many tossing their weapons to the ground and offering surrender.

Arrows picked off a few more. "Cease," called out Hayley. "We'll follow the Hearth Guard down into the pit."

She jogged along the edge of the quarry, Gryph loping along beside her. Revi remained where he was for a moment longer, then broke the connection with his familiar and followed.

. . .

Kasri halted her troops, expecting at least a token resistance, but none had been forthcoming. Instead, dozens of unarmed men waited to be taken into custody.

She dispatched warriors to gather weapons while others herded the prisoners together. From a small cave with a barred entrance, came calls in the common tongue of Weldwyn and Merceria. It took but a moment to smash the padlock, and then the door was opened, releasing those held within.

"Who are you?" Kasri asked.

One man stood a head taller than the rest. "We are men of Weldwyn," he replied, "taken after the fall of Summersgate and pressed into service to perform manual labour."

"Let me guess," she said. "You were widening a cave?"

"Yes. Then they brought that foul beast here, and we've been locked up ever since."

"A dragon?"

"If that's what you call it."

She noted the hesitation in his voice. "What else would we call it? Is it a dragon or not?"

"I don't know," he said. "What do you call a dragon with no wings?"

"No wings?" The words sank in. "Ah, that explains the massive cage." Kasri noticed Hayley's approach and walked over. "I'm afraid we're in for a bit of a disappointment."

"Oh?"

"It's not a dragon, merely a drake, although admittedly, a large one if that cage is any indication."

"And you think a drake would accept being caged up like that?"

"It would if it was under the effects of some type of concoction. All things considered, it would have to be, else its thrashing around would wreak havoc with whatever wagons they used."

"I'll have the rangers scour the immediate area. I suspect there's a camp up top somewhere, likely to the west where we haven't searched."

"It's not a drake!" called out Revi. "Remember the smell of sulphur?"

"But it has no wings," said Kasri. "That makes it a drake."

"Does it? I don't claim to be an expert in such things, but surely we cannot dismiss the possibility it's an aberration of some kind. Perhaps a defect at birth that left it flightless?"

"Then why bring it here?" said Hayley.

"Let's put it this way," said the mage. "If you lost an arm, could you still bear a healthy child?"

"I suppose I hadn't considered that possibility," said Kasri. "All right, so we have a crippled dragon of some sort. What's the next step?"

"You tell me. You're the one who wanted to come here in the first place."

"Hold on a moment," said Hayley. "Could your magic help it?"

"Help it?" said Revi. "Why in the name of Saxnor would we want to help it? The last thing we need is another dragon flying around, burning everything to cinders."

"Dragons are intelligent. What if we could reason with it?"

"Are you honestly suggesting we talk to that thing?"

"She has a point," said Kasri. "There are even rumours they can use magic."

"And do you speak dragon?" asked the mage.

"I speak Dwarvish. That should be close enough."

"I'm not sure I follow?"

"According to our ancient myths, a dragon taught the first races to speak. I don't know if that's true or not, but it would help explain why the ancient language of the Dwarves, Orcs, and Elves are so similar."

"And if it's not true?" asked Hayley.

"Then we waste a little time."

"Yes," said Revi. "With the added chance of getting burned to a crisp."

"I'm open to other suggestions? What do you think, Hayley?"

"It's worth a try."

"Good," said the Dwarf. "Then it's settled. Now, I suggest the rest of you keep well back, just in case this doesn't go as we hope."

They posted a dozen rangers to keep watch on the cave, then used the remainder to herd the prisoners into the newly vacated prison. They sent the released Weldwyn warriors out of the quarry, the better to ensure their safety. The Hearth Guard remained, ready to fight should it prove necessary.

Hayley even tried to send Gryph off, but the wolf proved unwilling to leave her side. She was trying to usher him away when he suddenly flattened his ears. Her attention immediately turned to the large cave. "Something's stirring."

Moments later, a large rumble echoed through the quarry. Rocks dislodged from the side, tumbling to the bottom, and then a nose poked out from the darkness. The beast was massive, far more so than the Tivilton drakes. Hayley was overcome with a desire to flee but held her ground.

The head emerged, a flattened snout topped with two protruding eyes and a crest running down its snakelike neck.

Rangers raised their bows. "Hold!" Hayley ordered.

There could be little doubt that this was a dragon, for when the bulk of the creature emerged, its four massive legs shook the ground. Then she spotted the terrible scarring where the wings should be. This creature was no aberration—someone had deliberately cut the wings from its back! It was hard to fathom, for who could possibly conceive of the idea, let alone see it to fruition? Was she then to believe that the mighty creature would sit idly by and allow this terrible mutilation?

The dragon stood there, its head whipping back and forth, its nostrils flaring. The smell of sulphur was everywhere, causing many to cough. Gryph let out a howl that echoed off the quarry walls.

Kasri stood firm. The creature before her was a beast of legends, the stuff of myths, yet here she was, face to face with one. Its head reared up, then the neck bent, allowing it to gaze down at her. Time seemed to stand still until the head moved closer, and then the creature's nose was less than an arm's reach away. It sniffed once before a deep voice rumbled forth, vibrating the very air with the language of the ancient races.

"*What have we here?*" it asked.

"*I am Kasri Ironheart,*" she replied, her voice unwavering. "*A warrior of Ironcliff. By what name are you known, oh great and wonderful serpent?*"

"*I am Melethandil the Great, conqueror of Rahad and scourge of the Isles.*"

"*Why do you serve the Kurathian prince? You deserve to live free amongst the mountains as did the dragons of old.*"

"*I was born into captivity many centuries ago. I have known nothing else.*"

"*Then come with me to the Thunder Mountains, where you can live out your life in peace.*"

"*And how would I do that? Are you suggesting I fly to these mountains? I no longer possess the power of flight. That gift was taken from me by my master.*"

"*Why?*" called out Hayley.

Melethandil swung her head in the ranger's direction, her penetrating gaze intimidating.

"*What could possibly merit this travesty?*" Hayley persisted.

"*How is it you speak the language of the ancients?*"

"*I am fluent in the Orcish tongue, not too different from your own.*"

"*Strange it is to see the mountain folk standing beside Humans and Orcs.*"

"*Please,*" said Hayley, "*we seek only to learn of how you came to be here.*"

"*Long have the Princes of the Isles fought amongst themselves. I destroyed the fortress of Rahad only to return to find my own home attacked in my absence. Three dragonets they killed, three precious hatchlings who no longer bless the world of the living. The burden was too heavy to shoulder. I lashed out in my grief, and in return, was chained and imprisoned, my wings cut to keep me from escaping.*"

"*And they brought you here?*"

"*My cruel master refused to leave me behind. He thought I might eventually*" *overcome my sorrow and once more bring life to this world, but I swore never again to put myself in that position."*

"But wouldn't they need to breed you with another dragon?"

Melethandil withdrew her head, raising it on high once more. "*Is that how you think it works? We dragons do not need others to birth young. Be gone, and I will spare your life. Remain, and I shall burn you to ash.*"

"What if we healed you?" said Hayley, desperate for a resolution.

Once more, the eyes bore into her, seeking her soul. "*You have such power?*"

"*No, but our Life Mage, Revi Bloom, does.*" She turned her head, seeking him out. "Revi, come closer," she called out in the common tongue.

"Why? What are you talking about?"

"You'd know if you ever bothered to learn Dwarf or Orc, for that matter."

"I'm far too busy with my studies for such things."

"Then cast your spell of tongues, but hurry, time is of the essence."

Revi stepped forward, looking frail against the massive dragon.

"*He's going to cast a spell so he can understand you,*" explained Hayley, reverting once more to Orcish.

The casting began, and then the familiar buzz as magic was released.

"*There,*" said Revi, now speaking the ancient tongue. "*Much better. Now, what have I missed?*"

"*This is Melethandil. Her wings were cut off. Can you help her?*"

"*You mean with a spell of regeneration? Of course, but it would take many days if not weeks to complete treatment on a creature of such size.*"

The great beast brought its muzzle close to Revi Bloom. "*Heal my wings, and I shall be forever in your debt.*"

"*I will heal you,*" he replied, "*but I ask nothing in return save that you never again attack our people.*"

Melethandil pondered the request, lifting her head once more to gaze over all assembled before her. "*I shall do better than that. Give me back my wings, and I shall help you defeat the forces of my former master. It is the least I can do in retaliation for my treatment.*"

"*And then?*"

"*Then I shall travel with Kasri Ironheart back to these Thunder Mountains she speaks of and dwell there forevermore.*"

Hayley turned to her rangers and spoke in the common tongue. "Put down your bows. There will be no further bloodshed this day."

"*I will need to get closer,*" said Revi.

"*How much closer?*" asked the dragon.

"*Close enough to touch you for the spell to work.*"

"I am no longer in the habit of letting mages so close, for they used that method to control me."

"Then I shall stand before you," said Kasri. *"If he harms you in any way, you may see fit to kill me in revenge."*

"You would do that for a Human?"

"I would. We are comrades in arms. I trust these Mercerians with my life."

"Very well," said Melethandil. *"You may approach."*

Revi drew closer, then called upon the words of power once again. His hands glowed with a deep orange hue as he pressed his fingers to the creature's back, the colour bleeding into the scales, concentrating on the stubs that formerly anchored the wings. Much to his surprise, small bones sprouted forth, a leathery coating covering them. It looked almost ludicrous, as if a bat's tiny wings had been placed upon the dragon's back.

"It is done," he announced. *"Although it will take many more such treatments. I'm afraid I can do no more for you this day. We must allow the magic to do its work."*

The embryonic wings wiggled slightly, and then the dragon spoke one final time, its voice echoing off the walls once more. *"Then I shall bide my time until I can exact my revenge."*

TWENTY-SEVEN

Incarceration

SPRING 966 MC

L ady Jane wore a puzzled look as she opened the door.

"Your Grace? This is an unexpected surprise." Her welcoming smile froze on her face as she noticed his look of displeasure, then her gaze beheld the note clutched firmly in his hand. Tears sprang to her eyes, and she knew, at that moment, her life was forfeit.

"Please," she pleaded. "Let me explain?"

"By all means," said the marshal. "Do tell me why you compiled a list of all our warriors."

"I had no choice."

He glanced around the room. "I see no one here forcing you to do anything. Quite the opposite, in fact. Since your arrival, we've shown you nothing but courtesy and respect. And you reward us with this?" He brandished the note.

She tried to compose herself, but her nerves got the better of her. Instead of answering, she slumped to the floor, wallowing in her misery.

He stood, crossing the room to stare down at her. "Come now. Your theatrics will do you little good."

Jane looked up, her tear-stained face pale and strained. "I didn't tell you the entire truth when I said I fled Summersgate."

"Clearly."

"I wanted to, I really did, but I feared you'd have me executed."

"For spying?"

She nodded.

He held out his hand. "Here. Come sit and tell me your story before I pass judgement. I would have the truth of it."

She took his hand and rose, allowing him to guide her to the chair. There she sat, dabbing at her eyes with the sleeve of her dress.

"As you know, my name is Lady Jane Goodwin, and as I told you, my husband died some years ago, leaving me to raise our son, James. All of that was true. My reasons for escaping the capital, however, are far more complicated."

"Go on."

"I told you my son was being watched—that much is true. What I didn't tell you was the hold they possess over him. His very life hangs in the balance unless I send them the information they seek."

"The information held within this note?"

"Indeed," said Lady Jane. "You've shown me nothing but kindness, yet I return your generosity with deceit and half-truths."

"How were you to send word?"

"The man I was supposed to hand this information to has yet to reveal himself. I can only assume he will approach me at some point in the future. I didn't expect to find Mercerians here in Kinsley."

"If not us, then who?" asked the marshal.

"I was told a small group supported a rebellion against the High Queen, supposedly led by Prince Alric of Weldwyn."

"Why didn't you come to me for help?"

"And tell you I was spying for the enemy? You would have simply clapped me in irons."

"If that's what you believe, then you don't know me."

"A burden I shall bear till my last breath."

"Who gave you the command to travel here?"

"My son, James. Originally, he was supposed to come, but he's been working at building the resistance in Summersgate."

"I find that difficult to believe."

"Why would you say something like that? Do you believe I'm making this up as I go?"

"No," said Gerald, "but just because someone tells you something doesn't mean it's the truth."

"What are you insinuating?"

He stared down at her, considering his words carefully. "Either he's being watched, or he's trying to raise a rebellion. I think the likelihood of both occurring would be terribly small, don't you?"

"I'm afraid I still don't understand?"

"If I suspected someone of urging on a rebellion, they'd be in irons before nightfall, yet somehow your son is still at large? Either he's not being watched, as he claims, or he's not trying to raise a rebellion. Tell me, has he much experience when it comes to battle?"

"None whatsoever. In that regard, he is much like his father."

"And you passed on no other letters?"

"No. As I said, no one has yet contacted me."

The marshal moved to the bed and took a seat. "You've given me much to think on."

"I'm truly sorry, but I felt I had little choice in the matter."

"So you say, yet I can't overlook this. You have actively worked against the Crown… and against me." He choked up as he spoke, necessitating a moment to gather himself.

She watched the tears forming in his eyes and knew she'd made the worst mistake of her life. "I never meant to cause harm," she said, "especially to you, Gerald. Can you ever find it in your heart to forgive me?"

"I wish I could." He stood. "You shall be placed under arrest pending a full investigation. I will inform Her Majesty of your actions, and I doubt she will be lenient. Yours is not the first act of treachery we've had to deal with, nor, I suspect, will it be the last."

She rose, trying to gather her composure. "Very well, I understand completely. Should I wait for your soldiers to come and arrest me, or shall I let you lead me to my incarceration?"

He cleared his throat. "I will take you."

"Very well. Then lead on, Marshal, and I shall trust myself to Mercerian justice."

Tempus set his massive head on Gerald's knee, staring up at him with a soulful look.

"He senses your heartache," said Anna. "He's always been good at knowing when he's needed."

"So he has," Gerald replied. "If only Humans were as easy to understand as dogs." He snagged a sausage from the table and passed it to the great mastiff. Tempus took it gently despite his size, then removed his head from where it lay and wolfed it down.

"You and he have a similar taste in food."

"That's nothing new. I've never seen him refuse a sausage."

"I could say the same for you, yet today, you've eaten little. You can't pretend to have breakfast if all you're doing is giving it away. Not that Tempus will object, of course."

She lifted a piece of toast and smeared on some jam. "What do we know about who's behind this?"

"Unfortunately," said Gerald, "nothing. She claims to have no idea who her contact is."

Anna took a bite. "And you say she was tricked into this?"

"So she claims. Though once again, there's no proof whether she's telling the truth or simply spinning another tale."

"I had thought these matters settled once we uncovered Lady Lindsey."

"Indeed, but I'm afraid this one may be my fault."

"How so?"

"I befriended her, took her to the tavern we use as our base. It would've been easy enough to find the information she sought there."

"Numbers that could just as easily be determined by counting our warriors. It's not as if we're hiding any behind the trees."

Gerald stiffened. "Are you explaining away her actions?"

"No, but it's obvious this woman's actions deeply wounded you. Have you feelings for her?"

"I would be lying if I said otherwise. It's precisely the reason I can't judge her crime. In fact, looking at how things turned out, perhaps I'm no longer fit to command the army?"

"Nonsense. Everyone makes mistakes."

"This one could cost us the war."

"You said she hasn't passed on the information. That means the enemy still lacks that which they seek."

"I'm not sure how that helps us."

"It might," said Anna. "One might even say it has given us a rather unique opportunity."

"To punish a spy?"

"No, to feed false information to the enemy. Hopefully, even lure them into a trap, if we can manage it."

"Are you sure you want to trust someone who was caught in the midst of spying on us?"

"You know her best. What do you think?"

He cast his gaze down. "Part of me would like to believe she can be entrusted with such a task."

"And the other part?"

"Wants her punished for her crimes."

"Is this Gerald the marshal talking, or the man?"

"What's that supposed to mean?"

"It means you feel betrayed, which is only natural, considering what's happened, but I need you to look at this with the eyes of my marshal, not a heartbroken soul. I know this is difficult for you, but there's too much at stake."

He nodded, although his gaze remained downcast. "You're right. I must look at this more objectively."

"Good. Now, first of all, do you believe this story of hers?"

"It would help if we had some way of checking up on this son of hers."

"That doesn't seem likely, considering our present circumstances."

"What about Prince Alric?" Gerald asked. "He might be able to give us some idea of the man's background?"

"I shall have Kraloch send word, but unless I miss my guess, he's rather busy assaulting Southport right about now. Once he's done there, he will bring his army north, joining us for the attack on Summersgate."

"Yes, I know. It was my strategy, remember?"

Anna softened her features. "I know, but you're emotional right now and thinking with your heart, not your head. Should I have Beverly deal with Lady Jane?"

"No," said Gerald. "It's my mess. I'll clean it up."

She leaned forward, placing her hand on his. "I realize how much this must hurt, Gerald, and my heart goes out to you. You've always been there for me. I want you to know I'm always available if you need to talk."

He finally looked up, the sadness in his eyes heartbreaking. "I know, and I thank you for that. I suppose I've always had scars from Meredith's death, but this feels like all the old wounds have been ripped wide open again."

"How do you want to proceed? Shall we try her for treason?"

"We can't," said Gerald. "She's not Mercerian."

"But she acted against Alric, and one day he'll be the new King of Weldwyn."

"You know as well as I that we have no right to do such a thing. Your reign is built on the rule of law. We cannot simply ignore that."

"Then there is little option other than to watch her closely. Should someone try to contact her, we shall know she speaks the truth."

"And if they don't?"

"That makes things a tad more complicated. Let me ask you this: deep down, do you trust her version of events?"

"Which version? Her original story of fleeing Summersgate, or her claims of being forced to spy on us?"

"Could there be truth in both versions?"

He was at a loss for words. He had not considered it, yet he knew the truth must be in there somewhere. "I wonder…" he said, his voice trailing off.

"Care to share your thoughts?"

"It occurs to me this whole thing might have been orchestrated without her knowledge."

"But you found her with a list of our troops?"

"I did, and she honestly believes she had no choice in the matter, but think about that for a moment."

"I'm not sure what you're suggesting," said Anna.

"If you were going to send someone to spy on the enemy, wouldn't you make sure they knew who to pass information to?"

"That would make sense. Are you suggesting someone sent her here to be caught? What would be the point of that?"

"I haven't quite figured that out yet. Perhaps to make us all concerned about spies?"

"But we're already on the lookout, especially after Lady Lindsey's escapades."

"Ah, but we already determined her efforts were motivated by her own desire for power, not machinations of a foreign queen. What if this whole thing is meant to draw attention away from the actual spy?"

"So you're suggesting there's another individual out there reporting back to Brida?"

"It would be easy enough, wouldn't it? If you recall, Prince Cuthbert plotted to seize the Crown of Weldwyn, and it's undeniable that the Clans backed him."

"But Cuthbert is dead."

"Yes," said Gerald, "but he may have had other supporters we never caught."

"Agreed, but who would they support without Alric's brother?"

"Brida, of course. What else could they do? They already threw themselves in with the Clans. No one else would trust them."

"I admit it's an intriguing possibility. It might also explain Lady Jane's activities. Let's face it, from what we've seen, she's not exactly the most competent at hiding her actions."

Gerald cheered up at the thought, something that didn't escape Anna's eyes.

"Be careful, Gerald. This is no more than mere speculation at the moment."

"I know."

"And there is still the problem of a spy amongst us."

"It doesn't matter anymore."

"What makes you say that?"

"We're about to march on Summersgate. Brida already knows we're coming. I doubt knowing our numbers will make much of a difference. Of course, they still have a dragon or two they can use against us."

Anna smiled. "Yes, about that. It appears we will soon have the services of one of our own."

"You heard back from Hayley?"

"I have. She and Kasri liberated one down at the quarry."

"Liberated?"

"It was crippled, but Revi has been using his magic to heal her."

"Her? It's a female dragon?"

"So it would appear."

"How big is it?"

"Immense, possibly even as large as the one that reduced the Royal Palace in Summersgate. You must give some thought as to how we might best utilize her."

"I must admit," said Gerald. "I know little of dragons. Of course, I've heard the legends, but such tales always lack the important details. Can we trust her?"

"Kasri definitely believes so. She's invited Melethandil to live amongst the mountains of her people once this campaign is over."

"Very well. I'll give it some thought. I assume she can fly?"

"Not yet. Her wings were removed, but Revi assures me they're making progress in regenerating them."

"And she breathes fire?"

"So I'm led to believe."

"How do we control her in battle?"

"That remains to be determined," said Anna. "In the meantime, however, you need to deal with Lady Jane. We must put this behind us so you can concentrate on taking the capital."

"I will. I promise."

"Good. Now, I have other things to attend to."

Gerald stood. "Of course."

Gerald approached the jail late in the evening. Kinsley was used to locking up drunks and miscreants, but dealing with a noble was an altogether different experience. Added to the confusion was the presence of Royal Guards to keep an eye on her.

Captain Wainwright greeted him as he stepped inside. The archer, usually commanding the Wincaster bowmen, sat at a table, partaking of a meal, but stood as soon as the marshal entered.

"Your Grace. I wasn't expecting visitors?"

"I came to talk to Lady Jane. Would you give us some privacy, please?"

"Of course, sir." Wainwright ordered the guards outside, ensuring he was the last out the door and closing it behind him.

Gerald moved closer to the bars, his gaze taking in his surroundings. The building was little more than a rectangular room, iron bars marking off one corner. Inside was a bed, along with a bucket for Human waste—not the type of lodgings a noble would be used to. Lady Jane bore her incarceration with dignity, rising as he came closer.

"Your Grace," she said, giving an awkward curtsy in the Weldwyn style. "You honour me with your presence."

"Please," said Gerald, "let's dispense with all this formality, shall we? We need to talk."

"It appears I have little choice in the matter, although I do welcome the company."

Gerald returned to Captain Wainwright's desk, dragging the chair over to the bars. "Please," he said. "Sit and make yourself comfortable."

She lowered herself onto the edge of the bed, her attention focused solely on him. Their eyes met, and for a moment at least, no words passed between them.

"You wanted to speak with me?" she prompted.

"I did... that is, I do. I've been thinking about your situation here. In truth, I have been able to think of little else. I'm torn between my duty to my queen and my own desire to be in your presence."

Lady Jane blushed. "I... feel the same way. I know what I did was wrong but—"

Gerald held up his hand. "No, please, let me continue." He paused to gather his thoughts. "Who was it that sent you here?"

"I told you, the High Queen."

"In person?"

"No, of course not. Why? What are you suggesting?"

"That you are as much a victim in all of this as are we."

Jane shook her head. "No, it couldn't be. My son told me of his plight."

"Yes, about that. You said he was concerned about being arrested?"

"Yes. He told me Brida's agents were watching him."

"I find that difficult to believe."

"That they should have concerns about his loyalty?"

"No," said Gerald. "That she wouldn't just arrest him if she suspected he plotted against her. In my experience, Brida is not one to use subtlety and definitely not the type to worry about such things as proof."

"But why would James lie?"

"Why, indeed? Tell me, is your son a loving individual?"

"I..." Her voice trailed off, leaving Gerald with no doubt as to the answer. "He can be distant at times, it's true, but I know, in his heart, he would wish me no harm."

"Is it possible he wanted you out of the way?"

"To what end?"

"Only he could tell us that."

"Perhaps he only sought to send me to safety?"

"Then why tell you to spy? Another thing that's been troubling me is how you got out of the city."

"I had a pass. James arranged—" Her voice caught in her throat. Tears welled up as she realized her own flesh and blood was working with the enemy.

Gerald nodded, although there was no pleasure in it. "My guess is that only a Royal Pass would allow someone to leave—it's certainly how we'd do things in Merceria. We heard rumours that Brida gathered up all the Weldwyn nobles she could lay her hands on. I think it noteworthy that your son was not amongst them."

He gave her a moment, continuing only when she finally looked up, her eyes red, tears streaking her face.

"Tell me of your son, James. What was he like growing up?"

"He was my only joy in life. My marriage was arranged, you see, and once James was born, my husband was inattentive. Admittedly, I doted on my son, but as he grew older, he became more distant, taking after his father, I suppose."

"Was he a loyal subject of King Leofric?"

"He never spoke of such things in my presence. He used to say it was unbefitting a woman to worry."

"Did he ever talk to you of military matters?"

"No. Never."

"Strange, then, that he would ask you to report on an army?"

Once more, her head went down. "I'm a fool."

"No, you acted out of love for your son. Understandable, in these trying times. It was not your fault he betrayed you."

"Wasn't it? I raised him. Who else would be to blame?"

Gerald turned. "Guards!"

Captain Wainwright returned, along with two other warriors. "Your Grace?"

"Release Lady Jane. She is no longer a prisoner."

TWENTY-EIGHT

Conflict

SPRING 966 MC

"So, we are agreed?" Brida looked at the other Clan Chiefs, at least the ones brave enough to make this pact.

"Yes," said Warnoch. "Then, if Kythelia does not accede to our demands, we'll move on the Dome."

"I still believe this a mistake," said Conner. "Confronting her will only alert her to our opposition."

"What other choice is there? Especially with those Elves of hers within the city."

Rurik grunted. "Timidity serves no one but the weak. If you're too afraid to act, then you should give up your position as chief!"

"I'm no coward," replied Conner. "In this, I shall follow the majority's wishes, even though I believe it wrong."

"Good," said Erlach. "Then it's decided. We'll confront this Elf queen and assert our dominance as we should've when she first arrived. Our warriors took this city, not hers, so it is our right to rule." He turned his gaze towards Calindre, who had remained quiet until now. "What think you?"

"It's a gamble," she replied, "but then again, what in this life isn't? The question is where and when? Do we invite her here, to our council chambers, or do we go to the Dome and face her in her own domain?"

"I think," said Brida, "we shall summon her here. If we are to show our dominance over her, then let that start from the very beginning."

"Bit late for that," offered Warnoch. "You should've done so right from the beginning, back in the Clanholdings when her emissary approached us. We could have avoided this entire debacle."

Brida fumed. "I don't recall you objecting at the time. Correct me if I'm wrong, but weren't you there along with the rest of us?"

"You know full well I was, but what was I to do? Tarak murdered people in your name, I might add, something YOU eventually must answer for."

"Please," urged Conner. "Can we not all agree to get along for a while? This constant bickering can only weaken us. Instead, let us band together in unanimous consent."

Warnoch snickered. "Unanimous, is it?" He swept his gaze over the room in an exaggerated manner. "I don't see the rest of the Clan Chiefs here."

"We are the ones who count," said Erlach, "as well you know."

"You mean the only ones who can be trusted not to talk of this to Kythelia!"

"I believe my words spoke for themselves."

Conner sighed. "We're getting off topic again!"

"He's right," said Brida. "Now, let us get to the details of it, shall we?"

"Very well," said Warnoch. "How do you see this unfolding?"

"We send word for her to attend us."

"Brilliant," said Erlach. "I hardly saw that coming!"

"Be quiet," snapped Calindre. "We are playing with fire here. Do you wish to be burned?" She paused, giving everyone a look of disgust. "There, that's better. Now, please continue, Brida."

"As I said, we send word we wish to speak with her. The letter will say nothing of our ultimate intentions, merely our desire for a face-to-face meeting of the minds. Naturally, warriors will be standing by in case things go badly."

"How many warriors?" asked Warnoch. "And from which Clan shall they be chosen?"

"Does it matter?"

"It does to me, and I suspect, to the others here as well. For all we know, once you dispatch Kythelia, you could turn on the rest of us."

"And why would I do that? I am already High Queen." She leaned in closer to stare at the Clan Chief of Drakewell. "Do you believe me unsuitable for the role?"

Warnoch paled. "No, of course not, but you must admit the history of our Clans has been a bloody affair. It wouldn't be the first time Clans turned against each other."

"And likely, won't be the last," muttered Erlach.

"Yes," said Conner. "We've had our differences in the past, but what's done is done. Let us not hold the actions of our ancestors as something to emulate. The matter before us is ridding ourselves of this Elven menace.

Once that's out of the way, we'll have all the time we want to sort out our differences."

"He's right," said Calindre. "Although I'm loathe to admit it, we must put our differences aside, if only for the moment."

"Very well," said Erlach. "But I believe we should have a pretext on which to summon this Elf queen."

"Perhaps," suggested Warnoch, "we could tell her we'd all like to pledge our allegiance to her?"

"That wouldn't work," said Conner. "If it were true, we would be going to her, not the other way around."

"Then let us take the fight to her."

"And try to kill her in her lair? Are you mad?"

"We need another excuse," said Conner. "Something that would intrigue her enough to entice her out of the Dome."

Erlach looked at Brida and smiled. "What about that brother of yours?"

"Lochlan?" said the High Queen. "What of him?"

"He's a scholar. Would he know some information that might be of use to her?"

"Like what?"

"I couldn't say, but there must be something?"

"It's worth looking into," said Calindre.

Brida had hoped to keep her brother out of harm's way, but confronting Kythelia was a risky manoeuvre. The more she thought about it, the more she began to see the wisdom in consulting him. With some sadness, she finally succumbed. "Very well. I shall talk to him."

"And the warriors?" asked Warnoch.

"Each of us here will contribute men to the task. Shall we say four each?"

"Twenty-four men in total? That'll be hard to conceal in this room."

"We'll tell her it's a guard in her honour," said Brida.

"And you think she'll believe that?"

"To be honest, likely not, but by the time she sees them, it'll be too late. They'll cut her down like a scythe through wheat."

"Aye," said Erlach. "I like the sound of that."

"Good," said Brida. "Now, let us look at the matter of when…"

Lochlan looked up from his book as his sister entered.

"What have you got there?" she asked.

"They found it in the rubble of the Palace—a book of Mercerian fables."

Brida snorted. "A story for children."

"Still," he countered, "it reveals a lot about the way the Mercerians think."

"How so?"

"Each story has a moral." He showed her a page. "This one here is most interesting. It's called 'The Mermaid of Colbridge'."

"How is it a book of Mercerian fables is found here in Weldwyn?"

"Apparently, a gift from Queen Anna to Princess Edwina."

"How in the Gods' name do you know that?"

Lochlan smiled. "Much as I would like to claim a superior intellect, the fact is there's an inscription in the front. Apparently, this book is one of the Mercerian queen's favourites."

"No wonder they're a race of degenerates."

"This book tells a vastly different story. As I said, it's a book of morals. The tales told within are a window into their souls."

"You place too much faith in written words."

"And you too little," he replied. "But you didn't come here to complain about my reading."

"No," said Brida. "I didn't."

"Then out with it. What do you want?"

"For you to apply that brain of yours to something useful for a change."

"Ah, now you have me intrigued. What, precisely, are you looking for?"

"We decided to make our move against Kythelia."

Lochlan paled. "I would not suggest it."

"You have little say in the matter. I am the ruler here, not you."

"Please, Brida. Heed my warning. I beg of you. You tangle with forces far beyond your understanding. She is a Necromancer; you have no idea of the power she commands."

"And you do? If so, tell me what it is I must fear. Otherwise, stand aside, and let me do what's right for our people."

"But you came to me for help. Make up your mind."

"I seek only information. As for the rest, well, you can leave that to the warriors amongst us."

"And precisely what information is it you seek?"

"Anything that might convince this Dark Queen to visit our council chambers."

"Not an easy question to answer. How much time do I have?"

"As long as it takes for me to eat my meal." She looked at a servant. "Well? What are you waiting for? Go and find me something to eat!" Her attention returned once more to her brother. "You've read more about Kythelia than anyone else here. What types of things would attract her attention?"

"I cannot say. She is an Elf. Her thoughts may well follow different paths than ours."

"Come now. She still lives a mortal life. Admittedly, there are some physical differences between Elves and Humans, but they still have hearts, don't they?"

"And brains," said Lochlan. "And that's what scares me."

"Explain yourself."

"We equate wisdom with age."

"And?"

"Amongst our own race, a man of, say, sixty years would be considered a wise man. How much more wisdom, then, would a man be able to accumulate if he lived to six hundred, or even six thousand?"

"Are you suggesting Elves live that long?"

"They are said to be immortal."

"Surely not?"

Lochlan kept his face neutral. "I do not say that in jest. There's ample reason to believe that no Elf ever dies of what we call a natural death."

"But weapons can still kill them, surely?"

"Most of them."

"Most? What's that supposed to mean?"

"When I returned from visiting Camrath, I brought back a large collection of books."

"I'm well aware. I've had people lugging them around for you for months."

"Yes. Well, I found some more references to Queen Kythelia."

"That say what?"

"It is said she can't be killed."

"That's ridiculous. Of course she can be killed."

"With all due respect, there are scholars who believe otherwise."

"But she's an Elf. Are you saying all Elves are impervious to weapons? And poison?"

"I can only relate what I read, but there are rumours she bathed in the blood of a dragon."

"And that made her invulnerable?"

Lochlan shrugged. "I suppose so. Let me see if I can remember the quote." He looked towards the ceiling, deep in thought.

"This is absurd," declared Brida.

"Ah yes, now I remember: 'No person, in all of Eiddenwerthe, can slay her.'"

"And this is based on her bathing in blood?"

"That's my assumption, although the two may not be related at all. Remember, she can call on dark magic. There may be a spell protecting her."

"This is all still mere speculation on the part of these scholars. Surely none of them sought to put their theories to the test?"

"No, of course not."

"Then there you have it. Kythelia created the myth herself to instill fear into others."

"It's not something I would take lightly."

"Can't you see those remarks were meant as jests?"

"I hardly think scholars would joke about such things."

"Nonsense. They are fables, no different from that book you hold."

"Kythelia is as real as you or I."

"Be that as it may, I still need a reason for her to come to the council chambers. Something to trick her into exposing herself."

"You play a dangerous game. The consequences, if you fail, are dire."

"Do you not think I know that? I am trying to save our people from a life of subjugation. Would you do any less for so noble a cause?"

"Noble? There is nothing noble in dying."

"Yet inaction could be the death of us all."

"Kythelia needs subjects," said Lochlan. "That alone would indicate she wants people alive."

"Perhaps, but how long until she turns her dark magic on us?"

"That is a question I cannot answer."

"Then at least tell me how we can lure her to us."

He thought it through carefully. Admittedly, it was difficult to separate myth and legend from history and fact, so how much truth was in the reports of these scholars? The question was impossible to answer.

"She is a queen," he said at last, "and has been so for thousands of years, if the records are accurate. Do not demand her presence. Instead, simply request it in as nice a way as possible."

"And you believe that will bring her to us?"

He shrugged. "It might. On the other hand, if she refuses, you lose nothing and may try something else."

"We waste our time," said Warnoch. "What else is there to discuss?"

"Much," replied Conner. "Or did you forget we still lack an excuse to lure the Elf queen here?"

"I forget nothing, but sitting around here all day will accomplish little. We must act while we still possess the upper hand."

The door opened, revealing Brida. "I see everyone has returned. Good. We can now complete our plans."

"You spoke with Lochlan?" asked Warnoch.

"Yes. He is of the opinion we are best served, not by demanding her presence, but by requesting it."

"Does that not make us look weak?" asked Rurik.

"What does it matter as long as she ends up dead?"

"She makes a good point," said Warnoch. "In the end, it doesn't matter how we accomplish our objectives, as long as we're successful."

The door flung open with a loud crash, startling everyone. Green-clad warriors stormed into the room, taking up positions surrounding the table, their swords drawn.

"What is the meaning of this?" demanded Brida.

The invaders remained silent behind their full helms. Footsteps echoed in the hall outside, and then Queen Kythelia entered, the Human woman, Margaret, following in her wake.

"Well, well," said the Dark Queen. "How convenient. You are all gathered together in one place, saving me considerable effort to round you up."

Brida opened her mouth to speak but was met with a withering glare. The very room grew oppressive as the Elf queen moved around, looking each in the eyes. All looked away, save for the High Queen of the Clans.

"Your time is up," said Kythelia. "I no longer require your services."

"Not true," Brida spat out. "The Humans of Weldwyn will never accept an Elf as their queen."

Kythelia wore a look of amusement. "You're right, of course, but that doesn't mean I need you."

"Who else could rule?"

"It just so happens I have someone." She stepped aside, revealing her companion. "Did you forget? I have Princess Margaret, rightful ruler of Merceria."

Brida stared, open-mouthed, for a moment before regaining her composure. "No, this is some type of trick. It has to be."

"I can assure you this is no ruse." She looked at Margaret and then nodded. The Human woman stepped closer, her gaze scanning over the Clan Chiefs.

"Which one?" the young woman asked.

Kythelia pointed at Warnoch. "That one will do."

Margaret closed her eyes and uttered a strange litany. The Clan Chiefs didn't understand the words, but the air grew so foul, several at the table began to cough. The candles all dimmed as a dark presence reached out from the shadows. Warnoch, his eyes wide, suddenly let out a gasp, his breath wheezing as if someone or something was throttling him.

Everyone watched in horror as he suddenly stood, then floated up above his chair as if hanging from a rope. A last rasp of breath came out of his throat, and then his body went limp, his limbs dangling, the rest suspended in the air.

Margaret made a slicing movement with her hand, and blood gushed from a cut that appeared on Warnoch's throat. She then pointed at the floor, and the body fell with a loud thud.

Kythelia smiled. "As you can see, she is well-versed in the ways of Necromancy."

"You murdered a Clan Chief!" shouted Brida. "The offence cannot go unpunished!"

The Dark Queen wore a look of amusement. "And who is to punish me? You?"

Brida stared back, defiant. She wanted to fight back, but the guards were close, their swords drawn. There was little she could do.

Kythelia looked directly into Brida's eyes. "Kill them all," she snapped, then watched as swords were plunged into the hapless Clan Chiefs. Leaning in, she watched the blood spill out of Brida.

"Such a waste," she mused. "I shouldn't have lost my temper."

"What else could you do?" asked Margaret.

"Why, drain the life from them, of course. It would have felt so nice."

"There are plenty of others who can fulfill that need, my queen."

"Yes, there are, aren't there. Very well, let us be gone from this place. It no longer serves any purpose."

"And the other Clan Chiefs?"

"The guards will hunt them down easily enough. In the meantime, we shall return to the Dome and continue with our plans."

"And the Mercerians?"

"They are little more than a nuisance," said Kythelia. "I have every confidence Prince Tarak is more than capable of dealing with them."

"You underestimated them before."

"You dare to question my methods?"

"No, Dark Majesty. I merely offer my warning in the hope that it serves your purpose."

"As well you should. If only my other advisors were as gifted as you. Now, come. There are other matters to attend to."

"And the bodies?"

"Leave them here to rot."

TWENTY-NINE

Turncoat

SPRING 966 MC

Lord Heath Morris, Earl of Shrewesdale, sipped his wine. "This sentiment has been on the increase of late?"

Lord Alexander stared back. "I said so, didn't I?"

"But Lord Caster could find no trace of it."

"Come now," offered the Earl of Eastwood, Lord Horace. "You didn't expect him to, did you? After all, he's one of those fellows who thinks the greenskins are worth having around."

Lord Markham grimaced. "I can't say I'm overly fond of the man's beliefs."

"Nonsense," said Lord Avery, "and stop calling them greenskins—they are Orcs. Why, if it hadn't been for their assistance, the queen would never have beat Norland."

"And is that a bad thing?" The young noble looked around the room. They sat in the parlour of Lord Alexander's Wincaster manor, a grandiose affair that boasted, amongst many things, a thick rug and a fireplace in every room. It was not that it was chilly—far from it, in fact, for with summer coming soon, it had turned decidedly warm, but Stanton liked to stand beside it, leaning his elbow on the mantel. In this way, he could be seen as the father figure, dispensing his wisdom to all who cared to listen, along with those who didn't, Lord Avery in particular.

"I don't know why you even invited me here, for Saxnor's sake," said the Duke of Kingsford. "It's not as though we're friends."

"True," said Stanton, "but we are colleagues, both interested in saving the kingdom from the influence of outsiders."

"Outsiders? I might remind you the Orcs live within the borders of Merceria."

"For now, but it's high time we gave them their own land."

"You want them out of the kingdom."

"What if I do? Is it wrong to feel a duty to keep our land free of strife?"

Avery finally lost his temper. "Free of strife? You're the one causing all these problems."

Stanton looked taken aback. "Me? Why would you ever think that?"

"Come now. We all know you're just pushing your weight around. You made it abundantly clear you objected to the presence of the elder races in this council."

"What if I do? Can you blame me? They dilute our power."

"So you said before, many times, yet there's no evidence their presence has caused any problems whatsoever."

"Yet," added Lord Horace.

"I've had enough of this ridiculous game." The Duke of Kingsford stood. "Why don't you work to maintain law and order instead of causing all this strife and chaos? Do you hate the queen that much?"

Stanton looked straight into his opponent's eyes. "I harbour nothing but the utmost respect for Her Majesty. I don't see how you could believe otherwise."

"I'm leaving."

"And you are free to do so."

Lord Avery glared back, locking eyes for only a moment before he turned and stormed from the room. Stanton took a sip of his wine, waiting until he heard the front door slam before returning his attention once more to his guests.

"Well, that was certainly interesting."

"Although not completely unexpected," said Horace. "I suspect he'll be trouble for us."

"Nonsense," said Stanton. "The man rants and raves all the time."

"I still don't see why you invited him. We all know he's a firm supporter of the queen and her band of commoners."

"Now, now," said Markham. "They may have been born common, but I must remind you they are all titled now, which means they deserve our respect."

"I respect their titles," said Stanton, "not the men themselves."

"Or women," added Spencer. "I still can't believe she allowed them on the council."

"Come now," said Markham. "There are only two, and if we are being honest, Baroness of Queenston is hardly a title worth fawning over. Now,

Lady Aubrey, on the other hand, at least has a legitimate claim to her title."

"It's not the women who trouble me," said Stanton, "it's the undue influence some of our colleagues maintain over the Crown."

"You're speaking of Lord Richard. I still don't understand the animosity you two have for each other."

"It goes back years ago when he slighted me."

"That's not the version I heard. According to my father, you and he had a falling out over a woman. Lady Evelyn Fitzwilliam, to be exact, although I believe in those days she was known as Lady Evelyn Brandon."

Lord Horace spat out his drink. "That's Lady Aubrey's family name."

"Yes," continued Markham, "and just think of it. Had she married Lord Alexander here, his children would have inherited Hawksburg."

"But he never married!"

"Precisely. Of course, things would be much different had Lord Richard not arrived on the scene. He was, after all, nothing more than the son of a minor baron."

"But Hawksburg is a barony too," said Horace.

"So it is, but the union of Lady Evelyn to Lord Alexander would have given him access to a lot more land, not to mention the income from raising all those horses."

"Don't be absurd," said Lord Heath. "Lord Richard didn't gain anything by the marriage. Why would Stanton?"

"Because he's an earl. Well, to be precise, in those days, he was the son of an earl, but it amounts to the same thing. In any event, the dowry would've been increased to account for the elevation in status."

"A reasonable expectation, given the circumstances," said Horace. "Why, then, did the Brandons refuse the offer?"

"Ah," said Markham. "That's the most galling thing of all. It appears Lady Evelyn fell in love with young Lord Richard."

"What has that got to do with anything?"

"That's exactly what I said," argued Stanton. "They should have done what was expected of them and approved her marriage to me. Instead, they allowed her to carry on with this upstart young baron who's spent a lifetime rubbing it in my face."

"Hardly that," said Markham. "Although I disagree with his politics, I've always found Lord Richard to be a decent and fair man."

"You don't know him like I do." Lord Alexander drained his glass. "I'll remind you he turned on the king, despite his pledge of loyalty, I might add."

"Only because he was told his daughter had been executed."

"She was a traitor to the Crown," snapped Stanton, "who should've been executed like the rest of those wretched Knights of the Hound."

A servant appeared at the door, causing Lord Alexander to interrupt his speech. "What is it?"

"You have visitors, my lord."

"Who?"

"Lord Richard Fitzwilliam, and he's not alone."

"What's that supposed to mean?"

"The Viscount of Haverston accompanies him, my lord, along with several armed warriors."

"That doesn't sound good," said Markham.

Stanton straightened. "Very well, show them in. In fact, bring them here, and we shall face them down."

"As you wish, my lord." The servant disappeared.

"Are you sure that's wise?" said Markham.

"I did nothing illegal," declared Lord Alexander. "Are we to be harassed simply because our opinions differ from those of the queen?"

They remained silent, everyone straining to hear what was said in the entranceway. The door to the room opened once more, revealing Lords Richard and Arnim, along with a third person, the witch Albreda.

The Baron of Bodden was most polite, scanning the area, and nodding at those present. "Gentlemen, I hope you're having a pleasant enough day?"

The room's occupants avoided his gaze, choosing instead to stare at their cups.

"Well?" said Stanton. "Do you have a reason for interrupting our little gathering?"

In answer, Lord Richard held out his hand, and Lord Arnim passed him a rolled-up parchment. "I have here," began Fitz, "an order for your arrest, Lord Alexander, on the charge of treason."

"This is outrageous!"

"And yet, here it is."

"You don't have the authority," insisted Stanton, pointing his finger to emphasize the point. "And don't try to tell me the queen has signed it. We all know she's off in Weldwyn."

"While it's true this document lacks her seal, it still carries the weight of the law."

"By what authority? Yours? You are merely a baron. You lack the authority to order my arrest."

"On the contrary," said Fitz. "I am a general in the Army of Merceria. As you well know, warriors founded our kingdom. You may peruse the laws if you wish, but I believe you'll find I am quite within my rights."

"I must protest."

"I expected no less."

"What's to happen to him?" asked Markham.

"If it were up to me, he would be hanged, but in accordance with the queen's law, he shall instead be held in custody until such time as his trial can be arranged." He nodded at Lord Arnim, who moved into the room, followed by two guards.

"I won't forget this," said Stanton.

"Nor would I expect you to."

The guards led him away without further protest.

"Lord Arnim here will expect statements from each of you in turn," said the baron.

"About what?" asked Markham.

"About the nature of this gathering."

"This is all political posturing, surely? You and Stanton have been bitter rivals for years."

"Is that what you think? Let me reassure you, gentlemen, this arrest has nothing to do with my personal feelings on the matter. I returned to Wincaster only this morning to learn your friend, Lord Alexander, has been sowing the seeds of dissension against the Crown. I feel I must warn you this is no idle speculation on our part. We have proof."

Lord Markham turned pale. "What kind of proof?"

In answer, the baron smiled. "That will all come out at his trial. In the meantime, I shall leave you in the company of Lord Arnim."

"And that's it? We're supposed to sit here and watch you cart him off?"

"It seems you already have."

"If I were you," added Albreda, "I would take advantage of Lord Alexander's generosity and drink up his fine wine while it's still his to offer."

Once more, the nobles stared down at their drinks.

"I believe our presence is no longer needed here," said the baron.

Fitz stepped outside, taking in the cool night air. "Well, that was quite interesting."

"Come now," said Albreda. "You've waited years to do that."

"Believe it or not, it gives me no pleasure. While it's true we've been political opponents for years, and for that matter, that he's been a pain in my backside for just as long, I had no desire to see him face a charge of treason. This time, however, he stepped over the line."

"I'm sorry I dragged you all the way back to Wincaster for this, but I felt it best you be the one to follow it through."

"You were right to do so," said Fitz. "In the hands of someone who doesn't know him as well as I, it could have easily resulted in a confrontation, and who knows where that could lead?"

"So you won't hold it against me?"

He looked at her and smiled. "I could never do that."

They continued down the street, back towards the Palace.

"How are things in the north?" asked Albreda.

"We've arranged a provisional government," replied Fitz, "and I convinced the earls not to take out their frustrations on their political rivals. It's a pity we can't do that here."

"And the throne of Norland?"

"Will soon be in the hands of Bronwyn."

"Surely, you jest?"

"I'm afraid we had to compromise," said Fitz, "or risk upsetting the delicate balance of power. The last thing we want is for them to be back at each other's throats."

"And what is the nature of this provisional government?"

"It's modelled on our own Council of Nobles, although I did insist on the inclusion of a Mercerian representative."

"You?"

"Saxnor, no," said Lord Richard. "Sir Heward is there for that."

"I thought Sir Gareth was to be their minder?"

"That's different. Sir Gareth is there to keep an eye on Bronwyn and rein in some of her more… eccentric ideas."

"Eccentric?"

"Yes. She wants to emulate Queen Anna's rule, but she hasn't the experience for it."

"Is that good or bad?" asked Albreda.

"Neither, or both, depending on your point of view. In any event, I've arranged for a copy of our laws to be made available for her to educate herself. That should keep her busy for some time."

"And our garrison?"

"That will remain in place for the foreseeable future. I had hoped to bring them back before summer, but I can't help but feel that would be a bit premature. I also don't want them to undo all the valuable work we put in over the last few months."

"Now that this arrest is out of the way, I suppose you'll want me to take you back to Galburn's Ridge?"

"No. I believe I'll stay in Wincaster awhile and look after things for Her Majesty."

"You've no desire to join the campaign to liberate Weldwyn?"

"Gerald has that well in hand. I doubt he needs me showing up and making a mess of it."

"Nonsense," said Albreda. "I'm sure he'd be happy to see you."

"He likely would, but there's little I can offer him. Unlike Norland, the liberation of Weldwyn is pretty straightforward. Not that I expect it to be easy, you understand, but there are only so many approaches to retaking Summersgate. I would, however, suggest that you travel to join them."

"Won't you need my magic to return north at some time?"

"We managed without your spells in the past. I'm sure we'll muddle through somehow. In truth, I believe your presence would be far more beneficial to retaking Weldwyn."

"Yes, I daresay you're right."

"Unfortunately, it's a long way to travel overland."

"Nonsense," said Albreda. "I can use the gate to travel to Queenston. It's not far from there to Kingsford, then I'll catch up with the army."

"But the Saurian gates cause madness? Their use was banned."

"That was before Aubrey and Kraloch came up with a way to remove its effects, and in any case, it's only prolonged exposure that's dangerous, not occasional."

"Still, I should very much like to believe you'll be careful about using it."

She smiled. "Yes, I shall be mindful of the consequences. I suppose we should consider continuing with those magic circles. One in Kingsford would be very useful right about now."

"But they sap your power, don't they?"

"They do, not to mention they're expensive to make."

"The queen wants one in every city of Merceria," said Fitz. "That would be quite an accomplishment."

"Indeed it would, but I fear that won't come about for some years yet."

"Why so long?"

"It's a simple matter of supply. If our mages use all their power to create these circles, they'll lack the power to use them."

"There's that much of a drain?"

"For some, yes. Empowering the circle at Wickfield almost killed poor Aldus."

"You created one in Galburn's Ridge with little difficulty?"

"I did," replied the Druid, "but I've been using magic for many years."

"So has Aldus Hearn," he countered.

"True, but his study of magic is much more… what's the word?"

"Strict?"

She laughed. "I suppose that word will do as well as any other. On the other hand, my magic is less constricted, more natural. You might even say

I'm more in tune with nature; thus, the power flows through me with little to obstruct it."

"Are you suggesting his training works against him?"

"It does. I worked very hard trying to convince others that their approach to magic is more limiting, but did they listen?"

"My niece, Aubrey, certainly did," said Fitz.

"Yes, she did, and I count it a singular success on my part. I have, in a sense, freed her mind of the self-imposed restrictions used by my fellow mages."

"What of the Orcs?"

"Their approach is similar to my own."

"Still, their magic is weaker."

"I wouldn't say weaker," said Albreda, "merely different. There's no denying their shamans are powerful, but I cannot speak of their other mages."

"I wasn't even aware they had other mages."

"Oh yes. The Orcs of Black Ravens have a master of earth—what we would call an Earth Mage, although I haven't seen him use his magic."

"Aren't you an Earth Mage?"

"I prefer the term Druid," she replied, "but the concept is the same. We both deal with animals and plants."

"And what do you make of Revi's plans to make an Arcane Academy?"

"You mean Aubrey's plan."

"I thought Revi came up with it first," said Fitz.

"He did, but it has fallen to your niece to work out the details. I understand the queen has given over custody of the old Royal Estate in Hawksburg for them to use."

"Has she, indeed? A most interesting development." He was suddenly struck by an idea. "Say, that wasn't destroyed by the king's men, was it?"

"No, only damaged. I imagine now that the city is pretty much rebuilt, they'll start concentrating on getting it up and running."

"There's still a war to settle first," said Fitz, "not to mention the matter of the Dark Queen."

"That will all be over soon enough."

"How do you know? Had one of your visions, have you?"

"Not at all," replied Albreda, "but I've spent enough time with you Mercerians to know you don't give up easily."

"You're a Mercerian too."

The statement took her by surprise, then she smiled. "Yes, I suppose I am, aren't I?"

THIRTY

Battle

Summer 966 MC

J ack Marlowe halted his horse. With the capture of Southport behind them, the southern army was preparing to move north, but Prince Tarak blocked their way.

Prince Alric reined in beside him. "Trouble?"

"It seems we're expected. See for yourself."

The Kurathian prince had formed a line of footmen between a small hill and the Mystic Woods. To the east, he had amassed his archers, along with his heavier horsemen.

"Send Lanaka to the other side of that woods," said Alric, pointing eastward. "We'll form our footmen up along a line between there and the Mystic Woods to our west."

"They badly outnumber us, Your Highness."

"At the moment, yes, but that will soon change."

"And where would you like me?" asked Jack.

"To the east with my Weldwyn cavalry. Get Tog to join you there with his Trolls."

"Aye, sir." The cavalier rode off, yelling out orders as he went.

Alric ordered his footmen into line, then watched as they marched into place. In the distance, the enemy advanced, moving slowly while keeping their positions relative to each other.

The captains urged the rest of the army into position. Had the enemy been typical Kurathian mercenaries, he would've been less worried, for those were lightly armed and armoured. These troops, on the other hand, were equipped much like his Mercerian warriors, presenting a far more formidable challenge. He cast his gaze around, taking in his position, and noticed Lady Aubrey riding towards him.

"Is all well?" he called out.

"It is, Your Highness. The enemy should soon notice our reinforcements."

Alric smiled. Just like his father back in the last invasion of Weldwyn, all he need do was hold the line and entice the enemy forward. The hope was to pin down this elusive Kurathian prince, allowing their allies to get into position for a killing blow.

"Where are his dragons?"

"There is no word of them," replied Aubrey.

"And our own?"

"Melethandil is not yet capable of flight."

"Not much point in having a dragon if it can't fly," noted Alric.

"On the contrary. She's a massive beast, and she can still breathe fire."

"True, but her presence could just as easily cause mayhem amongst our own army. I don't imagine there are too many men who'd be willing to bear its presence for fear of getting burned."

"In that case," said Aubrey, "I suppose it's a good thing there won't be any Humans joining her."

He looked at her in surprise. "Weren't there supposed to be warriors accompanying her?"

"There will be, just not of the Human variety." She grinned. "Who knows? You might even recognize someone amongst our allies."

"Who?"

"Now, now. I can't go spoiling the queen's surprise, can I?"

Prince Tarak kept his gaze locked on his pitiful enemy. "I must claim some disappointment with this Prince Alric. He could at least put up a credible defence."

"Yes, my prince," replied his aide.

"And you're sure this is the same one who captured Southport?"

"Yes, Lord, although admittedly, the garrison there wasn't at full strength."

"Well, he won't be so lucky this time."

A rider came thundering along the back of the line, drawing his attention. He watched as the fellow grew closer and then dismounted, making a great bow.

"Speak," commanded Tarak.

"There are men to the east of us, Lord."

"How many?"

"Five hundred or more."

"It matters not," said the prince. "For such numbers are insignificant."

The rider kept his eyes on his master. "There's more, Lord."

"Go on."

"They are Dwarves."

"Are you sure?"

"There can be no doubt, Lord. Their banners bear the crossbeams unique to the mountain folk."

Tarak stared towards the east, but the enemy was far too distant and the ground too uneven to see them from his present position.

"You have orders, Lord?" pressed the rider.

"Yes. Send in our heavy cavalry and drive them from the field."

"But they will be severely outnumbered, my lord."

"Then dispatch one hand of light cavalry."

"And the mages, my lord?"

"No. We shall need them here in short order."

"Yes, my prince." He rode off, yelling out orders. One hand's worth of troops—five companies of light cavalry—rode east to join their heavier cousins.

Tarak briefly considered holding off on the advance until he could deal with these interlopers, but the idea of doing so galled him. He outnumbered his foe significantly: better then, to crush them quickly, freeing up his warriors to turn on this new threat.

Commander Lanaka saw his chance. The other side's horsemen had been drawn eastward behind a large copse of trees that blocked his view. That could only mean one thing—reinforcements had arrived. From his vantage point, he spotted the mass of archers who'd taken up position on a hill that anchored the Kurathian prince's eastern flank.

He didn't hesitate, instead ordering his men to close up and charge the bowmen. Several of his riders fell to arrows, but they were soon in amongst the enemy, carving through their lines with ease. It was all over in a moment, the enemy throwing down their bows and streaming northward even as his riders cut them down.

Captain Haralan led Prince Tarak's cavalry eastward. As the enemy drew closer, he noted the presence of an immense dragon behind their lines. He had a hard time believing his eyes, for to his knowledge, only the Kurathian princes commanded such beasts. Yet one was here, following in the wake of this Dwarven host.

The distraction almost took his life. All around him, riders fell from their saddles as hundreds of arbalesters loosed their deadly bolts. Determined to put flight to the enemy, Haralan closed the range, but as he was about to make contact, his horse went wild, careening off to the side.

He struggled to rein him back in, but his mount was having none of it. Horses panicked throughout the prince's cavalry as the Dwarven line opened up. The last thing Haralan saw was the great beast opening its mouth, and then a glow as the flames consumed him.

Althea watched as fire consumed the enemy horsemen. Those who didn't perish in the initial onslaught panicked, many thrown from the saddle as their horses desperately sought to avoid the grim fate of a fiery death.

The princess stood in the stirrups attempting to gain a better view, but smoke and soot drifted in front of her. She needn't have worried, for the Dwarves knew their business. Even as the smoke cleared, the Hearth Guard moved forward, walking across the patches of burning grass as if it were an everyday occurrence.

Herdwin's Dwarves followed, along with Tulfar's own Mirstone warriors. Althea urged her horse forward, straining to see the battle. She rode past Melethandil in time to witness the complete destruction of Tarak's heavy cavalry. Beyond them, the lighter horsemen formed up for a charge.

Tulfar's Dwarves locked their shields, assuming the drake formation, while to their south, the dragon of Lyndenthorpe advanced.

Althea expected the enemy to charge. In fact, she was excited at the prospect of watching how effective this formation would be. Much to her disappointment, though, Lanaka's horsemen, wearing the red-and-green of Merceria, had somehow charged into the rear of the prince's second wave of horsemen. Sensing the opportunity, the Dwarves advanced, ready to tear through the enemy.

Unable to see what was happening in the east, Tarak ordered his last reserve of horsemen south, intending to pin down the pitiful line of warriors opposing him.

They advanced at the trot, passing through the Kurathian prince's lines as they'd trained to do. The Mercerians responded by sending their own cavalry to counter the move, resulting in a swirl of melee between the two opposing armies.

Tarak was forced to halt his advance as the horsemen struggled for dominance in the well-trampled fields. Overall, things were going well, but his view was now blocked by the very hill his archers manned. Unaware of what was transpiring in the east, he had complete confidence his footmen would soon rout the Mercerian forces.

The prince had studied warfare extensively, everything from the Campaigns of Aeldred to the more recent battles of the Petty Kingdoms. He considered himself an expert, even going so far as to promote himself as such to others. Yet the truth was, he possessed little actual battle experience. War was meant to be glorious, a shining example of honour and might where the virtuous triumphed over lesser men. As he watched the horsemen tear each other to bits, he began to have doubts. This was not a noble fight; it was a mad, desperate affair to see who survived and who perished.

Prince Tarak was the one who'd brought war to this land, and he suddenly felt vulnerable. Against the advice of his mages, he'd insisted on leaving his dragons in Summersgate, a choice he now wished he could undo.

His horsemen had been thinned out, but so had the Mercerians. He prepared to order the general advance, ready to swamp Prince Alric's meagre line, but a warning shout drew his attention. An additional threat had appeared from the north, lines of cavalry charging towards him.

He realized, with a start, he'd been lured into a trap. The pitiful army to his front was there to pin him in place, while another destroyed him from the rear. It dawned on him that this was not so much a disaster as the moment for him to demonstrate his command of tactics. He began issuing orders.

∾

Sir Preston led the cavalry south, directly towards the back of Prince Tarak's army. He had three hundred horsemen, one-third of that Orc cavalry, with another hundred Orc spears following along in their wake. To the east, the Dwarves mopped up what remained of the enemy horsemen, leaving the Knight of the Hound to deal the final blow.

His lighter mounts led the way, the heavier armoured cavalrymen following behind. He gave the order, and the horses increased their gait, yet he couldn't help but feel the enemy might still surprise them.

He was proven correct as the enemy footmen marched into a new formation, moving quickly and with great precision to form a large circle.

Preston noticed the enemy's bowmen running, seeking the safety of their brethren's new formation. After being cut off by Lanaka's taking of the hill, earlier in the battle, they'd been abandoned to their fate. The knight, unwilling to pass up an opportunity, gave the order to charge. The horsemen of Merceria descended on the enemy archers without mercy.

Prince Alric stared at the flames streaking out towards his men. "They're using their mages."

"So they are," agreed Aubrey, "but it will do them little good at this point."

"You don't judge them as a decisive tactic?"

"Not at all. Magic is powerful against individuals. That much is true but against hundreds? That's a completely different matter. See, there's Tog," she said, pointing at the leader of the Trolls in amongst the developing giant melee. "He's cutting through their lines with wild abandon."

"He'll overextend himself," warned the prince.

"No, he's fine. Tarak's forces have no crossbows to worry them, and the Mercerians following in his wake are there to support him."

They both watched the enemy line as it crumbled into disarray. Aubrey closed her eyes for a moment.

"Sir Preston has engaged their rear," she said, "and Kraloch reports the eastern end has been annihilated. The Dwarves are regrouping. It won't be long before it's all over."

"We can but hope," said Alric. The Mercerians suddenly surged forward as the Kurathian line disintegrated before their very eyes. One moment there was a recognizable formation, the next, nothing but chaos. The entire battlefield became one massive melee, with little to distinguish between the two sides.

Aubrey spotted the enemy commander running from the fray. "Prince Tarak is fleeing," she said. "Apparently, he's had enough."

Alric spit on the ground in disgust. "The coward. He's abandoning his men. The least he could do is surrender and spare them the pain and agony."

Jack Marlowe rode up to them. "It's a glorious victory, my prince. Shall we pursue?"

"I would advise against it," said Aubrey. "He still has dragons at his command."

"Good point," said Alric. He turned his attention once more to the cavalier. "Offer those who remain the chance at surrender and then round up the prisoners."

"And if they refuse?"

"I doubt they will, but just in case, Tog should bring his Trolls up. If that doesn't intimidate them, nothing will."

Jack smiled. "What about our dragon?"

"Yes. Admittedly, that would do the trick, but I'd prefer to keep her away, at least for now. I don't think our horses would appreciate being so close to such a beast."

"On that, we can agree. What are we to do with the enemy mages?"

"Have we captured any?"

"No, not yet, but it's not as if they have anywhere to go."

Alric turned his gaze to Aubrey. "What do you suggest?"

"Their power will be weakened after all that casting."

"Enough for you to negotiate their surrender?"

"I believe so. The question is, how do we guard them?"

"Can't we restrict their casting somehow?"

"We possess no magebane, if that's what you mean. I suppose we could bind their arms behind their backs. That ought to stop them from using their magic."

"Then do so, Jack," said the prince. "In the meantime, I'm going to need you and Kraloch to look after our wounded, Lady Aubrey."

"Of course, Your Highness. I shall see to it at once." She turned and rode off.

Prince Alric surveyed the battlefield. The fighting had ceased, save for the occasional spot here or there, where a few brave warriors fought on against vastly superior numbers.

He smiled. It had been his plan to pin the Kurathian prince in place while the Dwarves rolled up their flank. The added presence of Preston's cavalry hastened the enemy's demise. There would be a grand celebration in camp tonight, but not for Alric. He looked upon the dead and dying scattered around the field and thought of the families who'd lost so much this day. His father, King Leofric, had always spoken of battle as glorious and heroic. Looking at the death and destruction before him, Alric could think of little, other than pain and suffering. He longed only for days of peace and prosperity.

"To victory!" shouted Jack Marlowe.

Aubrey lifted her cup, and a great roar went up as everyone echoed his sentiments. They'd advanced up the road, occupying the abandoned village of Lyndenthorpe. Now, the captains and commanders gathered together to celebrate the occasion. The mood was festive, yet she knew it wouldn't be long before they would be called upon once more to make the ultimate sacrifice. The army of Prince Tarak had been routed, but the battle for Summersgate was yet to begin.

"It was glorious, don't you think?" said Jack.

"I'm not sure glorious is the right word."

"Then pick another! Magnificent, marvellous, heroic, one might even say superb! And all on the first day of summer."

"Is it?" said Aubrey. "I didn't realize how much time has gone by."

"Mark my words," said Jack. "This war will be over before the first leaves fall."

"Provided we can take the capital."

He waved it away with his hand. "What could stop us?"

"Dragons."

"Hah! Did you forget we have one of our own?"

"Yes, but they have two, maybe even more."

"You worry too much. You remind me of Dame Beverly."

Aubrey smiled. "I'll take that as a compliment."

"As it was meant." He bowed his head in a solemn gesture. "Say. What about all those mages?"

"From what I've been able to gather, there were six in total. We captured two Water Mages, a Pyromancer, and there are reports of at least one Fire Mage fleeing the aftermath in the company of Prince Tarak."

"And the rest?"

"Presumed dead. We'll know more once we're done interrogating the prisoners."

Jack took a deep drink of his ale before he turned to Kasri. "How's that dragon of yours doing?"

"That dragon has a name," she replied. "It's Melethandil."

"That sounds Elvish."

"Likely because it's in the ancient tongue, the one shared between the elder races."

"And can it fly yet?"

"Melethandil is a she, not an it," said Kasri.

"My apologies, Princess."

"That's Highness," said Herdwin. "I would have thought you would know better."

"He does," interrupted Prince Alric, "but I'm afraid he's a little into his cups this evening."

Aubrey closed her eyes, conjuring forth her magic, the spell easy enough to cast. Then she touched her glowing hands to Jack's arm, the magic flowing into him. The cavalier sat up with a start.

"What did you do that for?" he asked.

"What did she do?" asked Kasri.

"I simply neutralized toxins," explained Aubrey. "The spell treats strong drink the same as poison when it comes to such things."

"Meaning?"

"Meaning," said Jack, "that I find myself returned to a sober state."

"And that is a problem?"

"Of course. Now I must start drinking all over again!"

THIRTY-ONE

The Calm Before the Storm

Summer 966 MC

Gerald stared across the open field. At the other end lay the walls of Summersgate and their enemy. Somewhere in that city was Brida. He knew their occupation would quickly unravel if they could capture her or kill her. He heard someone approaching and wheeled to see Anna.

"Come to watch the play?" he asked.

"The play?"

"Yes. It occurs to me we are much like actors on a stage, each playing our role."

"And yet it's a play without an end."

He smiled. "I see what you did there. That's clever."

She moved closer, standing beside him to gaze out at the distant capital. "Will we get in, do you think?"

"Getting in isn't the problem. It's those dragons that have me worried. We need to lure them out."

"And how do we do that?"

"I have an idea, but it's risky."

"Do tell," said Anna.

"I thought we'd offer them a tasty target."

"Which is?"

"Massed troops rushing to assault the walls."

"That would be suicidal, surely? One breath from a dragon, and they'd all be burned to a crisp."

"Not necessarily. We have a secret weapon, or rather weapons."

"Let me guess—arbalests?"

"Yes, and Elven bows. I'm going to put some in amongst our regular troops."

"Do we even know if they can penetrate dragon scales?"

Gerald smiled. "If Melethandil is to be believed, then yes."

"And how many of these arbalests can we muster?"

"Over two hundred, with another hundred Elven archers. The problem isn't numbers, though. It's more about concentrating them where they're needed. Should the enemy dragons choose to attack elsewhere, it'll leave us vulnerable."

Anna glanced around the immediate area. "I see you authorized the construction of siege engines. Is Herdwin overseeing them?"

"He is, even though he knows they're not needed."

"Why would you say they're not needed? Don't you have to batter down the wall to gain entry? Unless, of course, you're planning to climb over the walls?"

"Not at all. The intent is to bring them down quickly, then rush the breach before the enemy can reinforce their defences."

"And how do you plan to accomplish that?"

He smiled. "I can't give away all my secrets, now, can I?"

It was Anna's turn to smile. "Now, that's what I like to see, you enjoying yourself. I hear you've been spending time with Lady Jane. Could she be the one responsible for this rush of energy you have of late?"

Gerald blushed. "I'm just concerned about the upcoming assault."

"Of course you are."

"Speaking of Lady Jane, I wondered if you'd made any decisions regarding her fate?"

"You mean will I have her tried for treason? The answer is no."

"No, you've made no decision, or no, you won't try her for treason?"

"I'm of the opinion she was forced into this against her will," said Anna. "Maybe it's because I'm a new mother myself, but I can't help but feel for her. However, I can't say I feel the same about her son. Once this war is over, I should like to see a full investigation into his affairs."

"You and me both," said Gerald. "I find it hard to imagine the amount of malice he harbours for his mother to send her out here like that."

"Of course you'd say that. You're falling in love with her."

"Whatever gave you that idea?"

"Come now. I recognize the looks that cross your face when you speak of your time with her."

"I am merely being a gallant host."

Anna chuckled. "Yes. A host who spends all his time doting on her. Mind you, I'm not complaining. You've deserved someone in your life for quite some time. I just don't want to see you hurt."

"I'm a grown man, Anna. I can take care of myself."

"Yes, you can, and I have complete faith that you will sort all this out in due course. Now, should we change the subject before you turn redder than the flag of rebellion?"

"Very well. What would you like to discuss?"

"You made it plain that you have some secret way of bringing down the walls of Summersgate. What I'm curious to know is how you intend to utilize our dragon?"

"Actually," said Gerald, "Kasri's been working on that very matter. The Kurathian custom is for an Earth Mage to ride on its neck, allowing them to control the beast at all times."

"Is that what we're doing? I have a hard time picturing Aldus Hearn atop a dragon, or Albreda, for that matter."

"I thought to use Aegryth Malthunen, but I've been informed she lacks the magic to control a dragon."

"Meaning?"

"We shall be taking a somewhat different approach."

"Are you going to tell me what that is, or just keep teasing me?"

"If you insist." Gerald chuckled. "Kasri has developed a close bond with Melethandil. She'll ride on the dragon's back."

"Will that even work?"

"It should. Melethandil is helping us of her own free will, but Kasri knows our tactics and can help interpret the battle."

"So she'll be a passenger?"

"Oh no," said Gerald. "Much more than that. She has Stormhammer, which means she can throw bolts of lightning. Add that to the dragon's breath, and we possess a devastating combination."

"Just how many times a day can a dragon breathe fire?"

"Not as often as you might guess. From the dragon's point of view, it's like spitting, but they first need to build up copious amounts of saliva to make it work."

"So you're saying their spit burns?"

"In a sense. It's more like regurgitating, then something in the stomach reacts with the air to ignite it."

"So it's not so much spit as vomit," said Anna. "How delightful. I can see why they wouldn't want to use it very often."

"Melethandil feels that two or three times a day would be all she could manage. Any more, and she risks burning her own throat. It's apparently quite a caustic substance. Oh, and you can expect them to drink lots of water afterwards."

"I imagine that has something to do with its acidic nature. We should send warriors to guard any nearby bodies of water."

"Already done," said Gerald.

"What else have you got planned?"

"As you know, we are blessed with many Dwarven arbalesters. I thought it might be prudent to steal some from the assault to guard those siege engines. You and I both know they're only for show, but the enemy will be keen to see them destroyed."

"More bait for the dragons?"

"I suppose that's one way of looking at it."

"You seem to have everything under control. It appears I'm not needed here. Would I have been wiser to remain in Wincaster?"

"No, not at all," said Gerald. "Your mere presence enhances morale tenfold. Of course, once the battle begins, you should keep your distance. You don't want to put Braedon at risk."

"Fear not. I'll have him sent to safety when the time comes. I, however, shall remain here, where my army can see me."

He was about to object but knew there was no dissuading the queen once she made her mind up about such things.

"Very well," he said. "I'll send word when the assault is to commence."

"And should I expect that soon?"

"Not today, if that's what you're thinking. I still have several things I need to see to."

"All right. I shall not take up any more of your time. I will, however, expect you for dinner." She smiled. "And I expect you to bring Lady Jane with you. You've told me all about her, but I have yet to actually meet the woman."

"I'm sure she'd be delighted."

"Make sure you tell her it's not formal. Saxnor knows, the last thing we need is for all that bother right now."

"Of course, Your Majesty." He made an exaggerated bow.

"Oh, and don't expect to stay clean."

He looked at her in surprise. "Why?"

"Your grandson has a habit of spitting up his dinner, and I can't keep changing my clothes."

He grinned. "Then I shall be happy to take on that responsibility, at least for one evening."

"Good. Then I'll see you this evening, both you and the mysterious Lady Jane."

Melethandil stretched out her legs as Kasri adjusted the leather straps crisscrossing the great dragon's torso, keeping the wings free. All along the straps were metal rings onto which ropes could be hooked, providing a safety harness of sorts. The plan was to bring along half a dozen Dwarven warriors and let their arbalests do the rest.

Kasri had no idea how practical it was to reload such a weapon while flying around on the back of a dragon. Still, she looked forward to trying. As if sensing her mood, the mighty dragon turned its head.

"*Is it ready?*" the creature asked in the ancient tongue.

"*As ready as it ever will be,*" replied Kasri.

Melethandil swivelled her head. "*It appears you have company.*"

The Dwarf princess turned to see a familiar face, then hopped down. "*Herdwin? What brings you here?*" she continued in the language of their ancestors.

The smith blushed. "*You, actually. I reckoned you might need some help with whatever it is that you're doing.*"

She smiled. "*How can you offer help if you don't even know what we're attempting?*"

"*You'd be surprised by the things I've gotten up to over the years.*" He peered around her, looking at Melethandil. "*I see you have some sort of harness. Do you intend to ride on her back?*"

"*Well, more on her neck and shoulders, to be honest.*"

"*Then you need a special type of clip.*"

"*A clip? I thought to tie myself to her using straps.*"

"*Aye, straps would work, but clips would allow you to move around at will. Think of them as a ring or clamp of metal similar to that found within chain-mail, except much bigger, and instead of using a rivet to attach the ends, you use a pin.*"

"*So that you can undo it?*"

"*Precisely,*" he replied.

"*But how would that make it safe? I'd still be required to undo it to move, wouldn't I?*"

"*Yes, but you'd have two of them. One stays attached while the other is moved. You already have those rings attached to the dragon.*"

"*We thought to use hooks.*"

"*Aye, hooks would work, but they can come undone if you're not careful. Dragons don't always fly straight and level.*"

"*How long would it take to make up some of these clamps?*"

"*All I need is a forge and some iron, and there's plenty of both back in the camp.*"

"*You two should go and see what you can do together,*" suggested Melethandil with some amusement.

"*Are you suggesting something untoward?*" said Kasri, staring back at the dragon.

"*Untoward? I am afraid that is an expression I am unfamiliar with. In any case, it's obvious he likes you. Why have you not coupled?*"

Kasri turned crimson.

"*Come,*" said Herdwin, taking her hand. "*The dragon doesn't understand the finer points of Dwarven behaviour.*"

She spun around. "*But that's just it,*" Kasri said. "*She does.*"

"*Meaning?*"

"*I should've been more careful with what I talked about around a dragon. Their hearing is apparently better than I realized.*"

"*So you talked about coupling?*"

"*Amongst other things.*"

"*What other things?*" asked Herdwin, a smile creasing his lips.

"*Forging,*" supplied Melethandil, her voice echoing through the glen.

"*For Gundar's sake,*" said Kasri. "*You don't need to tell the entire camp, do you?*"

"*Why not? Is it not the mountain folk's custom to announce such things?*"

"*No. It most definitely is not.*"

Gerald cut open the spicy sausage, the aroma drifting up to his nose. "One of my favourites," he announced. "How did you know?"

"It doesn't take a genius to know what you like," said Anna, "and you must eat all you want. I had them cooked up especially for you."

Alric waited as a servant placed a slice of meat on his plate. "Tell me, Lady Jane. How was Summersgate when last you saw it?"

"Quiet," she replied. "The High Queen announced a curfew. Anyone out after dark was subject to arrest."

"Was the city damaged much by the attack?"

"Other than the Palace, no."

"I find that hard to believe. Did the guards not hold the gates?"

"There was no fighting at the gates that I'm aware of. The Clansmen entered the city without opposition, as far as I can tell."

Alric frowned. "That suggests treason."

"Agreed," said Anna. "I would have expected at least some opposition."

"The garrison was relatively small," said Lady Jane. "Particularly in the wake of King Leofric's death."

"Yes," said Alric. "My father could be a stubborn man at times. He took the bulk of the army with him into Norland to prove we were better than the Mercerians. It made his loss all the more heartbreaking."

"I'm sorry," said Jane. "I didn't mean to speak ill of the king."

"I take no offence," replied the prince. "My experiences amongst the Mercerians has shown me a better way to move forward."

"I'm not sure what you mean, Highness?"

Alric put down his fork, the better to use his hands when explaining. "The Kingdom of Weldwyn, for all its long history, has several flaws, chief amongst them being the refusal to employ Dwarves and Elves in our armies."

"Or in the Earls Council," added Anna.

"Yes, that too. Should I become king, I shall seek to rectify that."

"Don't you mean 'when'?" said Gerald.

"The Weldwyn custom differs from that of Merceria. Yes, I am the logical heir to the Throne since the death of my brother, but the Earls Council has the final say on who shall rule."

"That's ridiculous."

"Agreed," said Anna.

"Be that as it may," continued Prince Alric, "it is how things are done in Weldwyn."

Lady Jane was intrigued. "But who else would even be considered?"

"Any of the earls could lay claim to the Throne. It's more a matter of political influence."

"Wouldn't they need Royal Blood?"

"In theory, yes, but the nobles of Weldwyn are all related, if you dig deep enough into their ancestry. In any event, they could insist on someone marrying Althea to become king. Not that she'd likely agree to that."

"Or Princess Edwina?"

"No. She is no longer an heir. Her magic saw to that."

"Magic?" said Jane. "What magic?"

"Oh yes," said Alric. "You wouldn't have heard. Right before my sister fled Summersgate, Master Tyrell discovered she possessed the potential to use Air Magic. As you are likely aware, since the founding of Weldwyn, mages have been barred from wearing the Crown. It's one of our most basic foundations of law."

"Why is that?" asked Gerald.

"The great mage Weldwyn always insisted on it."

"I know little about the fellow," said Jane. "Other than we named our kingdom after him, of course."

"He united the tribes against the invaders," explained Alric.

"Yes," added Gerald, "and by invaders, he means us Mercerians."

Jane smiled, a common enough occurrence these days. "And now we all live in peace and harmony. Or at least we will, once the Clans are driven back into the hills."

"We must do more than that," said Anna.

"What do you mean?" asked Alric.

"It's simple, really. The animosity between Weldwyn and the Clans is not too dissimilar from that which existed between our own people. We must learn more about them, bring them into our circle of friends."

"Circle of friends? The Clans?"

"I never said it would be easy, but we have to accept them for who they are, to assist them in developing a healthy relationship with their neighbours."

"You mean Weldwyn," said Alric. "What other neighbours could they have?"

"Actually," said Anna, "we know very little about them. For all we know, there may be another kingdom to their west. Not to mention the possibility of their lands adjoining those of other Dwarves or Orcs."

"Or Elves," added Gerald.

"Yes, or even some other race we've yet to meet. Ultimately, we all consider ourselves civilized people. We need to act that way in our dealings with outsiders."

"I must confess," said Alric, "it's not something I've ever considered, but the idea has merit."

"You know," said Gerald, "this whole discussion has made me think of something."

"Which is?"

"If you become king, then Anna would become Queen of Weldwyn."

"What of it?"

"That would make her a queen two times over. Has that ever happened before?"

"Not in these lands," said Anna, "and from what I've read about the Continent, not there, either. Mind you, our records of that distant land are quite old. What little we know mainly comes from the Orcs."

"The Orcs?" said Lady Jane.

"Yes," explained Gerald. "Their shamans can communicate over great distances. It's served us well during this campaign. I just wish we had more of them."

"Agreed," said Anna. "We need to see an end to this war so Aubrey can get that academy of hers up and running."

"Academy?" said Jane.

"Yes, to train mages."

"I doubt that would work. From what I've heard of the Dome's history, finding students has always been the toughest of chores. That's why we had such few mages when the Clans attacked."

"Ah," said the queen, "but they didn't have Lady Aubrey Brandon. She and Kraloch discovered a way to identify the magic potential in people. Saxnor willing, in ten years, both our kingdoms will be filled with those who can cast spells."

THIRTY-TWO

The Shadow of Darkness

Summer 966 MC

P rince Tarak looked out from the walls of Summersgate. "They are dangerous, these Mercerians."

"No more so than any other warrior culture," said Kythelia. "And that includes your own people. Admittedly, it is unfortunate they defeated you in battle, but we will still triumph over them."

"How can you say that when their army is at our very walls?"

"You believe an army could threaten me? I command dark forces able to destroy them in an instant."

"Then why not do so?"

"It does not suit my purposes."

"And being under siege does?"

The Elf queen smiled. "It is easier to destroy an enemy when they are within reach, is it not?"

The Kurathian was not amused. "You orchestrated all of this to bring them here?"

"It was one of many possibilities. The Queen of Merceria has long been a thorn in my side. By week's end, I shall be rid of her and those fools she calls her friends, for good."

"Are they not the same ones who defeated your army in the north?"

"I must grudgingly confess that they did, but not without paying a heavy price. Years of constant warfare have weakened their army. Crush them now, and they will be unable to resist your invasion of their homeland."

"And what army do I use to conquer them? They have destroyed my entire host!"

"You still have dragons at your command. Use them to annihilate the enemy."

He met her gaze, staring into inky black eyes that seemed devoid of a soul. It made him shiver. "Very well, I shall do as you ask."

"Good, but let's use them wisely, shall we? The last thing we want to do is throw them away."

"Might I ask how you suggest I should deploy them?"

"I would think that's the easy part, don't you? We start by having them destroy the siege engines. Without them, all they can do is stare at our walls."

"An excellent idea," said the prince. "We shall pay particular attention to where they are setting up, then attack at night. The dragons will be amongst them before they realize it."

"Be careful of their archers."

"In the dark? You give them too much credit."

"The warning is freely given," said Kythelia. "It is up to you whether or not you heed it. As you said earlier, these Mercerians are lucky. I would hate to see them defeat you a second time."

Prince Tarak was no fool. He knew how powerful this Elf queen was, and part of him suspected that his own time amongst mortals was now drawing to an end. His thoughts drifted back to the Island of Kouras, his home, where his princess, Olani, awaited his return. He'd hoped to bring back the riches of this land to lay before her feet, for she was a woman of unparalleled beauty—the perfect wife of a mighty prince such as himself.

He'd bet his future on the promises of this Elf, certain Weldwyn would fall beneath the swords of his warriors. Unfortunately, things had not gone as he had foreseen. To return home now would be to admit defeat; such an act could only result in the other princes destroying Kouras and plundering its treasures. Better to die here, a hero's death, than to return failed and impoverished.

One last look at the enemy army was enough to settle his mind. "No. I shall unleash the dragons when they attack," he declared. "That is when they will be at their most vulnerable."

Lochlan fretted. He'd narrowly avoided being killed by Kythelia's guards, but he knew she still viewed him as a threat. It wasn't that he was a warrior—far from it, in fact, or a leader, for that matter. His only crime was being brother to Brida; that alone warranted his death. The Clan Chiefs' murders had been utterly unexpected from his point of view. Now, those loyal to the chiefs were being hunted down. Any who failed to pay homage to their new Elf queen were deemed expendable, their lives forfeit.

He clung to the shadows, watching as a patrol marched by. It was well past curfew, a significant risk on his part, but a necessary one, for he needed the darkness to conceal his escape.

Down the street he went, using only the moon to light his way. More than once, he was forced to backtrack in the unfamiliar streets of Summersgate, but eventually, he found what he was looking for.

The steps before him led to the city's walls, and he took them two at a time. His heart was pounding by the time he reached the top, not through exertions but by fear. He could literally feel the blood pumping through his veins.

A guard strolled along the wall, his back the only thing Lochlan could discern. The young scholar held his breath and watched as the fellow continued on his way, disappearing into the darkness.

The young scholar approached the battlements, pulling the coiled rope from around his shoulders, looping one end over the merlon, and letting the other fall below. Saying a silent prayer to the Gods, he lowered himself over the edge, and the moon chose that exact moment to disappear behind a cloud, plunging him into darkness.

He climbed down, reaching the end of the rope while his feet still dangled below. Cursing, he realized in his rush to escape Summersgate, he'd misjudged how much rope would be needed. He had no concept of how far away the ground was. It might only be half his height, but then again, it could just as easily be three times that. He was literally stuck there, trying to decide on the better course of action. Should he climb back up and risk discovery, or let himself fall, possibly to his death?

The memory of his sister's body came to him, and he knew with a certainty that his only chance of survival lay with escaping Summersgate this night. He let go of the rope and fell.

Hayley watched the walls. "This is useless," she grumbled. "The clouds keep blocking out the moon. We'll try again tomorrow night."

"I agree," said Gorlag, "but before we return to camp, I would like to take one more look."

"Why? Did you see something of interest?"

"I am not sure," replied the Orc. "I thought I saw movement at the base of the wall, but the clouds hamper my night vision."

"Then we'll wait. It's not as if there's any pressing business for us back with the army."

"You sound disappointed."

"Do I?" said Hayley. "I suppose I'm on edge. I don't like the idea of a siege."

"Yet you've fought in them before?"

"That I have, but such affairs typically lead to a lot of bloodshed."

"I see someone," Gorlag called out as the moon emerged from the clouds.

"Only one?"

"Yes," replied the Orc. "They appear to be heading towards us."

"What are the chances of that?"

"Not us individually, I mean the Army of Merceria."

Hayley grinned. "I suppose that makes more sense."

"What shall we do?"

"Wait till they get closer, and then we'll confront whoever it is."

They waited and watched. The interloper was easy to follow for the Orc's eyes, but the High Ranger had no such advantage to assist her.

"Is he close?" asked Hayley.

"Yes," whispered Gorlag. He held up a hand and slowly put each finger down, one at a time, counting down the distance. As his last finger lowered, he leaped up, rushing forward into the darkness.

Hayley followed, her gait slower lest she twist her ankle, but she needn't have worried, for as she drew closer, the individual stood there with his hands in the air.

"Who are you?" demanded the High Ranger. "And what are you doing skulking around in the dark?"

"My name is Lochlan, brother to Brida, High Queen of the Clans. I must speak with your queen."

"What makes you assume she's willing to see you?"

"I bear important information for her."

"You'll need to be a little more specific if you expect to get through us."

"The city is under the control of a Necromancer."

Hayley looked at Gorlag. "That would do it, I suppose."

Led by his captors, a pair of rangers escorted Lochlan into the room.

"Queen Anna, this is Lochlan," announced the High Ranger. "Brother to Brida, High Queen of the Clans."

"And to what do we owe this honour?" asked the queen.

"I've come to warn you, Your Majesty. A great evil has descended upon this land, cursing us all."

"You must be more specific. We've dealt with a great many evils in the past. How is this one any different?"

"An Elf queen, Kythelia by name, has taken up residence in the Dome."

The room fell silent.

"An Elf queen, you say?"

"Indeed, Your Majesty."

"And what does your sister, the High Queen, think of this?"

"Brida is dead, slain by this very same Elf."

The Queen of Merceria looked at the old man to her right. "What do you make of this, Gerald?"

"If true, it presents us with a great opportunity."

"I don't understand?" said Lochlan. "Is this Elf known to you?"

"She is indeed," the man replied. "We originally knew her as Penelope Cromwell, mistress to King Andred, but later learned that was a ruse perpetrated by magic. She is, in fact, a Necromancer, and a dangerous one at that. One who has plagued the court of Merceria for decades. If what you say is true—"

"It is," insisted Lochlan. "Her warriors stand guard outside the Grand Edifice of the Arcane Wizards Council."

"And what is it you expect in return for bringing this news to us?"

"Only justice for my sister."

"You dare speak to us of justice?" said the queen. "You, whose people invaded this land?"

"My people were lured here with false promises. I tried to warn them against this invasion, but the animosity between our two people is too deeply ingrained. Many took the death of King Leofric as a sign from the Gods that the time for retribution was at hand."

The old man leaned forward. "Why do your folk hate the men of Weldwyn with such passion?"

"Because we Clansmen live in a poor land where we struggle to eke out a bare existence. Weldwyn is rich, with bountiful crops and fat livestock."

"Yet, it was not always so," shouted out another voice. A young man stepped out from the crowd, moving to stand before Lochlan. "Weldwyn was carved from the very same unforgiving land as the Clanholdings. The difference is, we were willing to work for our future, while you only saw fit to take what belonged to others."

"You do not know my people!" said Lochlan. "Who are you to make such a claim?"

"I am Alric, son of Leofric, Prince of Weldwyn, and well do I remember how your people corrupted my brother Cuthbert with your promises of power and wealth."

"That was not my doing, Your Highness. I am naught but a scholar. I know our people have long been enemies, but surely you can see that the presence of this Necromancer within the city spells nothing but our mutual doom?"

"Why should we take the word of a Clansman?"

Lochlan cast his head down in shame. "You shouldn't. I brought you no proof, and the Gods know there is little love lost between our people, but I swear to you I am telling the truth."

The prince turned to his queen. "I believe him."

In response, Queen Anna stood and stepped closer, surprising everyone. "Your people have given us few reasons to trust your word, but my husband has a good sense for these sorts of things. I, too, believe your story. The question now, is what do we do about it?"

Relief flooded Lochlan, for he would prefer to see his people ruled by Mercerians rather than some Dark Queen. At that precise moment, he was forced to consider his own fate. His eyes shot up, meeting those of the queen. "And what is to happen to me?"

"You shall be our guest for now. Dame Beverly will provide you with guards."

"So I am to be a prisoner?"

"No, but amongst our ranks are many men of Weldwyn who might otherwise take revenge by injuring or killing you. The guards will ensure your safety."

"Thank you, Your Majesty. I wish you only the greatest of success in your coming assault." The two rangers took him aside as the queen turned to her advisors.

"Well?" said Anna. "What does everyone think of this recent development?"

"I'm with Gerald," said Beverly. "It's an incredible opportunity."

"Yes, but can we take Kythelia on at the same time as assaulting the city? And how do we even get to her?"

"That," came a familiar voice, "is something that I can help with." Albreda swept into the room. "I'm sorry for my delay, but it has been a long journey."

"I am pleased to see you," said Anna. "You've come at a most auspicious moment."

"So I heard. Did I hear you speaking of Kythelia?"

"Yes," said Gerald. "She's apparently in the Dome."

"Then the time has come to finally push aside the shadow of darkness that has corrupted the four kingdoms."

"What are you proposing?" asked the marshal.

"That a small group enter the Dome and kill the Dark Queen."

"That's impossible," interrupted Lochlan. "There is said to be no person in all of Eiddenwerthe who can slay her."

"Says who?" demanded the Druid.

"Scholars," he replied, "and well-respected ones at that. They claim she bathed in the blood of dragons and that it protects her."

"What utter nonsense," said Albreda. "Anyone can be killed given the right circumstances. Still, it presents us with a difficult choice."

"Which is?" said the queen.

"Who to send on this perilous quest."

"Who would you suggest?"

Albreda cast her gaze around the room at the queen's closest advisors. All here would lay down their lives if necessary, yet she knew the choice would not be that easy.

"Your marshal is needed to lead your army," she said at last. "An army that must coordinate its attack with our own assault."

"Our?" said Beverly.

"Of course I have to go. How else will you recall to the Dome?"

"Then, with the queen's permission, I shall go too."

"Excellent," replied the Druid. "Although, admittedly, you were going to be my first pick."

"And who else shall you take?" asked Anna.

"Who indeed?" Albreda walked around the room, meeting the gaze of each in turn. "Dame Hayley should go, as should Lady Aubrey. We'll need her Life Magic."

She halted, turning to look at the queen. "Six is the magic number," she said. "It has special significance."

"In what way?" said Anna.

"Stone circles always consist of six stones, each inscribed with runes, and then there are the six schools of magic."

"But there are eight schools," said Aubrey.

"No. Necromancy and Hex Magic are but mirrors of Life and Enchantments."

"Then who shall take the last two positions?" pressed the queen.

"Tempus must be one. I once told you he had a task to complete before he passes from this land. I'm afraid that time is now at hand."

"No!" shouted Anna. "It can't be."

"It is not something over which we possess any control, Your Majesty.

This land is perched on the edge of an abyss. Each must play their part if we are to make things right."

"Then I shall accompany him," Anna announced. The room exploded with objections.

Albreda raised her hands in the air and called out one word that echoed off the walls. "Silence!" She waited as they all quieted. "There is no turning back. Six souls shall enter the Dome and seek out the Dark Queen. The rest of you have an equally dangerous assignment, for you must draw away the gaze of Kythelia. It will not be easy to withstand her magic, but if we are to win through, then we must make this sacrifice."

"She's right," said Anna. "I've known for years that Tempus and my fates are intertwined."

"No!" said Alric. "You can't do this. Who would rule Merceria?"

"Our son. With you to guide him, should it prove necessary. I shall not be dissuaded from this course of action, Alric."

"Then I pray for your safe return to us… to me."

THIRTY-THREE

Clash of Titans

Summer 966 MC

The assault began as the sun rose in the east. The Trolls led the way, moving slowly to allow others to keep up. Behind them, came the men of Merceria, spears and swords ready to take the fight to the enemy. The Elves of the Darkwood came next, followed by the Dwarves of Stonecastle, Ironcliff, and Mirstone. Amongst them marched the Orcs, their disciplined ranks in stark contrast to their savage reputation. Never before had this many races of Eiddenwerthe stood shoulder to shoulder, a testament to the power of a queen to unite people.

Gerald watched them march by. He was worried—not about the battle but Anna's fate. Taking on Kythelia herself was a far cry from leading her army. He feared he might never see her again.

"May I join you?" He turned to see Lady Jane.

"I'm surprised to see you here," said Gerald. "I would imagine a battle the last place you'd want to be."

"It is not the fighting I am here for. It's you."

"Me? Why? Whatever is the matter?"

"Nothing. I wish only to offer you companionship in your time of need. I know the queen can't be here, so I hoped I might suffice in her absence."

He smiled. "Thank you, Jane. That's very kind of you."

She gazed out at the army. "It's an impressive sight, but I must admit to little knowledge of such things."

"The foot will go first, although I put archers in amongst them, just in case the dragons make an appearance."

"And your horsemen?"

"They are to the rear, with little to do until we're inside the city."

"I see you have Orcs and Trolls in your army."

"We do," said Gerald. "What of it?"

"It wasn't so long ago people would take that as a sign of evil." She smiled mischievously. "Perhaps you Mercerians are the dark ones, coming to conquer our land?"

He laughed. "I like the Orcs," he said. "You can always take them at face value."

"And the Trolls?"

"They're a little more mysterious. The only one I've dealt with is their leader, Tog, but I've always found him to be insightful."

"Why do his people fight for you?"

"They don't fight for us. They fight for their home."

"I'm confused," said Lady Jane. "I thought they lived in the north?"

"Not anymore. The queen granted them land in the Great Swamp. It's their natural terrain, you see."

"And so they wander around a bog?"

"No, they built a city. They call it Trollden. Once this war is over, I intend to go visit the place."

"To what end?" she asked.

"To see what it's like. It'll make a pleasant change from all this warfare." He looked at her, adopting a serious expression. "You could join me. If that's something you'd be interested in, of course."

"I would like that, although I don't know when such a journey could be undertaken." She returned her gaze to the army. "Who leads this assault?"

"Tog."

"You must think highly of him to allow him such an honour, but is it not strange for Humans to follow such a creature?"

"You should put aside your fears," said Gerald. "Don't think of them as creatures. They are intelligent beings, much as us."

"I will try," said Jane, "but I'm afraid old prejudices run deep. You'll need to correct me if I slip into old habits."

He grinned. "I can do that."

A horseman approached.

"Sir Preston," called out Gerald. "What have you to report?"

"Herdwin has the siege towers moving up, Your Grace, and the men of Kingsford are standing by with ladders."

"Good. Now, all we need do is wait."

"Wait?" said Jane. "Your men are already marching towards the walls? Surely these others must follow?"

"Not yet," said Gerald. "We sent the invitation. Now, we must wait for the guests of honour."

"Guests?"

"Yes. By my reckoning, they should be here any moment." His eyes were glued to Summersgate's walls. "Ah, there's one of them now."

Jane followed his gaze. A large shape appeared from behind the city's defences, and as it rose into the air, it spread its wings, leaving no doubt as to its identity. She gasped. "A dragon!"

Gerald frowned. "Yes, but only the small one, by the look of it."

"Small?"

"Yes. The larger of the two collapsed the Palace. That one clearly lacks the mass for such an attack."

"It's still frightening!"

The dragon circled inside the perimeter of the city, gaining height with each pass until finally turning and heading directly towards the Mercerians.

Gerald realized he was holding his breath and forced himself to exhale. Everything was in place. He could do little now except watch the drama unfold.

The dragon gazed down at the warriors below before it descended, lining up for an attack, its wings thrust out for gliding as it swooped down on its prey. Gerald saw the throat glow slightly, the fire building within the creature until it spat out flames that struck the ground, splashing everywhere. Even from this distance, he heard the screams as warriors burned. He closed his eyes, trying to avoid the horror before him.

"Something's happening," said Jane.

Gerald snapped his eyes open. The dragon was having difficulty flapping its wings and suddenly went down, crashing in amongst his warriors, crushing some while sending others flying in all directions. He saw the creature flinch, and then he understood. The dozens of arrows and bolts protruding from its chest had done only minor damage, but the archers, much to their credit, had changed tactics, concentrating instead on the monster's membranous wings.

It reared its head up, trying to summon more fire, but the glow in its neck faded before it could complete its task, testament to the pain the creature was in. Instead, the dragon's head reached out, plucking a hapless Dwarf from the ground and snapping him clean in half.

The Dwarves moved closer, their arbalests sending bolt after bolt into the beast. It swung its tail to the side, knocking half a dozen warriors from their feet before it turned back towards the city. It lumbered along for some distance, flapping its wings, and for a moment, Gerald hoped the creature was dying, but then it launched itself into the air, letting out a primordial wail that echoed off the distant walls of Summersgate.

"Saxnor, give me strength," said Gerald. "It's getting away."

Jane kept watching. "No, it's fleeing."

"How can you tell?"

"It passed over the walls and is still climbing."

"It could come back for another pass."

"Would you, with wounds like that?"

He watched it for a little longer. "You're right, although I wonder where it will go?"

"Don't dragons like mountains?" asked Jane.

"I believe they do. Why? Where are the nearest mountains to Summersgate?"

"To the west, in the Clanholdings, but I have no idea how the dragon would know that."

"That's simple," said Gerald. "Prince Tarak likely landed them in Clan territory when they first arrived."

"Well," said Jane. "I suppose that means we won't be seeing that particular creature again."

"No, but to tell the truth, it's his comrade I'm dreading more."

"You mean the one that crushed the Palace?"

"I do, and I doubt a few crossbow bolts are going to chase it away."

As if Gerald had summoned it with his words, an immense shape rose from within the city, easily five times larger than the first dragon. Climbing at a steep angle, and looking like some armoured behemoth with scales of silver, it came directly towards the Mercerians, its mere presence spreading panic amongst the army.

Bolts sang out, but the creature was too high up to take any notice. Such was its size that it almost looked as if it were travelling slowly, yet its shadow rushed across the ground far faster than a cavalry charge.

Gerald watched the creature's throat glowing, points of light leaking out between the scales and knew the carnage was about to start, but the breath of fire never came. Instead, the dragon's head snapped up, spotting something to the east. Melethandil had arrived.

Kasri hung on for dear life. Even with the harness, she struggled to remain in her seat, but still, she risked a glance over her shoulder to check on her Hearth Guard. Six of them had volunteered for this attack, each firmly strapped into the harnesses that had been prepared. They were pale, resigned to death, for even a simple misstep here could send them plummeting to their doom.

Melethandil's eyes locked on her target. "*It is Degarath,*" she said. "*She who destroyed my eggs!*"

"*I thought you said someone from Rahad destroyed your young?*"

"*Yes. Degarath belonged to the Prince of Rahad. When Tarak's men conquered the island, the dragon fell under his control, but I never forgot her murder of my hatchlings.*"

"*Then let us finish this.*" Kasri gritted her teeth as the great dragon climbed higher and higher.

The Dwarf had spent a lifetime in the mountains, trod the mountain paths that littered her homeland, yet nothing could have prepared her for the naked fear that gripped her as they drew closer to their enemy.

"*Careful,*" she called out. "*Degarath will burn us.*"

"*No,*" replied Melethandil. "*It is not her breath we must worry about. It is her teeth and claws. Have you never seen dragons fight before?*"

"*Until I met you, I'd never even SEEN a dragon. How would I know how they fight?*"

"*Then watch and learn, and hold on tight.*"

The two great leviathans came straight for each other, then in the moment before impact, both turned up sharply, presenting all four sets of claws as they collided. Kasri heard a cry of dismay from one of her Hearth Guard as he slipped from his seat, dangling down the dragon's back, which was now perpendicular to the ground.

An awful rending sound reached Kasri's ears, and then she realized it was claws scraping along dragon scales. A great head loomed nearby, teeth catching on Melethandil's neck, blood oozing forth. Not the red blood so common to most creatures of Eiddenwerthe, but black, like the Orcs.

Kasri thrust out her hammer and called on its power. A bolt of lightning shot from its head, striking Degarath on the side of the nose. The creature released her mighty foe and pushed off, twisting into a dive.

Melethandil followed her prey, Kasri hanging on for dear life, one hand on her harness, the other with a death grip on Stormhammer. The enemy used her descent to gather speed, but even from above, Kasri saw the creature's throat glowing. Degarath suddenly made a sharp turn and twisted her serpentine neck to discharge a stream of fire, the flames headed directly for the Dwarf. Melethandil folded her wings and dove, the cascade of flame passing harmlessly to one side.

Degarath came at them again, this time from below, the impact knocking Kasri from her seat, straps straining to hold her in place as she rose in the air. Melethandril's body blocked her view of the melee, but the screams emanating from the beast beneath her told her all was not going well.

The enemy creature's mass had pushed them higher, but now, crushed together as they were, both unable to flap their wings, their ascent was about to come to an abrupt end. If something wasn't done soon, they would tumble to their deaths. Kasri looked over her shoulder at her Hearth Guard.

"*It's now or never*," she called out. She glanced down at her belt. Herdwin had insisted they all wore full harnesses rather than just a belt when they'd been discussing different tactics. She smiled at the memory and unwound the rope coiled at her waist. This was a desperate gamble and could kill her as easily as help, but she was out of options.

She connected the other end of the rope to the rings holding her in place before releasing her old restraints. It took only a moment to gather her courage before she leaped into the air.

～

Gerald watched, open-mouthed, as the two giant creatures battled it out in the sky above. Even here, far below them, the sound of their conflict echoed through the sky, their screams of rage deafening in their intensity. The entire army watched, frozen in awe at this clash of giants.

Jane gasped. "Oh no!" she yelled as someone fell from Melethandil's back. They both watched the figure descend, then suddenly swing inward, attached by some kind of restraint. Moments later, more figures followed in the first one's wake, hacking away at the titan below them.

Those on the ground ran in all directions, eager to be free from the impact zone. At the last moment, the dragons disengaged, spreading wings to swoop low over the ground, churning up dust and dirt.

Gerald watched as one unlucky Dwarf hanging from Melethandil was dragged along until the rope snapped, leaving a bloody mess.

The archers held their volleys lest they strike an ally, and then the dragons put some distance between them and began climbing once more.

"Malin's tears," said Jane. "This is horrific! I can't watch." She moved closer, burying her face in Gerald's chest. His arm unconsciously wrapped around her, holding her close.

～

Kasri looked down at the ground rushing past her at an impossible pace. Hanging from the long rope trailing beneath Melethandil, the leather went tight as the dragon once more climbed into the sky. Panic swept through her when she noticed her empty hands, her father's blessed Stormhammer no longer in her grip. Then she felt the comforting weight of it hanging from its wrist strap. She gathered her courage and began hauling herself back up the rope, along with the surviving Hearth Guards, who did likewise. Once back on the dragon, she took stock of their situation. Even with two of her warriors missing, she knew she must carry on. She helped the rest regain the relative safety of Melethandil's back and then moved up to the creature's neck.

"*I have a plan,*" she shouted.

"*Then speak!*" roared the dragon.

"*Can you attack from above?*"

"*To do what? My claws will have little effect on Degarath's scales.*"

"*True,*" said Kasri, "*but our weapons will make quick work of those wings.*"

"*Very well, but we shall need more height.*"

"*Why?*"

"*To ensure her death once she falls.*"

Kasri glanced around, seeking out their foe. "*You'd better hurry. She's coming back for another attack!*"

Up they climbed, the enemy close behind. Another streak of flame shot past, and Kasri felt the heat on the back of her helmet. The air cooled, and then she felt her ears pop. The surrounding noises grew faint, and for a moment, she wondered if her hearing had failed her.

Melethandil stopped climbing, levelling out into a glide. "*Get ready,*" she called out.

Kasri looked aft to check her warriors. They would only have one chance at this; they must make it count.

The great dragon of Kouras turned sharply and dropped. Degarath, caught by surprise, tried to angle away, but there was nowhere to hide. Kasri felt the impact and heard the claws once more screeching as they scraped across scales.

"*For Gundar!*" she yelled, sliding down the dragon's foreleg, spinning off into the air as she hit Melethandil's knee. The rope caught, and she swung back and careened into the monstrous beast's side. She had the presence of mind to grip Stormhammer with both hands, smashing the creature with all the might she could muster, but without planting herself first, she did little damage. The blow rang off a scale, and she released the weapon to grip the rope in an effort to climb up Degarath's back.

She realized her Hearth Guard was already at work, cutting into the creature's wings, when a piece of membrane flew by, accompanied by a roar of anguish. The dragons twisted in the air, and Kasri suddenly found herself lying down. Quickly getting back to her feet, she ran across the enemy dragon's back, her target now in sight. Just as she reached the base of a wing, the mighty beasts twisted again, and she grabbed at a scale to keep upright.

Kasri tossed Stormhammer into the air, then grabbed the handle, calling on its power once more. She swung the hammer, striking the root of the wing, sending lightning cascading along its length all the way to the tip. Degarath fell away from beneath her as the leathery appendage went limp, leaving the Dwarf dangling at the end of the rope.

Kasri had a brief glimpse of one of her warriors still hacking away at the other wing, and then the poor fellow was lost from sight as the great dragon spiralled out of control.

Degarath smashed into the ground, leaving a great rent in the dirt as she barrelled through a group of spearmen desperately seeking safety. She then careened into a tree, ripping its roots from the very ground.

Melethandil flew towards the body, using her wings to slow her descent, landing with a gentle footfall. Kasri abandoned her harness, staggering over to her warriors, who did likewise.

"*It is done,*" Kasri said. "*You have defeated her.*"

"*No,*" said Melethandil. "*Not yet.*"

She walked over to Degarath and paused. Everyone went quiet until the only sound to be heard was that of the fallen dragon's shallow breaths. Melethandil placed one claw on her opponent's neck, then reached out with her head and clamped down with her teeth. The breathing stopped, the light leaving Degarath's eyes.

THIRTY-FOUR

The Dome

Summer 966 MC

"Remind me again why only the six of us are going?" asked Hayley. "Surely we could take more?"

"It's a simple matter of energy," explained Aubrey. "While it's possible to bring more people using the spell of recall, it would require additional magic to do so."

"So Albreda would have less left to use against Kythelia?"

"Exactly."

"And why Her Majesty?"

"That," said Albreda, "is none of your concern."

"We're going into a place from which none of us might return. I think we've earned a little trust, don't you?"

"She's right," said Anna. "You should explain your reasoning."

The Druid sighed. "Very well. This all relates to a vision I had some months ago."

"You never mentioned it," said Aubrey.

"For good reason. I saw this very group standing beneath the Dome."

"And?" prompted Hayley.

"My visions don't always supply the details, but it would be prudent to be ready to fight the moment we appear."

"Easy for you to say," said the queen. "I'm still trying to don my armour."

Beverly moved to her side. "Here, let me help you."

"It fit last year."

"Yes, well, you've had a child since then. I imagine that hasn't helped."

Beverly pulled on the queen's belt, cinching it tighter. "Hayley, are you sure you don't want some armour?"

"I'm fine with my leathers, thanks. They don't hamper my archery skills."

"How about you, Cousin?"

"No," replied Aubrey. "I expect that I'll need to cast quickly. I doubt I'll be able to do that wearing unfamiliar armour."

"That's quite sensible of you," said Albreda, kneeling. Tempus came over to her, and she placed her forehead to his for a moment, then withdrew, the great mastiff padding back to Anna.

"What was that all about?" asked the queen.

"Just making sure Tempus knows what's happening."

"Care to tell the rest of us the plan?" asked Hayley.

"My spell will have us materialize in the magic circle that lies directly beneath the Dome itself."

"And is that where Kythelia will be?"

"I doubt it," replied Albreda. "The room has no windows, and she'll likely be watching the assault on the city."

"So," said the ranger, "we split up once the casting circle is secured?"

"No," said Beverly. "We must stick together if we want to defeat her."

"Beverly is correct," agreed the Druid. "Our strength is the bond we share. Only together can we take advantage of that."

"If things go badly," said Hayley, "do we have an escape plan?"

"Aubrey can use the spell of recall as easily as I, but you must all remember it takes some time to cast. Once engaged in melee, it will be very difficult to disengage."

"Fine by me. In fact, from a certain point of view, it makes things easier."

"How so?" asked Beverly.

"Well," said the High Ranger. "With retreat off the table, all we can do is attack. After all, it's what we're here for, isn't it?"

"My question is, how do we kill Kythelia? Isn't she immune to dying? You know the whole, 'bathing in the blood of dragons', thing?"

"Any living creature can be killed," countered Albreda. "We just have to find out how."

"I'm sure Nature's Fury would do some serious damage," said Beverly. "Assuming I could get close enough to use it."

"And therein lies the problem. I suspect you and Hayley will spend the bulk of your time fighting off her guards. Aubrey, you and I will concentrate on using our magic to our best advantage."

"What about Tempus and me?" asked Anna.

"Keep that Dwarf sword of yours close at hand. As for Tempus, he knows what must be done. Now, is that armour of yours ready to go?"

"It is."

"Good. Then draw weapons, and get ready for the fight of your lives."

Albreda moved to stand amongst them, then closed her eyes. At first, nothing happened, but then she began murmuring quietly, words that few could understand, save for perhaps Aubrey. A slight breeze picked up, the grass moving around as dust and dirt circled them. The Druid's voice got louder, the whirlwind picking up, flowing higher into the air and adding leaves and twigs to the mix. Soon, it became a raging tornado, just out of their reach, obscuring everything beyond its perimeter.

The ground shifted under their feet, and then the surrounding debris dropped suddenly, revealing the casting room beneath the great copper-coloured dome.

The room, much like the magic circle held within, was circular in nature, with two sets of double doors to the left and right. A trio of armoured warriors bedecked in green stood before each one. Obviously, Kythelia had foreseen a potential threat appearing here.

Beverly was first to react, smashing Nature's Fury to the floor. Vines creeped out from the point of impact, wrapping around the legs of two Elven guards on the group's left, pinning them in place.

Hayley, arrow nocked and ready, let fly as soon as the room coalesced around them, taking the third warrior in the upper shoulder, causing him to double over with a grunt.

Tempus launched himself towards the door to their right, ploughing into one and knocking him back. Shocked by the sudden onslaught, his companions backed up, drawing their swords.

The power built within Aubrey as she began to cast. Anna, meanwhile, rushed forward, coming to the aid of her dog, stabbing out with her Dwarf sword, but the Elven mail resisted. The guard countered, slicing down and driving her back. She parried as best she could, but a queen is no match for a trained warrior, and the Elf pushed past her smaller weapon, driving his blade into her shoulder. As he pulled back for another strike, his eyes closed suddenly, and he collapsed.

Tempus, having crushed the throat of one guard, turned on the remaining Elf. Before he could do much damage, however, an arrow took out the guard's eye, and he slumped against the door, sliding to the floor.

Anna recovered her wits and stabbed the sleeping guard beneath the helmet as Beverly finished off her two opponents with a pair of efficient strikes to their heads.

"Good," said Albreda. "The circle is ours. Now, all that remains is for us to find Kythelia. Beyond these doors, a corridor runs around this very room. I am positive that we can expect more guards there."

"And Kythelia?" asked Anna.

"Hard to say. A balcony runs along the outside of the dome. I suspect she may be there, for it would offer the best view of the area."

"How do we get there?"

"Out in the hallway, we'll find a wide set of stairs going down. From the top of those, walk down the corridor until you see a smaller set heading upwards."

Aubrey moved towards the queen. "Are you injured?"

"Only my pride. My armour stopped the blade from penetrating."

Beverly turned towards the door to their left.

"No, wait, Cousin," said Aubrey. "Let me use my magic to see what lies beyond."

"You mean to spirit walk?"

The Life Mage nodded.

"That could prove dangerous," said Albreda. "Remember, Kythelia and her minions enslaved an army of spirits. The realm of the dead is theirs to command. Who knows what creatures lurk in these halls?"

"Then I shall conjure a spirit companion."

"Can you take others into the spirit realm?"

"She can," said Beverly. "I've seen her do it before."

"Then take me," said the Druid. "I can help you, should you need it."

"What about the rest of us?"

"You must remain here to guard our bodies."

"Secure that door," Beverly said to Hayley, "while I keep a close eye on this one."

Hayley took an Elven sword, sheathed it, and then used the weapon to jam the door like a drop bar. "I can't guarantee how long this will last, but I suppose it's better than nothing."

Aubrey, for her part, was still within the circle, in the throes of casting a spell while lying prone.

Anna turned to Albreda. "You must lie down, lest your body falls when you enter the spirit realm."

The Druid heard a loud snap and then felt a tug as her spirit lifted from her. She looked down at her own lifeless body. There was a slight feeling of disorientation as her eyes adjusted to the muted tones.

"Is this what it's like to be a ghost?"

"You get used to it," replied Aubrey. The Life Mage looked drained of colour yet otherwise healthy. "It will take me a moment to call on my spirit companion, and then we can proceed."

Albreda stepped back, if stepped were the right word for it. She felt nothing beneath her feet and realized with a start that she wasn't even breathing. Her mind recoiled at the very idea, but then she got a grip of herself. Of course she wasn't breathing. In the strictest sense of the word, she wasn't even alive!

Aubrey was once again using her magic, the words of power falling from her lips in a cascade of sounds that echoed in the eerie world of the spirits. The sounds died away, but she remained still, her hands held out before her as if beckoning something.

A shadow lurked in the distance, becoming more distinct as it approached. It could have been any wolf who now tread the spirit realm, but the scar on its back told a different story. Albreda dropped to her knees, tears coming to her eyes.

"Fang! Is that you?"

Aubrey watched in fascination as the wolf ignored her, going instead towards the Druid. It placed a paw on Albreda's shoulder and licked her face.

"I don't understand?" said the Life Mage.

"This is Fang," said Albreda through tears of joy. "He is my oldest friend. We met when I first came to the Whitewood as a young girl."

"Incredible that I should be the one who summoned him. It almost makes me believe in fate."

"It is not fate but good fortune. I hope this is a sign we will be successful this day. In any event, we haven't time to visit. There's work to be done." She stood, wiping the tears from her eyes. "How curious. I wouldn't have thought one could weep as a ghost."

"There are many things we don't understand about the world of spirits," said Aubrey. "But we haven't got time to ponder them at the moment. As you say, we have work to do. The first thing is to step through the wall." She looked at the Druid. "It can be very disorienting. I find it best to close your eyes right before you make contact with it."

"Very well. Lead on."

Aubrey stepped close, then gathered her resolve and stepped right through the stone. Fang, eager to follow, rushed through as though nothing was there. Albreda moved to take up a similar stance to the Life Mage, and closing her eyes, took a step. She expected a strange sensation, as though something passed through her, but to her surprise, there was no difference. She opened her eyes to see the hallway beyond. The stairs leading down deeper into the Dome were on her left, but Aubrey's attention was focused on Albreda's right.

"You say the way up was over there?" She pointed.

"Yes. Although how we climb them in this state is beyond me."

"You must visualize yourself going up the stairs," said Aubrey. "It's a strange experience since you can't feel the steps yourself."

"Well, let's locate them first, shall we? And then you can show me the proper technique." She paused. "What about Fang? How will he climb them?"

"I gather he's been a spirit for some time. I doubt he'll have any problem."

They proceeded down the hallway. On the right was the wall making up the room with the casting circle, while on the left, windows overlooked the city of Summersgate.

Aubrey paused, her gaze coming to rest on an open shutter. She moved closer to view what was happening outside.

"What do you see?" asked Albreda.

"Warriors rushing to man the walls."

"Good. That means the attack is underway. It will keep everyone occupied while we make our way upstairs."

The Life Mage tore her eyes from the scene and continued on her way. The stairs leading towards the outside balcony were narrower than the others, requiring them to move in single file. Fang, understanding his role well, padded up first, proceeding to the top, halting at a small landing that ended at a door. He was soon joined by the two mages.

"This is it," said Aubrey. "Likely beyond this door is the Dark Queen. I cannot say what she will look like in the world of spirits."

"Still, we must persist, if only to establish her whereabouts. Remember, we're not here to fight her, merely to determine her exact location." Albreda paused for a moment, then nodded at her companion. "You may proceed."

Aubrey stepped through, with Albreda and Fang close on her heels. They emerged onto a narrow balcony that ran around the perimeter of the Dome. The Dome's magically enchanted, copper-topped roof was to the left, while a breathtaking view of the surrounding countryside was on the right. Albreda took this all in the instant before the very air grew dark. She turned, knowing full well that Kythelia was aware of her presence.

"So," said a rasping voice, "we finally meet."

Albreda had seen much in her long life, but nothing prepared her for the sight now standing before her. Kythelia was an Elf; that much was clear, but her spirit form possessed additional appendages growing from her shoulders like the arms of a giant spider. A dark mist swirled around her, obscuring her features, even as a purple glow floated above her head. This was Albreda's first visit to the world of spirits, but even she knew this Elf was an abomination, a very affront to the world of the living. The malevolence clung to the Elf's body like a wet cloak.

"What's taking them so long?" said Hayley.

"It's a big place," said Beverly, "and they must first find Kythelia."

"Should we go out into the hallway?"

"We can't," insisted the queen. "We must guard their bodies."

"We could take a peek, couldn't we?"

"Not without the possibility of alerting our foes."

"Sorry," said the ranger. "I'm not normally like this, but just standing around and waiting is driving me mad." She looked at Beverly. "How is it you're so calm?"

"Who says I'm calm?"

"You don't look worried."

"I'm not," said Beverly. "My cousin can take care of herself, and in any event, she has Albreda with her. I can't imagine two more powerful mages."

"Except," said Anna, "for Kythelia herself."

Hayley moved to the blocked door. "Did you hear that?" she whispered.

"Trouble?" asked Beverly.

The door rattled. "We've got company, and they're trying to get in."

Beverly moved up beside the ranger, her hammer at the ready.

"What can I do?" asked Anna.

The red-headed knight was quick to respond. "See if you can drag our two casters out of the circle and closer to the wall."

"To keep them out of danger?"

"Saxnor, no. The entire room will likely be flooded with warriors at any moment. We need the space to fight!"

"How do you want to do this?" asked Hayley.

"You stand back and use your bow."

"You'll be overwhelmed."

"You let me worry about that. Pick your targets carefully."

The door shuddered as someone tried to force it.

Anna was dragging Aubrey's body off to the side. "What if they come through the other set of doors?" she called out.

"Then we'll turn and fight there instead of here," said Beverly. Someone started battering the door. "Persistent, aren't they?"

The door rattled twice more, and then something solid hit it.

"Oh, great," said Hayley. "They have axes."

A large splinter of wood broke free, revealing a bevy of guards beyond. Hayley let fly with an arrow that hit a target, eliciting a cry from beyond. Beverly wheeled around unexpectedly, rushing for the other door as guards pushed it open.

She struck out with the hammer, taking one in the chest and knocking him backwards. She stepped into the gap, using her hand to push another to the side, letting out a yell, "For Merceria!"

Anna lowered Aubrey down, then pointed at the now open doorway. "Tempus, attack!"

The great mastiff rushed forward with a growl to strike a guard on the chest, his paws knocking the hapless warrior to the floor. Then the dog was in amongst a group of them, his teeth bared and bloody.

Hayley loosed off another arrow as the second door burst open. She dropped the bow, drawing her sword just in time to parry a blow.

Anna once more drew her Dwarf sword, prepared to continue the fight, but more and more Elves poured into the room. She swung out, only for the blade to be knocked from her hands. Her foe advanced on her, ready to deliver the killing blow.

THIRTY-FIVE

Into the Breach

Summer 966 MC

"The time to strike is nigh," said Gerald. "We need to take down that wall and get inside as quickly as possible." He looked around at his commanders. They were worried, and with good reason, for the walls of Summersgate were well-made.

"How are we to proceed?" asked Prince Alric.

"Now that we divested the enemy of their dragons, we can proceed with all haste. I have a plan, but first, I'm eager to see what others might suggest."

Lord Arandil nodded his head. "You are much more knowledgeable about this type of warfare than I, Marshal. I shall bow to your superior experience."

"As will I," said Althea. "I might have led a skirmish or two, but this is far outside of my expertise."

"Let us hear this plan of yours," suggested Urgon. "They have always served us well in the past. I see no reason we should doubt them now."

Gerald turned to Herdwin. "You're quiet."

"I don't wish to speak out of turn."

"Come now, we've known each other for years. If you're not comfortable speaking to me as a marshal, then speak to your friend."

"It looks to me like there's a weakness in the wall's design."

"In what way?" asked Alric. "I always thought Summersgate impregnable."

"Aye, well, you would, being from Weldwyn and all. Not that it's a bad wall, you understand, but the city is an irregular shape, and that bulge, just north of the gate, isn't properly supported."

"Meaning?" said Althea.

Gerald smiled. "The supporting towers don't have a clear view of the section. A blind spot, if you will."

"Can we exploit it?" asked the princess.

"I think so," said the marshal. "If we put our minds to it."

"But?" said Herdwin.

"We're not only assaulting the city," replied the marshal. "We're also trying to assist the others in taking down Kythelia."

"But getting in WILL help them, won't it?"

"Possibly, but my thinking was that we could bring down the wall right there." Gerald pointed to the distant city, a spot directly in line with the copper-plated Dome.

"That's a tall order," said Alric. "Are you sure we can bring it down?"

The marshal turned his attention to the other Dwarf. "Kasri?"

"Aye. We can."

"How?" said the prince.

"Melethandil will land on it. Trust me, if Degarath could destroy the Palace, then I'm sure our own dragon will have no trouble destroying a simple wall section. Of course, there'll still be a mountain of rubble to navigate."

"The Dwarven Brigade can do that," said Herdwin. "We'll climb up and secure the breach before moving out along the walls on either side, but you'll need someone a little speedier to make their way into the city."

"Allow me that honour," said Lord Arandil Greycloak. "Once inside, we shall make our way directly to the Dome and deal with this dark host, once and for all."

"I'm surprised you would offer your assistance," said Gerald. "For that will bring you into direct conflict with your own people."

"For too long have I let these outcasts bring terror to Eiddenwerthe. I shall permit it no longer."

"I would be pleased to assist," offered Urgon. "Provided our Elven lord has no objection?"

Lord Greycloak straightened his back. "I would be honoured to accept the help of your people. Let us put our past differences aside and now fight as friends rather than foes."

"Agreed," replied the Orc. They shook hands, much to the surprise of the others present.

"All well and good," said Alric, "but there's still the matter of retaking the streets of Summersgate."

"That," said Gerald, "will be the job of you and Princess Althea. You'll take in the Mercerian foot and secure the northeast gate. Once that's open, your sister will bring through the cavalry. You know the city better than anyone else here, so I'll be relying on your expertise when it comes to actual objectives."

"Marshal," said Sir Preston. "Might I suggest we cut off any chance of escape? We don't want these Clansmen rallying out in the countryside."

"An excellent suggestion. Use the Guard Cavalry and the remaining heavy cavalry to block the western gate. Kasri, once you and Melethandril destroy that wall, I'll need you airborne to keep an eye on things. Revi will help, but Shellbreaker can't be everywhere."

"What about the south gate?" asked Althea.

"Montak will take the mastiffs there. Horses or not, I doubt many people would be willing to risk running into them."

"And yourself?"

"I'll follow Prince Alric once he gets past that wall." Gerald looked around at the faces once more, recognizing their looks of determination. He knew they would do their best to see this through, which was all he could ask for. "All right, you lot. Let's not stand around here all day. You've all got things to do."

The meeting broke up, with everyone heading off to their separate commands. Gerald searched those nearby, looking for a familiar face. It didn't take him long to find it.

"Ah, Jane. There you are."

"Sorry," she replied. "I didn't want to interrupt your important meeting."

He shrugged. "I was hoping to hear their opinions, but they were content to let me do all the planning."

"That's because they hold you in high regard."

Embarrassed, he tried to laugh it off.

"No," she pleaded. "Don't do that. You really don't know the effect you have on people, do you?"

He was caught off guard. "What do you mean?"

"They love you, Gerald. They know you'll do whatever you must to keep them safe. It's the mark of a truly great leader."

"I'm just doing my job. I am the marshal, you know."

"You are far more than just the marshal. You are an inspiration, and not just for the warriors amongst us."

"What's that supposed to mean?"

"You are calm in the face of adversity, generous of spirit, and loyal to your queen: all admirable qualities. Any woman would be proud to call you hers."

"Any woman?"

She blushed. "Well," she said. "I definitely would."

Melethandril gained height, then circled while Kasri got her bearings. Six more Hearth Guards clung to the dragon's back behind the Dwarf, eager to make names for themselves.

"*You see that copper dome and the wall in line with it?*" Kasri called out in the ancient tongue. "*That's what we need to bring down.*"

"*Then hold tight,*" replied the dragon. "*I must make a steep descent.*" She held her altitude for a moment before folding her wings and plummeting towards her target.

Kasri, feeling the sudden drop, gripped her harness tightly. The wind rushed past her, whistling as it raced through her helmet, adding an eerie sensation to it all. With the buildings on the ground growing more distinct, Melethandril pushed her wings out into a steep glide. The Dwarf leaned to one side, the better to see past the dragon's back and was rewarded with the sight of Summersgate's walls drawing ever closer.

Arrows flew towards them, most falling short, but at least one sailed past her arm, catching in her cloak. Behind her, her warriors screamed out a challenge in the ancient tongue, telling all that the warriors of Gundar were fast approaching.

Another volley of arrows blossomed from the walls, many striking the dragon but doing no damage. In response, Melethandil let out a mighty roar as she lifted her head and flapped her wings to slow their approach.

Kasri aimed her hammer at a group of archers and let loose with a bolt of lightning, striking one, causing his body to twitch uncontrollably and then fall from the wall. More arrows flew towards her, one even striking her helmet, but it bore little force behind it, only making a dull thud before it was carried away by the wind.

Melethandil struck the wall with all four claws held out in front, landing as a cat might. With a powerful grip, she reached out and dug into the rock, then lowered her body onto it, allowing her mass to do its work.

Kasri felt them land, then all was still. She at first took the lack of destruction to mean they had failed, but then she felt a rumble as the dragon sank down about an arm's length. Bits of stone started falling from the wall, and then the massive creature dropped again, triggering an avalanche of debris that bounced off the distant buildings.

Melethandil, tilting to one side, stuck out her legs, trying to find some purchase. More rock went flying even as the enemy poured arrows into them. Kasri felt panic rising, for an uneven collapse could well mean a dragon trapped beneath a mass of rock and stone. The enemy archers moved closer, taking direct aim at the creature's wings. The Dwarf had the presence of mind to send another lightning bolt flying, with the satisfaction of a few more foes falling from the wall.

The sounds of destruction reached a crescendo just before the dragon dropped down once more. Bits of the broken wall shot up on either side even as a gigantic plume of dust flew into the air.

The archers, their view now blocked, ceased loosing their arrows. This gave Kasri an unexpected respite, but it also meant she could no longer target any foes.

"*Hold on tight,*" said Melethandil. "*Our job here is done.*"

The Dwarf hunkered down into her seat as the dragon flapped its wings once more. The action drove the dust into the enemy's eyes, making things all the worse for them. The great beast beneath her backed up, then twisted away from the wall and began climbing once more. She risked a glance behind her, spotting the long section of wall below them now in ruins. At the sound of a horn, the Dwarven Brigade rushed forward to take advantage of the breach.

~

The Dwarves of Mirstone led the assault, followed by those of Stonecastle. Kasri's Dwarves from Ironcliff acted as the reserve, ready to rush forward should opposition prove problematic.

Lord Tulfar was the first to arrive at the slope formed by the collapsed debris. The smaller rocks and stones at the bottom made climbing relatively easy, but as they went higher, larger chunks hampered their efforts. Unfortunately, the dust cloud drifted away as they advanced, allowing the enemy archers to resume their constant rain of arrows.

Herdwin ordered the arbalesters to take positions on either side of the slope, sending their bolts flying forth. Up the ramp he went, his trusty axe in one hand, his shield in the other.

An arrow whizzed by his ear, and he ducked behind a large piece of stone, his mind taking him back to Galburn's Ridge. He'd failed in the initial assault there, and the memory chilled him. He chastised himself, for he was a smith at heart, not a warrior, yet he couldn't bring himself to let the others down. Determined to do his part, he moved back out from behind his cover and continued his climb.

He spotted Lord Tulfar lying above him. The poor fellow had taken a shot to the chest and now crouched behind a rock, looking pale and disheartened.

"You two," shouted Herdwin, looking at a couple of nearby Dwarves. "Take His Lordship back down and find Revi Bloom."

Despite the disappointment on their faces, they did as ordered, carrying the injured lord down the hill of rubble.

"Ah, the passion of youth," said Herdwin. "I remember it well." The statement was said to no one in particular, but the sound of his own voice made him think of Kasri. He glanced upward, hoping to see the dragon rider, but she was far too distant to discern, hidden as she was by the bulk of her mount.

An arrow thudded into his shield. "Blast it!" he called out. "That's what you get for losing your concentration, you old fool!" He continued his climb.

The sounds of the melee drifted to his ears. Those in front of him had reached the summit and now dealt with the enemy. The volleys ceased as he arrived at the top, and he could see the clash of arms for himself. A Dwarf fell back, blood gushing from his helmet as he slid down the ramp, knocking Herdwin to the side.

"Confound it!" he yelled, struggling to regain his footing. He held his axe in a firm grip and charged on, his shield ready to block should the need arise.

A Clansman rushed forward, seeking to take advantage of the gap, but Herdwin's weapon smashed into the man's skull, slicing through the helmet to send him directly to the Afterlife.

The Dwarf threw up his shield as a spear jabbed out, the tip biting into the wood. He absorbed the blow, then twisted, ripping the weapon from the warrior's hand. Herdwin stomped forward, whirling his axe in a criss-cross pattern to drive back his foe, then finished him off with a severe cut to the arm that almost severed the limb. Blood spurted all over the place, blinding the Dwarf to his right. Herdwin quickly slid sideways, saving his ally with another shield block even as his axe swung out again. He felt resistance as the blade connected, then scraped down to the crossguard. His opponent, skilled with the sword, counterattacked with a thrust, the top of the weapon digging into Herdwin's chain hauberk.

The Dwarf grunted, taking the hit while driving the blade into his shield, the metal edge snagging it and ripping it from its owner's hand. The Clansmen bent low to recover his weapon, only to be head-butted by Herdwin. The Dwarf's head rang with the impact, but he heard his foe's skull crack, and then the poor fool was prone, blood streaming out from his ears.

The Dwarf to Herdwin's right, having recovered from his near blinding, rushed back into the fray, giving the smith a slight reprieve.

The enemy fell back, their weapons a poor match against the might of Dwarven steel. Warriors lay all around, their blood flowing down the ramp freely. The mountain folk had fared well, with only a few of his people down. Many more had been wounded but still carried the fight to their foes.

Herdwin grabbed the arm of a Dwarf passing by. "*Go down and inform Urgon the wall is ours,*" he said in his native tongue.

"*Urgon?*"

"*Yes. The Orc Chieftain.*"

The warrior turned, half running, half sliding down the slope. With that now taken care of, Herdwin turned his attention to the walls on either side of the breach. He soon spotted a familiar face, a rough-looking Dwarf with a yellow beard. "*I know you. We fought together at Galburn's Ridge!*"

"*Aye, so we did. The name's Naldurn Grimaxe.*"

Herdwin pointed with the head of his axe. "*Take these Dwarves, Naldurn, and head south, along the top of the wall. You're to clear away any opposition you see. Understood?*"

"*Aye, Commander.*"

"*And take some arbalesters with you. The last thing you need right now is enemy archers harassing you.*"

"*And you?*"

"*I'll take half of what's left and head north. The rest will hold the top until the Orcs arrive.*"

He waited long enough for Naldurn to move out before looking to his own self-appointed task. The enemy was atop the still-intact part of the wall, presenting a formidable obstacle. It would have signified an impossible task to anyone else, but to Herdwin, it was merely a challenge. He hefted his belt and shook out his arms.

"Well, boys," he called out, nodding at their target, "who's going to be the first to set foot up there?"

The Dwarf skidded to a stop before the Orc Chieftain.

"Commander Herdwin says to tell you the breach is ours," he reported.

"Good," said Urgon. "We shall begin the ascent."

He waved his troops forward, few as they were, before seeking out Lord Arandil.

"It is time," said the Orc.

The Elven leader turned to his own command. "Advance," he ordered. "Spears leading."

The warriors marched in perfect unison, their ranks tightly packed. Urgon wondered how they would climb the ramp in such a close configuration but held his tongue. Instead, he rushed to catch up to his own hunters, who were already passing through the debris.

"*About time you joined us,*" said Tarluk in the language of his people. "*I feared you would miss the hunt.*"

"*Fear not,*" replied the chieftain. "*I would never abandon my people.*"

Once they arrived at the top, Urgon spotted the Dwarves pushing along the walls while the entire city of Summersgate lay there, waiting to be reclaimed.

Urgon pointed at the distant copper rooftop. "*That which they call the Dome is our target,*" he said. "*It is not far now, but we must take care not to outstrip our allies, for we will find an adversary there who will prove most difficult.*"

"*More Humans?*" replied Tarluk.

"*No, Elves. Followers of the Dark Queen, Kythelia, and likely many more of them than us. We shall wait here until Lord Arandil's forces join us, then cover their flanks.*" His gaze drifted to the distant Dome, and he spotted a group of individuals up near the copper-covered roof.

"*Is that her?*" asked the Orc hunter.

"*More than likely,*" said Urgon.

"*I hear the Queen of Merceria herself is up there.*"

"*She is, and may the Ancestors protect her!*"

THIRTY-SIX

Confrontation

Summer 966 MC

K ythelia rose to her full height. "You are fools if you believe you can defeat me. No one in all of Eiddenwerthe can kill me. No weapon can penetrate my skin. Go back to your homes and cower in fear."

"We shall not," said Albreda. "For you are the very antithesis of that which I hold most sacred." She thrust out her hands, expecting to send vines crawling towards her foe, but the world of spirits proved no place for such magic.

Kythelia responded by sending a black tendril snaking out towards the Druid, wrapping around her, pinning one arm in place even as she tried to cast anew. Fang sprang upon the sinewy arm, sinking his teeth into the vile, inky blackness.

Kythelia cried out in dismay, her spell turning to ash to float away on an unseen wind. Aubrey cast, calling forth words of power that produced grey, shadowy figures that coalesced into Orc warriors who rushed forward, ready to strike down their enemy.

From behind the Dark Queen came Margaret, holding one hand, palm up, while the other made a cutting motion, weaving a spell of her own. Blood pooled in her hand, and then, as each drop fell to the ground, it blossomed into an obscene mockery of an Elf with ashen skin and twisted limbs.

Three of them lunged forward in time to meet the Orc hunters. The fight should've been short, for the Orcs were armed, while the spirit Elves bore no visible weapons, but as they clashed, it soon became apparent this was far from an unequal fight. The spirit Elves lifted their hands, revealing sharp, bony projections instead of fingers, that drove into their opponents, ripping armour asunder.

"Back!" shouted Aubrey. "We must get out of here."

Both Human mages turned and ran, Fang rushing along after them. The sounds of fighting were muted, as was everything in this strange world of spirits, yet they knew the conflict continued on behind them.

Albreda passed through the door to see Aubrey already descending the steps. The Druid picked up the pace, eager not to be left behind.

Aubrey reached the bottom, then ran directly through the wall, intending to return to the casting circle as quickly as possible. Albreda followed her lead, halting as she came upon the others.

A press of Elven warriors forced Beverly and Hayley to one side, fending off more and more attacks as they backed up. On the other side stood Anna, her Dwarven weapon on the floor as a foe advanced with his sword at the ready.

Albreda reacted instinctively, throwing herself into her physical body. It was a strange sensation, and for a moment, she wondered if it had failed. With the floor's coldness flooding into her bones, her eyes snapped open, no longer seeing the spirit realm's muted colours but the land of the living. She raised her hand towards the ceiling, tightly clenching her fist.

Vines sprang up from the floor, entwining themselves around the Elf warrior's leg. He looked down, letting out a scream of agony as it crushed him, forgetting the queen in his moment of panic. Slashing down in an attempt to hack away at the thorny growths, his sword made contact only to sink into the vines and become stuck fast. The vines crawled up his blade, crushing both flesh and steel.

Anna, seizing the opportunity, picked up her sword and stepped forward, driving it into her foe's stomach. The Dwarven steel easily slipped past Albreda's spell, and then the warrior fell, his blood staining the magic circle crimson.

Aubrey's hastily thrown spell of drowsiness failed to put one of Beverly's opponents to sleep, but at least it slowed his reflexes sufficiently for her cousin to take advantage of his delay.

Nature's Fury drove into his chest, collapsing his lungs through the armour. He stumbled backwards before falling down heavily. Seeking to gain the initiative, her second opponent struck out, only to find a shield blocking his attack. He pulled back his sword with amazing speed and struck again, this time at the knight's legs.

Beverly smashed the edge of her shield down on the blade, driving it to the floor along with her opponent's arm. Then came her hammer, hitting the elbow joint and shattering bone.

The Elf in front of Aubrey was fast, far faster than she thought possible. All she could do was parry over and over again, never getting the opportunity to take a swing herself.

The Life Mage blocked once more, but this time she felt the weight behind the attack as the two swords locked, and it became a test of strength. The blade edged closer to her face, and then her opponent fell back with a scream as Tempus's jaws clamped on the fellow's leg.

The Elf wheeled around, attempting to stab at the beast, but suddenly Hayley was there, thrusting into his side, the links parting beneath the onslaught. All resistance melted away as her blade sank halfway up the hilt in Elven flesh. Her opponent stiffened before toppling away from her, taking her sword with him.

More guards came, bearing large, two-handed axes. The first one through the door took a Dwarf blade to the leg, a thrust that cut through the straps of his greave, drawing blood. Anna backed up, barely avoiding the Elf's axe as it struck stone, ringing out like a bell, the sound echoing off the walls.

Albreda turned to meet this new threat, calling on more vines to block the door. Two more enemies halted their advance, Earth Magic pinning them in place.

Beverly ran at the other door, where more guards rushed in. She didn't give them time to organize. Instead, she pushed right into them, using her mass to knock one from his feet, another to back up. She struck out with Nature's Fury, feeling the power surge as its sky metal head sank into an arm. Her attacks gained speed as the magic took hold. Another guard fell to her weapon, and then she was in the corridor, charging towards the steps that came up from below.

She placed herself at the top while half a dozen Elven warriors clustered below. When two archers stepped into view, their large Elven bows nocked and ready to take her down, the threat came too late for her to react. The arrows flew up the stairs. One bounced harmlessly off her helmet as she twisted away, while the second pierced her side, penetrating the gap between chest and backplate. Blood bubbled up into her lungs, and she coughed. Her legs went weak as she collapsed to the floor, Nature's Fury all but forgotten. The last thing she heard was Kythelia's mocking cackle of glee.

Aubrey rushed to her cousin's aid, but the Elves were faster. A blade struck out as she left the doorway, slicing into the flat of her stomach. The skin parted way, blood staining her dress, and then she fell, clutching the wound. Unbidden, words of power came to her mind. Her hands glowed with magical energy, but before she could complete her spell, the hilt of a sword was bashed against her forehead, the force sending her spinning to the floor just as everything went black.

Albreda scrambled to fight back, closing her eyes for a moment as she pulled forth the magic of the earth. Her fingernails grew, tearing flesh as they did so, blood splattering onto the floor as she gave a howl, releasing the fury of the forest. She rushed forward, knocking an axe aside, screaming with rage as animal instincts overwhelmed her. With hands that were now claws, she ripped through chainmail better than any axe could hope to match. The Dark Queen's voice drew closer, and Albreda charged at her, using her newfound talons to rip into a guard's arm. Chainmail links tore asunder, a fine mist of blood filling the air.

Onward, the Druid charged, ripping another's throat open but not stopping, keeping up the momentum that was bringing her closer to her ultimate prey. Behind her followed Tempus, his teeth tearing at the throats of those knocked aside.

Kythelia watched as her personal bodyguards rushed forward.

"How curious," she said, turning to Margaret. "Come. We shall let my warriors dispatch this witch. It is time you claimed what is rightfully yours."

Hayley cut down another Elf, then scanned the room for Queen Anna. The place was a scene of carnage, with bodies and blood strewn around everywhere. While most of the others were out in the hallway, an axe wielder loomed over her queen. As the Elf raised his weapon, the High Ranger ran forward, bowling him over and sending them both to the ground, weapons flying from their hands.

Before even gaining her feet, Hayley had her knife in hand, stabbing out, seeking to get beneath her foe's helmet. He tried to push her off, but his helmet hampered his ability to see her clearly. His clumsy attempts to fend her off came to an abrupt end as she pushed her dagger into his neck.

The Dark Queen entered the casting room, two warriors in black surcoats flanking her while Margaret followed, her eyes opening wide at the sight of the carnage.

Hayley rolled off the limp body and charged forward, desperate to kill Kythelia. The Elven guards intercepted her, driving her back with their swords. Hayley felt a blade sink into her thigh, and then her leg collapsed beneath her, throwing her to the floor. A blade hovered over her face, ready for the killing blow.

"Don't kill her yet," ordered Kythelia. "I want her to witness the end of Merceria." She turned to face the Mercerian queen. Anna backed up against the wall, her Dwarf sword still in hand.

Kythelia moved closer, taunting her. "Go ahead, try to kill me. There's isn't a weapon in all of existence that can take my life."

Anna thrust out, the blade easily penetrating the Elf's skin, yet as she withdrew it, no blood issued forth. Kythelia looked down at the tear in her dress.

"Is that the best you can do?" A large purple cloud appeared overhead as the Dark Queen uttered the ancient words of power. The spell absorbed the light from the room, illuminating all within with its eerie glow. Kythelia reached out, pointing at Anna. "Now," she said, "you—"

"No!" screamed Margaret, dashing forward as the energy erupted from her dark mistress's hands. Intended for Anna, it engulfed her sister instead, a purple light illuminating her as it cascaded around before sinking into her, glowing as it settled in her bones.

Margaret's agonizing screams reverberated throughout the room as her body seemed to shatter. Flesh exploded until the only thing left of the former Mercerian princess was a red smear on the floor and bits of skin and bone plastering the walls.

Albreda ripped open an Elf's stomach, then turned, ready to face another challenger, but the hallway was nothing but bodies. She rushed back to the casting room only to behold Kythelia standing before Queen Anna, naught between them but a pulpy mess of flesh and bone.

The Druid readied another spell, but the Dark Queen was quicker, turning and thrusting out a hand to send forth a thin black tendril that sank into Albreda's chest. Kythelia made a fist, pulling Albreda's arms in tight, every muscle in her body screaming out in agony as if the very flesh was being torn from her bones.

Kythelia's other hand shot out, this time targeting the Queen of Merceria. Anna tried to use her sword to ward off the attack, but it was of little use.

"Ahhh," the Dark Queen cackled. "This is most satisfying." She looked at what little remained of Margaret. "A pity. She had such potential."

"What are you doing to Albreda?" Anna shouted.

"The same thing I'm about to do to you, my dear. Syphoning off her life force and drinking it in. I thought I'd let you watch her die before you suffer the same fate." She smiled. "Go ahead. Struggle if you wish. It will do you no good."

Time seemed to stand still as Anna was forced to listen to Albreda's heart-wrenching wails of torment.

Hayley watched in horror as Albreda's body began to shrivel as if the Druid were aging year by year in a mere matter of moments. Starting as a low growl, a sound broke through the Druid's screams, then Tempus, covered in blood with cuts all over him, burst into the room. Without hesitation, he launched himself at Kythelia, taking the Dark Queen by complete surprise as his teeth sank into her neck. Unable to control her spells while defending herself, Anna and Albreda dropped to the floor, magic no longer holding them in place.

The guards rushed forward, sinking their swords into the noble beast. Still, the mighty Kurathian Mastiff hung on, determined to do what he must to save his mistress.

Kythelia's hand gripped the dog's head, struggling to pry him loose, her shrieks of pain calling forth dark powers that caused the very air to grow foul with a green mist that enveloped them both, Elf and hound alike.

Anna tried to rush forward, but Hayley was there, holding her back, even as flesh bubbled and burned. One last wail was all that remained, and then Kythelia, the Dark Queen, was dead.

Albreda crept forward slowly, waiting as the acid cloud dissipated before she could reach out to Tempus. The poor soul's breathing was weak, his life almost spent. She placed her forehead on his, ignoring the blood, then closed her eyes. Anna, Hayley's grip on her now released, ran over, staring down at her faithful companion.

"Can you do anything for him?" she asked, her voice quivering.

"I'm afraid his time amongst us has come to an end, my child."

"No!" cried the queen. "It can't be. You must help him!"

"No one can help him now. He is ready to take that final journey to the Afterlife. Say your goodbyes, Majesty. You haven't much time."

Anna moved to the side of her oldest friend and held him close, tears streaming down her face. "I shall never forget you, Tempus."

The great hound let out one final breath, then lay still.

THIRTY-SEVEN

Aftermath

Summer 966 MC

A ubrey opened her eyes to see Kraloch staring down at her.

"Cousin Beverly?" she squeaked out, for her head felt like it was going to explode.

"She is alive," announced the Orc, "but her wounds are severe. It will be some time before she is up and about."

An Elf drew close, causing the Life Mage to recoil.

"You may rest assured you are safe," said Lord Arandil. "Kythelia's reign is over, her soul banished to the Underworld for all eternity."

"And the rest of her army?"

"My warriors are rounding them up even as we speak. They have little fight left in them after the death of their mistress."

"And Queen Anna? Is she safe?"

"She is," said Kraloch. "Although she has taken the loss hard."

"I don't understand."

A tear came to the Orc's eyes. "Tempus has taken his place amongst the Ancestors. He gave his life to destroy the Dark Queen."

"It seems the prophecy was correct after all," said Aubrey.

Lord Arandil looked at her with a quizzical expression. "I am not sure I understand?"

"It was claimed there was no person in all of Eiddenwerthe who could slay her. How appropriate then that it should be a dog that finished her off."

Hayley appeared, concern on her face. "How are you feeling, Aubrey?"

"Like my head is going to explode."

"You've taken quite a wound there," said Kraloch. "The flesh is restored, but it will take some time for the mind to recover."

"Are you saying I can't cast magic?"

"Not for a bit, but do not worry. I expect you will make a full recovery. In the meantime, you must excuse me. There are many other patients to tend to." The Orc shaman moved on.

Hayley sat down beside the Life Mage, shaking her head. "I still can't believe it's finally over."

"Over? What about the Clans?"

"Urgon says they're all throwing down their weapons and surrendering. They lost their appetite for a fight after the death of Brida and the other Clan Chiefs."

"So the war is finally over? It feels like we've been fighting forever."

"Not quite, but I can see how it looks that way. In any case, there's still the matter of retaking the rest of Weldwyn, but I'm certain it will simply be a matter of diplomacy."

They sat in silence for a while as the wounded Elves were escorted past under guard.

"What happens now?" asked Aubrey.

"We'll supply garrisons for most of Weldwyn until they can train replacements."

"No. I mean for us?"

"Well, I don't know about you, but I'm still the High Ranger. That alone will keep me busy for quite some time. What about you? You can open up that magical academy you've been talking about for years."

"That was Revi's idea."

"Maybe," said Hayley, "but he's going to be far too busy doing other things to run it."

"Other things? Like making another monumental discovery?"

"No," replied the ranger, blushing. "Like getting married to me!"

Gerald picked his way up the steps. Littered with the dead, the front of the Dome was a testament to the fury with which the battle had been carried out. The vast majority of the slain were Elves, causing him to stop and ponder things a moment.

"Grisly, isn't it?" said Sir Preston. "It appears the Elves don't take prisoners."

"I can't imagine the followers of Kythelia were willing to surrender."

"Nor did Lord Arandil's warriors ask, from what I heard."

Gerald turned to the knight. "Who said that?"

"The Orcs. They witnessed the assault first hand."

The marshal turned his gaze to the building before them.

"Their animosity must run deep," offered Preston. "Then again, we see Kythelia only for what she did to Merceria, but in truth, she's been a scourge on this land for centuries."

The marshal's gaze wandered back to the dead. "Perhaps it's better like this. How does a person return to the world of the living after thousands of years of worshipping death?"

"It is an enigma, to be sure."

"I'd best get inside and report to the queen."

"Aye, sir. I'll take care of disposing of the bodies. On that note, do we know the Elven custom for their dead?"

"If I remember correctly, they see the body as merely a vessel."

"Meaning?"

"Burn them or bury them, whatever is more convenient, but whatever you decide on, don't do it within the city walls. We don't want a spectacle." He made his way up the rest of the steps and entered the Dome, passing by several of Lord Arandil's Elf warriors along the way.

He continued through the magnificent structure, taking the stairs upward, only to come across a pale Lady Aubrey, clutching the arm of Dame Hayley as they descended.

"Glad to see you two made it," said Gerald. "Did we lose anyone?"

"Only Tempus," said Aubrey. "He gave his life to save the queen, and in so doing, saved us all."

"I'd best go to her. She'll be devastated."

"Beverly's with her," added the mage. "As is Albreda."

Gerald found the last few steps a burden. Having known the loyal mastiff for years, his loss would forever leave a hole in his heart. He topped the stairs to see Anna putting on a brave face, ordering about the guards who were cleaning up after the battle. At the sight of her old warrior friend, though, she ran towards him, hugging him tightly.

He held her as her grief poured out in great, wracking sobs. Finally, she pulled away, straightening her dress in a manner that said the queen was in control once more.

"How are you?" said Gerald.

"I'll be fine," she replied, her voice quivering ever so slightly. "I should have seen this coming."

"And if you had, would you have done anything differently?"

She stared back at him, and he noted the resolution settle across her features.

"No," she said, closing her eyes. "He had his part to play in all of this. Without him, we never would've defeated her. I shall always remember the sacrifice he made for me… for us all."

"As will we all."

"Look at me, falling apart like a scared little girl. You'd never know I was the Queen of Merceria."

"Even a queen is allowed to mourn."

"Where's Alric?"

"Rounding up the Clansmen."

"So the fighting is over?"

"It is," said Gerald. "Lochlan called for a truce on behalf of the Clans."

"A truce?"

"Yes. They're leaving Weldwyn and returning home."

"To cause problems down the road?"

"No. They agreed to leave emissaries for both the Weldwyn and Mercerian courts, in addition to having our people join their chiefs in the Clanholdings. It's all subject to Royal Approval, of course, but Alric has already agreed in principle. Now all that remains is for you to decide if it's what you want."

"I shall agree," replied Anna. "Saxnor knows, there's been enough bloodshed over the last few years. Our land deserves a lasting peace for a change."

Beverly looked up from her bed. "Father. What are you doing here?"

"Hello, my dear," replied the baron. "I thought I'd drop by and see how you're faring."

"But weren't you in Norland?"

"I was actually in Wincaster, but Albreda thought I might like to look into how you were faring. With the Dome back under our control, it was a simple enough matter."

"How is Albreda? I haven't seen her since the fight."

"She is well, although a little tired. Kythelia tried to drain her energy, but it all came rushing back once the Dark Queen died." He stared at his daughter a moment. "That reminds me. I brought you a present."

"You didn't have to do that."

"Oh, I think I did," said Fitz. He turned to the door. "You can come in now!"

Aldwin entered, wearing the biggest smile Beverly had ever seen. "What's this I hear about you getting wounded?" he asked.

Tears of happiness poured down her cheeks as he moved to embrace her. "It's true," she finally said. "An arrow slipped in between my chest and back plates."

"Well, it's a good thing I learned how to make plate armour, then. We'll just have to get you back to Bodden where I can make you a set."

"I would like that very much."

"I see you two have a lot to catch up on," said Fitz, "so I shall leave you to it."

Queen Anna and Prince Alric held court two days later to celebrate the victory. It would take years, possibly even decades, to rebuild the kingdom, but with the Clans defeated and Kythelia finally dead, that work could now begin.

It still remained to crown Alric King of Weldwyn, but many insisted on pledging their allegiance to him despite only being a prince.

Once they finished, Anna had some surprises of her own. She stood, waiting for the crowd to quiet before beginning.

"I have the honour, this day, of rewarding those who served the Crown of Merceria. I name Sir Heward as Baron of Redridge in recognition of his unwavering loyalty. Unfortunately, Lord Heward can't be with us today, as he is busy in Norland, but we send him our warmest regards and congratulations."

Polite applause erupted. Heward was well-known amongst the Mercerians, but to the people of Weldwyn, he was simply another one of those foreigners.

"In addition," she continued, "considering Wickfield's growth, I name it a barony and place it in the capable hands of Sir Preston, who shall henceforth be known as the Baron of Wickfield." The queen paused long enough to catch the eye of her lady-in-waiting. "Congratulations, Lady Sophie, on your elevation to baroness."

Alric turned to face his wife. "Have you considered what to do with Tewsbury?" he asked, his voice low.

"I have, as a matter of fact." She turned her attention to the crowd, once more raising her voice. "Commander Lanaka!" she called out.

The Kurathian made his way through those assembled, halting before his adopted queen, to bow deeply. "Your Majesty."

"Do you, Lanaka, swear to be faithful and bear true allegiance to the Crown of Merceria, forsaking all others?"

"I do."

"Then I name you Earl of Tewsbury." She lowered her voice. "You shall act in this capacity from this day forth, but on our return to Wincaster, we shall have a proper investiture ceremony."

"But he's a Kurathian," said Alric.

"No, most noble prince," replied Lanaka. "I am Mercerian, as are my people."

"You have more than proved your worth in service to this realm," added the queen. "I'll expect your presence at the next meeting of my Nobles Council. In addition, your fellow countrymen will be granted land within your new domain."

"You honour us, my queen." The new Earl of Tewsbury withdrew back into the crowd.

Alric looked at Anna. "You are enjoying this far too much."

She grinned in reply. "And why shouldn't I? There is much to celebrate. While it's true I shall forever miss Tempus, I know a part of him will always be here, in my heart."

She turned to Sophie. "Did we forget anyone?"

"Lord Arandil wishes to speak privately with you at your earliest convenience, Majesty."

"Very well. Have him meet us back at the Dome once the celebration is underway."

"You don't wish to remain?"

"No." She looked at Alric. "I should instead prefer to spend some time alone with my family."

"I shall make the arrangements, Majesty."

"Excellent... Baroness Wickfield."

Gerald paced the room. They were ready to use the magic circle and return to Wincaster but still waited on Lord Arandil.

"What could be keeping the fellow?" he said. "Does he not realize we're on a tight schedule?"

"Hush, now," said Anna. "We're not in that much of a rush. The Elves were a great help to us. We at least owe them the courtesy of waiting."

"Don't bother arguing," said Alric. "We both know it will do no good." Braedon let out a giggle, and the prince looked at Althea, who held the young princeling. "He seems to like his aunt."

"And why wouldn't he?" she responded. "Did you tell him I was an ogre or something?"

"No, of course not. I'm just not used to seeing you look so..."

"So what?" she responded.

"So mature." He smiled. "You've grown up so much since the invasion began. I sometimes forget you're not a little girl anymore."

"She's a warrior princess," said Anna. "And a seasoned one at that. Wouldn't you agree, Lady Aubrey?"

The Life Mage simply nodded in agreement.

"I see a bright future ahead for her," the queen continued. "Perhaps eventually as Marshal of Weldwyn?"

"Let's not get too carried away," said Alric. "I don't want her head to get any bigger."

A guard opened the door. "Lord Arandil is here, Your Majesty."

"Send him in," said Anna.

"Your Majesty," said the Elven lord. "My apologies for the delay."

"I shall not trouble you for details, Lord Arandil, but I trust it was something of the utmost importance. You indicated you wanted a private audience. Is this private enough? You may rest assured everyone here is completely trustworthy."

The Elf lord looked around the room, his eyes meeting each in turn. "That would be acceptable, Majesty."

"Then, please, tell us what it is that you consider so important?"

"I came to apologize for the strife my people caused."

"Your Elves did not plot against us, my lord. It was those of Queen Kythelia. There was nothing you could have done to make it any different."

The Elf cast his gaze down to the floor. "I am afraid that is not entirely true. You see, I should have stopped her millennia ago when I suspected her studies had taken a dark turn."

"You knew Kythelia back then?"

"Indeed. She was my sister."

Everyone stared at Lord Arandil.

It took the queen some time to gather her thoughts after that revelation. "Why didn't you say something sooner?"

"I had no idea Lady Penelope and Kythelia were one and the same."

"How long ago was this?" asked Anna.

"Over two thousand years," replied Lord Arandil. "It led to a rift within the Elves of Vaerendril."

"Vaerendril?"

"Yes. It's the ancient name for this land."

"You mean Eiddenwerthe?"

"Not at all, Your Majesty. I meant the land that now comprises Weldwyn, Merceria, and Norland."

"And the Clans?"

"Indeed. Theirs is part of the lands of our forbearers, although it was shared with the Orcs and Dwarves."

"And the war that wiped out the Orc cities?"

"That was all my sister's doing. That very war drove me to choose exile, although I now see I should have resisted her efforts. It would have spared much sorrow."

"We cannot undo the past, Lord Arandil," said Anna. "Only plan for the future."

"And in that spirit, I promise to be more open with the Crown of Merceria. I shall honour the sacrifice of my daughter and supply warriors to the Army of Merceria permanently."

"And in exchange, I look forward to you taking your seat on my Nobles Council, that you may have a say in our policies going forward. After all, the combined might of all our armies led to our success."

"Yet in the end," said Lord Arandil, "you faced down the greatest threat this land has ever seen. It truly was a triumph of the crown."

Epilogue

Autumn 966 MC

B raedon giggled as Gerald lifted him up into the air.

"Careful," said Jane. "You don't want to drop him."

"Don't worry. I've got a good hold of him."

They sat on a blanket with Anna and Alric, in the middle of the hedge maze at Uxley.

"So many memories," said Anna. "I first met Gerald here."

"So you did," he replied. "That seems like a lifetime ago."

He passed Braedon over to Jane, who looked down fondly at the infant. "He looks just like you," she said.

"Nonsense," said the old warrior. "We're not related."

"But I thought you Anna's father?"

He looked at her and grinned. "If I were truly her father, wouldn't that make me king?"

"Oh yes. I should've realized that. I'm sorry. I've gone and embarrassed myself."

"Not at all," said Anna. "The fact is I consider it an honour to call Gerald my father, and whether or not he's related, he shall be grandfather to my children."

Prince Alric piped up from where he lay. "Children? Does that mean we're going to have some more?"

"Eventually, but let's not rush things. I still have a kingdom to run, as do you, eventually."

Gerald looked at Anna, and an understanding passed between them. "I think he'd like it here," he said. "Don't you?"

"I do."

"What are you two talking about?" asked Alric.

"Gerald and I have been talking of late."

"Oh? Anything the rest of us should know about?"

"As a matter of fact, yes. We decided to commission a statue in honour of Tempus."

Alric sat up. "That's an excellent idea. You could put it right out front of the Palace in Wincaster."

"No," Anna replied. "It shall go here, where friends and family can see it. He loved it here, in the maze, and I can't think of anything he'd like more."

The sound of voices echoed off in the distance.

"It appears we are about to have company," said Jane.

"Sounds like Beverly and Aldwin," said Gerald. "I wonder what they're doing here." He tried to maintain a serious expression, but Anna saw right through it.

"What are you hiding?" she said.

"What makes you assume I'm hiding something?"

"Come now. How long have we known each other?"

He laughed. "Far too long, it seems. Very well. I'll come clean. I arranged a little surprise for you."

"What kind of surprise?"

"You'll just have to wait and see."

Beverly's voice drew closer, then she appeared at the edge of the clearing. "Hello. I trust everyone is well?"

Anna's eyes danced with excitement. "Never mind all that. What have you brought me?"

The knight stepped aside to allow Aldwin entry. In his arms, he cradled a pup. He moved up to the queen and set the tiny creature down. "This is for you, Your Majesty. Of course, you must name him, but we felt it only fitting that you have him. After all, Tempus was his sire."

Tears came to Anna's eyes as she lifted the wee thing, cradling him in her arms.

"There," said Gerald. "Finally, a gift suitable for our queen."

<<<<>>>>

REVIEW TRIUMPH OF THE CROWN

∽

ON TO BOOK ELEVEN: GUARDIAN OF THE CROWN

∽

If you liked *Triumph of the Crown*, then *Temple Knight*, the first book in the *Power Ascending* series awaits your undivided attention.

READ TEMPLE KNIGHT

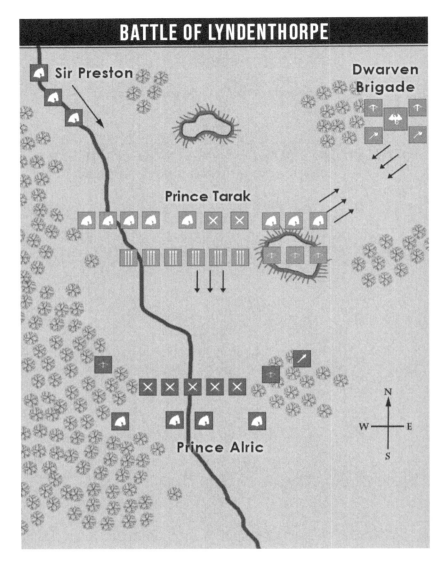

Battle of Lyndenthorpe

Cast of Characters

- Hayley Chambers - Baroness of Queenston, High Ranger, Knight of the Hound
- Heath Morris - Earl of Shrewesdale, former carpenter
- Henry (Deceased) - First son of Andred IV, previous King of Merceria
- Heward 'The Axe' Manton - Knight of the Hound, Northern Commander
- Horace Spencer - Earl of Eastwood
- Kendall - Captain
- Kiren-Jool - Kurathian Enchanter
- Lanaka - Kurathian Commander of Light Horse
- Lightning - Beverly's Mercerian Charger
- Lily - Saurian, friend of Princess Anna
- Linton - Captain, Mercerian Light Cavalry
- Manson - Stable hand, Tewsbury
- Markham Anglesley - Duke of Colbridge
- Mathers - Ranger
- Matron Crawley - Nanny to Prince Braedon
- Meredith (Deceased) - Gerald's wife
- Montag - Kurathian Masstiffs handler
- Nathaniel - Servant to Lord Alexander Stanton
- Nevin - Captain, Mercerian Light Cavalry
- Nicole 'Nikki' Arendale - Advisor to Queen Anna, Married to Arnim Caster
- Orlan Turnbull - Guard Cavalry
- Preston Wright - Knight of the Hound, married to Sophie
- Revi Bloom - Royal Life Mage, Enchanter
- Richard 'Fitz' Fitzwilliam - Baron of Bodden, father of Beverly, mentor of Gerald
- Sally (Deceased) - Gerald's daughter
- Samantha 'Sam' - Former archer of Bodden, Queen's Ranger
- Shellbreaker 'Jamie' - Revi Bloom's avian familiar
- Sophie Fairborn - Queen Anna's Lady-in-Waiting, married to Sir Preston
- Telethial (Deceased) - Elf, daughter of Lord Arandil
- Tempus - Kurathian Mastiff, the queen's pet
- Tog - Leader of the Trolls
- Vivian - Wagon Driver
- William Blackwood - Bodden Sergeant-at-Arms, aide to Gerald
- Zale Halfen - Commoner, Tewsbury, Frequenter of the Lucky Dog

THE ORCS:

- Orcs of the Black Arrow - Located in Artisan Hills
- Orcs of the Black Raven - Located in Ravensguard
- Wolf Clan - Netherwood Tribe of Orcs
- Andurak - Shaman, Netherwood Tribe
- Ghodrug - Chieftain, Black Raven Tribe
- Gorath - Aide to the High Ranger, Black Arrow Clan
- Kraloch - Shaman, Black Arrow Clan
- Kurghal - Shamaness, Black Arrow Clan, older sister of Urgon
- Lahzak - Guard of the Hawksburg magic circle, Black Arrow Clan
- Tarluk - Hunter, Black Arrow Clan
- Urgon - Chieftain, Black Arrow Clan, bondmate to Zhura
- Zhura - Ghostwalker, Black Arrow Clan, bondmate to Urgon

THE DWARVES:
- Agramath - Earth Mage of Ironcliff, Master of Rock and Stone
- Begrin - Engineer in Queenston
- Brogar Hammerhand - Warrior of Mirstone, guard to Princess Althea
- Caldrim - Dwarf of Mirstone, Brother to Haldrim
- Haldrim - Captain of arbalesters, from Mirstone, Brother to Caldrim
- Herdwin Steelarm - Smith, from Wincaster, friend of Queen Anna
- Kasri Ironheart - Daughter of the King of Ironcliff
- Naldurn Grimaxe - Blond Dwarf from Stonecastle, Fought at Galburn's Ridge
- Thalgrun Stormhammer - King of Ironcliff

OF WELDWYN:
- Aegryth Malthunen - Earth Mage
- Alric - Prince, husband of Queen Anna of Merceria
- Alstan (Deceased)- Crown Prince, older brother of Alric
- Althea - Eldest daughter of King Leofric and Queen Igraine
- Edwin Eldridge (Deceased) - Earl of Farnham
- Edwin Weldridge (Deceased) - Earl of Faltingham
- Edwina - Youngest daughter of King Leofric and Queen Igraine
- Erick Lanford - Earl of Falford
- Godfrey Hammond - Noble, friend of James Goodwin
- Gretchen Harwell - Enchanter
- Igraine (Deceased) - Queen, wife of Leofric
- Jack Marlowe - Cavalier, friend and protector of Prince Alric
- James Goodwin - Noble
- Jane Goodwin - Mother of James Goodwin
- Leofric (Deceased) - Former King

- Lindsey Martindale - Viscountess Talburn
- Nigel Wharton - Retired barrel maker, Kinsley
- Parvan Luminor - Elven Baron of Tivilton
- Roxanne Fortuna (Deceased) - Life Mage
- Stafford - Baron of Almswell
- Tulfar Axehand - Dwarven Baron of Mirstone
- Tyrell Caracticus - Water Mage, Grand Mage
- Woodward - Captain of Summersgate militia

OF THE TWELVE CLANS:
- Angus - Warrior
- Brida - High Queen of the Twelve Clans, daughter of High King Dathen
- Calindre - Clan Chief of Windbourne
- Camrath - Scholar of Glanfraydon
- Carmus (Deceased) - Fire Mage in the employ of King Dathen
- Conner - Clan chief of Hillsfar
- Dathen (Deceased)- High King of the Twelve Clans, Clan Chief of Dungannon
- Erlach - Clan Chief of Glanfraydon
- Lochlan - Younger brother of Brida, son of King Dathen
- Rurik - Clan Chieftain of Halsworth
- Toby Whitaker - Warrior
- Warnoch - Clan Chief of Drakewell

OF NORLAND:
- Calder - Former Earl of Greendale
- Creighton - Earl of Riverhurst
- Halfan (Deceased) - Former King of Norland, Grandfather of Bronwyn
- Hollis (Deceased) - Former Earl of Beaconsgate
- Marley (Deceased) - Former Earl of Walthorne
- Marley the younger - Earl of Walthorne
- Princess Bronwyn - Granddaughter of King Halfan, Leader of the Norland rebel army
- Rutherford - Former Earl of Hammersfield
- Thurlowe - Former Earl of Ravensguard
- Waverly - Earl of Marston

THE OTHERS:
- Aeldred - First King of Therengia
- Degarath - Prince Tarak's dragon

- Gundar - God of the Earth
- Haralan - Kurathian Captain in service to Prince Tarak
- Kythelia (Dark Queen) - Elf, Masqueraded as Lady Penelope, Necromancer
- Lysandil - Elf Emissary to the court of the Twelve Clans
- Malin - God of Wisdom, revered by the people of Weldwyn
- Margaret - Older sister of Queen Anna
- Melethandil - Dragon
- Olani - Princess, married to Prince Tarak
- Saxnor - God of Strength, revered by the Mercerians
- Tarak - Kurathian Prince of Kouras

PLACES

MERCERIA:
- Artisan Hills - Hills east of Eastwood
- Bodden - Town, Barony
- Colbridge - City, Dukedom
- Darkwood - Forest east of Wincaster
- Eastwood - City, Earldom
- Erssa-Saka'am - City in the Great Swamp, home to the Saurians
- Great Swamp - The southern edge of Merceria
- Haverston - Town, Vicountcy
- Hawksburg - Town, Barony
- Kingsford - City, Dukedom
- Old Oak Tavern - In Uxley
- Shrewesdale - City, Earldom
- Tewsbury - City, Earldom
- The Grand - Theatre in Wincaster
- The Lucky Dog - Tavern in Tewsbury
- Trollden - Town, Great Swamp, mainly Trolls
- Whitewood - Forest north of Bodden
- Wickfield - Town
- Wincaster - Capital City

NORLAND:
- Beaconsgate - Earldom, City
- Galburn's Ridge - Capital of Norland
- Marston - Earldom, City
- Ravensguard - Earldom, Fortress city
- Riverhurst - Earldom, City
- Thunder Mountains - Range close to Ironcliff

- Walthorne - Earldom, City

- Ironcliff - Dwarven Stronghold, Kingdom
- Kouras - Kurathian principality, Prince Tarak
- Kurathia - Collection of Island principalities
- Mith-Drunuin(Destroyed) - Elven city, where Summersgate now sits
- Petty Kingdoms - Collection of Kingdoms on the Continent
- Rahad - Kurathian principality
- Stonecastle - Dwarven Stronghold, Kingdom
- Vaerendril - Ancient Elven land encompassing the Four Kingdoms

BATTLES

- Battle of Uxley (964 MC) - Defeat of the Norland invasion
- Campaigns of Aeldred - Ancient military campaign that created Kingdom of Therengia
- Great War - Ancient war between Elves and Orcs

OTHER THINGS:

- Heartseed - Herbal concoction for anxiety
- Nature's Fury - Beverly's magical hammer
- Stormhammer - Kasri's magical hammer
- The Hearth Guard - Elite Dwarven company
- *The Mermaid of Colbridge* - Book of Fables
- Vard - Dwarven term for leader, roughly translates as 'ruler'

A Few Words from Paul

Triumph wraps up a storyline that spans ten books. Ultimately, it is about the final battle for supremacy, but at its heart, it's really about the people who determine the outcome and what influences them. It also marks the end of the journey for at least one character, an end that was foreshadowed way back in book 2.5, Stories of the Past. By far, it was the most difficult scene I've ever had to write, and one which will likely hit my readers very hard. But a conflict of this magnitude leads to death, and without the sacrifice of some, we wouldn't be living in the world we are today. This loss, in a sense, represents the heartache suffered by so many in times of war.

Life goes on, of course, as do relationships, and this story deals with two in particular. First, there is that of Lady Jane and Gerald, which has been queued up for some time now. The original character of Lady Jane dates back to the original RPG campaign, and I knew she would eventually make it to the pages of this series. The other pair, however, came as a complete surprise. Herdwin and Kasri just seemed to hit it off as I was writing them. The next thing I knew, they were a couple. Their story will continue in Mercerian Tales: Into the Forge, book 10.5 in the series.

The land of Merceria is finally at peace, and the future looks promising. There are still issues to settle with the Clans and Norland, but the war is over, and the warriors can return to their homes. This is not the end of their story, for even as they settle back into everyday life, a new threat emerges from the east, one that has plagued the Petty Kingdoms for years.

Gerald, Anna, Beverly and the others return to face new threats and challenges in Heir to the Crown, Book 11: Guardian of the Crown.

This book would not have been possible without the assistance and support of my wife, Carol, who is my editor, media coordinator, inspiration and best friend throughout the process. It is her presence, more than any other, that has allowed us to take this trip together to tell the tale of Merceria.

I should also like to thank Christie Bennett, Stephanie Sandrock, and Amanda Bennett for their encouragement. Also, I must give a shout-out to Brad Aitken, Stephen Brown, and the late Jeffrey Parker for their character inspirations.

As always, my BETA team proved to be most helpful, so I thank them for their suggestions and comments. Thank you to: Rachel Deibler, Michael Rhew, Phyllis Simpson, Don Hinckley, Charles Mohapel, Lisa Hanika,

Debra Reeves, Michell Schneidkraut, Susan Young, Joanna Smith, James McGinnis, Keven Hutchinson, and Anna Ostberg

Most importantly, I must thank you, my readers, without whom these later tales would never have seen the light of day. Your comments and accolades are the fuel that powers my writing, and I look forward to sharing more stories in the future.

About the Author

Paul J Bennett (b. 1961) emigrated from England to Canada in 1967. His father served in the British Royal Navy, and his mother worked for the BBC in London. As a young man, Paul followed in his father's footsteps, joining the Canadian Armed Forces in 1983. He is married to Carol Bennett and has three daughters who are all creative in their own right.

Paul's interest in writing started in his teen years when he discovered the roleplaying game, Dungeons & Dragons (D & D). What attracted him to this new hobby was the creativity it required; the need to create realms, worlds and adventures that pulled the gamers into his stories.

In his 30's, Paul started to dabble in designing his own roleplaying system, using the Peninsular War in Portugal as his backdrop. His regular gaming group were willing victims, er, participants in helping to playtest this new system. A few years later, he added additional settings to his game, including Science Fiction, Post-Apocalyptic, World War II, and the all-important Fantasy Realm where his stories take place.

The beginnings of his first book 'Servant to the Crown' originated over five years ago when he began a new fantasy campaign. For the world that the Kingdom of Merceria is in, he ran his adventures like a TV show, with seasons that each had twelve episodes, and an overarching plot. When the campaign ended, he knew all the characters, what they had to accomplish, what needed to happen to move the plot along, and it was this that inspired to sit down to write his first novel.

Paul now has four series based in Eiddenwerthe, his fantasy realm and is looking forward to sharing many more books with his readers over the coming years.

Printed in France by Amazon
Brétigny-sur-Orge, FR

14109034R00192